**It was fright...in
its pure state!**

Suddenly Rivas was certain that something out
there in those miles of darkness was aware of him,
was watching him. And he knew he could see *it*
if he cared to, for he wasn't seeing with his eyes
now...

The thing out there knew he was retreating, and
he could feel its amusement.

Soon, it said, though without words. *It's always
been me you loved best. Only.*

He didn't choose to see it, but he realized that
it didn't matter, for he knew precisely what it looked
like. It looked like himself.

Ace Science Fiction Books by Tim Powers

THE ANUBIS GATES
DINNER AT DEVIANT'S PALACE

DINNER AT DEVIANT'S PALACE

TIM POWERS

ACE SCIENCE FICTION BOOKS
NEW YORK

DINNER AT DEVIANT'S PALACE

An Ace Science Fiction Book / published by arrangement with
the author

PRINTING HISTORY
Ace Original / January 1985

ISBN: 0-441-14879-4

Ace Science Fiction Books are published by
The Berkley Publishing Group,
200 Madison Avenue, New York, New York 10016.
PRINTED IN THE UNITED STATES OF AMERICA

To The Thursday Night Gang:

Chris Arena, Greg Arena, Bill Bailey, Jim Blaylock, Jenny Bunn, Pete Devries, Phil Dick, Jeff Fontanesi, Don Goudie, Chris Gourlay, Dashiell Hamster, Rick Harding, K. W. Jeter, Tom Kenyon, Dave Lamont, Tim Lamont, Steve Malk, Phil Pace, Brendan Powers, Serena Powers and Phil Thibodeau...

...and the honorary members: Russ Galen, Dean Koontz, Roy Squires, Joel Stein, Ted Wassard and Paul Williams...

...and with thanks to Beth Meacham, most perceptive, persuasive and tactful of editors.

DINNER AT DEVIANT'S PALACE

BOOK ONE:

WHATEVER I CAN CARRY IN ONE HAND

And suddenly there's no meaning in our kiss,
And your lit upward face grows, where we lie,
Lonelier and dreadfuller than sunlight is,
And dumb and mad and eyeless like the sky.
—Rupert Brooke

CHAPTER ONE

CROUCHED WAY UP at the top of the wall in the rusty bed of the Rocking Truck, Modesto tugged his jacket more tightly across his chest, pushed back his hat and squinted around at the city. At the moment there was no one in particular that it would be lucrative to watch for, but just to keep in practice the boy liked to climb up here and keep track of the comings and goings in general. Below him to his left was the South Gate area, not quite its usual crowded self because of the recent rain, and beyond that to the southeast—the direction that was nearly always downwind—he could see the ragged shacks and black mud lanes of Dogtown, canopied by the snarls of smoke rising from the eternal fires in its trash-filled trenches.

The boy clambered over the collapsed cab to sit on the hood and look north. The broken-backed truck, as immov-

able as the age-rounded concrete wall it straddled, didn't
shift under him; nor had it ever moved in the memory of
anyone now living.

The towers made ragged brushstrokes of black down the
gray northern sky, and at the skeletal top of the Crocker
Tower he could see bright orange pinpricks that he knew
were torches; the night watch was coming on duty early,
and Modesto knew that their various spyglasses would be
turned to the east, watching for any sign of the army that
was rumored to be approaching from San Berdoo. And
though even Modesto couldn't see them from here, he knew
that out beyond the north farms there were armed men on
horseback patrolling the Golden State Freeway from the
Berdoo Freeway in the north to the Pomona in the south.

Thirty feet below his perch he noticed a grotesque vehicle
moving south down Fig Street toward him, and with a grin
half-admiring and half-contemptuous he identified it as the
carriage of Greg Rivas, the famous pelican gunner. Like
most kids his age, Modesto considered gunning a slightly
embarrassing historical curiosity, conjuring up implausible
images of one's parents when they were young and foolish. . . . Modesto was far more interested in the more defined
and consistent rhythms of Scrap, and the new dances like
Scrapping, Gimpscrew and the Bugwalk.

With a creaking of axles and an altered pace in the clopping of the horses' hooves, the vehicle turned west onto
Woolshirt Boulevard, and Modesto knew Rivas was just
arriving early for his nightly gig at Spink's.

Bored, the boy turned his attention back to the thrillingly
ominous lights in the Crocker Tower.

The carriage was an old but painstakingly polished
Chevrolet body mounted on a flat wooden wagon drawn by
two horses, and though the late afternoon rain drabbed the
colors and made the streamers droop, it was by far the

grandest vehicle out on Woolshirt Boulevard. Old super-stitions about rain being poisonous had kept the usual street crowd indoors today, though, and only two boys emerged from a recessed doorway and scampered up to cry, some-what mechanically, "Rivas! Hooray, it's Gregorio Rivas!"

Rivas pushed aside the beaded curtain that hung in place of the long gone door, stepped out onto the flat surface of the wagon and, squinting in the light drizzle, braced himself there as his driver snapped the reins and drew the vehicle to a squeaking halt in front of the building that was their destination.

Like most of the structures that stood along the north to south midcity line, this one was a well-preserved shell of old concrete with neat sections of woodwork filling the gaps where plate glass had once fabulously stretched across yards and yards of space. The building was three stories high and, again typically for this area, the wall at the top, now dec-orated with a profusion of spikes and ornaments and sun-faded flags, was jaggedly uneven with an ancient fracture. Over the doorway strips of metal and colored glass had been nailed to spell out, in letters a foot tall, SPINKS.

"Here," Rivas called to the boys, "never mind it today, no one's around. Anyway, I think I need a couple of new prompters—lately the goddamn parrots sound more enthu-siastic than you guys."

As if to illustrate his point, one of the parrots nesting in the top of the nearest palm tree called down, *"Rivas! Rivas!"*

"Hooray!" added another one from a tree farther up the street.

"Hear that?" Rivas demanded as he reached back inside the car for his hat and his vinyl pelican case. "I think it's because they work free, just for the art of it." He put on his hat, glanced around below him for unpuddled pavement, spotted an area and leaped to it.

"We don't, though, man," one of the boys pointed out

cheerily. Both of them held out their palms.

"Mercenary little mules," Rivas muttered. He dug a couple of small white cards out of his vest pocket and gave one to each boy. "There's a jigger apiece, and you should be ashamed to take so much."

"You bet we are, man." The pair dashed back to their sheltered doorway.

Rivas paused under the restaurant's awning to set his antique hat at the proper angle and comb his fingers through his dark Van Dyke beard. Finally he pushed open the swinging doors and strode inside.

A moment later, though, he was pursing his lips irritably, for his careful entrance had been wasted—the chandeliers, which had been lowered after the lunch crowd, still sat on the floor unlit, and the room was so dim that if it weren't for the faint smells of stale beer and old grease the place could have been mistaken for a between-services church.

"Damn it," he yelped, stubbing his toe against the edge of one of the chandeliers and awkwardly hopping over it, "where are you, Mojo? How come these things aren't lit yet?"

"It's early yet, Greg," came a voice from the kitchen. "I'll get to 'em."

Rivas picked his way around the wooden wheels of the chandeliers to the bar, lifted the hinged section and stepped behind it. By touch he found the stack of clean glasses, and then the big room echoed with the clicking of the pump as he impatiently worked the handle to prime the beer tap.

"There's a bottle of Currency Barrows open," called Mojo from the kitchen.

The edges of Rivas's mouth curled down in a sort of inverted smile. "The beer's fine," he said in a carefully casual voice. He opened the tap and let the stream of cool beer begin filling his glass.

Old Mojo lurched ponderously out of the kitchen carrying a flickering oil lamp, and he crouched over the nearest chandelier to light the candles on it. "That's right," he said absently, "you're not crazy about the Barrows stuff, are you?"

"I'm a beer and whiskey man," said Rivas lightly. "Fandango or the twins here yet?"

"Yeah, Fandango is—them's some of his drums on the stage there. He went for the rest."

There was a shuffling and banging from the direction of the back hall just then, and a voice called, "That you, Greg? Help me with these, will you?"

"Whatever I can carry in one hand, Tommy." Tucking the pelican case under his arm and sipping the beer as he went, Rivas groped his way to the back hall, relieved the puffing Fandango of one of his smaller drums and led the way back across the already somewhat brighter room to the stage.

Fandango put his drums down carefully and wiped sweat from his chubby face. *"Whew,"* he said, leaning against the raised stage. "Spink was askin' me this morning when you'd be in," he remarked in a confiding tone.

Rivas put down the drum he'd been carrying and then glanced at the younger man. "So?"

"Well, I don't know, but he seemed mad."

"How could you tell? He probably *sleeps* with that smile on."

"He said he wanted to talk to you about something." Fandango avoided looking at Rivas by concentrating on tightening a drumhead screw. "Uh, maybe about that girl."

"Who, that Hammond creature?" Rivas frowned, uneasily aware that Fandango had been seeing the girl first, and had introduced her to him. "Listen, she turned out to be crazy."

"They all do, to hear you tell it."

"Well, most of them *are* crazy," Rivas snapped as he climbed up onto the stage. "I can't help that." He untied the knots that held the vinyl case closed, flipped up the lid and lifted the instrument out.

Though not even quite two feet long, it was said to be the finest in Ellay, its neck carved of mahogany with copper wire frets and polished copper pennies for pegs, and its body a smoothly laminated half sphere of various woods, waxed and polished to a glassy sheen. The horsehair bow was clipped to the back of the neck, and in profile the instrument did look something like a pelican's head, the body being the jowly pouch and the long neck the beak.

He put the case on the stage floor, sat down on a stool with the pelican across his knees, and plucked out a quick, nearly atonal gun riff; then he swung it up to his shoulder, unclipped the bow and skated it experimentally across the strings, producing a melancholy chord.

Satisfied, he laid the instrument back in the open case and put the bow down beside it. He picked up his glass of beer. "Anyway," he said after taking a sip, "Spink wouldn't be bothered about any such crap. Hell, this is the eleventh year of the Seventh Ace—all that chastity and everlasting fidelity stuff left by the Dogtown gate before you and I were born."

As was very often the case, especially lately, Fandango couldn't tell whether Rivas was being sincere or bitterly ironic, so he let the subject drop and set about arranging the drum stands around his own stool.

"Say," he ventured quietly a few minutes later, "who's the guy by the window?"

Mojo had got several of the chandeliers lit by now, and the kitchen corner of the room glowed brightly enough to show a heavy-set man sitting at a table just to the right of the streetside window. Rivas stared at him for a moment, unable to tell in that uncertain light whether or not the man was looking his way, or was even awake; then he shrugged. "Jaybush knows."

"And he ain't tellin'," Fandango agreed. "Say, is it still gonna be mostly gunning tonight? I've been practicing some newer songs, some of these bugwalk numbers, and it seems to me—"

Rivas drained his beer. "Catch!" he called, and tossed the glass in a high, spinning parabola toward Mojo, who looked up wearily, clanged his lamp down and caught the glass before it could hit the floor.

"Goddammit, Greg . . ." he muttered, getting to his feet and shambling toward the bar.

"Yeah," said Rivas, frowning slightly as he watched the old man's progress, "it'll be gunning. They don't pay to hear Rivas doing bugwalk." No, he thought. For that you want those savage kids coming out of the southeast end of town—Dogtown—the kids who rely on the ferocity of their voices and ragtag instruments to make up for their lack of musical skill. "Why?"

"I still can't get the hang of the beat on it," Fandango complained. "If you'd just let me bang away in the same time as what you're playin', or even the time of what you're singin', I could handle it, but this third and fourth layer stuff, all at different paces but having to touch the peaks and bottoms together . . ."

"We're going to gun," Rivas said firmly.

After a few moments, "Are you gonna do 'Drinking Alone'?" Fandango persisted. "It's the hardest."

"Christ, Tommy," said Rivas impatiently, "this is your *job*. Yes, I'm going to do that song. If you don't want to learn the whole trade, you may as well grow a beard and beg out on the street."

"Well, sure, Greg, except—"

"Think I moved back here from Venice working like that?"

"No, Greg."

"Damn right. Maybe we'd better go through it now, before the show, to give you some practice."

Before Fandango could reply, a chair rutched back in the corner and the man at the windowside table stood up and spoke. "Mr. Rivas, I'd like to have a word with you before you start."

Rivas cocked a wary eyebrow at the man. What's this, he wondered, a challenge over some despoiled daughter or wife? Or just a bid for a private party performance? The man was dressed respectably, at least, in a conservative off white flax shirt and trousers and a dark leather Sam Brown belt—in contrast to Rivas's own flamboyant red plastic vest and wide-brimmed hat. "Sure," said Rivas after a pause. "Shoot."

"It's a personal matter. Could we discuss it at the table here, perhaps over a drink?"

". . . Okay."

Mojo bumbled up to the stage with the refilled beer glass just as the pelicanist hopped down. "Thanks," said Rivas, taking it from him. "And a glass of whatever for the citizen yonder."

Mojo turned toward the stranger, who said, "A shot of that Currency Barrows, please."

Rivas walked over to the man's table, holding the beer in his right hand so that his knife hand was free, and when he got there he hooked back a chair for himself with his foot.

Mojo arrived with the glass of brandy a moment later, set it down in front of the stranger, then stepped back and cleared his throat.

"On my tab, Mojo," said Rivas without taking his eyes

off the stranger—who, he noticed, had no hair on his head at all, not even eyebrows or lashes.

"No, I insist," the man said, "and Mr. Rivas's beer, too. How much?"

"Uh . . . one ha'pint."

The stranger took a bugshell moneycase from his belt pouch, snapped it open and handed Mojo a one-fifth card. Mojo took it and lurched away.

"Never mind the change," the man called after him.

Mojo slowed to a more comfortable pace. "Thank you, man," he called back in a voice from which he was unable to keep a note of pleased surprise.

"Well?" said Rivas.

The man gave Rivas a distinctly frosty smile. "My name is Joe Montecruz. I'd like to hire your services."

Though still a little puzzled, Rivas relaxed and sat back. "Well, sure. You want a backup band too, or just me? It's twenty fifths a night for me, and for this band it's seven fifths ha'pint extra. If I put together a better group it'd be more, of course. Now I'm booked solid until—"

Montecruz raised a hand. "No no. You misunderstand. It's not in your musical capacity that I wish to hire you."

"Oh." I should have guessed, he told himself. "What, then?" he asked dutifully, just to be certain he was right.

"I want you to perform a redemption."

He'd been right. "Sorry. I'm retired."

Montecruz's not quite friendly smile didn't falter. "I think I can make an offer that will bring you out of retirement."

Rivas shook his head. "Look, I wasn't being coy. I've quit. I make plenty now with the music—and anyway, I'm thirty-one years old. I don't have that kind of reflexes and stamina anymore." Or luck, either, he thought sourly. "And it's been three years since my last one—the country will have changed. It always does."

Montecruz leaned forward. "Rivas," he said quietly, "I'm

talking *five thousand Ellay fifths*."

Rivas raised his eyebrows in genuine respect. "That's handsome," he admitted. "There can't be fifty people in Ellay that can even hope to borrow that much." He took a long sip of beer. "But I'm *retired*. I just don't want to risk my life and sanity for strangers anymore. There's other redeemers around, though. Hell, five thousand would buy Frake McAn ten times over."

"Is McAn as good as you?"

"Infinitely better, since I don't do it at all now. Thanks for the beer—and now I really should try to show that damn fool drummer what I want." He got to his feet.

"Wait a minute," Montecruz said quickly, holding up a pudgy hand and beginning to look a little less confident. "You're the only guy that ever performed eight redemptions—"

"Six. Two got to the Holy City before I could catch them."

"Okay, six. You've still got the record. The girl's father wants the best, and listen, this won't be as difficult as the others. All you've got to do is locate her, her family will do the kidnap and breaking—"

"Her family can do the whole thing," said Rivas, straightening up. "I'm not kidding about being *out* of that game. Hire me as a pelicanist or songwriter anytime—they're my only occupations nowadays."

He turned and started back toward the stage, but Montecruz, agile for a fat man, scrambled around the table and caught Rivas's elbow when he'd taken only four paces.

"We'll go *ten thousand!*" the man hissed.

Exasperated, Rivas turned back to face him. "I told you my answer."

For a couple of seconds Montecruz's face was expressionless, and looked oddly childlike; then, "To *sing?*" he demanded, his voice shrill with incredulous scorn. "You'd stop saving lives—souls!—to sit in a bar and sing? Oh, but you only did it while you needed the money, isn't that right? And now that you can fiddle for it, everybody else can... can be gutted and skinned, and it won't disturb your self-satisfaction even as much as a wrinkle in your precious costume would, huh? It must be nice to be the only person worthy of your concern."

A crooked, unmirthful grin had appeared on the pelicanist's face during Montecruz's speech, and when the man had finished, Rivas said, "Why don't you go home and just deal with things you know something about, sport."

He'd spoken quietly, but Mojo and Fandango heard him and looked up in alarm.

The insult, especially deadly in view of Montecruz's hairlessness, hung in the air for several seconds and hardened jaw muscles made Montecruz's suddenly pale face seem even wider.

Rivas yanked his arm free and took two steps back, the skin over his cheekbones taut and his left hand near his knife sheath.

Finally Montecruz, whose hand had darted for his own knife, took a deep breath, let it out, and then whispered, "I don't *take* that, Rivas—I'll just *hold* it for a while." He turned and stalked out of the building.

When the swinging doors had creakily flapped shut after him Rivas looked at the ceiling and exhaled a long, descending whistle. That, he told himself, was loss of control. Better slow down on the beer, old buddy—you've had enough already, at home and here, to keep you oiled for the rest of the evening.

"God, Greg," said Fandango in some awe as the pelicanist walked back to the stage, "you were *mad,* weren't you? I just realized, I never seen you *mad* before—just, you know, grouchy about something not being done right. What'd he say to make you call him out that way? That stuff about singing, and your clothes? And whose life did he want you to—"

"Oh, shut *up,* Tommy," said Rivas wearily. Mojo had got the bright lamps lit at the front of the stage, so he put on a look of only mild annoyance as he climbed back up onto it. "He didn't make me mad, all right? I'm tired of everybody thinking they've got a right to my time, that's all. And I didn't mean to call him out." He picked up his instrument and the horsehair bow, and was embarrassed to notice that his hands were trembling; he lowered them quickly and shot a freezing look at the drummer, but Fandango was shaking his head and tapping out a quick burst on one of his drums and clearly hadn't noticed.

"But you called him a *sport,* " the drummer said. "I mean, sure, you call me that when I screw up sometimes, but that guy *was* one—I could see from here he was a baldy."

"I'm going to think you're a mental one if you still can't grasp the tempo of this," said Rivas. "From the beginning now, and make it rattle." He tapped his foot three times while Fandango frowned attentively, then began playing.

They had to stop a few minutes later when Mojo began turning the noisy, ratcheted wall cranks that hoisted the lit chandeliers up to the ceiling, and in spite of his earlier resolve Rivas put down his pelican and went to the bar for another refill. He came back and perched cross-legged on his stool and then just stared absently into the still dim corners of the ceiling, where long, dusty festoons of paper dolls were draped like huge cobwebs around three of the walls.

Only a few customers had wandered in and sat down by the time Mojo finished his tour of the wall cranks, and Fandango glanced inquiringly toward Rivas, but the pelicanist seemed to have forgotten his dissatisfaction with the drummer's playing. More people drifted in, and the chandeliers slowly stopped swinging as the ripple of conversation grew louder and the laughter and clinking of glasses more frequent; but Rivas remained oblivious, and when the pair of typically mute Chino twins who were the steel guitarist and chimes-banger arrived and climbed onto the stage, Rivas's hand-jive greeting was as unconsciously automatic as the twitch of a horse's flank when a fly lands on it.

Finally Fandango had to nudge him and hiss, "Heads up, Greg!" when the owner appeared and began threading his way around the tables toward the stage.

Steve Spink and Rivas were of about the same age and build—thirty or so and rangy but tending a little toward plumpness over the belt—but Spink with his ready smile and undisciplined tumble of blond hair fairly radiated boyish cheer, while Rivas's dark hair and beard and deeply lined cheeks gave his face in repose an almost theatrical look of disdain.

Spink leaned toward the stage as Rivas, looking only startled at the moment, hastily hopped off his stool and picked up his instrument and blinked around in some surprise at the filled room.

"You okay, Rivas?" Spink asked pleasantly.

"Uh, what?" Rivas stepped to the edge of the stage, inadvertently kicking over his forgotten beer glass. The glass broke, and beer spattered Spink's expensive leather coat.

"Damn it, I asked if you were all right. You don't act like you are. Can you still perform?"

Rivas scowled and straightened to his full height. "Of *course* I can perform! What do you mean *still?* My God, just because I kick over one cheap beer glass—"

"Since when is glass cheap? There was an old guy in here at lunch talking to me. Said you were a Jaybird once. Any truth to that?"

"Yes," Rivas said haughtily. "I don't make any secret of it. I've been a lot of things in my life."

"You talk about all the other things, though. Did you take the sacrament very often?"

For the second time that evening Rivas felt real anger kindle in him. "Just what are you trying to say, Steve?"

Spink let his habitual eye-narrowing smile relax into a frown. "I'm sorry, Greg. But you can understand my concern, can't you? I can't have any of the people I rely on going birdy."

"Start worrying about it when I can't fill your damn place to overflowing for you anymore."

"You're right, Greg. Sorry. I shouldn't have listened to the old guy." He turned to the audience, and Rivas glimpsed the smile flashing back on. "Ladies and gentlemen," Spink said loudly, "tonight once again we're privileged to have with us Gregorio Rivas, of Venice."

The applause came right on cue and was satisfactory in volume and duration, and Rivas grinned as arrogantly as ever as he bowed in acknowledgement—but under it he was uneasy. How would the applause sound, he wondered, if I didn't have a few paid prompters in the crowd to lead it? And how much longer can the dangerous glamor of Venice plausibly cling to me? I've been out of Venice for five years, after all, and while it's true that Steve's standard intro still gets raised eyebrows and shocked whispers from strangers, old Mojo the other day was actually surprised when I mentioned having worked at the Bom Sheltr Bar in Venice—he said he thought that story was just flash for the tourists, like the fake hooter skulls on spikes on the roof.

As the clapping and whistling was tapering off, Rivas turned to Fandango and the twins and impulsively hand-jived the signal for "Everybody Wants to Smoke My Comoy," his trademark song, which he usually saved for reviving an apathetic audience. Fandango hammered out the staccato opening of the song and the crowd reacted with unmistakably genuine enthusiasm, and for the next few minutes Rivas forgot his doubts and let his singing and playing absorb him totally.

During a lengthy alternation between the steel guitarist and the drummer—a sequence Rivas knew they had no trouble with—he took the opportunity to scan the audience—a little nervously, for he was afraid the Hammond girl might have shown up to make a scene. Spink might have liked it, as being evidence of what a genuine Venetian rake-hell the pelicanist was, but Rivas dreaded such encounters, inevitable though they seemed to be. He peered at each face that he could make out by the illumination of the chandeliers and the tabletop candles, and was relieved not to see her.

And she'd be sure to sit where I *would* see her, he thought with a slightly drunken shiver. Damn her anyway. Why can't a girl grasp the fact that a breakup *can't* look tragic to the one initiating it? It can only seem tragic to the one being ditched; to the one doing the ditching it's ... fresh air, a load off the shoulders, a spring in the step and a whistle on the lips—the very opposite of tragic.

And hell, he thought, it's not as if I haven't drawn that hand as well as dealt it; only once, granted, but I had naively invested so much that time—much more than this Hammond creature ever could have—that I carry the loss with me still, as helplessly as I carry my skeleton, and like the old-time stainless steel it doesn't rust away with time into camouflage colors, but is always as bright as new, and mercilessly reflective.

Rivas turned to the chimes-banger and hand-jived, *Remind me later—stainless steel—rust—camouflage colors.* The man nodded.

Yes, thought Rivas with some satisfaction, a nice image. Ought to fit well into a song, with some dramatic way of having lost the girl ... death, maybe ... suicide even, sure ...

... Anything but the way I actually did lose Urania. ...

He shied away from the memory of himself at the age of eighteen, crouched behind a bush, in the ruins of a rented suit that stank of brandy and vomit, and, to his everlasting horror, barking like a dog.

Once or twice in the years since, during unusually objective moods, it had occurred to him that he might someday find the memory funny. It had certainly not happened yet.

In any case he was glad the Hammond girl seemed willing to disappear painlessly. He'd found her interesting for a while, but she was no Urania. None of them ever were.

It was nearly time for the pelican to re-enter, and he had just gripped the neck and poised the bow over the taut strings when he noticed at the bar a well-dressed old man who was watching him; and his belly went cold several seconds before he even consciously realized who it was, and he missed his cue.

The steel guitarist looked up in mild surprise and without a falter smoothly began the phrase again.

He had to begin it one more time, though, and let the more attentive members of the audience catch on that something was wrong, for Rivas had now remembered who the old man was and was staring at him with astonishment and hatred and, even after more than a decade, a bit of fear.

"Greg!" whispered Fandango urgently. "Hop aboard!"

Rivas blinked, returned some of his attention to the music, and then at the correct moment slashed the bow across the strings, and the song continued as usual.

He signaled to the other musicians to drop the time-consuming flourishes from the end of the song this time, and, as Fandango obediently rattled out a quick conclusion phrase, Rivas, much soberer now than he'd been a minute ago, lowered his instrument and stepped to the front of the stage.

"We'll be taking a short break now," he said curtly, and leaving the pelican beside his stool, he hopped down and strode to the bar—and he was able to do it fairly quickly, for even the bleariest of the drinkers seemed to sense a dangerous tautness in him, and pulled in their legs and scooted their chairs closer to the tables to get out of his way.

By the time he stopped in front of the old man his shock had receded enough for him to have deduced what must have happened to bring the man here.

"There's a private room off the kitchen," Rivas said to him in a voice from which conflicting emotions had leached all inflection. "Wait till we get in there to tell me about it. Whiskey," he added, more loudly, to Mojo. "Double, with a chaser, now."

Mojo provided the two filled glasses quickly, and Rivas picked them up and led the old man away from the bar to a door in a shadowed corner.

"Go fetch us a lamp from somewhere," the pelicanist snapped at the old man as he held both glasses in one hand to open the door with the other. "Hurry now—chop chop!"

The old man's face had been pinched into the expression of someone who has learned that his dinner will consist of the stable boys' leftovers, and the change it underwent now was as though he had been told that he'd have to express gratitude for it too; but he silently did as he was told and went back to get a lamp from the corner of the bar.

Rivas stood by the door and shut it behind them when the old man had returned with the lamp and carried it into the little room. All but filling the chamber was a plastic table with half a dozen chairs around it, and Rivas sat down in one of the chairs and set his drinks in front of himself.

"You should have told Spink who you were this afternoon," he said. "He'd have been impressed to meet the man who distills Ellay's money."

The lamp clanked down onto the table and the agitated flame made the two men's shadows fragment and then reform on the wooden walls. "It would do neither of us any good," came the rasped reply, "to let people know that Irwin Barrows has business with Gregorio Rivas."

Rivas took a gulp of the whiskey and chased it with a long draught of the beer. "Right," he said coldly, "in fact why let even Rivas himself know, eh? Who *was* your touchy negotiator this evening? Some jumped-up vineyard foreman? He didn't handle the approach in a terribly businesslike way—almost wound up challenging me to a duel."

Irwin Barrows stared at him speculatively. "I considered not telling you this," he said finally, "but I will, because I don't think it will alter your decision. Montecruz can be excused, perhaps, for showing some heat—you see, he's her fiancé. They're to be—they *were* to be—married next month."

Rivas was surprised by the gust of unhappiness that battered at his control—and even shook it, for he could feel the color draining from his rigidly expressionless face—and he realized wearily that the grief he'd been tending like a garden for thirteen years had gradually become domesticated, ceased to be the wild, naturally occurring sort. And then a moment later he was disgusted with himself for having such an obsessive focus on the feelings of Gregorio Rivas. My God, he told himself, that Montecruz son-of-a-bitch was right: for you, everything exists only to the extent that it pleases or displeases your favorite person—you.

Still, I won't fetch her back for him.

He hastily downed the remainder of the whiskey, but instead of the obscuring fog he'd hoped for, it brought an unwelcome clarity to his thoughts; and he knew, despairingly, that he couldn't let the Jaybirds have her.

If only I didn't know, he thought, if I hadn't been one myself for almost three years, I could probably turn him down. If I hadn't seen for myself Jaybush's methodical disassembly of human minds, his consumption of souls as if they were firewood, I could probably spit in Barrow's face this minute and stalk out of here in a grand gesture of rejection. *You exiled me from her thirteen years ago—now I exile you from her. How do you like it?* Yes, to rub his hitherto celestially superior nose in it . . . to send his smug complacency out the Dogtown gate . . . to let *him* beg *me* for her, and be contemptuously dismissed . . .

If only I didn't know!

But when he replayed that last thought and considered the several things it indicated about himself, he had to suppress a shudder, for it had momentarily sickened him simply to be Gregorio Rivas.

Finally he looked up. "You're right," he said, wishing his voice hadn't hoarsened for the occasion. "It doesn't alter my decision. I'll do it."

Barrows inclined his head. "Thank you."

"So when did they get her?"

"Last night, late. She was at a party north of here, at Third and Fig, and somehow she wound up alone out front, and a gang of them started talking to her—I guess you should know their stinking arguments and tricks as well as anyone—and when her lazy and now unemployed bodyguard finally caught up with her, it was just in time to see Urania climbing into the back of a Jaybird wagon as the horses were being whipped up."

"It took off in what direction?"

"East on Third."

"One wagon alone?"

"That's what the bodyguard said."

Rivas sat back and drummed his fingers on the table and his eyes lost their sharp focus as, for the first time in three years, he began planning one more redemption. "You should have come to me right away," he said, "and not wasted time trying to undermine my job here and sending that clown in here this evening. Still, it's a good sign that it was a

single eastbound wagon; that implies the shepherd wanted
to recruit at least another one or two people before returning
to his caravan camp. They might still be in the area, camped
in one of the neglected districts outside the wall."

"Can you find out tonight?"

Rivas smiled at the naive question. "No way. You don't
just ask the nearest Jaybird where one of their wagons went.
And even if they are right outside—even if there were a
full moon out tonight, instead of this rainy overcast—do
you know how many square miles of ruins there are out
there?"

"Tomorrow morning, then. Now as Montecruz evidently
started to explain to you, all you'll have to do is—"

"—Locate her. Yeah, he did say that, but that's not how
it's going to be. I'll do the kidnap and breaking too."

Barrow's eyes narrowed and his face assumed the stony
cast Rivas remembered so well. "No," he said firmly. "That
is simply out of the question."

Rivas pushed his chair back and stood up. "Frake McAn
lives over Mister Lou's on Sandoval Street. Don't tell him
I sent you—it'll only prejudice him against you. And don't
waste time," he added, poking a finger at Barrows. "Some
of those recruiting caravans go directly to the Holy City."
He picked up his beer glass and reached for the door latch.

Barrows raised a frail hand. "All right," he said tiredly,
"wait, sit down, you can have it. The whole thing, like you
say."

Rivas opened the door and leaned out. "Mojo!" he called.
"Another beer here!" He closed it and resumed his seat.
"Then I guess we've got a deal, Barrows." Unconsciously
he ran his fingers through his hair, disarranging it. "Ten
thousand fifths of your Currency brandy; a bank draft for
five thousand now, and another of the same when and if I
can bring Urania back inside the Ellay walls."

"You misunderstood. Five thousand is the total price."

"Montecruz went up to ten."

"Montecruz must have got carried away in his anxiety. I think that's understandable. But there's no—"

"That's something you can take up with him later," Rivas said. "I'm taking the offer that was made to me."

"The price I'm offering," said Barrows angrily, "is still much more than you've ever been paid before."

The door was pulled open from the outside and Mojo hobbled in, set the fresh beer on the table, took the old glasses and exited.

"Evidently she's worth five to you," Rivas remarked matter-of-factly, "but not quite ten. Did you catch McAn's address? Over Mister Lou's on—"

Barrows was staring at him with loathing. "This is interesting," he interrupted in a tight voice. "I had thought that extended use of the Jaybird sacrament always simply eroded the *intelligence* of the communicant, but I see it can do far worse than that—I see it can destroy the person's empathy, his very *humanity*, leaving just a . . . sort of shrewd, cunning insect."

Rivas knew that anger was what Barrows wanted, so he leaned back and laughed. "Not bad, Barrows! I like it, write it down so I can use it in a song sometime." He leaned forward and let his smile unkink. "And I hope you realize that a 'shrewd, cunning insect,' as you so diplomatically put it, is exactly what you need right now. Yes, I was a Jaybird for nearly three years after that night you drove me off the Barrows estate, and I *have* taken their devastating sacrament a number of times—as Urania is probably doing at this very moment, quite a thought, hmm?—though I pretty quick figured ways to blunt its effects, make my mind inaccessible to it. But that's why I'm the only guy who's been any kind of successful at prying people out of Jaybush's hands . . . or off his dinner plate, let's say; I'm sure you like that better, you being such a fan of colorful metaphors, right?"

The door was pulled open again, but this time it was the furiously grinning Steve Spink that leaned in. "You gonna get back out here, Greg? People are beginning to leave, and I remember what you said about always filling the place to overflowing."

Rivas had a quick, involuntary vision of himself as he'd probably be if he lost this job *and* blew the Barrows redemption deal—a no longer young man fiddling for jiggers on a Dogtown corner, his beard thick and bushy and no longer a daring, carefully trimmed symbol of straddling the line dividing the upper classes from the lower—but he took a leisurely sip of the beer and managed to sound unconcerned when he said, "I'll be back up there in a minute, Steve. They aren't going to forget who I am between now and then."

"Hope you're sure of that, Greg," Spink said with a couple of extra teeth showing in his grin. Then he noticed Rivas's companion. "Say, that's the old guy who was—"

"I know, Steve. One more minute."

The door closed again, muting the crowd sounds, and Rivas turned to Barrows with raised eyebrows. "Well?"

"Okay," the old man said quietly. "Ten. Five now and five when you bring her back."

"Done. See me after the show tonight to set up the details."

Barrows nodded, got to his feet and edged around the table to the door, but paused. "Oh, by the way," he said uncertainly.

Rivas looked up, clearly impatient.

"Uh, there's something that's been . . . puzzling me for thirteen years. Maybe I shouldn't ask."

Rivas was afraid he knew what was coming, but he said, "Yes?" casually.

"Why—excuse me, I don't by any means insist on an answer—but on that night I had you driven off, *why* were you behind those bushes on your hands and knees, throwing up and . . . barking?"

Rivas was humiliated to realize that his face was turning red. Why, he thought, can't he and I forget that damned incident? "You've been wondering about that for thirteen years?" he asked.

"Yes."

Rivas shook his head and waved at the door. "Keep on wondering."

After Barrows had left, Rivas sat back and tilted up his glass again, and then, gingerly, he gave in and allowed himself to remember that disastrous night—the first and last time he'd ever tasted the Currency brandy.

It had been in the fall of—Rivas counted the years on his fingers—the sixth year of the Sixth Ace, and Urania Barrows had decided to invite Gregorio, her fieldboy lover, to her gala seventeenth birthday party. Though only the son of one of the tenant farmers, the eighteen-year-old Gregorio had managed to save some money—a fifth and some change, big money to a field hand—and on the day of the party he spent it all on renting a suit and getting a haircut and a presumptuously aristocratic shave. And he went to the party, and in spite of being terribly nervous in the sophisticated company, he had made a good impression . . . until the brandy was served.

Young Gregorio had been drinking wine since childhood, but distilled spirits were new to him, and he didn't know that one was supposed to drink them more slowly. He eventually realized that he was foolishly drunk and embarrassing

Urania, so he left the party...and as soon as he was out in the fresh air, it occurred to him that he was sick.

Not wanting to be seen vomiting, he'd reeled off the path into a tiny clearing behind some bushes and then, on his hands and knees, begun the lengthy process of expelling the brandy from his stomach.

And at one point, when he'd paused for breath, he heard a lady on the path asking someone about the peculiar noises coming from behind the bushes. A man's voice replied that it sounded like a dog.

Rivas shuddered now, and drained his beer. He remembered that he had desperately wanted the people to forget about the noises and go away, and somehow he'd concluded that the best way to accomplish that would be to convince them that it was indeed only a dog, and not anything that needed investigating. So he'd begun...barking.

He stood up now and opened the door, but he was unable to avoid remembering the rest of it, his last conscious moments of that disastrous evening...when he'd finally opened his eyes and seen Irwin Barrows's boots six inches from his face.

He left the little room, swinging the door shut behind him, and as he reeled back toward the stage—the alcohol had caught up with him again—his eyes only half saw the dim bar and the stage ahead and the uneasy faces watching him; overlaid on that scene like a second transparency he was seeing again the One-a-One Freeway, seeming because of the thick fog to be a solitary track across the chilly sky, down which he'd fled on foot on that awful dawn thirteen years ago. He'd been shivering with cold and dizzily sick from a concussion as well as a hangover, for the outraged Irwin Barrows had given him a solid kick in the head before dragging him out from behind the bushes and ordering the kitchen crew to carry him away and dump him somewhere outside the Barrows land boundary.

He'd walked all that day, and as the sun rose and gradually scattered the fog, he'd seen for the first time the weathered and vine-hung ruins of big old Ellay, noisy now only with the chatter of parrots and monkeys. Decrepitude lent the still imposing building shells an air of tragic grandeur that they couldn't have had in life, and the sheer number of them—they stretched like ranks of uncared-for tombstones to the horizon—awed the young Gregorio; several times his curiosity had outweighed his sickness and haste and numb sense of loss, and he'd gone exploring through old rooms and up and down alarming, rubble-strewn stairways. By the time he finally sighted the high west wall of Ellay, only its top trim of crenelations was still lit by the low red sun. The summer-shrunken river beyond the city was invisible in the darkness, and fear of hooters and hemogoblins made him ignore his headache and cover the last couple of miles at a run.

That had been the first night he'd ever spent out of his father's house, and, after a couple of hours of unhappy wandering through the streets, he'd spent it in a corner of a shed in Dogtown. He hadn't been the only vagrant to seek shelter there, and he was awakened several times by the abrupt awareness of, and then the weary effort of refusing, the affectionate attentions of one or another of his shedmates. One young man, offended at having been rebuffed, had asked Gregorio if he'd care to leave the city right at that minute by the Dogtown gate. Rivas had politely refused . . . and been very glad of his refusal when he learned, years later, that there was no such gate, and that the phrase "leave by the Dogtown gate" meant to disappear, figuratively or literally, into one of Dogtown's ubiquitous, feculent trash trenches.

The next morning, stunned by hunger and exhaustion, he'd set out walking, and in the South Gate area by Sandoval Street he'd met the group of the zealots popularly known as Jaybirds . . . the wonderfully concerned, shoulder-patting, sympathetically smiling Jaybirds.

Steve was right, he thought uneasily when he stepped back up onto the stage and surveyed the crowd—quite a few people have left. How long was I in that room talking to Barrows? It'd probably be an error to ask, admit I don't know. Goddamn whiskey. No more beer or anything for you tonight, man!

He started to signal for "Everybody Wants to Smoke My Comoy," and then remembered that he'd already used it and signaled instead for "Drinking Alone."

Fandango sighed audibly as he started the song. Oh, look on the bright side, Tommy, Rivas thought—the next main attraction performer they get in here will probably want to do nothing but Scrap and Bugwalk.

CHAPTER TWO

SOMEHOW THE CLEAR blue sky visible through the unglassed windows only made the interior of the Toothtalker's room look shabbier. The Toothtalker herself, it occurred to Rivas, looked like just one more piece of faintly morbid antique trash to avoid tripping over. The thought made him smile in spite of his headache. Yes, he thought, among all these pictures and specimen jars and rotted books and bits of incomprehensible old-time machinery, she looks like a desiccated old mummy. The lower jaw, perhaps due to some error in taxidermic technique, had gradually pulled away from the face as the unwholesome memento dried out, finally leaving the effigy frozen forever in a stressful but inaudible scream.

A mummy which, he added as once again she treated her guests to some of the eerie low gargling she was so good at, has become inhabited by baritone mice. In spite of being irritable and grainy-eyed from a nearly sleepless night, Rivas had to strangle a chuckle. The effort made his headache worse.

He glanced at the chair beside him and saw that Irwin Barrows was sitting hunched forward, anxiously watching the motionless, gargling old woman. Rivas was surprised— he had thought that Barrows's insistence that they consult a Toothtalker before Rivas embarked on the redemption was nothing more than a formality, a traditional gesture like letting a wagon "warm up" for a few minutes on cold mornings before flicking the reins and getting started . . . but the old financier was obviously as credulous as the stupidest scavenger who ever shambled up these tower stairs to hear the judgment of the spirit world on which beyond-the-wall districts were particularly favored or imperiled by the configurations of the stars.

Rivas felt almost betrayed to realize it. Come *on,* he thought, you're one of the wealthiest men in Ellay, surely *you* can see through this nonsense if *I* can.

He leaned back and looked out the window at the sunlit but still damp landscape. To the west he could see a green band that was the edge of the south farms, but to the south was nothing but the spread of tumbled, empty buildings, a scene lost somewhere between cityscape and landscape, animated by rolling tumbleweeds and, once in a while, the ragged figure of a scavenger too weak to venture very far from the city walls. Further to the south he could see the gleam of San Pedro Harbor. And beyond that, he knew, was Long Beach Island and then the open sea, and, way down the coast at the mouth of the Santa Ana River, Irvine.

I hope I can catch her, he thought, before having to travel too far in that direction. He shuddered, remembering one redemption—one that had not succeeded—that actually brought him within sight of the high white walls of Jaybush's Holy City at Irvine. I never, he thought firmly, want to be that close to that damned place again. It wouldn't be so bad if I didn't more than half suspect he *is* some kind of messiah. My father used to swear he'd seen the spray of shooting stars that lit the sky on the night of Jaybush's conception, thirty-some years ago—and even rival religions admit that before he retired from public life he several times did, verifiably, bring dead people back to life...though of course the rival religions claim he had Satan's help.

A patch of morning sunlight had been inching its way across the wall, and when Rivas glanced again at the old woman in the corner, he saw that the light had reached her face, and, in her gaping mouth, was glittering on all the bits of metal glued to her teeth. Well, Barrows can't say he isn't getting his money's worth, he thought. There must be half a pound of scrap metal in there. Rivas knew—as Barrows evidently didn't—that this was just a gaudy prop, that real toothtalking was supposed to be a consequence of having tiny metal fillings in the teeth. In years past a few people with such fillings *had* reported hearing faint voices in their mouths; but they said it happened very seldom and only on mountain tops, and Rivas hadn't heard of a verified case of it showing up within at least the last ten years.

It was, though, a priceless piece of popular superstition for fortunetellers to exploit.

Rivas yawned audibly—so that for a moment he and the old woman seemed to be yawning in tandem—but he closed his mouth with a snap when Barrows darted an angry glance at him, and he had to make do with just arranging himself more comfortably in his chair. He'd given up trying to sleep last night after a dream about Urania had sent him jack-knifing out of bed just as the one o'clock bell was being rung. He'd spent the remainder of the night on the roof of his building with his pelican, sawing and strumming increasingly fantastic gun improvisations on the tune of *Peter and the Wolf*.

Perhaps because Rivas seemed unimpressed with her routine thus far, the old Toothtalker let her jaw relax and hurried to a closet from which, after knocking a few things over, she produced a yellow plastic telephone with a receiver which began buzzing and clicking after she gave it a couple of shakes. She frowned reprovingly at Rivas as she began whispering into it.

For a few minutes he tried to pay attention, if only to figure out what she was saying about him to the spirit world, but the interrupted dream from last night seemed to cling to him like a faint, disagreeable odor, ignorable most of the time but intruding itself whenever he shifted position. Finally he sighed and gave in, and let the recollection take him.

In the dream Urania had been one of a row of people kneeling in a typical Jaybird nest, a cramped room out in the ruins somewhere, littered with the sort of relics that aren't worthy anybody's time to scavenge. The priest— known as the jaybush, for during administration of the sacrament he was supposed to become an actual, literal extension of the Messiah, Norton Jaybush himself—moved down the line, pausing in front of each communicant just long enough to touch him or her on the forehead.

Every one of the kneeling figures at least jerked at the touch, and many pitched over in violent fits. Rivas still remembered very clearly his own first receiving of the sacrament—remembered watching the jaybush work his way down the line toward him, and wondering how much of the gaffed-fish response was just hysteria or outright faking; and then the jaybush had come to *him*, and touched *his* forehead, and the rending physical shock of it had blacked him out, leaving him to wake up on the floor, dazed and bruised and stupefied, half an hour later.

In the dream, when the jaybush came to Urania and touched her, she had raspingly exhaled a cloud of pink vapor, and then had steadily kept on exhaling more of it, long after her lungs should have been wrung completely empty, and when Rivas rushed up in concern and took her in his arms he could feel her flesh diminishing inside her clothes like an outgoing tide; for a long time he cradled the still impossibly exhaling and ever-lighter girl, and when the emptying finally stopped and he raised his head from her shoulder and looked down into her face, it was nothing more than a naked skull that gaped blindly up at him.

And, he recalled now with something like nausea, that discovery had not in any way altered his determination to bring her back to Ellay and make her his wife. He rubbed his eyes and pushed a stray lock of hair back into place.

"Ah," the old woman said, nodding and pacing back and forth with the telephone receiver pressed to her ear. "Neutrons, you say? Goddamn. And . . . *master cylinders?* Lord have mercy." She squinted down her nose at Rivas to see if he was properly impressed by these esoteric terms. He noticed that she hadn't bothered to connect the end of the telephone cord to anything, and it was dragging around on the floor behind her. He wondered whether she'd trip over it. "Ten-four," she said finally, and then put the telephone down on the window sill, apparently to cool off.

She turned to her guests. "Well, the spirits had a lot to say. You, sir," she said, pointing at Rivas, "are the focus of a lot of uncertainty. You see, in every equation there's an *unknown* factor—the hex, as we mathematicians say— and in order to untangle the various lifelines involved and see which one comes out healthy at the end, it's necessary to . . ."

She went into a long speech then, full of "identity resonances" and "orbital velocities of the soul," frequently waving toward her dust-covered and obviously random collection of shabby books to support her statements. Presently she dug out a deck of playing cards and, while shuffling them, explained that Matt Sandoval, Ellay's legendary First Ace, had designed the fifty-two cards on his deathbed as a means for mystically savvy people to be able to consult him even after his demise. The four "aces," she informed her guests, were called that because they represented the four natures of the Ace himself. She then began laying the cards out on a tabletop in a significant-looking pattern, scowling or nodding as each card was added.

Rivas stopped paying attention. During the last several years he had laboriously learned to read the old-time writing, with all its silent letters, superfluous tenses and fabulous, credulity-straining words; and he'd actually read a number of the books and magazines that were just decorations in the more affluent households, and props for fortunetellers. And though he had arrived at no very clear understanding of the bright, crowded, "electrical" world of more than a century ago—even their maps described a southern California coastline that didn't exist—he'd gleaned enough to know that most people who made their livings by claiming to know about the ancient wonders actually knew less about them than he did.

Her story about Sandoval having invented playing cards, for example, and naming the aces after his own title, was, Rivas knew, exactly backward. Rivas had read a journal kept during the First Ace's reign, and had learned that the citizens of Ellay had wanted to confer the title of king upon the man who had founded the currency, had the wall built, broken the terror hold of the piratical "motorcyclists" known as the hooters, and re-instituted agriculture. Sandoval had accepted the job but not the title. "There've been too many kings," he was reported to have said; "and Queen or Jack or Joker won't do—I'll be the first Ace."

The old woman seemed to be winding down anyway. "I see success for you both," she said. "The spirits say you're cookin' with gas. For you, man," she went on, pointing at Barrows, "I see an increase in your fortune, I see those old brandy bottles just a-rolling toward you."

Rivas looked over at Barrows. Yes, the chance of mention of brandy had firmly set the Toothtalker's hook—the old man's eyes were wide and his knuckles were white on the arms of the chair.

"And for you," she continued, now pointing at Rivas and eyeing his bare wedding ring finger, "I see . . . a reunion with a long-lost lover, a wedding and . . . six unsporting children."

Rivas blinked. You old phony, he thought in instant panic, don't say *that,* he *believes* your idiot predictions! The musician glanced apprehensively at the old man and, sure enough, Barrows was staring at him coldly and nodding.

"I wondered how great the risk of that would be," Barrows murmured.

Rivas abruptly decided that he'd go after Urania unpaid and independently if he had to—but leaving to perform a redemption right now would almost certainly cost him his job, and Barrow's payment would mean the difference between a leisurely, well-fed year or two in which to court another position on the one hand, and poverty and bad food and the selling off of possessions and hasty, undignified begging for *any* sort of job on the other. And if at all possible he wanted to prevent Barrows from hiring some other redemptionist who'd certainly only manage to muddy the water and put the Jaybirds on their guard.

"Look," he said evenly, "this old lady's a fraud, and no more able to tell the future than I am. Now just because she—"

"Don't try to claim *that,* Rivas," rasped Barrows. "After she knew—"

"She just said you'd get a lot of money! That's a standard fortuneteller's line, dammit, same as the one she gave me! She *didn't* know you're the guy that distills it."

The Toothtalker, disconcerted that so innocuous a prediction had caused such rancor, had been listening closely, and her eyebrows went up at Rivas's last sentence. "Yes I did," she said instantly. "The vibratory dimensions told me everything. Greg Rivas and Irwin Barrows, you two are."

Smothering a curse, Rivas sprang out of his chair, crossed to the window and picked up the telephone receiver, which had quieted down but began buzzing again when he jiggled it. "Damn it," he shouted at Barrows, "none of this is real. Look." He unscrewed the perforated plastic cap on the earpiece and a large wasp flew out; it looped a confused figure-eight in front of his eyes and then lighted on his cheek and stung him. "Ow, goddammit."

"You see?" cried the Toothtalker triumphantly. "You can't mess with scientific machinery with impunity!" The wasp found the window and disappeared outside. "Look, you made me lose my . . . high frequency receptor."

Rivas saw that Barrows, who evidently didn't know how telephones were supposed to have worked, was even more impressed with the Toothtalker's powers now than he'd been a minute ago. "Holy smokes," the old man exclaimed, "Rivas isn't going to die, is he?"

Rivas started to say, scathingly, "Of a *wasp sting?*" but the old woman, with the reflexes of a veteran entertainer used to quelling troublesome audiences, whipped a squirt gun out from under her robe and squeezed off a blast of raw high-proof gin straight into his face; Rivas squawked, reeled blindly to the window and hung on the sill, gasping and spitting.

"He would have," she said serenely, "if I hadn't given him that. Radio liquor, distilled from isotopes. He's lucky I had some handy—that was no *ordinary* wasp."

Feeling defeated, Rivas straightened up, took a deep breath and turned around to face Barrows. "Listen to me," he said. "I'll promise to bring her back to your house—assuming I can get her away from the Jaybirds—if *you'll* promise to let her go with me if she understands what she'd be doing . . . and if she should happen to want to, after all these years. How's that? We'll leave it up to Uri to decide whether this lady's prediction was accurate." Barrows started to speak, but Rivas interrupted him by taking a firmer grip on the telephone receiver, which he somehow hadn't let go of, and slamming it very hard against the concrete window sill. The receiver exploded, and bits of yellow plastic buzzed through the air and clattered around among the piles of incomprehensible old junk. "And of course," Rivas went on, "keep in mind the fact that I'm the only redemptionist with any real chance of getting her at all."

Barrows squinted at him for several seconds, and Rivas was a little surprised to see that the old man actually looked uncertain and even a little sick—as if the price of this redemption had begun to involve something more than his Currency.

"You make it hard on both of us," Barrows said softly.

Rivas wasn't sure he knew what the old man meant, but he said, "I'm just divvying up the weight." He crossed to where Barrows was sitting and stuck out his right hand. "Promise?"

Barrows sighed. "I truly hope she doesn't decide to join you. Yes, I promise." He reached up and with the slow emphasis of a weary judge rapping a gavel, shook Rivas's hand.

• • •

Few of his sophisticated friends would have recognized
the lost-looking fellow standing in the rain-puddled square
by the South Gate as Gregorio Rivas; he had spent the hour
since leaving the Toothtalker's parlor at a tailor's and a
barber shop. Now, looking years younger with his half beard
shaved· off and his hair pulled back and funneled into a
tarred stump at the back of his neck and his wild clothes
replaced by a neat suit of off white flax, he was the very
picture of a well-born youth bewildered at finding himself
alone, jiggerless and hungover in the nastier end of the big
city.

He wasn't the only person loitering there. In general
parlance the South Gate consisted of the area immediately
roundabout as well as the actual gate through which Sandoval Street entered the walled city, and it was perhaps the
busiest and most crowded fifty square yards in southern
California. At the moment Ellay's most successful lumber
scavenger was bringing several wagons into the city, each
one piled high with wooden beams, most of them gray and
caked with concrete but a few still bright with ancient paint.
The musty smell of freshly resurrected lumber contended
in the morning air with the aroma of the hot tacos being
sold on several street corners, the stench from Dogtown
every time the wind faltered, and the smoky pungency of
the charcoal and lye guilds out on eastern Woolshirt; and the
big old buildings on the west side of Sandoval echoed back
the cacophony of daily life among the barrows and gullies
and shacks on the other side. Rivas's aching head was as-
saulted with an auctioneer's jabbering from the big wooden
warehouse that was the Relic Exchange, the ringing of ham-
mers in the various blacksmith booths, and even, he half
suspected, the clink, clank and curse of the steel miners under
the streets, struggling to free and bring up pieces of the vast
steel beams that lay tumbled and rusting under the fine soil

of the whole eastern half of Ellay. And there was even, Rivas noted with a wry grin, a street balladeer playing a pelican and ineptly singing "Everybody Wants to Smoke My Comoy." Rivas rubbed his smooth chin and wondered if he wasn't leaving more of himself in the city than he was taking with him.

And because the little white cards that represented brandy changed hands so frequently in this quarter, much of the crowd consisted of scavengers of a less respectable sort than the lumber merchant and the miners. Though continuing to behave like a scared young man in unfamiliar surroundings, Rivas watched with concealed amusement the specialized dance of an expert pickpocket—strangely insectlike in its series of hesitant touches culminating in a darting garb, the whole body spring-poised for the possible necessity of flight—and the indolent progress of a somewhat overripe prostitute who had come to terms with the consequences of time and knew how to make the most of shadows and selectively revealing clothes. It occurred to Rivas that he was, at the moment, just as much a web-spinner, just as much a patient angler, as either of them.

The difference between us, he thought as he hefted his knapsack and wandered in an aimless fashion to a different corner, is that I'm fishing for predators.

During the next fifteen minutes he saw, too, a number of people who were genuinely in the sort of plight he was mimicking. Hunched down in a doorway near where he'd been standing before, Rivas noticed an obviously malnourished, no more than teenaged boy muttering angrily to several imaginary companions, and Rivas wondered what it was that had brought the boy to this state. Liquor or syphilis generally took decades to ruin a person's mind, but dope could have—especially the Venetian Blood—or the Jaybird sacrament, though the Jaybirds nearly never let strangers see any of their very badly eroded communicants.

There was a drunken girl stumbling around, too, who seemed at first to be with the inexpert pelican player but was eventually led away by a grinning baldy-sport who, Rivas happened to know, was a Blood dealer. What's the matter, thought Rivas sourly, the dope trade so bad you've got to pimp in your spare time? I'd go rescue her if I wasn't certain she'd drift right back here to one of you.

Some people, he thought, simply have no will to survive—they're walking hors d'oeuvres waiting for someone who can spare the time to devour them. And while it's probably some such unattractive quality as egotism or vanity that has kept me clear of . . . that catastrophic relaxation, it's the reason I'm still alive and able to think, and I'll work on keeping it.

Rivas smiled, remembering his response to his first taking of the Jaybird sacrament—while the rest of the recovering communicants had been praising the Lord Jaybush and making sure they knew when the sacrament would be administered again so as not to miss it, young Gregorio Rivas, though stunned, exhausted and glad to have found shelter and company, was coldly appraising the situation. He didn't doubt that the mysterious Norton Jaybush was certainly more than a man and possibly a god, but the prospect of abandoning his individuality in order to "merge with the Lord" was profoundly repugnant to him.

The Jaybird band that picked him up had taken him to a nest in one of the neglected structures outside the wall and introduced him to the Jaybird way of life. He had, that first day, watched several of the far-gone communicants "speaking in tongues," and he was disturbed not so much by the gibberish pouring out of the slack faces as by the fact that they were all doing it in precise, effortless unison, as if—and Rivas still recalled the image that had occurred to him then—as if each of them was just one visible loop of a vast, vibrating worm. Rivas had had no wish to graft himself on, and soon discovered that an alcohol-dulled mind was inaccessible to the sacrament. Thereafter, despite the Messiah's ban on liquor, he had been careful to take the sacrament only when he was, unobtrusively, drunk. This let him parry the alertness-blunting effects of the damaging communion . . . though it wasn't until he got the idea of incorporating his musical skills into the Jaybird services that he found himself able, if only furtively, to riposte.

And then, when he'd finally left the Jaybirds and drifted northwest to Venice, there had been Blood.

Venice was a savage carnival of a town that had sprung up like crystals in a saturate solution around the semicircular bay known as the Ellay-Ex Deep, in the center of which was a submarine pit that was reputed to glow with fantastic rainbow colors on some nights. A person who had a lot of money and could take care of himself could sample some amazing pleasures, it was said, in the rooms above the waterfront and canalside bars—Rivas had heard stories of "snuff galleries" where one could strangle to death people who were actually volunteers, frequently but not always goaded to this course by the money that would subsequently be paid to their families; of "sporting establishments," brothels whose inmates were all physically deformed in erotically accommodating ways; of sport-seafood restaurants, whose long-time patrons eventually could be conveyed inside only with some difficulty, being blind, decomposing and confined to wheeled aquariums . . . but eager for just one more deadly, fabulously expensive meal; and of course he'd heard whispers about the quintessential nightclub of the damned, the place about which no two stories were consistent but all attributed to it a horrible, poisonous glamor, the establishment known as Deviant's Palace.

As a jiggerless young vagrant, Rivas was in no position even to verify the existence of such fabulous places, and even a tortilla with some beans rolled up in it was the price of a day's hard labor—but Blood was cheap.

The drug was a reddish brown powder that could be snorted, brewed, smoked or eaten, and it sucked the user into a semicomatose state, comfortingly bathed by the triple illusion of great deeds done, time to rest, and warmth; longtime users claimed to feel also a vast, loving attention, as if it was God himself rocking the cradle.

In Venice it was daringly fashionable to sample Blood, perhaps because the genuine Blood freaks were such an unattractive crew. Many of them simply starved to death, unwilling to buy food with money that could be used to get more of the drug, and none of them ate much, or bathed, or shambled any farther than to the next person that could be wheedled out of a jigger or two, and then back to the Blood shop.

After Rivas found himself a steady job washing dishes in one of the many restaurants and got a little money, he wandered one evening into a narrow little Blood shop beside one of the canals, curious about the drug because in Ellay it was illegal and expensive. The man who ran the shop was a user himself, and delivered such a glowing panegyric in praise of the stuff that Rivas fled, sensing that this all-reconciling drug would rob him of his carefully constructed vanity, his painful memories of Urania, his budding musical ambitions ... in short, everything that made him Gregorio Rivas.

"Beautiful morning, isn't it?"

Rivas jumped realistically and looked with wary hope at the man who'd paused beside him. Though not as tall as Rivas, he was a good deal stockier, and except for his nose and his eyes his whole face was hidden by a hat and a bushy copper beard.

"Uh, yeah," said Rivas in a nervous tone as he shifted

his knapsack to a more comfortable position on his shoulders. "Kind of cold, though."

"Yeah, it is." The man yawned and leaned against the wall beside Rivas. "Waiting for someone?"

"Oh yes," said Rivas quickly, "I—" He paused and then shrugged. "Well, no."

The man chuckled. "I see. Listen, I'm on my way to get some food. You hungry?"

Rivas hoped that the quick gesture of touching his wallet looked spontaneous. "Uh, I guess not."

"You sure? The place I'm thinking of will give us each a big plate of *machaca con juevos,* on the house, no charge." He winked. "And I can get us a table right next to the fire."

Rivas frowned. This was beginning to sound wrong. "Yeah? Where's this?"

"Oh, it's a little place on Spring, run by some friends of mine." The man yawned again and stretched his arms over his head and then let them fall—one of them landed, and stayed, around Rivas's shoulders.

Rivas's mouth became a straight line. "Spring and what?"

"Huh? Oh, only a couple of blocks from here, Spring and Main. A five minute—"

"Right." Rivas stepped out from under the man's arm. "That would be the Boy's Club. No thank you." He strode off to find a different wall to lean on.

But the man came hurrying after him. "You know about the place, huh? Well, listen, lad, this is no time for false pride. Let me just—"

Rivas spun to face him, and he let the man see the knife he'd snatched from his right sleeve. "I can have it in your heart so fast you won't have time to yell," he remarked, not unkindly. *"Vaya."*

"Jesus, kid," the man exclaimed, stepping back, "okay!" Once out of range of the knife he permitted himself to amble away insouciantly, and he called back over his shoulder,

"But you could have had a friend!"

I like the way, thought Rivas in almost honest puzzlement as he settled the knife back in its sleeve sheath and walked on, that every person in the world thinks his or her friendship is worth something. My God, if I really was a broke, hungry kid, I'd be a lot more chagrined at the loss of that breakfast.

Earlier Rivas had noticed a gang of young people crouched around a fire under a canted stone arch beside the Relic Exchange, and when he glanced in that direction now he saw that one of the girls was walking toward him, smiling, her hands in the pockets of her long, pavement-sweeping dress.

"Lost a friend, huh?" she asked when she was close enough to speak quietly and be heard.

"Oh." Rivas waved vaguely. "I didn't know him. He just came over and started talking to me."

"Are you hungry? Come and share our breakfast."

Rivas's heart was thumping, for he suspected this might be the baited hook he'd been looking for, but he made himself look wistful as he said, "Well, I don't have any money...."

The girl put her hand on his shoulder and looked into his eyes. "Money is just the checkers in a game played by unhappy children," she told him earnestly, and he turned away in case his sudden burst of feral satisfaction might show in his face—for he recognized her statement as one of the standard Jaybird come-along lines, unchanged since he'd first heard it on that lonely morning thirteen years ago. He'd later used it himself when out on recruiting expeditions.

"That may be true," he said, reciting a response to it that he remembered as being easy to counter, "but you need money to live."

"No," she said gently, pulling him toward the leaning

arch, "you're exactly wrong. You need money to *die*. It's love you need to live."

He laughed with sophomoric bitterness. "That's even harder to find."

"Anything's hard to find," she told him, "if you don't know where to look for it or what it is."

This girl's smooth, Rivas thought as he allowed himself to be led toward the group of Jaybirds, who were all looking up now and smiling at him; the grime around her neck and wrists has been there a while, and the dress has been slept in, but the figure's adequate, she delivers her lines with fair sincerity, and, despite her teeth, that smile is as bright as a lamp in a window on a stormy night, and it's the only thing a hungry stray would notice anyway.

The Jaybirds in the circle shifted to make room for Rivas, and he looked around sharply as he sat down on the damp dirt, but Urania wasn't one of them. It seemed to be a typical band—mostly young people, their faces ranging in expression from the timid optimism of the new recruit through the sunny confidence of those who, like the girl that had snagged him, had been with the faith for a while, to the vacuous inattention of a couple of long time communicants, on whose faces the obligatory smile sat like a welcome mat in front of an abandoned house.

"This is a new friend of ours," his guide told the group as she sat down next to him, "who's been kind enough to accept our invitation to breakfast."

There were quietly delighted exclamations, and from all sides Rivas was warmly assured that his arrival had brightened their day enormously. Rivas set about the task of responding as they would expect him to.

Abruptly he realized that he was shaking hands and grinning like an idiot *spontaneously*—for at least several seconds there he had not been acting. He felt a faint stirring of uneasiness—no, genuine fear—deep inside himself, for this had happened to him only twice before in his life, this warm, happy surrender of personality: once thirteen years ago when as a scared runaway he had first been approached by the Jaybirds, and then once only three years ago while performing his last redemption. He had finally located the girl he'd been hired to snatch, had finalized his plan for the escape late that evening, and had incautiously permitted himself the luxury of relaxing in the crowded Jaybird nest in the meantime. Both times it had been just a brief slip, and he'd only been vulnerable at all because of extreme fatigue—but what was his excuse this time?

"What's the matter, brother?" A skinny Jaybird girl had noticed Rivas's sudden chill and was leaning forward solicitously, stroking his cheek with one hand and, he noticed out of the corner of his eye, furtively twitching the other hand at her companions in the tighten-the-net signal. Instantly the gang closed around him, expressing concern and as if by accident blocking all the directions in which he might make a run for it.

Rivas looked around at them all and decided it was time to find out which one was the boss here. "I, uh, was just thinking," he stammered, "I really should be trying to find a way to get back home; to my family."

He knew this called for a strong block, and that he'd learn now who their leader was; and as he'd guessed, it was Sister Sue, the girl who'd found him, that now knelt in front of him and took his hands and, leaning almost close enough to kiss, stared hard into his eyes.

"Trust yourself," she said to him in a low vibrant voice that seemed to resonate in his teeth. "You realized that they weren't your real family, didn't you, saw that there are qualities and depths in yourself that they can't share or recognize? Questions they not only can't answer, but can't even understand? That is why you left them—no, don't interrupt—think about it, and you'll realize I'm right. I knew the moment I saw you that you had a real soul and that you were seeking the family that you can join *totally*. I don't say trust me, or them, or anyone; I tell you that the only person you dare trust is yourself. And where did your need to find love lead you? To me. To us."

Her eyes were glistening with tears, and the other Jaybirds, even the deteriorated ones, were nodding at him and humming deep in their throats, half of them on a very low note and half on a very high one, and the insidious two-toned buzz seemed to get right in behind his eyes and set all the contents of his brain vibrating into softened blurs.

It was hard to remember anything . . . nearly impossible to hold onto a thought for more than a few seconds . . . but he knew he didn't *need* to anymore. The self-consciousness, the anxious policing of his personal boundaries, could at last be relaxed.

He felt tired—his knees didn't seem to have their usual spring—but of course he hadn't gotten much rest last night, and he didn't have any reason to stand up anyway. He was among people he could trust.

He was aware of some inconsistencies between his memory and his perceptions—he remembered this Jaybird band as consisting of different people, and he thought he'd been sitting with them at a different corner, and the gray overcast he remembered seemed to be gone, and his clothes were somehow clean and pressed again, no longer caked with dust and dried blood—but his own personal memories and perceptions no longer seemed crucially important.

He smiled into the pair of eyes that seemed to fill the whole world, and he realized that he felt better already. The loss of Urania might have happened years ago for all the pain it caused him now, and even the aches and stiffnesses from the beating Barrows and his men had given him last night, after Urania's birthday party, were gone.

"You've found your real family now, haven't you?" Sister Sue asked softly.

If there was a part of his mind screaming in horrified denial, it was well buried. Rivas, totally at peace for the first time in many years, happily breathed the single word, "Yes."

When the Jaybird band left the city at noon they took Rivas with them. One of the guards at the South Gate, a grayed veteran who had seen this sort of thing many times over the years, wearily walked out of the guard shack and extended his staff across their way to stop them.

"Alto," he said. "Whoa."

Sister Sue beamed at him. "Is there anything wrong, man?"

The guard nodded toward Rivas, who had bumped into the man in front of him when the group stopped, but was smiling benevolently at everyone.

"Who's the blurry boy?" the guard asked sternly.

"He's one of us," the girl said. "His name is Brother Boaz."

"Is that right, son?" he asked more loudly. "Son? Jeez, one of you nudge him, will you? That's got it. Listen to me, do you *want* to leave the city? You don't have to."

"I want to go where these people go," Rivas explained.

"Where are they going?"

"I don't know."

"What's your name?"

"Uh . . . they told me, but I forget."

"Well, that's fine," the guard said bitterly, letting his staff tip clack onto the flagstones. He looked at the girl. "And him still dressed respectable. You all sure didn't waste any time on him, did you?"

"Some are more ready than others to give themselves to

the Lord," she told him serenely.

He opened his mouth for an angry retort, then apparently couldn't think of one, for he just said, *"Vaya,"* and turned back to the guard shack.

"Vayamos," Sister Sue replied, and led her band forward under the high arch of the gate and then across the cobbled wall road and down the gravel slope west toward the Harbor Freeway. The day being clear and sunny, a number of beribboned tents and booths had been set up in random patterns across the face of the slope like some kind of colorful mushrooms brought out by yesterday's rain, and some of the vendors hooted at the group of pilgrims.

"Hey, *señora,*" yelled one fat old tentkeeper to Sister Sue, "let me give you a bath and a little lipstick and I swear to Jaybush you could knock down three fifths a day!"

The other vendors within earshot laughed, and the laughter doubled when one added, "A jigger at à time!"

Some of the newer Jaybirds looked embarrassed or angry as they plodded their winding course through this irreverent gauntlet, but the smiles on the faces of Sister Sue, Rivas, and the several deteriorated communicants never faltered.

One small time vice-caterer vaulted the counter of his booth and sprinted across the slope to Rivas and waved a piece of paper at him. It was a faded black-and-white photograph of a nude woman, a shabby example of the sort of relic that, bigger and more explicit and in color, could sell for cases of fifths in the fancy galleries in the city.

"You like that, eh?" cackled the merchant.

Rivas's gaze crossed the picture and then returned to it, and for the first time in a couple of hours his eyes focused and his smile relaxed and was replaced by a frown.

"Oho, don't like girls, eh?" said the merchant loudly, playing to the delighted audience. "I'll bet this is what you like, am I right?" And he yanked out of his pocket a pint bottle of cheap Ventura gin and waved it alluringly.

Rivas stopped, and the man behind him bumped into him as Rivas hesitantly reached for the bottle. The attentive vendors roared, pounding on the counters of their booths and rolling on the ground.

"Not all the way birdy yet!" yelled the prancing merchant. He was tugging at the stopper when a hard slap knocked the bottle out of his hands; Sister Sue was in front of him now, leaning toward him, her smiling gaze so intense that the man actually squinted before it as though it were an intolerably bright light.

She whispered to him for a few seconds and then said, "We'll be back for you, brother."

She turned to Rivas and said softly, "Follow me, Brother Boaz." He nodded, and fell into step when the band began moving forward between the now silent vendors, but Sister Sue kept looking back at him, for the tiny creases of frown hadn't left his face.

The vice-caterer, who'd been wobbling ever since Sister Sue turned away from him, all at once sat down heavily on the gravel, and the ancient magazine clipping slipped from between his fingers and fluttered away across the slope.

Chapter Three

ALL MORNING THE little group moved south along the shore of the great inland sea that, though its broad surface now extended north nearly to the walls of Ellay, was still called San Pedro Bay; and though Rivas didn't particularly slow the group—he climbed over fallen building sides, waded down streets reclaimed by the sea, and plodded across the occasional stretches of gray powder as tirelessly as any of them—his pace remained somnambulistic, his gaze unfocused.

They'd moved into the Inglewood Desolate, a wide band that extended east all the way from Venice; plants grew poorly in the Desolate, but the main reason for its almost complete lack of population was the spectrum of illnesses suffered by long term residents, and the impossibility of

having unsporting children here. Several times during their
trek lean faces peered longingly down at them from glass-
less windows or up from sewer vents, but the hunched,
hungry, scarcely human creatures that would have attacked
other travelers let Sister Sue's band pass unmolested, for it
was only in and around the cities that the Jaybirds pretended
to be pacifists, and the dwellers in the Desolate had learned
to stay away from even the most defenseless-looking group
of them.

They passed a few piers that had been built recently
enough not to have been swallowed by the ever-rising water,
but one could only speculate about what businesses might
be practiced by the men who moored their boats at them,
for the furtive sailors never yelled or waved, and all carried
long knives and slingshots.

The area around the Gage Street pier, though, was a sort
of Jaybird settlement. Several tents had been erected, and
every month a different group of shepherds took over the
task of maintaining the boats and making sure all new recruits were shipped on across the bay.

Sister Sue's group presented no problems. Along with
the rest of them, Rivas shambled docilely out to the end of
the pier. The Jaybirds' pier was a result of luck rather than
construction, for it was a big, ancient truck lying on its
side; the uphill end of it, which was the cab, was half buried
in the layers of soil that a dozen winter floods had flung
over it, and out at the far end the top side of the box-shaped
trailer was nearly awash in the water of the bay. The surface
of this pier was rusted and scuffed and riddled with finger-
sized punch holes, but a big cross that might once have
been red was still dimly visible painted on it, along with
fragments of words, after a hundred baking summers. Ordinarily Rivas would have tried to read the words and guess
at their meaning, but today they were just patterns on the
pavement. Beyond the rear of the truck, silhouetted against

to his new masters earlier that day ... but now it only deep-
ened his frown. He glanced at Sister Sue and saw that she
was watching him, and he looked away quickly.

The nearest horizon was a ragged line of bone-white
buildings three miles away across the bay, but the shepherd
at the end of the pier was squinting south, where the bay
broadened out and one could see, this being a clear day,
the distant dot that was Long Beach Island. At the seaward
end of the pier Rivas hung back, seeming to find something
disquieting about traveling on the water, but a shepherd
stepped up impatiently behind him and gave him a hard
shove between the shoulders. Rivas wound up making a
flailing jump down onto one of the benches, but once he
was in the boat he sat down quietly.

Sister Sue stared at him, then turned to the shepherd,
shrugged, and resumed getting the rest of her group aboard.

In the midafternoon the boat tacked in to a Jaybird dock
at Cerritos, which, being a good two miles below the southern edge of the Desolate, presented an almost tropical front
to the bay, with tall trees trailing flowers and vivid greenery
over the water. The harsh cries of monkeys and parrots rang
for hundreds of yards through the trees up and down the
coast, and the warty top halves of a few amphibian heads
poked up out of the water to see what the commotion was,
but there was no hitch as the shepherd helped everyone up
out of the boat and onto the dock. As he pushed away and
let the wind fill his main and jib sails for the skate back
northwest to the Gage Street pier, Sister Sue's band plodded
up the foliage-roofed highroad that split the narrow band of
coastline jungle and led the group finally to the crest of a
hill from which they could look down on the Cerritos Stadium. Other groups of Jaybirds were arriving from north and
south and inland, and there was a considerable crowd at the
gates. Sister Sue led her group down.

Over the stadium's entrance gates some agile devotee
had painted, with more fervor than skill, a mural of the
Messiah Norton Jaybush welcoming all of humanity with
outstretched, misproportioned arms; and the painted crowd
on which he was looking down became, below the long
lintel over the gates, the real, animate crowd of smiling
Jaybirds jostling up to get inside. They were all silent, and
the only sounds were panting, and the scuff of shod or
callused feet, and the occasional uncomplaining grunt of a
member of the faithful being momentarily compressed against
a wall.

Once inside the huge weathered bowl of the stadium,
Rivas absently noticed eight rickety wooden towers set up
at even intervals around the periphery of the wide field, and
on the little railed platform at the top of each tower stood
a brown-robed, bearded man holding a crook-topped staff.
Once free of the press at the gates, the various Jaybird groups
became distinct and separate again, and each group set out
walking toward the base of one or another of the towers.

There were no visible differences among the hooded,
tower-top shepherds, and in this orderly dispersal it was,
for once, the most deteriorated and imbecilic member of
each group that determined on a specific tower and led his
or her band across the weedy field toward it. The tower
toward which Rivas's group plodded was on the far side of
the enclosed field, and most of the other bands were already
standing at ease in the shadow of other towers by the time
his band came to a halt.

As if at a signal, all the tower-top shepherds abruptly
opened their mouths and began producing a low, steady
note, and a moment later every deteriorated Jaybird in the
stadium joined in with a shrill *"eee"* sound; though a ground-
rumbling roar now instead of a buzz, it was the same in-
sistent two-tone note that had aided Rivas's acquiescence

to his new masters earlier that day . . . but now it only deep-
ened his frown. He glanced at Sister Sue and saw that she
was watching him, and he looked away quickly.

As suddenly as it had started the sound stopped, and in
the moment that the last harsh echoes were rebounding away
among the high tiers, Rivas took an involuntary step forward, as if the sound had been something physical he'd
been pushing against.

The shepherds slung their staves through their belts and
climbed nimbly down from the towers, and Rivas watched
the one his group and a couple of others were clustered
around. When the man got to the ground he straightened
up, hiked his staff free and then strode up to Sister Sue and
spoke to her quietly.

She indicated Rivas with a nod of her head and then
whispered to the bearded shepherd for nearly half a minute.
The expression on the man's tanned, craggy face didn't
change, but he slowly lifted his head to stare at Rivas, and
when Sister Sue had finished he walked over to the new
member.

"Welcome to your real family, Brother Boaz," he said
in a deep voice.

Rivas glanced around uneasily, then nodded. "Uh, thank
you."

"How old are you?"

". . . Eighteen? I think eighteen."

The shepherd raised an eyebrow and looked more closely
at Rivas's face and hair. "Hmm. Take off your knapsack,
please, and let me have it."

Rivas looked over at Sister Sue, who smiled and nodded.
With evident reluctance he reached up, slipped the canvas
straps off his shoulders, shrugged the knapsack off and held
it out toward the shepherd.

The man took it, stepped back and began undoing the

buckles. Around the arena the other shepherds were also busy taking stock of new recruits, and, except for the low mutter of those conversations, the wind in the ragged high tiers was the only sound.

"Or thirty-one," said Rivas.

The shepherd looked up. "What?"

"Maybe I'm thirty-one years old."

The man had got the flap open, but paused to squint at him. "Maybe thirty-one, eh? Have you ever...been with us before?"

"No, sir. I ran away from home yesterday. My father's a tenant farmer for Barrows. The Currency brandy estates."

"Let me get this straight," said the shepherd curiously as he pulled a large cloth-wrapped bundle out of the knapsack. "You leave home at thirty-one and call it running away?"

Rivas was breathing deeply now, clearly trying to resist panic. "No, eighteen," he said tensely. "That's right, eighteen. For sure."

The shepherd opened his mouth to ask another question but shut it again when he saw what was wrapped up in the cloth—Rivas's second-best pelican.

The gaze he now turned on Rivas was full of suspicion. "What the hell is this?"

After a pause Rivas said, almost in a whisper, "Somebody's pelican."

"Somebody's? It's not yours?...Damn it, answer me!"

"No, sir." Rivas rubbed his hand across his mouth. "I have one, but not as nice as that."

"Well, Brother Boaz, music is one of the things we have to sacrifice." He opened his hand and the instrument fell to the ground with a discordant *bwang,* and then he lifted a heavy boot and stamped the thing flat.

The shepherd started to turn away, then froze, and an

instant later he had whirled back to face Rivas again. "Say, what's your name?"

For a moment Rivas's apprehensive frown left his face and, proud of knowing the answer, he said, "Brother Boaz."

"No, damn it, I mean before, what *was* your—"

A strident trumpet note suddenly split the air, and a voice from the far side of the arena shouted through a megaphone, "Make yourselves ready for the Lord!"

The shepherd craned his neck and saw that an old man in a white robe had entered the stadium. "The jaybush is here," he said. "You walk out into the center of the field. We'll talk some more after the sacrament." He gave Rivas a push and then turned to the other groups around his tower. "All new members follow this brother!" he called. "I'll greet you all personally afterward."

Rivas plodded out across the uneven ground, which was stippled now with fresh green weed shoots after the rain, and though he walked as slowly as any of the hundred or so new members who were approaching from all sides of the arena in a steadily shrinking circle, his mind was racing.

That wasn't my pelican, he thought, I remember mine, I saved up my jiggers and bought it when I was sixteen— okay, so why do I *remember* the one he stomped? Hell, I even remember that its E-string screw didn't bind properly, and needed to be readjusted after every set.

Set? What do I mean *set?* That's right, I play at the . . . what's the name of the place? The Bom Sheltr, that's it, in Venice; of course, and I'm twenty-five—why in hell was I thinking eighteen or thirty-one?

And what in God's name am I doing back among the Jaybirds? And lining up for the communion while *sober?*

He paused for a moment, but a dim suspicion that he did have some presently forgotten purpose in being here made him reluctantly resume the quasi-ceremonial pace. He surreptitiously touched his wrist and was reassured to feel his knife strapped there as usual. Okay, he thought, I'll play this scene up to, but not including, the point of receiving the sacrament. This seems to be the Cerritos Stadium, and from my old birdy days I remember where the kitchen exit is; with surprise, speed and my knife, I should be able to be out of here and into the hills within two minutes.

The white-robed figure of the jaybush had been walking toward the center of the field at a slightly quicker pace than the tightening ring of communicants, and just before shoulder to shoulder contact caused the ring to stop shrinking he slipped between a couple of them and then made his way to the very center. For ten long soundless seconds he scrutinized the nervously eager people in the ring.

Then, "Kneel," he said, in a voice like concrete blocks rubbed together.

Everyone in the stadium did, with a rustling and thudding that seemed loud in the silence. Rivas squinted up at the jaybush, and the man's robe shone so in the afternoon sun that the sky looked darkened to purple behind him. The man looked around the congregation again, then slowly crossed to stand in front of a young girl six places away to Rivas's right.

"Merge with the Lord," the jaybush said, then reached out and touched her forehead.

She *oomphed* as if she'd been punched in the belly, and a moment later she was rolling on the damp ground outside the circle.

And suddenly it all came back to Rivas: Barrows hiring him to perform the redemption of Urania, the nightmare he'd had about her, and his own alarming susceptibility to this predatory religion.

Let me *out* of here, he thought, instinctively reaching

into his sleeve for the knife; if the plain recruitment tricks can make a grinning zombie of me so easily, what would a dose of the sacrament do?

But you can't run, he realized a moment later—not without blowing your hard-won earnest-new-boy cover and wrecking your chance of finding Urania.

But I can't take the sacrament sober either, he thought desperately. His heart was pounding in his coldly hollow chest, and when he darted a glance to his right he saw that there were now only two people to be disposed of before it was his own turn. He noticed that he was whimpering deep in his throat, and with some difficulty he forced himself to stop it.

"Merge with the Lord," said the jaybush, touching the forehead of the boy who was next in line. The boy slumped limply to the ground, and Rivas heard his jaw clack shut as his face hit the dirt.

Rivas dug up inside his sleeve and tugged slightly on the knife grip so that an inch of blade was free of the sheath, and then he pressed the nail of his thumb up against the bottom edge. He took a deep breath and closed his eyes.

"Merge with the Lord." *Gasp. Thud.*

As he heard the jaybush's boots scuff to directly in front of him, Rivas exhaled . . .

. . . and then drove his thumb up against the blade edge, which split the nail and grated against the bone. The pain was a bright, hot flare that brought a metallic taste to his mouth, and he forced his mind to cling to the agony and focus on it to the exclusion of everything else.

He didn't even hear the jaybush say, "Merge with the Lord."

There was a silent, stunning impact and then he was falling through an abyss so frigid that what lived and moved here—and he knew something did—partook of an ani-

mation below freezing, as he'd read that liquid helium was
said by the ancients to begin to crawl at temperatures approaching absolute zero; his own warmth was being violently wrung out of him, but more kept on coursing into
him through his left hand—specifically through his thumb.

He was being stretched both toward the bottomless cold
and toward the heat, and though he sensed a tearing in
himself, in his mind, he willed himself to move in the
direction of the heat; then he seemed to be rushing upward,
though whatever had been on the other side of the rip in
his soul had now broken free of him and, alive but separate,
was pacing him. It became more distant and soon he wasn't
aware of it anymore, nor of the sentience in the black cold
below.

What he was aware of was an aching hip and pebbly,
damp dirt against his cheek. He sat up and looked around—
the jaybush was gone, though the crowd around the field's
periphery was still out there, and all of them were still
kneeling; then he let his gaze fall onto his fellow communicants.

Only a couple had regained, or kept, consciousness, and
they were blinking around stupidly like people lately roused
from sodden sleep. Most were still stretched out on the dirt,
several of them twitching, the rest limp and conceivably
dead. Of the ones near enough to see closely, quite a few
were bleeding from injuries sustained during falls or fits;
his gashed thumb probably wouldn't excite any comment.

And then he realized that he was still clear-headed—as
alert as he ever was, and with his memory and personality
intact. This new-found pain defense worked even better than
the drunk defense, for though the latter insulated him from
the sacrament, it did leave him drunk.

The thought of drink reminded him of the pint of Malk
whiskey concealed behind a flap in his knapsack, and brought

him to his feet. He walked across the field to his own Jaybird group, being careful to act dopey and clumsy.

Sister Sue watched him approach, but the shepherd kept his back turned until Rivas paused a few feet away—then he turned around, and he was holding the pint of whiskey.

"You recover fast," the shepherd said.

Rivas put on a foolish grin and brushed some stray strands of hair off his forehead, leaving a smear of blood over one eyebrow. "Murphy's still playing in the yard," he said thickly, "even though Mom told him to come in." It was the sort of thing people said when recovering from the sacrament.

"You're bleeding, Brother Boaz," said Sister Sue in a concerned tone, at the same time giving the shepherd a hand signal that Rivas didn't catch.

"Yeah?" Rivas stared at his split thumb with what he hoped looked like foolish astonishment. "Gee."

"Piece of old glass, probably, out there that he fell on," said the shepherd. "Say, brother, what's this?" he asked Rivas, holding up the flat bottle.

Rivas peered at it. "Whiskey," he said finally. "I think it's mine."

"It *was* yours."

The shepherd let it fall. It didn't break when it hit the ground, but it did when the man stamped on it. Rivas forced himself not to let his chagrin show.

"Liquor's another thing we have to sacrifice," the shepherd told him. "You're lucky it was still full, and that the sister here says you were sober when she picked you up this morning. Still, liquor and a musical instrument, both on one novitiate." He shook his head thoughtfully. "What's your name again?"

"Joe Wiley," said Rivas at random. "Uh, no, sorry, I mean Brother Boaz."

"And how old are you?"

"I . . . forget."

The shepherd nodded, then smiled. "Did you like taking the sacrament?"

Rivas closed his eyes and inhaled the fumes of the lost whiskey. "Oh, yes sir."

"Good, because I'm going to set up a special treat for you. Most people only get to take it once a day at the very most, but we're going to let you have it *twice* today, isn't that great? I think you'll be able to talk to me more . . . frankly, afterward. How does that sound?" Before Rivas could answer, the shepherd added, "Oh, and we'll have you sitting down, so you won't fall and hurt yourself this time."

Rivas widened his eyes. "I'd love it," he said. Then he whispered, "But won't everybody else be *jealous?*"

"Naw. It'll be our little secret. Follow me."

He led Rivas across the dirt to a door in the stadium wall, and through it and down a dim corridor to a room with a bolt on the outside of the door. "Sorry there's no window or lamp," he told Rivas, "but you've got the Lord Jaybush watching over you now, so there's no need to be scared of the dark. There's a chair in there—find your way to it and sit down."

Rivas hesitated. Once again, he thought, I could knife him and run. Easier now than before. But, once again, that would blow my cover.

Do I *really* want Urania back this much?

"Yes," he sighed, and stepped into the room. The door was instantly slammed shut behind him, the buffet of air pressure letting him know that the room was indeed windowless, and very small, too. A tool storage room once, probably. A moment later he heard the bolt clank solidly home.

After a bit of cautious shambling and groping, his split thumb collided agonizingly with the promised chair, and he sat down. Okay, he told himself, let's get one thing straight, there's no way you're going to take that damned sacrament again. Don't even *consider* worrying about that. I'll kill the jaybush if I have to...but maybe I can whistle him out, and then sprawl on the floor, so that when he regains consciousness he'll think he already gave it to me.

He pursed his lips and in a simultaneously hesitant and hasty gunning rhythm, whistled the first six notes of *Peter and the Wolf*—the bright adventurous tune sounding constricted and out of place in these surroundings—and then, satisfied, he sat back to wait.

He remembered how he had come to discover this special property of music, and of *Peter and the Wolf* in particular.

In the hills north of the Seal Beach Desolate the Jaybird band he was with had followed a column of smoke until they found, broken up and still burning and scattered across one of the little dry riverbeds, the remains of a Santa Anan merchant caravan. The raiders, whoever they'd been— probably the self-styled modern hooters, who had to ride weirdly customized bicycles instead of the fabled motorcycles ridden by their historical namesakes but did still carry the dreaded hooter swords, painstakingly slotted to produce a loud hooting when whirled in the air at high speed—had taken everything of particular value, but the Jaybirds had lots of time and would be content with meager pickings. They rooted and scrabbled patiently among the blood-spattered wreckage, and came away with a modest haul of metal pieces and wire...but Rivas came across a pelican, miraculously unbroken.

And so for a few minutes the nineteen-year-old Rivas forgot the ruin around him and treated the sprawled corpses to a few of the old melodies he'd learned from his father; and the calculatedly uneven rhythms that he eventually evolved into gunning startled the carrion birds overhead and made them circle a little higher.

The other members of his band somehow didn't guess

that he'd owned and played one before, and assumed that his modest proficiency was a miracle. Rivas had let them think it, and that evening when they'd returned to the nest he had set about writing new, pious lyrics to accompany the handful of tunes he knew how to play.

A month or so later a circuit-riding jaybush had passed through to administer the communion, and Rivas had self-lessly offered to forego the joy of receiving the sacrament in order that the event might be graced with music. The jaybush had had no particular objection, and proceeded with the ceremony while Rivas sawed and plucked his way through *Blue Moon, Can't Always Get What You Want,* and other traditional favorites—and he played them at a fairly traditional tempo—but something happened when he wearied of that sort of thing and began to do an emphatically gunned rendition of *Peter and the Wolf.*

At the first bouncing notes the jaybush had paused, and as the tune continued the man's eyes had unfocused and his outstretched hand had fallen limp to his side. Rivas had of course noticed it, though he didn't suspect that his music was the cause, and glancing around he saw that all the far-gones had ceased their usual speaking-in-tongues background rumble and were also inert. The jaybush snapped out of it and resumed working his way down the line as soon as the tune came to an end, and the far-gones started up their eerily synchronized jabbering again, and young Rivas thoughtfully put his instrument away for the evening.

In the next couple of weeks he'd managed to prove to himself that that tune, when rendered at a gunning tempo, did reduce the very deteriorated communicants from near to total unconsciousness, and when the next circuit-riding jaybush passed through, Rivas found an opportunity to verify the effect with him, too.

From then on it had been his secret last-ditch defense against the sacrament, and in later years, after his stay in

Venice and his eventual return to Ellay, it became the trade secret that made him the best redeemer in the business.

But, he reminded himself worriedly as he sat now in the lightless little room, now they're down on music. Is that just for the sake of deprivation, or are they onto my trick?

After a long time in the dark he heard footsteps in the corridor and saw a wavering line of yellow light appear and brighten under the door, and then the bolt rattled and snapped back and the door was pulled open. The jaybush stood in the doorway with a flaring torch in his left hand, looking like some Old Testament prophet with his robe and wild white beard, and for a few seconds he just stood there— presumably staring at Rivas, though his face was in shadow down to his prominent cheekbones and it was hard to be sure. Rivas took the opportunity to glance around the room. Some stringy webs in the corners implied big spiders, but his chair was the only piece of furniture.

"A great privilege is yours," the jaybush grated.

"Yes, sir," said Rivas, trying to sound eager. "I mean, father. Or whatever. I'm just glad you all think I'm worthy of it."

The white-robed figure stepped into the room and, reaching out to the left, fitted the butt of the torch into an old can that had been nailed to the wall. Now the long right arm lifted, with the pointer finger extended like the stinger of some oversized insect.

Rivas puckered his lips and began whistling *Peter and the Wolf.*

The arm remained up, the feet kept moving and the finger stayed pointing at him.

He whistled a few more notes, more shrilly, and then kicked the chair over backward and rolled to his feet behind it, not even caring if he roused some spiders.

Another robed figure came into view behind the jaybush and laid a restraining hand on the old man's shoulder. The jaybush stepped back, turned and left the room. Rivas heard his steps receding away up the corridor as the by now familiar shepherd entered the room, smiling and holding a pistol trained at Rivas's stomach.

Though frightened, Rivas was a little surprised that the man would use so awkward and unreliable a weapon—antique pistols refitted to shoot spring-propelled poison darts were a trendy item among the high society ladies in the city, but the darts frequently got fouled up in the barrel and at the best of times had nearly no range nor accuracy. Rivas tensed, and calculated how he would jump.

"He's deaf," the shepherd remarked. He cocked the gun and raised it. "Now, no hard feelings, but we don't care if you're McAn or Bailey or Rivas or just some creep trying to kidnap his wife away from us. We can't have you around."

"Oh Jesus, mister, don't shoot me," quavered Rivas, falling forward onto one knee and snaking his left hand up into his right sleeve—and then from the half-kneeling position he lunged strongly upward, whipping the knife free and driving it at the shepherd's chest.

The pistol exploded beside his ear as he came up and a hot lash ripped his shoulder a moment before he slammed heavily against the shepherd. Together they thudded into the wall and rebounded, knocking the torch loose and spattering both of them with scalding wax, and then Rivas had spun away in the sudden darkness, lost his footing and tumbled to the floor. He heard the shepherd lurch forward, collide with the chair and go over it and then fall thrashing and gasping in the corner.

Christ, thought Rivas frantically as he slapped the floor around himself for the lost knife, the goddamn gun *shoots bullets,* he *shot* me, he's probably aiming it at the noise I'm making right now, where's the goddamn *knife....*

All his muscles were tensed in useless anticipation of the next bullet, and even after he heard the harsh exhalation from the corner and the staccato knocking of one of the shepherd's boots against the wall and floor, and realized what it meant, it took him nearly a full minute to relax enough even to get to his feet.

Live ammunition, he marveled. Where on earth can he have got it? I thought it all went stale half a century ago.

After a while he stopped panting. The torch had gone out when it fell, and the room was illuminated only dimly by the light that filtered down the hall, but after some peering he saw his knife on the floor and picked it up. It was slippery with warm blood. He shoved it back into its sheath, promising himself he'd clean it later.

He took a deep breath, tried not to pay attention to the hollow feeling in his belly and the sudden sweat on his face, and then he forced himself to walk around the fallen chair, get down on his knees, and grope for the pistol.

He thought his eyes would become accustomed to the dimness, but somehow as the minutes went by he could see even less than before. The shepherd's death spasm had left his corpse smelling very bad, and when Rivas's fumbling search forced him to move the body he had no idea what his hands were getting wet with. Webs stretched and tore under his fingers in the darkness, and his thumb had started bleeding again, slicking everything he touched, and the dead body seemed to have gotten huge, so that Rivas could hardly move without bumping into an arm or a leg . . . or maybe it had, spiderlike itself, grown more limbs in the dark . . . or maybe there was more than one corpse in here, maybe there were dozens, all over the floor, behind him, getting silently to their feet, wide-eyed in the dark, reaching for him with cooling hands. . . .

A spider or something tapped across his hand, but instead of exploding in a scream Rivas imploded into a sort of mentally crystallized state. His jaws were clenched together so hard that his whole head hurt, and his knees were helping push against his lower jaw, both kneecaps jammed under his chin and his arms wound tightly around his shins.

Hang on, he thought dimly, just hold it all in, maintain stasis, until Jaybush can take the whole thing away. Don't want agitation, motion, stuff, people . . . come soon, take it all away from me.

But he hadn't backed far enough away from it all, and he knew he was lying on his side on the floor like a knocked-over barrel, and that his elbow was in agony. He released the grip of his hands, and his knees fell away from his chin and he coughed.

Alarm quickly replaced the crystalline stasis as he struggled to his feet. There was more light in the corridor outside, as if approaching torches were only a corner or two away, and voices were getting louder. He reeled to the doorway and hurried down the corridor in the direction away from the light.

He wished he'd found the pistol, but he was fairly confident that he could find the kitchen—and the kitchen exit!—from here.

An hour later he was crouched on the shaded balcony of a half-collapsed apartment building a few miles south of the stadium, wishing he hadn't lost the pint of whiskey, which he'd brought along as much for its disinfectant properties as for its relaxing ones. Though his bullet-furrowed shoulder had stopped bleeding, it was hot and aching, and he was afraid that it—or maybe his thumb—had got infected and was responsible for his present feverish dizziness.

You can't get sick now, he told himself angrily, you've got to decide with a clear head what to do. I'm blown with the Jaybirds, Sister Sue's band, anyway, and all my supplies are gone. What any smart redemptionist would do at this point is go home, refund half the client's advance, apologize and recommend a colleague; especially a redemptionist who has every reason to believe he's begun losing his mind.

But they've got Urania. If I'm not willing to risk it for her, then what am I saving it for?

He stood up, flexing his hot, throbbing shoulder against the weight it seemed to have on it. The only thing I can do, he thought bleakly, is to move much further southeast, along the shore of the Long Beach Channel and into the Seal Beach Desolate—assume the worst, that Urania is being taken directly toward the Holy City in Irvine, get well ahead of her and then slowly try to work my way back northwestward without letting any Jaybird group get past me unobserved.

The realization that it was a nearly impossible task didn't make him change his mind about attempting it.

Rivas sighed, plodded out of the shade to the end of the tilted balcony and was about to climb back down the outward-leaning stairs, when out of the corner of his eye he caught a glimpse of his shadow on the stucco wall.

And then despite his dizziness he had instantly vaulted over the rail with a hoarse yell of fear, and he landed heavily on his side but forced himself to go rolling and somersaulting across the yard, scraping against walls and grinding his wounded shoulder across the dirt . . . for in blurry silhouette against the wall he had seen an as-yet-only-tenuous shape crouched on his shoulder, the shadow of a thing still mostly transparent but clearly man-shaped.

After a few frantic, spasmodic seconds Rivas scrambled to his feet, wheezing, and peered around fearfully behind him, afraid the dislodged thing might still be near enough to pounce on him and reattach itself.

Then he saw it, a dozen feet away. Its ectoplasmic substance had been torn and crumpled in Rivas's slithering progress across the yard, but it was hunching itself up into a crouch, and though it was as hard to get a good look at as a jellyfish in clear water, Rivas could see the thing's faintly pink-tinged face curl in an idiot grin.

He was desperately trying to remember what he'd heard—and naïvely scoffed at!—about the creatures known as hemogoblins: that they were mostly commonly encountered in the southern hills, and started out as almost invisible cellophanelike bags that drifted through the air until they could attach themselves to an open wound; they expanded and took on human shape and a reddish color as they ingested more and more of the blood of their host, until finally the host expired and the vitalized hemogoblin was able to walk around and hunt rather than just fly randomly, like a dandelion seed, on the wind. He'd even heard stories of them speaking.

The indistinct anthropoid shape started toward him, and he scooped up a handful of dirt and lashed it at the thing. The dirt tore through it like shrapnel, but in a few seconds it had re-knit itself and was grinning at him again.

It began hissing, in bursts, and then it whispered, "Rivas."

"Get the hell away from me," he told it in a voice shrilled by tension.

"Need little blood," the thing pointed out.

Rivas pulled loose his clotted knife and tossed it onto the dirt. The move reminded him of tossing a crust of bread to a stray dog to keep it from following you. "Take that first," he said unsteadily. "I'll wait right here until you're done with it." He'd seen a gravelly stretch a few yards to his right, and as soon as the thing began to suck the knife he planned to dive over there and then just keep flinging handfuls of rocks until the thing was so shredded and scattered that it wouldn't ever be able to pull itself back together.

But when the hemogoblin reached out and touched the bloody knife it instantly became much more clearly visible, and Rivas saw that its face, impossibly, was a perfect caricature of his own; and a moment later he was running away with the boundless energy of absolute panic, his knife and all thought of strategy forgotten.

When he rolled to a gasping halt five minutes later—having followed the last street of his zigzagging course past the point where, undercut by the bay, it ended in a muddy slope—his panic had thinned out to mere apprehension, and he was able to note with chagrin the mud that now caked his once white clothes.

He sat up, gingerly rubbing his abraded palms together, and stared back up the slope he'd just cartwheeled down. The black ash band exposed in the soil's cross section was clearly visible, and he remembered his father saying that it was always about two feet under the surface anywhere one went, so it wasn't difficult for Rivas to calculate how far he'd tumbled—about twelve feet, he decided. Lucky I didn't break a leg, he thought as he stood up, suppressing a groan—or my neck.

It occurred to him that he was hungry, and he stared out across the broad wrinkled face of the water, which was beginning to glitter gold under the late afternoon sun. He was far enough south so that the fresh water of the Ellay River would be fairly well mixed with the sea, and there might be some salt-water fish out there; he wasn't nearly hungry enough to experiment with the sort of fresh-water specimens that somehow throve in the Inglewood Desolate. But how was he to catch anything?

Then to the north he saw a sail, and when he squinted at it he recognized the sophisticated rigging the Jaybirds used. All at once thankful for the broad smears of mud on his clothes, he carefully but quickly picked his way along the shoreline until he came to a gap in the bank, a water-cut cleft choked with age-rounded chunks of broken concrete. He clambered up over them, pausing a couple of times

to admire the line of decorated tile that ran across one edge
of a few of them, and up at street level he shambled toward
the clustered, tumbled, vine-hung buildings, hoping at least
to find edible vegetation.

He didn't seem to be able to keep his mind on the con-
cerns of the moment, though; just as he'd paused to peer
at the century-old decorations on the broken stones, he found
himself shading his eyes to look up at the rooftops and
balconies around him, where now only lizards, birds and
the occasional cat sunned themselves, and he was imagining
what it would be like to waste an afternoon picnicking up
on one of them with Uri on the return trip. He wasn't
considering the odds against his finding her, nor the fact
that a lot of hard psychological crowbarring was required
to even partially free a person's mind from the Jaybird
template. He finally found an avocado tree and managed to
knock down a couple of avocados and then he climbed a
fire escape to the top of a three-story building and sat there
and stared at the slow sunset while he chewed them up.

Two distinct lines of smoke stood up from Long Beach
Island in the south, and when the sky began to get dark he
thought he could glimpse the winking yellow dots of distant
fires.

CHAPTER FOUR

THE NEXT MORNING was cold; fog, like the ghost of stone, had spread another sedimentary layer over the already mostly buried old landscape, so that the building Rivas had taken shelter in stuck up out of the indistinct gray flatness like the last spire of a city reclaimed by desert sand. He stood on the roof with one foot up on the crumbled coping, and as the sun made the fog band glow a ruddier and ruddier pink in the east and then rose above it and began to dispel it, he studied the emerging view and wondered where evening would find him.

At last he decided that the fog had thinned enough for travel to be practical, and he started to turn toward the fire escape—but he'd caught a suggestion of motion out of the corner of his eye, and he turned back to the landscape that stretched away below his perch.

A vertical line was slowly moving over the fog far away
to his right, which was north, and after he'd stared at it for
a few minutes he decided that it was a boat's mast, and that
it was approaching. Nothing in that for me, he thought, and
he had again started for the stairs when a thought struck
him. How, he wondered, can that mast be approaching so
steadily when it seems to carry no sails? The river certainly
provides no strong current this far south, and at least when
I last passed through these parts any oceanic currents would
only be moving the other way on this side of the bay.

Curious in spite of himself, he limped stiffly back across
the roof to the coping and stared at the mast, which was
much closer now, perhaps only a mile away. It was rocking
back and forth, and sinking and rising, much more than
could be caused by the surface of the bay, and at last Rivas
realized that the mast must be attached to a wagon that was
moving down the uneven bayside roads.

He watched it until he was pretty sure where it would
pass, and then he hurried down the fire escape to wait for
it, not sure yet whether he meant to hitch a ride, steal a
horse, or just satisfy his curiosity about the vehicle. When
he got to street level he hid behind a clump of bougainvillea,
confident that the bush and the remaining traces of fog made
him invisible.

If he hadn't heard the clopping of hooves first, he might
have thought he'd miscalculated his position and was down
on the bay shore, for the vehicle that soon appeared out of
the fog, first as a shadowy silhouette and then with proximity
gaining detail and color, was more boat than wagon in spite
of the four horses pulling it. A wide hull flared like an up-
blown skirt above the axles, with cowls around the wheels,
and the pole that projected up from the front of the cabin
was indeed a mast; from his hiding place Rivas could see
the horizontal boom stretching away behind, over the roof
of the cabin.

The cabin itself was a wooden shed as compact and solid as a Jaybird recruiting wagon, and Rivas thought he could guess what business these early morning travelers were in. His suspicion became virtual certainty when the vehicle approached close enough for him to see the freshly splintered and dented spots along the hull, and a couple of broken ropes that swung in the air and flicked an occasional drop of dew from their fog-wet, frayed ends.

As Rivas mentally put together a cover story that might make him seem to be a useful hitchhiker, he squinted now at the men themselves, who were slouched on the high driver's bench, which was shielded at the rear and the sides by sheets of aluminum so frequently dented that they now had a uniformly hammered look. The men seemed to have fared about as well as their boat-wagon: they too were battered but evidently still functioning. The wagon was close now, and would pass him if he waited much longer.

Rivas took a deep breath, crossed his fingers and then stepped out from behind his bush. "Good morning," he said cheerfully.

The driver snapped the reins and pulled a brake lever, and the wail of the brake shoes echoed away up and down the street as the wagon ground to a halt, the mast swaying overhead.

"What do you want," the other man said, looking down without enthusiasm at Rivas. "We don't pick up hitch-hikers." A bowler hat sat loosely on top of a blood-speckled turbanlike bandage, and under it his tanned face was so lean and pinched that it was hard to imagine him ever having eaten a decent meal, or even ever having smiled.

"Too risky," jovially agreed the driver, a white-haired old man wearing a baseball cap and overalls. Like his companion, he too wore several bandages.

Rivas smiled at them. "I was just wondering if you ran into the same gang of Jaybirds that jumped me last night.

I managed to run clear, but they got my wagon and all my . . . stock."

The old man stared down at him. "Stock," he said thoughtfully.

"What, uh, do you gentlemen deal in?" Rivas inquired, his eyebrows high.

After a pause in which he glanced cautiously around at the nearby buildings, the old man said, "We're *redeemers*, son."

His partner nodded absently.

And I know what sort, thought Rivas. "Ah," he said. "Commendable. I'm a . . . pharmacist, myself."

"You're a Blood dealer," said the old man.

"And you're pimps," said Rivas affably.

After another pause, the old man nodded. "Correct, son. And yes, it was a gang of Jaybirds—those damn shepherds, resenting us cutting a few ewes out of their flock. They get all your Blood?"

"All I had with me. And my horse and wagon. I'm lucky I still have my head."

"Ah. Too bad. Blood's the only thing that'll quiet 'em down when they've got the birdy fits."

"Yeah." Hence my story, thought Rivas. "You know Ratty Frazee?"

"Sure," said the lean man. "You know he's dead?"

"I heard something about it. What happened?"

"Some damn redeemer."

"One of the out for hire redeemers," the old man clarified. "They say it was Greg Rivas, snatching some girl for her parents. You knew Frazee?"

Rivas shrugged. "Did some business with him."

The two men up on the bench seemed to relax a little. The lean man took his hat off and peered into it. "Where do you go for more Blood?" he asked, apparently addressing the hat.

"I've got some stashed in a sewer outside Hunningten Town." Rivas guessed that this pair had at least a couple of girls in their wagon—the Jaybirds wouldn't have sling-shotted the vehicle so savagely otherwise, and the fact that these two were alive was proof that the Jaybird shepherds hadn't caught up with them—and hijacked Jaybird girls were nearly always routed to Hunningten Town and then by sea up to Venice, because the pacifying Blood was so plentiful there. Perhaps the main complaint the average pros-titute runner had about the universe was the fact that *female* communicants, unlike the less readily saleable males, never did reach the placid, tractable far-gone stage, and in order to be used had to be regularly tranquilized with doses of Blood.

The lean man put his hat back on. "Hunningten's on our way."

"Yeah, you can ride there with us if you like," the old man said.

"Thanks," said Rivas, climbing over the wheel cowl . . . a bit awkwardly because of his mangled thumb. "I'll pay for the ride when we get there."

"Sit by me," the old man added. "Nigel will sit on the roof behind."

"I'd be cautious too," acknowledged Rivas as he settled himself on the bench Nigel had just vacated. The last of the fog had drifted away down the bay and he savored the smell of eucalyptus on the warming air as the old man flicked the reins and the wagon lurched into motion.

"If you need to re-stock," the old man said, "you could sail north to Venice with us too—can always use an extra pair of hands on a boat, and I think this old barge needs some patching up this time. I think the shepherds messed up the keel hinge, and half the line's shot."

"Sure, sounds good," said Rivas, though reflecting in-wardly that no power on earth could ever get him to enter

Venice from its seaward side, where the most altered of the city's denizens limped, hopped and swam about on un-imaginable errands in the canals of poisonous Ingle-wood . . . on the narrow, ever-shifting beaches whose mulitcolored sand was sown with lumps of fused glass and occasional ancient but undecaying bone fragments . . . and even in the very shadow of the structure known as Deviant's Palace.

Though in his years in Venice Rivas had prided himself on being a particularly wild, nothing-to-lose young man, boating by moonlight down canals sane people shunned even at noon and participating in several foolish duels, he had taken care never to venture within blocks of Deviant's Palace. But the stories he'd heard about the place still colored his nightmares: stories of fantastic towers and spires that threw dark stains on the sky, so that even at noon stars could be seen twinkling around the warped rib-cage architecture of its upper levels; of nonhuman forms glimpsed weeping in its remoter windows; of what creatures were sometimes found dying in the canals that entered the place through high arches, and what things these creatures some-times said; of wooden gargoyles writhing in splintery agony on rainy nights and crying out in voices recognized by passersby as those of departed friends. . . . The place was supposed to be more a nightclub than anything else, and Rivas remembered one young lady who, after he'd impa-tiently broken off their romance even more quickly than he'd instigated it, had tearfully told him that she was going to get a waitress job at Deviant's Palace. He had never permitted himself to believe that she might really have done it, in spite of the evening when a walruslike thing that a gang of fishermen had netted and dragged to shore and were butchering by torchlight rolled its eyes at him and with its expiring breath pronounced the pet name she'd always called him. . . .

The boat-wagon rattled on southward along the old streets, putting on a little more speed as the sun came up and let the old man see where the potholes and washouts were. For the first half hour of the ride Rivas didn't ask about the girls his companions had rustled, for he didn't want to seem too interested in their business; but the thought that Uri might be in the wagon right below him made him unable to consider anything else, and finally forced him to speak. "How many have you got?" he asked with feigned casualness, jerking his wounded thumb downwards.

"Four," the old man said. "Or maybe it's three now. Nigel overthumps them sometimes."

"Vermin," commented Nigel from behind.

"Nigel doesn't care for ladies."

"'Specially birdy ones," Nigel explained.

"I see," said Rivas, nodding.

Jesus, he thought, what a pair. If I can think of a way to work them ill before I ditch them, I'll do it. And if Uri's in this wagon, I'll kill them. And if Uri's in here and dead, I'll . . .

He turned away as if to look at the inland countryside, for he feared that his amiable smile was turning into some less reassuring expression. Several tumbleweeds were rolling across a field parallel to the wagon like skeletons of some spherical species; and as the things crested a grassy rise and spun free in the air for a moment Rivas thought he saw a faint rosy shadow or stain on one of them . . . but the old man was speaking again and Rivas had to turn and face him.

"My name's Lollypop," the old man said.

Given ten tries, thought Rivas, I think I might have guessed that. "I'm Pogo Possum," he said on the spur of the moment, it being a pretty safe bet that neither of these fellows would be well read. "You been in this . . . trade long?"

"Since the sixth year of the last Ace, Nigel and me both. We were around when young Jaybush first appeared and started recruiting followers. Hell, I used to live in Irvine, in a house that's behind the white walls today—or was, I guess, until the big explosion in the last year of that Ace."

Rivas nodded. The rumors of the midnight flash and deafening roar behind the white walls—and speculations that Jaybush himself had died in the blast, for he subsequently went into cloistered seclusion in the Holy City—had shaken the whole structure of the faith, and Rivas, at the age of twenty-one, had taken advantage of the confusion and quietly left the Jaybirds and fled to Venice.

"Did you ever *see* Norton Jaybush?" Rivas asked.

"Oh hell yes, in those days before he retired into his damned city he was everywhere." Lollypop shook his head wonderingly. "Can't really blame people for following him, you know? That man was hard to beat. Still is, I suppose, just doesn't have to prove it anymore. Yeah, I seen him make a dead man get up and walk around and talk to his family—and I *mean* dead, this guy was bloated up and stinking."

"Trees bent over when he walked by, like bowing," said Nigel. "We seen it."

"It wasn't any big thing at all for a hundred birds at once to circle around over his head neat as the rim of a dish, like a big damn whirling halo, and not a peep out of one of 'em."

My rival for Uri's devotion, thought Rivas uneasily. And one time father figure of my own, too; though luckily only through the jaybushes, the surrogates, the representatives of him. I probably wouldn't have had the—the what? Strength of character? Certainty of my identity?—to leave the faith if I'd been dealing with Mister Messiah Jaybush himself. And I'd *never* have dared to disobey him so directly by going straight to Venice as soon as I ditched the faith. Jaybush had nothing but condemnations for that sinful place.

He was startled then by a quick, rhythmic thumping from inside the wagon under him, and it wasn't until Nigel, at the rear of the roof, pounded his fist on the wood and yelled, "Save it, slut—they gonna teach you a new dance," that Rivas realized what the noise had been. One of the girls was evidently having doubts, losing a little of her confidence that the world was in Jaybush's hands and all was well; for the peculiar running-in-place, arm-waving activity known as Sanctified Dancing was the recommended means to clear the mind of uncomfortable thoughts. Like speaking in tongues, it had never held any attraction for Rivas.

He knew it couldn't be Uri—this would be only her third day in the faith, and she wouldn't have been taught Sanctified Dancing yet—but if she actually was in this wagon he wondered what she was making of the spectacle. Often, he recalled, it was kind of scary when someone erupted into it, stamping and waving and gasping, eyes generally screwed tight shut, and it had to be scarier still when it started happening in a dim confinement and you didn't even know what it was.

He remembered being with her once when her cat dragged itself into the yard, its hind legs useless because of a broken back. Rivas and Uri had been breathlessly rolling around in the grass behind a toolshed in the Barrows yard, and when Uri leaped up and ran to the struggling cat, her eyes were still a little unfocused, her lips swollen—and then when she'd tried to pick it up, the cat had screeched and spun in the grass and Uri had lurched back with bright drops of blood already rolling down her slashed fingers and pattering onto the grass.

Rivas had put the animal out of its agony with a shovel, and then tried to comfort the appalled and weeping Uri. What had shocked her, he remembered now, was not the blood everywhere, nor even the pain of the several deep scratches she'd gotten, but the *abruptness* of it; the way grotesque, horrible violence had appeared in their midst with no warning, as if a chunk of icy iron had plummeted out of the cloudless summer sky.

For several miles the boat-wagon rattled along peacefully, while the day grew warmer; at one point a flicker of motion above the verdant ruins ahead caught Rivas's eye . . . and his belly went cold a moment later when he saw that it was one of the big-as-your-fist punch-bees looping toward them out of the high branches of a carob tree, the rattling buzz of its six-inch wings audible even a couple of hundred feet away. He'd seen a man hit by one of them once, knocked right off his feet by the impact and dead before he hit the ground because of the three-inch stinger driven right up to the bug's rear end in his eye.

Rivas was about to jump off the wagon and run when he heard a twang behind him and felt the air beside his right ear thrum like a plucked rope, and a split second later the punch-bee exploded with a wet smack and was suddenly just spray and bits of meat spatting onto the pavement and iridescent shards of wing spinning away like glassy leaves.

Very slowly Rivas turned around on the bench. Nigel, sitting astride the boom, was fitting a second pebble into his wrist-brace slingshot, and then he put the weapon back in his bowler hat and put the hat on his head. He met Rivas's gaze with eyes as cold and incurious as marbles.

"Good with that thing, Nigel is," observed Lollypop.

"Yes," Rivas agreed, re-evaluating his chances of disabling these boys soon and getting a look at the girls in the wagon.

As the wagon went rolling past the carob tree Rivas breathed through his mouth, for the air was sharp with the metallic smell of the killed bee.

•   •   •

Several hundred yards behind, the tumbleweed caught against a metal post from which still hung a few curly strands of a barbed wire barrier that, a century ago, had apparently blocked the whole street. The bush heeled around to a stop. A pinkly translucent head disattached itself from the twiggy ball and blinked around, then snuffed the air. A smile stretched its face like a breath stretches a smoke ring, and a pink arm less substantial than a snakeskin reached down and with some difficulty freed the bush from the barbed wire. The head and arm were retracted again as the tumbleweed began to roll, resuming its interrupted southward course.

Late in the afternoon Lollypop left the at least somewhat maintained succession of bayshore roads and turned east up one of the old highways that mounted inland through the band of jungle and into the dry hills beyond.

"Why the shift?" asked Rivas, watching the water move around from the starboard side to the stern, and then begin to recede.

"There's a big damned army been moving up the coast last couple of days," said Lollypop. "Supposed to have come south overland, sacked Santa Ana and Westminster, and now they're heading toward the bay, along the shore and in boats, burning everything in their way."

Rivas remembered the fires he'd seen on Long Beach Island last night. They're at the mouth of the bay now, he thought. "Huh. Who are they supposed to be?"

The old man didn't answer until he'd guided the horses around a dangerously undercut-looking section of pavement. "Well," he said, relaxing when they were past it, "we were in Hunningten Town a couple of days ago, and people were saying it was an army from way up north, like San Berdoo." He shrugged. "I guess it's possible."

"Huh." Rivas leaned back, absently enjoying the coolness on the right side of his face where the sun had been shining on it all day. So, he thought, Ellay's got soldiers patrolling her western and northern borders, and here comes San Berdoo up from below. I wonder if the Berdoo boys really think they can take her by surprise. Maybe they can. Nearly all the traffic across the Inglewood Desolate is of fairly furtive, untalkative types—Jaybirds, hooters, pimps like my pals here. Maybe they can, at that.

The girls were getting restless by the time Lollypop parked the wagon in a garagelike structure with a roof high enough to let the mast in, and Rivas was trying to hear their voices, for he was sure he'd recognize Uri's, even after thirteen years. During the long afternoon he'd considered and reluctantly dismissed the idea of asking to see the captives, even on the pretext of suffering a sudden fit of lust; a genuine Blood dealer would know better than to ask, and suspicion seemed easily kindled in his two traveling companions. The voices fell to muttering when the wagon stopped, though, so Rivas hopped down and looked around the big echoing chamber.

Square sunken areas with truncated metal pillars in them seemed to confirm his guess that this had once been some sort of garage, but there were indications too that it had seen other uses not quite as long ago. Several cots and stretchers, their fabric spiderweb-frail after all the desiccating years, were tumbled in the corners, and when Rivas crouched down on the littered floor, hoping to find a weapon, he picked up a tiny squat bottle with a rubber diaphragm instead of a lid. The diaphragm broke to dry bits when he touched it, and whatever fluid the bottle had once contained was long gone.

The unoiled-axle cries of homeward-bound parrots were ringing in the sky faintly—though very loud when, every now and then, a half dozen of the busily flapping green and

orange birds would pass over the street in front of the garage — and the shadows were lengthening and the light outside was turning apricot when Nigel scuffed away with a
roll of twine and a bag full of old jewelry and aluminum
cans to set up some intruder alarms.

"Do you generally sleep in the wagon?" Rivas asked
Lollypop.

"Yeah," said the old man as he tossed some cloth bags
to the pavement and then jumped down from the driver's
bench. "The girls inside the cabin, Nigel and me on deck."
He sat down and opened the bags and began pulling out
heavy waxed-paper packages. "Hope you like pork," he
said. "Oh," he added, looking up, "and hitchhikers sleep
off the wagon."

"Makes sense," said Rivas, who'd hoped for that answer.
"I think while there's still some light I'll check for snakes
and scorpions."

"Probably a good idea," the old man allowed.

Rivas wandered deeper into the building, looking around
again for something that could serve as a reliable weapon.
The inland detour had been a bit of luck for him, but he
knew this was about as far east as his companions would
be going — from here they'd begin to bear back west, toward
the bay and away from Irvine. He'd have to find out tonight
if Uri was in the wagon, for if she wasn't, he'd have to get
moving south.

Against one wall an ancient engine block and an equally
ancient bed frame seemed to have formed the seed of a
particularly convoluted litter pile, and he walked over to it
and noisily wrenched some things away: an old chair, a
teevee box, the hood of a car, a refrigerator shell so rusteaten that he could spin it away one-handed. . . .

He was exposing a sign stencil-painted on the bricks of
the wall — he could already see the word "AVAILABLE" —

so he pulled over a set of metal shelves, making a hellish clatter and sending a million little glass rectangles tinkling out across the concrete floor. He could read the sign now.

CD GUARANTEED SAFE FOOD
AVAILABLE HERE_____

There was still chalk dust in the pits in the brick surfaces over the stenciled line, but the only legible notation in that spot seemed to be the last applied, and it was scratched in as if with the point of a knife:

nevermore

Rivas looked over his shoulder at Lollypop, who had gathered wood for a fire and was laying pieces of pork out onto a metal grate. The old graffitist spoke too soon, he thought.

At last he found something that looked possible—it was a whippy length of flat aluminum with a heavy, rusted bolt at one end, and he slipped it up his sleeve so that the bolt was nestled in his armpit and the end of the strip was just concealed by his cuff. And, just as carefully, he was rehearsing in his head a word he didn't know the meaning of, but which he had heard many times: *sevatividam,* pronounced gutterally with the tongue against the edges of the teeth on the *t* and *d*.

"I guess there's nothing gonna bite me," he said, ambling back toward the wagon in the wide doorway. He noticed that his hands were visibly shaking, so he added, "You guys got any liquor?"

"Sure, a fifth of Currency up under the driver's bench," said Lollypop. "A cup, too. Don't take more'n one cupful."

Rivas opened his mouth to voice the response that had become automatic with him over the years, but then he just nodded. "Okay." He climbed up to the bench, and as he reached under it for the bottle and cup he risked whispering, *"Uri?"* hoarsely at the floor. There was no reply, and he filled the cup, re-corked and replaced the bottle, and then managed to climb back down without spilling a drop or banging his thumb.

The old man had got the fire going and Rivas sat down on the concrete floor near it and with some trepidation took his first sip of Currency Barrows since the night thirteen years ago when he'd done his imitation of a barking dog.

He was a little disappointed that it didn't bring back any memories. It was just a mouthful of hard liquor, a bit perfumy and biting, without the clean grain taste of whiskey. Oh well, he told himself; better than gin. He relaxed and, having given up on feeling dramatic about it, set about enjoying it simply for its alcohol content.

"How is it?" Lollypop enquired.

"Root of all evil," said Rivas with a satisfied smile. Wouldn't Mojo be surprised, he thought, to see me knocking this stuff back.

And what, he forced himself to wonder, is Mojo doing right at this moment, do you suppose? Drawing infrequent beers and making frequent apologies for the absence of the legendary Venetian pelicanist? Or hopping and sweating to fill the drink orders of the huge crowd attracted by some new performer? No, Steve couldn't have got someone else *yet.*

Rivas rolled another sip of the brandy around on his tongue—he was beginning to get used to it—and wondered if he'd ever stand on the stage at Spink's again. He closed his eyes and tried to visualize the place—the high ceilinged room with the bar on the far side and the doors to the left, the lamps, the tables, the strings of dusty paper dolls way up there higher even than the chandeliers. . . . He wished now that he'd taken the time to really *look* at those strings of little figures holding hands and touching toes. He'd always been curious about them, even before he'd learned that they were the last work of some genius sculptor—Noah Almondine, Rivas seemed to remember his name was—who lost his mind and killed himself in the last year of the Sixth Ace. Rivas had never been able to keep straight the names of all the genius painters and poets and doctors and engineers—and even politicians, for the Sixth Ace was supposed to have been the best Ellay had had since Sandoval himself—who crowded into prominence when Rivas was about seventeen, and then all wound up leaving by the Dogtown gate at about the same time the Sixth Ace was assassinated. Though there weren't ever any *musicians* in that crowd, Rivas thought, and thanks be to Jaybush for the lack of competition.

All too soon the distant rattling and clanging was replaced by the scuff of Nigel's returning footsteps. Rivas put down the cup and got up into a crouch, his heart pounding, and frowned dubiously at the pork to explain the move.

Nigel walked into view from around the corner.

"How long have you guys been carrying this pork around?" Rivas asked, trying not to talk too fast or too shrilly. "It looks a little old to me, yes man, little bit old. Don't need, what, worms, do we, hey? Why, I knew a guy ate some old pork one time, and listen, worms woulda been a blessing to him; he'd 'a' begged you for 'em, compared to what he got. He came down with—"

Nigel was close enough now, and looking annoyed rather than suspicious at this jabbering.

"—*sevatividam*—"

As Rivas had hoped, the captive girls instantly began shrieking when they heard those five syllables and Nigel, startled by the sudden din, spun toward the wagon.

Rivas sprang up out of his crouch, whipping the length of metal from his sleeve in one motion and whirling it around and back, over his head; when his right foot hit the pavement he was moving at running speed, and though Nigel looked back in real alarm when he heard it, Rivas was already upon him, and with all the strength of his arm and momentum of his rush Rivas lashed the heavy bolt directly into the bridge of Nigel's nose. Even as Nigel's head snapped back and his body folded backward, Rivas let go of the aluminum strip and let himself fall with the body, and as they hit the floor together he snatched Nigel's hat and when he rolled to his feet on the far side of the body he was fitting the slingshot into his hand and over his wrist and aiming it at Lollypop, who'd drawn a knife and taken a couple of steps forward.

The old man skidded to a stop when he saw Rivas draw the pebble back against the increasing resistance nearly to his ear.

"Drop the knife," Rivas panted.

The knife clattered on the floor. "What have you done to Nigel?" the old man moaned.

"Maybe I overthumped him," said Rivas, beginning to catch his breath. "Open the cabin."

"You're a Jaybird," said Lollypop.

"No. Open the cabin."

The old man didn't move. "That was that speaking in tongues gibberish."

"Right. I can kill you and open it myself."

The old man started toward the wagon. "You're a redeemer, then."

"One of the out for hire ones," Rivas agreed. He turned slowly to keep the slingshot aimed at the man, but took a couple of steps back and let the rubberized netting go slack for a moment while he crouched and snatched up the knife. He had the knife wedged into his wrist sheath and the pebble drawn back again before the old man could do more than look around.

As Lollypop turned back toward the wagon Rivas glanced down at Nigel. One eye was wide open and staring up into a darkening corner of the ceiling, the other was nearly closed, and between them was a deep indentation. Rivas's outstretched arm began to shake, and he wished he was anywhere else on earth.

Lollypop had climbed up over the wagon's stern and unbolted the cabin door, and Rivas hurried forward as it swung open. Three girls were standing inside, blinking in the orange firelight; they were smiling uncertainly, evidently still supposing that Rivas's imitation of a far-gone receiving the sacrament had been genuine.

He peered closely. None of them was Uri.

"Step down, girls," he said with weary gentleness. "You're free."

Their smiles disappeared, but they climbed down and wandered aimlessly toward the fire.

"Climb in there," Rivas told Lollypop, "and, carefully, bring the fourth girl forward."

The old man disappeared inside the cabin. After a moment he called out, fearfully, "She's dead."

"Bring her forward."

"You'll kill me."

Maybe I will, thought Rivas helplessly. But, "Don't be silly," he said. "This is just a job to me."

There was scuffling and thumping in the darkness, and then he saw a long, dark-haired body rolled to the cabin's threshold.

"Let me see her face."

Lollypop lifted the head and turned it toward Rivas. It wasn't Uri.

Rivas wasn't aware of how tense he'd been until his shoulders relaxed. "Not the one I'm after," he told Lollypop. "Get inside and shut the door."

There were tears on the old man's face. "You can't lock

me in here! This cabin's built tough, I'd starve to death, just shoot me right now—"

"I'm not going to lock it, relax. I'm just going to pile some stuff in front of the door so I'll hear it if you come out. The dead girl you can leave in there with you or roll out onto the deck."

Lollypop rolled her back inside. "I can't be alone," he muttered as he pulled the door closed.

Rivas let the slingshot go slack and tucked it into his shirt, then ran back into the dark garage, picked up the old bed frame and carried it back to the boat-wagon. He threw it onto the deck, climbed up himself, and leaned it up against the closed cabin door. "There," he called. "If I'm still around when this falls, I'll hear it and come back and kill you, okay?"

The old man was mumbling inside, possibly to the dead girl, but there was no specific reply.

Rivas let the slingshot go slack and tucked it into his belt, walked around to the driver's bench and grabbed the bottle of Currency, then hopped down to the floor. During the day's ride, he had noticed that the harness of the horses was an unusual style, with some sort of hinge and pin arrangement as well as buckles on the harness straps, and a light English saddle on each horse; now he put the bottle down, carefully, and walked up to the front right horse to get a closer look at the harness.

Each of the pins, he saw, had a ring on the top end; he yanked one out of its hinge and the harness strap fell away. He smiled almost sadly. Ready for anything, you boys were, he thought; Jaybird shepherds, punch-bees, the necessity of having to take to the water . . . even, I see, for having to abandon your vehicle altogether and proceed on horseback without unbuckling anything. I'll bet old Lollypop is going to be a little more careful about picking up hitchhikers, though. Rivas yanked out another pin and tried to remember what length he liked stirrup leathers to be.

"Where's the jaybush?" came a voice from right behind him, making him jump and gasp.

He turned to the girl. She was tall, with pale hair; she was silhouetted against the comparative brightness outside, and so he couldn't see her expression, but, knowing Jaybirds, he didn't figure there would be much to see anyway. "Sorry, miss," he said. "There isn't one anywhere near." He looked past her. "Where'd the other two go?"

She shrugged.

"Good luck to them." He went back for the bottle and tucked it into his shirt and then pulled the last pin, freeing the horse from the wagon. "And good luck to you," he added, wondering if she'd know how to give him a leg up.

"Where are you going?"

He looked back at her in exasperation. Why couldn't she have wandered away with her friends? "South."

"South?" she said with sudden eagerness. "To the Regroup Tent?"

"No, dammit, I—" He paused. Why not? What better cover could he hope for than the role of a Jaybird who'd become separated from his band and was waiting to be caught up with or reassigned? Especially if he was accompanied by an obviously genuine stray Jaybird girl. "I mean yes," he said.

"Can we start tonight?" she asked. "I feel terrible being away from everyone."

"Yes," said Rivas, leading his horse around so that he could reach the harness pins on the left front one. "I'd like to get away from this place as soon as possible."

The girl glanced around blankly, apparently giving Nigel's corpse no more attention than she gave the neglected pieces of pork. Obviously home was wherever the Jaybirds were, and every other place was simply a place where they weren't, only to be passed through and not worth a second look. Rivas had read somewhere that toads could perceive only two categories: a fly, and everything that was *not* a fly. This girl seemed to have the same sort of two-position attention switch.

"Since it's not where everyone is," he amended wearily. She smiled and nodded, and he went on, "Sure, there's still enough light for us to cut a couple of miles out from between us and the Regroup Tent." He handed her the reins to the second horse. "Can you ride?"

Her smiled disappeared. "Yes," she said, taking them.

He realized that it must have been a skill she'd acquired before becoming a Jaybird, during her renounced old life, and that while she was willing to use it to get back into the bosom of the church, she'd take no pride or joy in it.

"Well," he said, "if I fall off, come back for me."

Without replying the girl hiked her left knee up, got her sandalled foot into the left stirrup, and effortlessly swung up onto the horse; Rivas noticed that her legs, under the coarse cloth robe, were long and graceful. She'd have fetched a good price in Venice, he thought—and I'm glad I saved her from that. And what the hell am I looking at a girl's legs for when I'm trying to find Uri?

At his second try Rivas got into the saddle. "Follow me," he said, and led the way out onto the street.

When the quiet tick-tock of the hooves had receded away down the street, the garage was silent . . . but not quite still. The sunlight became redder and dimmer as it slowly advanced across the concrete floor, the remaining two horses blinked incuriously from time to time, and a shadow without a body drifted from the street into the garage, hard to see because it was the same color as the twilight glow. It turned like an unhurried underwater swimmer and tensed slightly when it saw the raw pork, but moved eagerly forward when it saw Nigel's corpse. It lifted its legs in a crouch, and when gravity finally coaxed it down to the floor its insubstantial fingers fluttered over Nigel's face and hands, trying to find an open wound.

Then finally the wagon's cabin door was pushed open, and a bed frame toppled onto the deck with a tremendous crash. The transparent creature, immensely startled, darted away like a minnow, and by the time the snuffling Lollypop had shuffled across the deck and climbed down to the floor, the thing was clinging upside-down to one of the ceiling beams, as tight and still as a pink glass bat.

The old man sat down beside the body and began haltingly whispering to it while the light crept further into the garage and grew dimmer and the creature on the ceiling beam blinked and rolled its big eyes and one of the Jaybird girls, outside, made a steady clanging racket but no vocal complaint as she tried patiently to extricate herself from one of Nigel's intruder alarms.

At last Lollypop picked up Nigel's body, carried it to the wagon and laid it on the deck. He climbed back aboard, rolled the dead girl out of the cabin and dumped her over the gunwale, and then gently dragged Nigel inside and closed the door behind them.

Five minutes passed, then the ceiling-clinging thing let go and spread its arms and legs and spiraled down like an autumn leaf and touched down, silently, on the dead girl's face.

There was no further motion in the garage; and after a while the Jaybird girl outside got free of the alarm and wandered aimlessly away into the night, and then the silence was unbroken.

CHAPTER FIVE

WHEN A SUDDEN clatter of hoofbeats spilled Rivas out of the night's web of dreams, he decided that he'd been premature yesterday in deciding that his fever was abating. His skin was hot and dry and tight and his breath was arid in his head and the bright morning sunlight seemed to be making faint rainbow auras around everything. His head was murky with the sort of unspecific depression left behind by a night of heavy drinking or the worst sort of nightmares.

He rolled over into a crouch on the pile of cardboard that had been his bed, and he squinted around at the weedy yard. A collapsed, rusty swing-set leaned against a fence near him, and the cardboard freshly shoved under it reminded him that when he'd gone to sleep last night the Jaybird girl had been sleeping there. So where was she now? He stood up, feeling dangerously tall and fragile, and stumbled out of the yard to the tree he'd tied the horses to.

One of the horses was still tied to it. Rivas peered around, blinking tears out of his eyes and wishing that his nose would either produce a sneeze or stop tingling, and finally saw her, fifty yards down the street, riding the other horse.

"*Hey!*" he yelled. "Uh..." Why hadn't he learned her name? "Hey, *girl!*"

She looked over her shoulder, then reined in and rode back to the tree, which he was now leaning against. "What?" she said.

"Where are you going?" He had to squint to look up at her against the bright blue sky.

"The Regroup Tent," she said impatiently. "Where did you think?"

"Well, Christ...you weren't going to wait for me?"

"I thought you were sick."

"*Oh!*" he said, nodding in exaggerated comprehension. "*I* see. You thought I might slow you *down*."

"Right."

He throttled his anger by reminding himself that she was a vital stage prop in his role as a stray Jaybird...and just for a moment, though he suppressed the thought almost instantly, he knew he'd have ditched *her* in an instant if she'd been sick and of no use to him.

"Well, I'm *not* sick," he said. "This is just an allergy. I'm allergic to these...bushes, here. Okay? So wait for me. And don't run off without me again, hear?"

She blinked at him in some surprise. "It's the duty of every strayed follower of the Lord to return to the fold as quickly as possible."

"Well, sure," he said, intrigued by the hint of an Ellay accent in her voice, "but not so hastily that you're likely not ever to get there at all. One girl alone, why...you wouldn't get two miles before you'd run into a snake or a punch-bee or a rapist or another couple of pimps."

She seemed genuinely puzzled. "But my soul would be in the Lord's hands. Why should it upset *you?*"

He spread his hands and opened his eyes wide to show her how sincere he was. "Because I care what *happens* to you, that's why." She waited while he saddled his horse and got onto the animal by half climbing the tree.

The girl didn't speak as they rode slowly down the sunlit street, but she looked vaguely troubled.

"Didn't I save you from those two guys who killed your friend?" he reminded her after a couple of minutes.

"Yes," she said. Phone poles stood every few hundred feet along the left side of the road, and sun-rotted rope rings dangled from some of the cross pieces, way up there where only birds could get to, and a couple still held yellow sticks of forearm bones. At about every twenty-fifth hoof clop the horses passed through the shadow of another pole. "But . . ." the girl said after a while, "we aren't supposed to care about each other that way. . . . That's for the shepherds, rescuing is . . . and even they don't do it because they care about us but just because the Lord wants us."

Rivas glanced at her with some respect. Very good, sister, he thought. You've got clear eyes for a birdy chick. She caught his look and smiled uneasily before looking away.

Rivas let his gaze drift to the buildings in the middle distance ahead, standing out there among the heat shimmers like broken, discolored teeth in green gums, and he let his eyes unfocus so that it all became just blurs of color. As the morning wore on, he wished he'd taken Nigel's hat as well as his slingshot. The hot sun made it feel as if his fever had spread out from him and infected the whole world, like a spilled beer gradually soaking through a whole book, so that the pages tore or stuck together in clumps, and all continuity was gone. He *could* remember, if he tried very carefully, who he was, how old he was, and what his pur-

pose was in being here; but during this monotonous southward ride he didn't need to keep all those things in mind,
and so he just rocked with the motion of the horse and,
unless something roused his attention, thought about nothing
at all.

*Don't put on the act for me, old boy. I know you hate
'em all, every one of 'em.*

He frowned and focused his eyes. Where had he heard
that recently? Who was it that had said that to him? He
couldn't have been sober at the time, or he'd remember.
Unless he'd been overpoweringly sleepy...?

It's me you love. Me only.

It was last night. A dream? Yes, of course it had been
a dream, a fever-warped one. He tried to remember something more about it, but couldn't.

At midmorning he killed two doves with Nigel's slingshot, and as he was awkwardly butchering them another
sentence from his dream came to him. *You're too ashamed
to admit it,* the voice had said.

Rivas paused, the bloody knife hovering over one of the
half-dismembered birds, and he tried to remember what the
dream had been about and who in it had been saying these
things to him. Then he remembered seeing something in
the dream...a person...himself? Was he looking in a
mirror? And why, of all things, did he see himself sucking
his thumb?

He finished butchering the birds, and started a fire by
dampening some shredded cloth from his shirt with Currency and then banging together various rocks and bits of
scrap metal until some sparks fell on the shreds and ignited
the alcohol vapor. Then he spitted the doves and cooked
them over a fire of powdery old lumber pieces. His companion didn't seem surprised when he let her have one of
the birds, served with a mock flourish on a Ford hubcap,
but she didn't look pleased either.

"What's your name?" Rivas asked her between bites as he leaned back against the big splintered sign that shaded them. He'd whimsically chosen it for their lunching spot because of the archaic message painted on it in big stark letters: ALL CANNIBLES HEREABOUTS CRUCIFYED— *NO* EXEPTIONS.

She gnawed a charred breast for a few moments, then said carefully, "Sister Windchime."

He smiled. "I like that. I'm Brother—" What, not Pogo, "—Thomas."

"It's nonessential for you to like my name," she said irritably. Rivas remembered that *nonessential* was a pretty harsh term of disapproval among Jaybirds. "And why do you have that bottle of money?" she went on.

"To sterilize wounds and start fires," he said virtuously. "Why? You don't think I'd *drink* it, do you?"

"How long have you been a follower of the Lord?"

"I was recruited when I was eighteen," Rivas told her, truthfully.

"Huh," she said. "You can't have taken the sacrament very often if you're still walking around at your age."

Unable to think of a reply, he just shrugged.

She leaned back against the sign and pitched the breast bone into the fire. "I don't—what's the matter?" she asked, frightened, for he'd leaped to his feet and his face was gray.

"Uh—" He turned and squinted back the way they'd come. "Nothing. But we're wasting time. Let's get moving—if we crank, we can be at the Regroup Tent tonight."

He didn't begin to relax until they were mounted and riding south down a well-preserved highway, and even then he kept glancing back anxiously; for he'd suddenly remembered a little more of his dream and he was pretty sure now that it hadn't been a dream at all, that he really had been mockingly spoken to, very late last night, while he was feverishly half awake—spoken to by the hemogoblin whose face was somehow a caricature of his own.

And he was sure, too, that the glimpse he'd remembered earlier, the glimpse he'd thought was of himself sucking his thumb, had actually been a fevered memory of seeing that thing sucking its sustenance from his self-inflicted knife wound.

When the sun was near meridian two columns of smoke appeared in the south, and a third began upwardly staining the blue sky within the next half hour. Rivas and Sister Windchime couldn't hear anything but the grasshoppers and lizards in the dry grass around them, but every time a long straight length of street offered a chance to see some distance, Rivas stood up in the stirrups and peered, trying to see through the mirage ripples and guess whether the troubles ahead—whatever they were, some consequence of the advance of the San Berdoo army, he supposed—would obstruct his progress toward the Regroup Tent.

After a while the street they'd been following turned sharply to the southwest, and they had to strike out across the fields and flattened housing tracts. Eventually they were fortunate enough to find a southward-snaking dry riverbed, and they rode down the middle of it for almost an hour before noises from ahead made Rivas call to Sister Windchime, softly, "Stop."

"What is it?" she asked, already a little nervous herself.

"I don't know exactly, but I'm pretty sure it's people coming this way. Whoever it is, we don't need 'em. Come on," he said, quickly hopping out of the saddle to the gravelly dirt, "let's get up the slope here."

Sister Windchime dismounted and they led the horses up the eroded slope. After the first few minutes of dusty scrambling they were in shade among trees, and at the crest of the slope they found a segment of narrow paved road still not quite reclaimed by colonies of tall asphalt-crumbling weeds and the downhill tug of the annual floods.

"Quiet now," Rivas whispered. "We'll just let 'em move on past us and then be on our way again."

Over the rustling of the branches around them he could now hear a sort of windy ululation and a faint metallic clatter—but it wasn't until the first scream raised startled crows from the trees ahead that Rivas realized what must be going on. It's a band of hooters, he thought.

Though he'd several times talked to people who'd survived hooter attacks and once or twice come across the remains of people who'd run afoul of them, Rivas had never seen a band of them himself, and he wasn't eager to. He was glad he and the girl had found concealment, and he hoped everyone down there in the riverbed would be too busy to note the tracks of two horses on the dusty bank.

Again, and more loudly now, came the eerie fluting sounds, discordant and choppy.

"It's hooters, isn't it?" the girl whispered.

"Yeah," he said. More fervently than ever he wished he'd grabbed Nigel's hat. The shift from motion in sunlight to stillness in shade had got him disoriented again, and thoughts were as hard to hold onto as lively fish in a bait tank. He caught one, and was able to add, "Probably running down some luckless fugitives from the troubles along the coast."

Branches framed a segment of the gravel riverbed below, and as the hoarse yells and thudding footsteps and the clatter of bicycles got louder, Rivas kept his eyes on it. Almost unconsciously he had taken out the loaded slingshot and hooked it over his wrist. He felt Sister Windchime's hand close tightly on his shoulder, but he couldn't spare her a glance to see what her expression was.

"What are you going to do?" she whispered.

"Nothing, don't worry. This," he whispered, raising the slingshot, "is just in case they try to come up here."

Minutes passed and the sounds grew louder and sweat tickled his forehead and neck. Damn, he thought tensely, why do there have to be all these *obstacles?* All we want is to get to the Regroup Tent, get back to where we belong, in the hands of the Lord. The affairs of the world are ephemeral, I believe that, and the ways of the Lord are all important, I believe that too—so why must the world's ways always be so *noisy?*

A particularly raw scream erupted only a short distance ahead, and seemed to shake the leaves. Someone was cursing exhaustedly and a child was sobbing.

"We've got to help them," Sister Windchime whispered.

Rivas glared sternly at her. "Are you backsliding, sister? Everyone dies, and if they are of the Lord it's a cause for rejoicing, and if they're not then their death means less than that of a fly." Though it's noisier, he amended. "Perfect yourself before you take it upon yourself to improve the condition of others."

Tears glittered in her eyes. "Well, that's," she faltered, "that's all . . . *true,* of course, it's *logical* . . . but this"—she waved downward—"this is real."

"The world *seems* real, sister," he told her gently. "With the cleverness of its illusions it tempts us to participate in them. Why, this show today is probably just a test which the Lord has sent to measure our strength. Be brave and do the right thing."

He had turned to look at her, but now a motion below made him snap his head back. A horse had appeared below; a little girl rocked in the saddle and a man was jogging alongside with the side-to-side weaving of total exhaustion. All three creatures were covered with dust and spattered with blood.

Then a rattling, glittering construction had flashed across his view, and the man fell to his knees with a sob, and coins of bright red blood began rapidly appearing under him and around him on the smooth stones—

—and in the same instant Sister Windchime put her heels to her horse's flanks and went avalanching down the slope.

Rivas, though swearing with fright and rage, was right behind her.

The cloud of dust they raised in sliding and scrambling down to the riverbed made it hard to see anything, but to his left Rivas heard the skid and clatter of one of the hooter bikes turning around, and he lifted the slingshot and faced that direction. Then he could see the thing through the dust: the two high-wheels that stuck out to the sides at an upward angle looked like the eye-stalks of some big metal insect, and under the cross bar that connected them he could just see the rider, hunched over the pedals; the bike was still leaning way over from its sharp U-turn as it bore down on Rivas, and the starboard high-wheel was spinning from having touched ground.

Rivas held his arm straight out, and fright made him risk the slingshot's elastic by drawing the stone all the way back to his mouth. He let fly and then without waiting to see the effect vaulted off his horse and landed in a crouch on the gravel. As he squinted around for Sister Windchime he fitted another stone into the slingshot's leather pouch, and when he heard quick, rhythmic fluting ahead of him he drew the stone back and peered.

One of the marauders was off his bike and running forward, whirling his slotted sword over his head to produce the alarming, nearly musical noise, but before Rivas could aim at the man, the bike whose rider he'd shot at careened past between them, leaning all the way over so that its starboard high-wheel was rolling along on the ground and the left one stuck straight up in the air like a dish being spun precariously on top of a pole. The rider was gone. When the bike had rolled on past, Rivas saw the slotted sword glittering as it tumbled away through the air, and the

man who'd held it was in the process of sitting down; the
seat of his pants hit the gravel only a moment before the
back of his head did, and then Rivas saw Sister Windchime—she too was off her horse, and with an expression
of horror on her face was straightening up and stepping
forward like a pitcher following through after a fast ball.

The harsh squeak of pebbles grating together made him
look to his right. Another of the weird bicycles was racing
along a course diagonal to him, its rider pedaling furiously
and holding his sword back for a chop at either the girl on
the halted horse or Sister Windchime. Both possible victims
looked off balance and confused.

Knowing that he wouldn't have time to reload and try
again, Rivas turned carefully on his heel, tracking the bike
and trying to aim at a point a bit ahead of the rider and
wishing he'd spent the day practicing his marksmanship.
When he saw that in another moment it would be too late,
he let fly, and then yelled with triumph when the rider
seemed to dive off the bike; the man tumbled along right
beside the riderless bicycle for a few yards, then lagged
behind, rolling more slowly over the stones.

Quickly Rivas crouched and fumbled another stone into
the sling, then tensely turned all the way around, scanning
both banks and the riverbed in both directions, and while
he was doing that he heard the first bike roll to a stop fifty
yards away, and a moment later heard the second one crash
janglingly into the bank. He saw the three sprawled hooters,
and Sister Windchime, and the girl, still on her horse, and
the man still kneeling beside it . . . and there didn't seem to
be anyone else. Rivas straightened and let the slingshot's
elastic relax, and the wind that was sweeping the kicked-
up dust away was suddenly cool on his sweaty face and
chest.

He tucked the slingshot back into his belt and trudged
over to the kneeling man, who had begun yanking at the

tail of his own shirt, presumably trying to make a bandage for the jagged, energetically bleeding gash in his upper arm.

"Here," croaked Rivas, then got control of his voice and went on, "let me get that with a knife."

"Thanks," the man whispered.

As he ripped Lollypop's knife through the cloth, Rivas looked up at the little girl on the horse. She was staring off into the distance with a half frown, as if trying to remember where she'd left something. He decided that there was nothing to be gained by speaking to her and focusing her attention. He'd cut a wide strip of cloth free and was knotting it around the man's arm when Sister Windchime gave a little startled scream.

"This one's still alive, brother!" she called fearfully.

Rivas gripped the knife more firmly and looked up. The second man he'd shot had rolled up onto his hands and knees and was coughing a lot of blood out onto the stones. The line of his profile seemed too straight from forehead to chin, and it occurred to Rivas that the front of the man's face, including his entire nose, was gone. Rivas stood up and walked over to the nearest sword, picked it up and looked at the other two fallen marauders. The first one he'd shot at was lying somewhat bunched-looking against a rock, and had pretty clearly suffered a fatal injury of the spine; the man Sister Windchime had flung a rock at was staring wide-eyed and unblinking straight into the sun, and Rivas felt safe in ignoring him too for now. He approached the crouching, retching one.

Though his face was a horrid red tangle of exploded flesh and bloody beard-fringe from the bridge of the nose on down, the eyes were bright and alert. He gargled something that sounded to Rivas like, "Go ahead."

Rivas did, and then with sick, weary disgust flung the fouled sword away and plodded back to the kneeling man. He had to keep fighting off a dizzy, fatalistic certainty that this hot afternoon, characterised by dust in the throat and fingers sticky with drying blood, wouldn't ever end.

The man had finished tying and adjusting the bandage, and though it seemed to have cost him half his soul, had stood up and was hanging weakly onto the saddle horn.

"I've got," said Rivas, "money. Brandy. To sterilize your wound."

"Screw that," the man said. "Let me . . . sterilize . . . my stomach with it."

"Right."

Peripherally Rivas noticed that Sister Windchime didn't evince any disapproval at all as he walked to his horse, unstrapped the bottle and carried it back to the man. He uncorked it and handed it over.

"Cheers," Rivas said.

"Happy days," the man responded, then tilted the bottle up to his mouth. Bubbles wobbled up through the amber inside, but not a drop spilled. The man finally lowered it and handed it back, with a sharp exhalation and a breathless *"Thanks."*

"Sure you don't want to splash some on your bandage?" Rivas asked. "It kills germs."

"Germs," the man echoed contemptuously. He looked around. "They all dead?"

"Seem to be."

Sister Windchime had quietly moved up behind Rivas, and now she shyly asked, "Why were they after you?" She pointed at the horse, whose harness bore cut straps but no pouches or saddle bags. "You haven't *got* anything."

"Not anymore, no," the man agreed. "They started after us just north of Stanton. Everybody's running from the Berdoo army, hooters as well as city citizens. We had some supplies originally, but had to cut 'em loose—less weight for the horse, and we kept thinkin' we could lose these boys while they were grabbing our scattered food. We kept going up steep hills and across bad terrain, but they'd always find a parallel street and be right back on us in a half hour at the most. And then this afternoon when they knew we had no supplies left but they still kept after us, that's when I knew they were as hungry as everybody else and our poor couple of pounds of salted pork hadn't done them enough good. They wanted fresh meat."

"Well," said Rivas, "now they *are* fresh meat."

The man gave him an unreadable stare. "Not for me, thanks." He cautiously let go of the saddle horn, and reeled a little but didn't fall. "They killed my wife—this kid's mother—a hundred yards back. We'll head back and bury her and then be on our way. We're much obliged to you people for saving our lives."

Sure, thought Rivas helplessly as he watched the man take the horse's reins and begin to walk back. I'll bet we bought you and your little girl another whole two days of life. Six hours less for you, maybe, and six more for her, but averaged out, say two days. Jesus.

Sister Windchime touched him hesitantly. "I'm sorry, brother," she said. "I feel terrible about it. Of course you'll report me to the disciplinary committee."

At first Rivas thought she was sorry for having put a fast rock into the face of the dismounted hooter, but when he looked at her he realized that she was apologizing for having intervened in a worldly quarrel; and for having done it even as he was virtuously pointing out to her the doctrinally correct course.

"It was a singularly strenuous test," he told her with kindly condescension, now faking the tone he'd somehow been sincerely taking earlier. "I'll report that fact to them."

"Thank you, brother," she said earnestly. With a humble, short-stepping stride she walked back to her horse and, with an ease that infuriated Rivas, swung up into the saddle.

After he managed to flounder onto his own horse they

set off down the gravel track. Rivas waved as they passed the slow horse with the girl in the saddle and the wounded man walking alongside—there was no answering wave—but Sister Windchime, he noticed, frowned unhappily and looked away.

A few minutes later they passed the collapsed, ripped-up body of a woman. They didn't alter their pace.

"They," said Sister Windchime after a while, "are going to die, aren't they? Soon?"

Rivas glanced at her. "One way or another, yeah. They won't make it to a town."

"Then it didn't do any good, did it? Interfering. All we did was ... delay them a little, in their trip to the Dogtown gate."

Rivas was busy worrying about his episode of unfeigned birdy orthodoxy up on the hidden slope-crest road, and even this slang confirmation of his guess that she was an Ellay girl didn't make him want to talk. "Right," he said shortly. "Goddamn waste of time."

For another half mile they rode on in silence while the sunlight began to cast a warm light on the greenery to their left and silhouette it to their right; then Sister Windchime said, "Why do I feel like you have to do what you can to help? Even when you know in advance it won't do any good."

"Because you're sinful," said Rivas impatiently. "Now shut up, will you?"

"Would it be all right," she ventured a little later, "if we stopped for a few minutes? I think I need to do some more Sanctified Dancing."

Rivas groaned. "We're in a hurry, okay? Do it in the saddle."

After that they rode on in silence, Sister Windchime stiff with resentment and Rivas frightened—frightened of what he was getting into and of what was happening to his mind.

• • •

They carefully avoided all other groups of fugitives and by early evening they'd reached their destination. Viewed from above as they crested the last of the rounded, brush-covered hills, the huge Regroup Tent in the valley below them looked, Rivas thought dizzily as he swayed on the back of the horse, like a vast bony beast huddling under a patchwork blanket big enough to drape around God's shoulders. Up where they were, Rivas and Sister Windchime were still dazzled by the red sun sinking over the Pacific Ocean, but the tent was already in shadow, and lamps and torches bobbed like fireflies in the valley.

In spite of himself, Rivas slowly turned his head to the southeast, knowing what lay in that direction. And yes, there it was on the far side of the Seal Beach Desolate, the Holy City, its wall just visible as a pale rectangular segment on the horizon. He shivered, not entirely because of the cold sea wind that stirred the dry grass on the miles-separated hilltops.

With no sensation of relief he let his gaze fall back into the dark valley that lay open to him below his horse's hooves. He remembered how easily and totally he had succumbed to the mind-sapping techniques of Sister Sue and her band, and how difficult it had been to float back up into his own identity. I didn't even know how *old* I was, he thought now with a tight mix of sadness and panic. And this afternoon I delivered all those birdy homilies to this girl *sincerely!*

Only for you, Uri, he thought as he nudged his horse forward and down, would I do this.

In less than a minute the chilly sea wind and the sunlight and the view of the ocean were behind and above him. Up from below came warmth and the smell of rancid cooking oil.

"Not so fast, Brother Thomas," called Sister Windchime behind him. "Your horse will trip in the shadows."

"How nonessential of you to remember my name," he snarled without looking back.

Rivas had been to the Regroup Tent only once, more than a decade ago, and in the years since he'd forgotten how big the thing was. Now as his horse slid and clattered down the slope, kicking up a plume of gray dust that was red lit at its breeze-flattened top, he began to remember details: that there were streets and tents inside it, and that the highest sections of the roof were seldom visible from inside because of the upwardly pooled smoke from all the cooking fires, and that for half an hour or so at night, especially after a hot day, you could hear a low whistling that was the warmer interior air escaping through the stitching of the million seams.

The path leveled out and, having given vent to some of his apprehension by his plunging descent, Rivas reined in and waited for Sister Windchime to catch up. It'd be idiotic to ditch her *now,* he told himself, after you've put up with her all the way down.

She stared at him when she rode up alongside. "You're a strange one, Brother Thomas. You act so bitter, but I've never seen anyone so anxious to get back to the Lord."

He made himself smile. "Being away makes me bitter. I'm sorry. I'll be perfect when we get there."

"I think we should both take the sacrament as soon as we get in, don't you?"

"Well—of *course,*" he said wildly. "Let's go. You can lead for a while—I think I may have lamed my horse a little there."

As she nudged her mount ahead, he let his horse follow at its own pace and weighed his choices. It *would* look good, he had to admit, to rush in begging for the sacrament; the problem was that they'd probably be given it. So did he want to use the drunk defense—there was the third of a bottle of Currency—or the newly discovered pain defense?

Somehow, taking into account his weariness and fever—and the fact that he couldn't approach the tent with the liquor—the answer was inevitable. He pulled the bottle out of his shirt, held it down where the girl wouldn't see it if she turned around, and with his good hand he thumbed the cork out. He heard it rustle in the dry grass. And then every time it was clear that her attention would be devoted for a few moments to guiding her horse, he'd raise one arm as if pointing out emerging stars to her, and behind this cover—in case anyone below might be looking up—he'd raise the brandy bottle and swallow a couple of mouthfuls. The warm fumy liquor choked him, but he forced down gulp after gulp, and when he knew that one more drop would undo all his labor he let the nearly empty bottle fall noiselessly into a thick green bush. He'd ridden a few yards further before he realized that the bush was wild anise. He halted his horse and goaded it back, then with a cry toward Sister Windchime he swung his leg over and jumped into the bush.

He buried his face in the greenery and as he heard the thudding of her horse's returning hoof beats he ripped up handfuls of the ferny plant, shoved them into his mouth and chomped them up.

To his surprise he felt her hand on his shoulder and realized that she'd actually dismounted to help him, or at least to satisfy curiosity. "Are you all right, Brother Thomas?"

He got up unsteadily, his recent actions having accelerated the alcohol's invasion of his blood stream. "Yeah, thanks, I was dizzy—" He brushed bits of greenery out of his hair and spat out a leaf or two. "Dizzier than I thought, not really well enough to ride all day, I guess . . . went to sleep and fell off, and I . . . banged my head a good knock on the ground just now."

He grinned foolishly at her. Perfect, he thought. I killed
the brandy smell on my breath and at the same time established an alibi for any drunken lurching or babbling I may
do: *Poor guy—evidently a concussion.* And I get to be
drunk, too.

"Let's walk the rest of the way," said Sister Windchime.
"Wait here while I get the horses."

The sky was a deep cobalt blue by the time they'd wound
their way down the increasingly well-constructed path to
the valley floor, and when Rivas looked up he saw that a
lot of stars were already visible, seeming to hang not too
far above the highest peak of the tent. Lowering his head,
a bit jerkily, he saw several makeshift towers like the ones
that had ringed the field in the Cerritos Stadium, and, closer
at hand, an approaching figure silhouetted by the cooking
fires behind it. The figure was tall and broad and carried
a staff, and for one moment of drunken panic Rivas thought
it was the same shepherd who had stomped his pelican and
shot him, and whom he'd killed, the day before yesterday.

"Children," rumbled this shepherd, "welcome home. What
band are you from?"

"I'm from Brother Owen's," said Sister Windchime.

"I . . . don't remember," said Rivas. He remembered Sister Sue vividly, but he wanted to get the concussion established right away.

Sister Windchime came in right on cue. "Brother Thomas
has been feverish all day," she explained apologetically.
"And on the way down the path a little while ago he fell
off his horse and bumped his head."

Good girl, thought Rivas. "We'd like to take the sacrament, please," he said.

The shepherd clapped him on the shoulder. "Of course.
I imagine you've missed merging with the Lord."

The man had turned toward the light now as the three of
them approached the tent, and Rivas could see the kindly

smile curling the mouth behind the beard. Careful, he told himself; they *practice* that you're-home-now smile. *Don't* relax.

A dozen cooking fires hazed the air of the valley floor and made the many lamps and torches glow like lights seen through fog, and as the shepherd escorted Rivas and Sister Windchime on a looping course toward the tent, unseen people called greetings to them through the smoke and glare and darkness: "Welcome home, stray sheep!" "Merge with the Lord!" and "May you enter the Holy City soon!"

Oh, thanks, thought Rivas, nervous in spite of the brandy. He was trying to figure out what it was that had changed since his previous visit. Something—some smell or noise— was missing.

Under wide hooked-back flaps the tent's main entrance was a twenty-foot-tall arch spilling out a delta of yellow light against the increasing darkness, and as they approached it Rivas could see brightly painted canvas tents inside and robed figures striding about. It occurred to him now what the missing piece of furniture was—there weren't any far-gone communicants speaking in tongues. The other time he'd been here, the valley had echoed day and night with their babbling.

"A jaybush will be administering communion before very long," the shepherd told them as he led them inside, "so it might not be a good idea to put anything in your stomachs right now, but I'll find you a tent where you can relax for a—are you all right?"

Goggling around at the lanes of colorful tents and the spiderwebs of cables far overhead, Rivas had stumbled and fallen to his knees, but as he got up, muttering apologies, he saw only concern in his companions' faces.

"Merging with the Lord will help clear your head," the shepherd assured him.

Rivas nodded solemnly, trying to re-establish his dignity.

"It will be a well-attended ceremony," the shepherd went on. "Several bands are here to pick up their strays, and one of the bands is going directly from here into the Holy City!"

"Called home at last after their hour of wandering in the wilderness," quoted Rivas drunkenly.

"Amen, little brother," said the shepherd.

To someone perched on those high cables, thought Rivas an hour later as he peered up into the smoky heights of the tent, this line of Jaybirds would look like the outline of a huge snail, all looped around and around in a spiral.

He stood up on his toes and craned his neck, but he couldn't see the white-robed jaybush anymore. The old man had wordlessly entered the tent and begun walking through the coiled gauntlet toward the center; Rivas had nervously dropped his gaze when the jaybush passed directly in front of him, but when a few minutes later the man made his next pass on the other side of the line of people in front of Rivas, he sneaked a look . . . and reflected, not for the first time, that it was hard to tell jaybushes apart. Like every other one he'd ever seen, this one had a craggy, browned face and an ivory-colored beard.

Suddenly from the center of the coil he heard an agonized gasp and the clopping thud of a heavy fall, and he realized that the distant mutter he'd heard an instant earlier had been the jaybush's formal exhortation: "Merge with the Lord." He could now hear the faint creaking of clothes and the change in everyone's breathing as the people in the spiral tensed in anticipation. Many closed their eyes and seemed to go into a trance, and Rivas knew that if any of the far-gone men present were on the brink of entering the speaking in tongues stage—women, of course, never deteriorated that far—it would happen about now. Got them old *seva-tividam* blues, thought Rivas.

And, sure enough, two men in the line ahead of him

started up at the same instant, in such effortlessly perfect unison that even their inhalations were exactly synchronized. *"Hmmm,"* they said. *"Hmm?"* Now joined by two more, they went on in a rush: *"Yes, yes, it's boiling down nicely now, let me see—yes, I think I can even taste the heaviness.... Help me boil it, children, gently, each of you lend me your little flame...."*

Quickly but calmly several shepherds trotted into the spiral, pausing in front of each speaker in tongues just long enough to deliver, with all their strength but apparently no animosity, a devastating punch to the belly.

Finally there was just one speaker still working—*"Always welcome, newcomers are, oh, quite a group, how tasty, tasty ... yes, children, let's see if we're strong enough to squeeze it, shall we? Summon a triton for your sea-king to make a hot dinner of, ho ho ho...."* and then an echoing punch silenced him too. All through these noisy interruptions the metronomic "Merge with the Lord," and subsequent thumping collapse, had been continuing without any change in pace.

Rivas wished he could sober up just for a minute and think clearly. My God, he thought, they speak in English now! It's a much eerier-seeming trick now that when it was just gibberish. How do they *do* it, so perfectly in step with one another? Do they rehearse it? Impossible, most fargones can't even feed themselves....

And why do the shepherds silence them now? They never did when it was gibberish.

What are they afraid might be revealed?

"Merge with the Lord." A scream, then a rattling thud.

Rivas wondered where Sister Windchime had wound up. Some of the new recruits were crying—the sacrament *was* a fairly scary spectacle to someone not used to it—and he wondered how deeply that vein of worried doubt ran in her, and what would be the effects on her of today's events and conversations. He looked around as much as he could without turning his head but didn't see her. Oh well, he thought. She's not my responsibility. He closed his eyes as if in a trance and waited for the jaybush to get to him.

When he opened his eyes again and blinked around, he was startled to see that considerable time had passed. In front of him was a circular clearing littered with bodies, some limp and some twitching and huffing as if with bad dreams; a few people were on their feet out there, gaping around in a sort of drugged bewilderment. The jaybush was only two people away to Rivas's left, and he wished he'd stayed in his nap or trance or whatever it had been just a minute longer, so that he wouldn't have seen the sacrament coming.

"Merge with the Lord." A young man jackknifed forward, and the tremendous crack as his head hit the hard-packed dirt made Rivas guess he was killed. He tried to concentrate on how he wanted to fall himself—bending the knees so he'd sit down first, try to get the arms up around the head—but a woman behind him was crying so loudly that he could hardly make his drink-fogged mind work.

The jaybush stepped up to the boy next to Rivas. "Merge with the Lord," spoke the white-robed figure, extending a hand. The boy hissed sharply as the touch was made, seemed to struggle to remain upright, then blew out a noseful of blood and went down like a dropped armload of firewood. Some of the red spray dotted the jaybush's robe, but there was already some drying blood spattered on the hem.

"No," wept the woman behind Rivas. "I don't *want* to go to the Holy City. Not so soon."

Something about her voice struck the drunken Rivas as familiar, and he turned to look at her. She was about thirty, a bit overweight, and tangled black hair hung over her reddened eyes.

He heard the jaybush step in front of him at the same

moment that he recognized the woman as Urania Barrows, and even as he opened his mouth to say something to her the jaybush's cold, bony finger touched the back of his neck.

He wasn't drunk now, though he was vaguely aware that he had been recently and would be again soon, as soon as he got back into his body. In the meantime it was pleasant to be able to see in the dark and move without using any muscles . . . though he was careful not to move too fast or too far, for he knew it would be easy to scoot right up into the sky and forget the way back.

The big tent was far below him. He was level with the hilltop where he and the girl had paused earlier this evening, and he was still rising—must have bounced hard off the ground back there—but so slowly now that he knew there was no cause for alarm. It was nice to be alone up here, distantly aware of all the others way off there to the southeast. They were linked now to the cold, sentient thing that couldn't reach him; every few seconds he perceived yet another of them going there . . . no, more like *becoming* there, and stopping being in the tent . . . and much more distantly there were a few isolated awarenesses in the darkness to north and east . . . one fairly conspicuous one, as a matter of fact. . . .

Suddenly he was certain that something out there in those miles of darkness was aware of him, was watching him. And he knew he could see *it* if he cared to, for he wasn't seeing with his eyes now. . . .

But he was frightened, and was willing himself down, trying to put some hills between himself and that awareness out there in the dark; it was all he could do to move, and it occurred to him that fright in its pure state, without the hormones and reflexes of a physical body, was paralyzing, and that if he hadn't just been in a body recently he probably wouldn't have been capable of any motion at all.

The thing out there knew he was retreating, and he could feel its amusement.

Soon, it said, though without words. *It's always been me you loved best. Only*.

He didn't choose to see it, but he realized that it didn't matter, for he knew precisely what it looked like. It looked like himself.

And just before the hill rose up and blocked the night sky in front of him, he caught a faint hint, more an attitude than a thought, of the thing's ambition: below him, in the tent, was a physical body steadily deteriorating; out there in the hills was a physical body steadily solidifying. Was there a link, was there some sort of transference at work that was only *symbolized* by the transfer of blood? Was that thing becoming him? Would it one day complete itself and walk off, leaving him in a mindless little cellophanelike bag sharing the wind currents with dandelion seeds?

Just as he was about to be swallowed up by the tent that had been growing nearer and nearer beneath him, he realized that he had picked up another half thought from the distant thing: it was glad he had used the drunk defense rather than the pain one, because the thing didn't want any . . . any . . . what word, he wondered, expressed the flavor of the concept? Something like brothers, he decided as, inside the smoky tent now, he let himself be drawn down to his body; something like . . . rivals.

Sound crashed back in on him so abruptly that he jumped like a startled cat, and his brandy-fouled digestive system rebelled at the sudden movement; he rolled to his feet and with clenched teeth and sweat-cold forehead sprinted out of the tent without looking at anything, and on the dirt track outside rid himself of a lot of the brandy and a surprising amount of wild anise. Fortunately it wasn't an uncharacteristic response to the sacrament.

After a while he walked back, dug his heels into the dirt and leaned his weight back against the fabric of the tent. It gave a little, and he wound up resting comfortably at a twenty-degree angle, facing east. Well, he thought, at least I didn't get down on my hands and knees this time and go *woof woof woof*. He closed his eyes and took several deep breaths of the dawn-chilly air.

Suddenly it stuck him—*dawn* air? And yes, the sky behind the black hill was a little paler than black. Christ, he thought with instant panic, was I out all night? *Has Uri's band left?*

He floundered back upright and looked around. A few hooded figures were still hunching back and forth across the clearing in front of the tent, and he made himself walk swayingly over to one of them.

He grabbed the person by the shoulder. "Listen," he babbled, "I . . . was supposed to be . . . I'm a member of that band that was supposed to go to the Holy City, you understand, but I just now recovered from the goddamn communion. They haven't *left* yet, have they?"

The person—Rivas couldn't tell in the dimness if it was a man or a woman—yanked its shoulder free of his hand. He couldn't see tears on the blur of the face but he could hear them in the voice as the person choked, "I—don't know. Ask the ones there by the entrance." The figure hurried away from him and was almost instantly enveloped in the shadows of the eastern hill.

Not feeling at all reassured, Rivas reeled to the tent entrance, which was still brightly lit from within. "Has the band heading for the Holy City left yet?" he croaked at the half-dozen people clustered there. "I'm, uh, supposed to be, like, with them, all right?" He glared around belligerently.

Dark hoods turned toward him, but against the light from inside the tent he couldn't see faces. "They left hours ago, brother," a man said in not a very friendly tone. "And their shepherd oversaw the loading of them all into a wagon, and he made sure he had every one of them, even the unconscious ones." The man took a step closer. "What's your name, brother? Trying to get into the Lord's city by lying is a pretty serious sin."

Another robed and hooded figure stepped forward from the group. "His name is Brother Boaz," said Sister Sue. "Grab him, he—"

Rivas was off and running through the darkness toward the path that led up the hill, hearing nothing but the hard quick thumping of booted feet close behind him and his heart laboring in his chest, and he was wishing he'd done some exercise during his years in Ellay; and then an open hand slapped him solidly between the shoulder blades and he went flailing forward, off balance, his feet unable to keep up with his plunging body, and he hit the ground in a long grinding slide that left him retching in a cloud of dust as he struggled to get air into his impact-emptied lungs.

Strong hands yanked him roughly to his feet; he'd have collapsed again immediately but the two men held him up and turned him around, back toward the tent. Sister Sue was walking up to the swaying trio, and in the brightening light Rivas could just see her broad, savage smile. "He's a redeemer," she told the figures following her. "He's the one who killed our shepherd in the Cerritos Stadium. He knows a way to resist the sacrament." She stopped in front of him and her ferally happy gaze made him squint defensively. "But he's . . . susceptible, aren't you, little brother? He can be made to be uncertain about things like who a musical instrument belongs to, and how old he is. Yes." She laughed softly and reached out and touched Rivas's abraded, bleeding cheek. "Yes, I think that after a couple of administrations of the sacrament while you're securely tied up, and then being kept awake and chanted over for about seventy-two hours, you'll be completely repentant, don't you think, and eager to tell us all the details of your sins."

Rivas realized that he'd never been *truly* scared before now. "Look," he quavered, trying to keep from breaking down and crying and probably wetting his pants too, "look, you don't have to. I'll tell you right now, Christ, everything, all of it, I swear, please—"

Sister Sue laughed again, affectionately. "No no, little brother. We'll do it our way—the Lord's way." She turned to the four figures behind her. "He's strong with fear. All of you hold him. Get a rope around him—but not around his neck. Soon enough he'll be happy to merge with the Lord, but right now he'd certainly rather take his own life."

With stout leather thongs they tied him to two big timbers which had been crossed and bolted together to form a big standing capital X, and a wide basket of woven bamboo was wedged over the tops of the beams as a sort of roof. The X stood over on the seaward side of the big tent, by the trash pits and the latrines; people seldom lingered on this side normally, but the sight of someone being disciplined roused morbid curiosity even in Jaybirds, and when the news about Rivas got around the shepherds had to set up a sticks-and-string boundary fence to keep the crowd back. The bright dawn had given way to an overcast sky, and the clouds whirled occasional skirts of rain across the valley, leaving patterns of round, dark pockmarks in the dust.

Rivas's ludicrous spread-eagled position was uncomfortable from the start, and during the morning it became increasingly painful in his shoulders and back; his arms would eventually have become entirely numb if he hadn't kept flexing them against the bindings, and wiggling his fingers...though by midmorning he had to roll his head around and look up to see if the fingers really were moving as ordered. The most tormenting things were aches and itches that he couldn't do anything about, and the way his nose kept tickling as if leading up to a sneeze which never came, and his consuming hangover thirst. Blood and sweat slowly dripped from him or soaked into the wood, and he couldn't get rid of the idea that as every drop left him the hemogoblin out there in the wilderness became stronger and more solid, and that as every dragging hour eroded Rivas's alertness and capacity for connected thought, the thing out there became more intelligent.

At around noon the rain became steady, and soon after that it began coming down hard in battering sheets that raised a foggy spray of splashes from the muddy ground and rattled a loud, continuous drum-roll on the tent and the hillside and the basket above Rivas's head. His black hair was slicked across his forehead and his clothes were darkly plastered against him and the breath seemed even hotter in his head because of how cold he was. The crowd of Jaybirds dispersed reluctantly, and before long they had all gone back inside the tent.

Rivas had by now become almost calm. He knew he was not as strong, mentally or physically, as he'd been at twenty-one, and that if he became a Jaybird again now he probably would not again succeed in escaping the dreadful faith. But he knew too how short was the lifetime of the average far-gone—and he suspected that he'd be gone, and definitely far, in record time. Sister Sue had been right this morning in guessing that he'd gladly have killed himself rather than wind up here . . . but now he could see little difference between the two courses. And it seemed to him that there was something fitting about not dying until everything one ever had was used up . . . not dropping the glass until it was empty and even gnawed a little. . . . There was a term he'd heard once . . . test to destruction. . . . To learn how much punish-

ment something can take before breaking, you eventually
have to break it. . . .

. . . He could think of a lot of smooth rhymes for "break
it". . . .

At least, he thought feverishly, I won't wind up an old
man. He spoke hoarsely into the rain: "I never did *want* to
wind up an old man."

Then, and it scared him even though he could tell it was
just delirium, he thought he heard the hemogoblin's voice
from miles away across the rainy hills: *Well then* I'll *come
over and wind him up.*

He shuddered, and shook his head to clear it of all these
morbid, self-pitying ideas. There you go again focusing only
on Rivas, he told himself. You're just fascinated by the
Gregorio Rivas story, aren't you? Especially the tragic end-
ing.

What about the Urania Barrows story? She may be just
a supporting actor in your story, but what about *hers?* Or
is yours the only one there is, and when you're not actually
looking at people they disappear or collapse like stage cos-
tumes that aren't currently in use? Now *that* would be an
interesting position for you to take, Rivas; maybe even if
you somehow get out of this you'll just end up as Noah
Almondine's main successor in the art of cutting out paper
dolls.

He couldn't hear over the thrashing hiss of the rain, but
through the deeply moored timbers of his rack he could *feel*
the thudding of approaching footsteps. He closed his eyes
so that they might think he was unconscious. . . . The jaybush might just touch him anyway, but it was worth a try.

"Brother Thomas!" came a sharp whisper.

Rivas's eyes snapped open. A robed and hooded figure
stood in front of him, holding a knife. "Sister Windchime?"
he rasped.

"Yes. I don't want to get my hair wet or they'll know I'm the one that did this." Quickly she plowed the knife edge down the gap between Rivas's right arm and the wood, and as he shook off the slimy loops of wet leather she did the same for his left arm—and then had to hold him up with her free hand, for he'd started to fold helplessly forward. Reaching down, she cut his legs free too, and Rivas reflected dazedly that this was one strong young lady. "Now run," she said. "No one should ever be *forced* to take the sacrament."

"Thank you," Rivas gasped. "I—"

"Go, damn you!"

"Right, right."

Rivas ran wobblingly toward the seaward hill, his shoes splashing in the new mud, and when he got to the slope he crouched behind one of the scrawny bushes at the foot of the hill until he got his breath back and stopped seeing a rainbow glitter seeping into his vision from the sides.

After a few minutes he scrambled to the next bush, then to a boulder he could lie behind, then to a shallow gully. . . . Half an hour later he thought he heard shouting in the wind, but it was hard to be sure, for by this time he was well up into the inland end of the valley, and the patter of the rain on stone and leaves, and the trickle and splash of newborn streams, tended to drown out more distant sounds.

He paused, though, and looked back down the valley. The Regroup Tent was a gray mushroom far away, difficult to distinguish from the bulks of the hills because of the mile of veiling rain that hung between it and him.

He grinned. Redeemer, redeem thyself. So long, Sister Sue.

Late in the afternoon he found a building—once some kind of office, apparently—and decided that smoke against this gray-mottled sky would not constitute much of a risk, so he frictioned up a fire of plywood shelves and antique invoices in the open doorway and warmed himself and baked his clothes dry. He tried not to torment himself with thoughts of food or—though he had managed to slake his thirst at a pool of rain water—liquor. Finally, dry and warm and at least not much sicker than he'd been this morning, he admitted to himself that there was nothing he could do right now except, with massive reluctance and not even a drink, review his situation.

Well, he told himself, Uri's gone now, but everything you could do you did do. You not only *have* Barrow's five thousand fifths, you *earned* them: you took the sacrament twice; you were actually shot, though nobody'll believe that; twice a hemogoblin attached itself to you; you had to kill four men; and if it weren't for the unlikely intervention of that girl, Sister Windchime, you'd be a grinning, babbling moron at this very moment. Oh, and that guy knocked you down this morning, and damned hard, too. And you cut hell out of your thumb. And God knows if you still have a job at Spink's.

He glanced around at the rusty, dusty old filing cabinets and wondered if any of the generations-dead people who'd worked here had been in the habit of caching some liquor somewhere. One heard of such finds occasionally.

Suddenly and shamefacedly he remembered the incomparably greatest suffering he'd sustained during the course of this last, unsuccessful redemption: the loss of Uri herself! For thirteen years he'd planned to go find her as soon as he'd got some real money and could give her the kind of life she deserved, and for these last three days he'd been out actively risking his life to find her . . . and now she was gone, snatched from him just at the very moment—what a touch—the very moment when his three-day search, no, *thirteen-year pilgrimage,* was within seconds and inches of being completed!

He was sure to get some good lyrics out of all this.

Then with an unwelcome clarity that memory can rarely manage, he re-heard how Barrows had described him four nights ago: ". . . Just a kind of shrewd, cunning insect." And though he'd laughed then, all at once he was astonished at how thoroughly Barrows had understood him. My God, Rivas thought now, you're going to get some *lyrics* out of this, are you? Sister Windchime may be birdy, but she's twice the human being you are, boy.

Well, he replied to himself defensively, I'm a professional songwriter—what am I supposed to do, pretend I *don't* derive my songs from the things that happen to me?

No, clown, what you're supposed to do now is the same thing you were supposed to do yesterday. Go get Uri.

But they took her into the Holy City.

So?

So no one has ever come out of the Holy City except a few jaybushes and shepherds. Even Norton Jaybush himself hasn't been seen since entering there ten years ago. Everyone knows that a redemption attempt ends when the quarry goes in there. And no, I *don't* think such an unheard-of effort is called for by the unheard-of price I screwed Barrows into paying. (Though how on earth could I have *bargained* for Uri's soul?)

Now memory replayed a statement of his own, one he'd made to Barrows that same night: "Evidently she's worth five to you, but not ten." So what do you tell *yourself,* boy? he thought. Evidently she's worth a cut thumb and a few scares, but not worth putting your life on the table on a long-shot chance?

Against this question he involuntarily held up a sheaf of treasured images: his apartment on First by the North Gate, with rain and night outside and himself inside with warm lamplight and a pipe and a drink and a book; long summer afternoons with the feet up on a sunny balcony rail, and a friend or two, and a cool beer standing right where his hand could reach it; the pleasant certainty of new pretty girls to charm and impress and possibly take to his bed, and the equally pleasant certainty of being comfortably alone in that bed later. . . .

And at length he realized, bleakly, that all this did not balance the scale. Not when Uri's life was what was being weighed. He had to go to Irvine and get into the Holy City and get Uri out.

God damn her, he thought fervently, for getting us into this.

BOOK TWO:

LEAVING by THE DOGTOWN GATE

"...And when he glimpsed a patch of sky
   above,
Fearing the sight would startle her, he
   turned—
But saw, behind him, no one..."
                              —Ovid, *Metamorphoses*,
                              Book X, lines 55-7
                              the W. Ashbless translation

CHAPTER SIX

FRACAS MCAN SCOWLED fiercely at a harmless couple of Jaybird girls who were ambling down the other side of the street, and was edgily gratified to see them register alarm and duck into one of the ubiquitous prayer parlors, for the response indicated that his shepherd disguise was convincing—at least to the rank and file. And he only had a couple of blocks still to go before he got to the imminent-departure yard, and it looked like he wouldn't have any trouble getting there while the morning dew was still wet on the wagon he was after, and before today's fresh batch of wagons began to be wheeled in. Just so he didn't run into a genuine shepherd! He supposed they probably had some system of passwords or winks or some damn thing that would instantly expose him as a phony. What a damnable advantage Rivas had in actually having *been* a Jaybird for a few years!

McAn was scared. In all his previous redemptions he'd been careful not to go anywhere near Irvine, and now here he was only a long stone's throw from the high, inward-slanting white walls of the Holy City itself.

He touched the knife strapped to the inside of his left wrist, but it didn't give him quite the confidence it usually did. He'd been feeling less than confident ever since the parents of this quarry had reluctantly explained to him that the first redeemer they'd hired to retrieve their son had limped back to Ellay with a bullet in his leg and a story of having been shot at by Jaybird shepherds armed with real working guns and live ammunition.

McAn had asked for five hundred fifths with half payable upon agreement, the most he'd ever asked for a job, and he had explained that he would search only in the areas north of the Seal Beach Desolate. They had objected to that at first, as his clients aways did, but he gave them his standard explanation: that the residual radiation—an impressive phrase—was simply so great in those distant regions that no sane person would spend the kind of time there that even the easiest redemption would require, and that even if a Jaybird *could* be found and snatched at that point, he or she, and probably the redeemer too, would die like a Venetian fish-eater long before they got back to Ellay.

McAn had always known that the story wasn't entirely true, but until the day before yesterday he'd never worried about how much of an exaggeration it might be.

He'd been following a caravan of several loosely connected Jaybird bands who'd been moving south from the Flirtin hills; he wandered along with them, imitating a birdy imbecile whenever anyone tried to speak to him, and he waited for them to stop somewhere and stage one of their big communion spirals so that he could see if anyone present particularly fitted the description of his quarry.

Finally, just as he'd been about to give up on them and

retreat back north, they did all stop for a communion, in a parking lot at the Anahime Convenshin Centr. It had been about noon of the day before yesterday.

The shepherds had climbed to the tops of the old light poles and the weird two-tone roar had started up as the old man in white showed up and walked into the spiral, going around and around as he got closer to the center. McAn had watched the whole spectacle while sitting comfortably on the roof of a truck, remembering to wince occasionally and glance with chagrin at his hand, which he'd wrapped in the realistically red-spotted rag he always took with him now on redemptions. People in severe pain, he'd learned, were disqualified from taking the sacrament.

During the parking lot ceremony he spotted two possibles, and when the sacrament hammered them down he noted which of the sprawled shapes they were, so that after they recovered he'd be able to approach each of them and spring one of the questions the quarry's parents had primed him with.

Though his luck, as he now knew, had been about to run out, it had not quite abandoned him yet. The second of the boys, still somnambulistic from the communion, had not only shown clear recognition of the family dog referred to in the question—"Lucy's chewing all her fur off and she's covered with sores, what can we do besides have her killed?"—he'd even given the correct answer: "Put garlic in her food, like we did last summer."

McAn had been eyeing the nearby fences and walls and doorways, looking for a hidden spot where he could knock the kid out and then carry him away unseen, when the shrill metallic whistling began. Because he'd been peering around he was among the first to see the several dozen Y-shaped bicycles racing across the pavement toward the Jaybird crowd, and he grabbed his quarry's arm and pulled him along in the opposite direction through the confused crowd.

An irregular *pop-pop* began punctuating the screams behind the fleeing pair, but it wasn't until McAn and his quarry had broken away from the crowd and begun running south along a sheltered sidewalk that he realized the noise must have been gunfire.

The Jaybirds had been at two disadvantages when the attack occurred: most of their number were unconscious or disoriented, and, secure in the knowledge that hooters never dared to attack Jaybird bands, the shepherds had set up the communion in an open, paved spot.

McAn couldn't get the boy to run for more than a minute at a time, and the fleetest Jaybird fugitives quickly caught up with and passed them, and soon McAn and his quarry were just two bobbing heads in a packed crowd that was being herded south by grim-faced shepherds on horseback. The shepherds held drawn pistols, and kept standing up in the stirrups to look back, and they took every opportunity to drive their herd up steep hillsides and through narrow gaps in the eternal aluminum chain-link fences—clearly they expected the starving hooters to try again. McAn assumed that the wagons, and all the still unconscious communicants, were being taken south too by some other route, but he couldn't see anything—his horizon was the close heads of the Jaybirds who jogged uncomplainingly along all around him. All he could do was trot along with them and maintain his grip on his quarry's arm.

They passed the wide street which was Chapman Av. They were in the Seal Beach Desolate now, and showed no sign of slowing down.

McAn still wasn't too worried. Obviously there would be some opportunity between here and Irvine for him to grab the boy and slip away.

McAn paused now when he came to the alley that he'd reconnoitered last night. He knew it looped around to the square where the wagons stood, and he swept a disapproving glance over the street before he stepped out of the patchy, unwarm sunlight and into the shadows of the alley.

But of course, he thought, no such opportunity came, and here we are in actual goddamn Irvine. I've stumbled onto a couple of small pieces of luck—having been healthy-looking enough to be assigned to the detail that loaded wagons with the people, including my quarry, who passed out during the two-day forced march; and being able to salvage this robe from a shepherd killed yesterday, in the confusion of the hooters' second attack—but now it's time to *make* some luck. My disguise is good; they never iron these robes, so you can't tell that this one spent twelve hours crumpled in my pack, and with the hood up you can't see the cropped patches on my head where I cut off hair to make this fake beard with.

Think about that second two hundred and fifty fifths! And the unparalleled stories you'll be able to tell once you get yourself and the kid out of this loony, bottom-of-the-world town.

I think the thing about this place that most puts my teeth on edge, he thought as he silently picked his way along the trash-littered alley, is that there's nobody in the whole damn ramshackle settlement who's not birdy as a bedbug. The real shepherds have to hop just to keep slugging all the guys who click over to the speaking-in-tongues channel, and piling them onto the wagons heading into the Holy City. I suppose I ought to punch somebody, just to seem in character. I wonder if there's a back gate to the city somewhere, where they bring the empty wagons out. There must be otherwise you'd be able to see the piles of old wagons over the top of the wall. Heh heh. Unless they—

He froze, for a ragged figure was crouched tensely at the courtyard end of the alley, apparently staring at the wagon McAn had to get to. Well, McAn thought, his heartbeat beginning to accelerate as he flexed his right hand and stole silently forward, here's where I start behaving in character.

But with an alertness uncharacteristic of Jaybirds the figure spun to face him when he was still several yards away, and with no hesitation the man drew a knife from his sleeve and lunged at McAn. McAn managed to knock the knife arm aside, but the man collided hard with him and they both tumbled to the filthy pavement. McAn's false beard was hanging from one ear and was badly unraveled, but he'd sat up and got his own knife out now, and had begun a feint to draw a wide, flank-exposing parry from his opponent—

"Frake!" his opponent gasped, and McAn hesitated.

He peered at the gaunt, red-eyed face. "Who are you?" McAn asked in a clipped whisper, not lowering his knife.

"Rivas."

"Tell me who you are, or—" McAn looked more closely. "Really?"

Rivas nodded, leaning back against the alley wall and obviously trying to pant quietly.

"What on earth's *happened* to you, Rivas? And I thought you'd retired."

"I did." He took several deep breaths. "This is . . . special circumstances."

McAn got painfully to his feet. "You're awful hasty with a knife. *You* I was only going to *hit.*"

Rivas had got his breath back, and stood up too. "That's why you were always the second-best redeemer."

McAn smiled coldly as he carefully re-hooked the beard across his lean young face. "Yeah. I sure do envy what being number one has done for you."

To McAn's surprise, Rivas actually reddened. What's this, Greg, he thought—did you shed the cynical armor too when you shaved off that silly, affected, half beard?

"You're on a job, I gather," said Rivas quietly. "Someone in that wagon?"

"Right. The skinny kid just inboard of the right rear wheel. I put him there late yesterday. Which one's yours?"

"Mine's already in the city. How's this—you make some kind of commotion out in the street to get the attention of anybody who may be hanging around here and I'll drag your boy over to this alley for you, and then I'll take his place in the wagon."

McAn stared at him with genuine horrified awe. "You're going *in there* to get yours?"

Rivas nodded hopelessly.

And I thought I was walking the farthest, most insanely dangerous edge just by having come *this* far, thought McAn. Impulsively he tossed his knife to his left hand and held out his right. "Rivas, I've always figured you for a posturing, slimy son-of-a-bitch, but by God, I'll tell anyone who'll listen that you're the best damn redeemer there ever was."

Rivas gave him a fragile smile and took the extended hand. "Thank you, Frake." He sheathed his knife. "Let's get moving before they bring the conscious members of this band over here."

Rivas didn't know how McAn did it, but no more than half a minute after the young man had loped back up the alley there came a splintering crash from the street, followed by a lot of screaming; he even heard one voice, evidently that of a far-gone startled right over into the last stage, begin babbling about how tasty it was when everybody helped to boil down the heavy water.

Thanks, Frake, thought Rivas. He sprinted to the wagon, rolled the luckily emaciated boy over the rail, crouched to get him draped across his shoulders, then straightened up and, gritting his teeth against the possibility of losing consciousness himself, plodded to the alley. At the last possible instant he changed his mind and instead of simply heaving the kid like a sack of gravel, squatted down and rolled him almost gently onto the pavement.

The unconscious young man was wearing clothes very similar to his own, so Rivas just hurried back to the wagon, climbed in and lay down in the same position the boy had been in, with his face well concealed under someone's limp shoulder, and then let his breathing and heartbeat slow down. After a while he heard a muted scuffling from the direction of the alley, and thought he heard a whispered, "Thanks, Greg. Good luck."

The morning began gradually to warm up, and Rivas heard the rumble of other wagons arriving in the enclosed yard. From time to time he heard desultory conversation, though he didn't catch any words. He actually fell asleep for a while, but came instantly awake when closely approaching boots and hooves clocked on the pavement and the wagon shifted as someone—and then a second person—climbed onto the driver's bench. "These all still out?" someone asked. Rivas heard the jingling of harnesses.

"Yeah, looks like. Buckled up there? Okay, let's go, the rest of you walk alongside.

The wagon jerked, then the axles began creaking and it was moving. Rivas could hear the footsteps of the conscious members of the band walking beside the vehicle; to judge by the snifflings and hitches in breathing, at least one of them was quietly weeping.

He felt the grating shifts of a couple of slow turns, and then all too soon the rattle of the wheel rims became a soft hissing and he realized they'd left the pavement and were crossing the hundred yards of pale sand that ringed the Holy City like a gritty moat, presumably merging with the real beach sand on the seaward side. It occurred to him that it would be very easy to break out in a high, keening wail that could be maintained indefinitely by doing it while inhaling too... and as soon as he thought of it, it became difficult not to do it.

One of the plodders alongside must have felt something similar, for the hot noon air was abruptly shaken with glossolalic jabbering.

Rivas wasn't particularly surprised when no one silenced this babbler—he'd already come to the conclusion that the shepherds did that to keep them from revealing something... but who cared what might be learned by people who were in the very process of entering the Holy City?

"*Annoyances!*" croaked this far-gone now. "*What do I care? Deal with it yourselves, you idiots, I'm not to be interrupted in my cooking.... Sevatividam can't be bothered with these provincial problems... far places, long ago times, I take a longer view.... What if it was your dreaded Gregorio Rivas? He can't impede me....*"

Rivas had stiffened with panic, assuming that they knew who he was and were only conducting this performance to let him know, albeit a bit elaborately, that he was caught; he assumed the wagon would now stop, the bodies slumped around him would leap up, and he'd find himself surrounded by triumphant shepherds with drawn-back slingshots. But the wagon kept rolling and the plodders kept plodding and the speaker in tongues babbled on: "*This stinking boat, you're trying to kill me, careful, ow...*"

Rivas began, one muscle at a time, to relax. Could it simply have been a coincidence? Who the hell was it that was talking, anyway? Obviously not the individual Jaybirds. Was it Norton Jaybush himself? *How?* And why in English now, when a few years ago it was all just gargling? Though the word—or name—*Sevatividam* showed up in both versions. . . .

"*...Leave me alone, I'm about to give the sacrament in Whittier,*" the helplessly babbling man went on. "*Oh, look at them all, turn around, you damned old carcass, I*

*want to see them all. . . . Sevatividam's blessings on you,
my dears . . . give me your push, children, your at-a-distance
strength . . . you never use it yourselves, you don't need
it . . . I wish I could just take that from you, not use you all
up so fast . . . but it seems to be linked to your minds, so
maybe you do need it . . . hard luck. . . . Oh, some first tim-
ers, how tasty. . . .* At this point the stuff became more the
way Rivas remembered it from his own days as a Jaybird,
just grunts and burping and conversational-tone yodeling.

The sweat from his moment of panic cooled him and he
had nearly relaxed back to the degree of tension he'd been
in before it, but suddenly he tensed up with fear again, for
the light had dimmed and the air was a degree or two colder
and he knew that they were even now under the high stone
arch of the gate . . . and when the brightness returned and
the chill passed he felt only worse, for he knew he was now
on the inner side of the high white walls. As if to emphasize
it for him, the gates slammed loudly behind the wagon.

The vehicle was riding perfectly smoothly now, the wheels
making a featureless noise like water being slowly poured
into a metal pan. Rivas had begun shivering among the
tumbled bodies in the wagon bed, for he could tell by the
very scent of the air—a sort of garbagey sweetness with
burned overtones mixed with the fish smell of the sea—
that he was in entirely unknown territory. He was pretty
good at faking and bluffing the Jaybirds in the camps and
stadiums and meeting places out there in the hills, though
not even too successful at that lately, but now he was in
the house of Norton Jaybush himself, the man—if he was
a man—through whose generosity the Jaybirds had whatever they had of power and fearsomeness. In here he might
find anything.

There are only two things, he thought, that I can be reason-
ably sure are in here to be found: Uri, and my own death.

The wagon slowed, and a man's voice said, "All of you—this way," and the sounds of the wagon's pedestrian escort—the babbling of the far-gone, the snuffling and sobbing, and the thudding of all the footsteps—receded way to the right while the wagon resumed its course straight ahead, in a silence that only strung Rivas's nerves tighter.

Quite a while later reins flapped and the wagon came to a stop—after a weird sensation of sliding that made Rivas wonder if they were on a vast sheet of glass—and the shepherd in the driver's seat spoke: "One dozen as promised, Mister Trash Heap, sir." Rivas heard the other man on the driver's bench laugh nervously.

And suddenly there came a sound that made Rivas's eyes open wide for a moment in pure astonishment; it was as if a man had channeled a whole valleyful of wind through one mouth-sized hole, and then for years experimented with holding all sorts of inorganic but flexible instruments up to that focus point of wind, exploring all the ranges of sound that could thus be produced, cooings and whistlings and bass rumblings, until finally he was able to approximate human speech.

"Yess," sighed this implausible voice. "Run along you now, shepherds. Roentgens and rads like to bald you here in minutes only."

"Right," agreed the driver cheerfully. "Rags and rajahs gonna make me bald. Probably why rajahs wear rags on their heads, do you think? To cover it. Help him get the sleeping guys out of the wagon, will you, Bernie?"

"Okay," Rivas heard Bernie say in a strangled voice.

The wagon rocked as Bernie hopped down, his boot nails audibly clicking on the ground. Bernie began hoisting up a body on the far side of the wagon from Rivas, but a moment later there was a sound like someone trying hard to sweep a tile floor with tree branches, and then Rivas felt something thrusting between himself and the floor of the wagon bed. It rolled him over, and he had to open his eyes just a slit.

After a few seconds of stunned staring he decided that the thing prodding at him wasn't a tall fat man with a bucket over his head and bits of cardboard and rusty metal attached all over himself, for Rivas could see blue sky through many gaps in the thing's neck and chest. He saw now that it had bits of glass for eyes, and some arrangement of rusty tanks and dented copper tubing inside the stripped baby carriage that was its chest, and its head was mainly an oversized cocktail shaker in which, in this silence, Rivas could hear something sloshing.

Somehow it didn't occur to Rivas that this was the source of the windy voice, that this thing was in some sense *alive*, until it spoke again. "Wakeful, this one is," it whistled, "or near."

Then without any clear transition, though obviously much later, Rivas was thrashing with nightmares on a cold hard bed in darkness.

His head throbbed painfully and he was terribly thirsty, but every time he got up and went into the kitchen and filled a cup from the water tank and started to drink it, he realized he had only dreamed of getting up and was still in the comfortless bed. Finally he actually sat up—and knew he hadn't done it before because of the unprecedented way it increased the pain in his head—and blinked around at a dim, long room with beds standing every few feet along both walls. The air was stale, and smelled faintly of fish and garbage.

For a while he had absolutely no idea where he was. Then he remembered his fear of losing the job at Spink's, and he tried to get his memory to let him know if that was what had happened. This looks like one of those jigger-a-week rooming houses in Dogtown, he thought, and to judge by how my head feels I've been abusing some truly horrible liquor.

He rubbed his face, and was dismayed to feel a four or five day growth of beard—all over his jaw, too, not just on his chin. That's it, he thought sadly. You're ruined, Greg. Drunk and bearded in the gutter. Bound to happen eventually. If Uri could see you now, wouldn't she be sorry! The fresh-faced boy her father drove away thirteen years ago now nothing but a . . .

He paused in this bathetic reflection, for thinking of Uri had reminded him of something. Of course! How could he have forgotten all *that?* She'd gone birdy, and he'd risked his life to save her but she'd been taken into the Holy City. That made it an even sadder story—young lovers trampled to bits by an indifferent world—though it would be better if there was someone to know about it, a properly anguished audience . . . maybe he'd go birdy himself, voluntarily this time, just to be to that minimal degree with her at last. . . . What a touch!

Someone in a nearby bed had been gasping and sniffling for a while, and now let go a couple of loud sobs.

"Shut up," whispered Rivas impatiently. Goddamn noisy bums, he thought.

He heard the person sit up. "You're awake?" came a whisper.

"Think I could *sleep* in this damned outhouse?" The other person sounded like a girl. If she only knew who I am, he thought bitterly. She probably grew up singing my songs.

To his annoyance she stood up and shambled over to his bed. Jesus, he thought, she's not only sloppy fat but a sport too. Bald as a stone. "I wasn't sure you'd make it," she said. "You looked real bad when they brought you in. One of the trash men hit you?"

So I've descended to getting into fights with trash men, Rivas thought with something like satisfaction. "I wouldn't be surprised," he told her. He felt the back of his head. His hair was stiff with dried blood, and there was a lump back there.

"I guess you tried to run."

"Oh, yeah?" said Rivas, stung. "Bastard probably snuck up behind me."

"Snuck up behind you," repeated the girl in a tone of polite but absolute disbelief. "Right." He was about to argue, but she went on. "I'll be one myself soon," she said sadly. "Lost my hair a while ago, and got the fever bad now. They'll probably put me in one I helped to build."

"Probably," Rivas agreed, not caring what she was talking about. "Now if you'll excuse me, I'd like to—" He stopped talking, for he'd glanced at the window in the far wall, and all he could see through it was night sky . . . and there was no place within Ellay's city walls, except up in the ragged towers, from which one could get an absolutely unobstructed horizontal view of the sky. He stood up, breathed deeply until the sudden dizziness passed, then hurried to the window and looked out.

A glassy plain, flawed with yards-long cracks here and there, reflected the bright stars, and in the distance was the straight white line of a wall dividing the glass from the sky. And then he remembered his decision to follow Uri inside, his meeting with Fracas McAn, the thing that was made of old litter but walked and spoke. . . . He could remember nothing beyond that, but clearly this girl must be right, he must have tried to run, and been chased down. . . .

He was thankful that he couldn't remember.

At length he turned away and stared at the form beside his bed that was the girl. "I'm sorry," he said. "I must not have been making much sense just now. I had . . . forgotten where we are."

"I wish I could forget," she said.

"What do you—what do we—do here?"

"Oh"—he saw her spread her hands—"work. There's machines that need tending, and the helium balloons always need patching—"

"*Helium* balloons?"

"Yeah, big old things for observation along the coast. I don't like that job. I always burn myself with the iron, and the glue makes me dizzy."

"Ah." Obviously she means hot air balloons, he thought.

"And we build the trash men too, to do the really heavy work, though I understand we're not making 'em as good as they used to be made. People say the Lord is getting tired of everything and doesn't care so much that things be done just right anymore. And down at the beach the men mainly build and repair boats. That's probably where you'll be sent."

Something was moving, way out there on the glass plain, and Rivas turned back to the window. In the middle distance a thing was limping wearily along. It looked like a huge misshapen puppet that someone had made of papier-mache stretched over a wire framework and had then partially burned, and it plodded along on its uneven legs as if on an errand that would take centuries to complete.

Rivas turned to the girl again, feeling like a child lost in a strange, cold house. "You said," he began, but his voice came out soprano and he tried again. "You said put you in one of the ones you made. What did you mean?"

"What's good for the Lord isn't good for ordinary people," she said. "We get sick here—and at his temple in the sister city, too, I hear—our hair falls out, and we get, like, sores, mostly on our feet and legs . . . and any that are pregnant don't stay that way long . . . and so when we get so bad we're gonna die, he—Jaybush—puts us into the . . . trash men." She began crying again. "They call 'em trash men even if it's a girl they put in it. Don't make no difference, it ain't anything, not in that way. . . ."

Rivas was breathing fast. "What the *hell,* can't you . . . can't you *kill* yourselves, at least? Christ, they let you use tools, right?"

"Yeah," the girl admitted, nodding. "But... it's a sin, of course, suicide is, though somehow here in the city people don't worry much about sins anymore... and anyway they... the trash men... gee, they do last practically *forever*."

"Well, that's *fine*," Rivas whispered. "Listen, did a girl arrive here a couple of days ago? Slim and dark-haired with... I mean, a woman with dark hair...." He tried to remember the glimpse he'd caught of Uri in the Regroup Tent night before last. "A little bit heavy," he finished lamely.

"Everybody in all the wagons before yours, for a week, nobody's been brought here. They all went straight on south, the men to work on the boats and the women to be shipped direct to the temple in the sister city... that's where the Lord is right now... and of course all the far-gones were took right to the bleeder huts."

"Where's the sister city?"

"I don't know. We better get back in our beds. They don't like it when we talk among ourselves."

"Is it north of here, or south? The sister city," he added, seeing her blank look.

"Oh. I don't know." She shambled back to her bed, yawning.

Rivas looked out the window. The limping thing was a distant unrestful figure far out across the plain. "What goes on in the—what did you call 'em?—bleeder huts?"

The boards under her mattress creaked as she climbed ponderously in. "Oh," she yawned again, "bleeding, I suppose."

Well, yeah, Rivas thought, not moving toward his own bed. I had to ask?

"Tomorrow, probably," the girl said sleepily. Then, after

he'd given up on hearing any more from her, she added, "They'll take you to the beach settlement." After another long pause, she went on, "And weld your leg irons on."

Zat so, thought Rivas. Leg irons, is it, and welded on. But of course, Greg, it'll just be until you get so deteriorated that they put you in a trash man. My God. Well, I leave *tonight*.

"Of course," said the girl, so sleepily that Rivas knew this would be her last statement of the night, "if they make you a trustee, you only gotta wear one."

That doesn't change my mind, kiddo, he thought. He went back to his bed and lay on it until he was sure the bald girl had fallen asleep, and then he got up silently and tiptoed down the central aisle to the end of the room. The door there was locked, but it was the work of a moment to poke his knife blade between the door edge and the jamb, lift the bar out of the slots outside and ease the door open. Evidently the authorities didn't expect the inmates to have any tools—or initiative, probably.

He edged half his face past the door jamb, peered around with that eye, and then stuck his whole head out. It was brighter outside, with the stars and faint webbing of cloud reflected on the plain, and there seemed to be a faint glow emanating upward from under the glass. He didn't see any of the trash men.

To his right was the same bleak, unearthly vista he'd seen from the window, but the view to his left, which was south, was more conventional; rows and rows of barracklike shacks, pretty clearly identical to the one he was crouched in the doorway of, receded away in the dimness.

He noticed that each one seemed to be casting a very faint shadow of light, like a building in a photographic negative, but when he peered in wonder he saw that the "shadows" were just even, abraded patches of glass, which reflected the starlight and the subsurface glow in a faint, unfocused radiance. Evidently the shabby buildings were unmoored, and being gradually shifted toward the sea by the wind, like a fleet of very old and slow ships.

Rivas ran silently to the next row of sheds, and snoring from inside the nearest one confirmed his guess that it was a duplicate of the one he'd left. One row at a time, with much fearful peering-about between sprints, he passed ten rows of the long shacks, and except for the one he'd been in and the next two, they all seemed to be empty.

Once there had come a mournful, windy wail from far away across the glass plain, but though he'd snatched out his knife and then frozen, the sound had not been repeated and no motion had been visible anywhere, and he'd eventually moved on.

The tenth row of sheds was the last, and south of him now was only a number of small round huts on stilts. Unlike the barrack buildings, these were arranged in irregular clusters, like huge mushrooms or termite towers, and it was hard to guess how many there might be. The bleeder huts, he thought uneasily.

The shore lay somewhere beyond them, so after making sure his knife was both firmly sheathed and easily drawable, he set off at a careful jogging pace from which he could almost instantly stop, break to the side at a wide angle, or double his forward speed.

He passed a dozen clusters of the little raised buildings during the next ten minutes, but when he drew near the very last one, with only featureless glass beyond, he slowed, and when he was next to it he let his pace falter, and then finally he stopped.

What's this, he asked himself sourly, pure *curiosity?*

Well, hell, he thought, how can you not stop and at least peek into something called a bleeder hut?

He moved toward the structure's four-foot-high ladder as silently as a shadow . . . and in the sudden subjective silence, without his own breath and heartbeat pounding in his ears, he became consciously aware of something he'd subliminally noticed several seconds earlier.

Soft, regular breathing, not quite snores, could be faintly heard issuing from these stilted huts—and every pause between inhalation and exhalation, every hitch and sigh and occasional grunt, was exactly identical, from hut to hut, in perfect, effortless unison, a subtle prodigy being quietly performed out here on this lake of glass with no audience but Gregorio Rivas and the remote stars.

I'll be damned, he thought as he approached, then touched, the wooden ladder—at any moment now I may become the first person I've ever heard of to be a witness to people *snoring* in tongues.

The ladder was lashed together with wire and old rope, and creaked when he put his weight on it, but he was certain nothing inside the hut could hear any noise he might make; he wasn't sure exactly what there was to fear in this vitreous wasteland, but he knew there was nothing threatening nearby . . . certainly not in this lonely, southernmost hut.

The door swung open quietly at his touch—there was not even a token latch here. Inside he dimly saw five beds, but they were leaned up against the walls at steep angles, and when his eyes adjusted to the darkness he saw that each sleeping body was belted to the bed frame; and when he stepped closer to one, he saw that a narrow dark tube was attached to the inside of the person's elbow, and curled down to the floor, where it disappeared through a hole drilled in the boards.

Rivas felt a little queasy at the sight. Bleeder hut, he thought; I get it. But why drain off the blood of far-gone Jaybirds?

He went to the ladder and climbed back down to the glass, and then bent over and peered under the hut. All five tubes, he saw, fed into a central tank which was connected by metal pipes to a couple of smaller tanks. Something that looked like an old-time air conditioner was attached to the front of the main tank, and it had a metal nozzle projecting from it. He put his finger in the nozzle and felt the grooves of screw-threading . . . and when he took his finger out there was a dry powder on it.

He sniffed it . . . and was suddenly reminded of his days as a destitute dishwasher in Venice, for the powder was, unmistakably, Blood.

He looked back at the hundreds of other bleeder huts, standing nearly silent in the starlight, and he was sure that each of them, too, held sleeping far-gones whose blood was steadily being drained through tubes into a tank and somehow being refined into the deadly Venetian drug.

Rivas shivered with fear, but for once it wasn't for himself. This is big, he thought unhappily, bigger than anyone dreams. I wonder if even the shepherds know.

Blood is manufactured in the Holy City.

The bald girl back there said that all newly arrived women—including, presumably, Uri—have been shipped to the sister city. I think I know now what the sister city is.

And, God help me, I'm afraid I may know what place, there, is Jaybush's temple.

He paused indecisively, trying to assimilate this new knowledge, and he remembered wondering who was talking when the far-gones spoke in tongues—what was the origin of the signal for which they were just passive receivers. He had guessed that it might be the voice of Norton Jaybush himself, who, having so to speak eaten their souls from within by means of his devastating sacrament, couldn't then entirely withdraw his psychic teeth from the shells of the many bodies, so that they resonated when he spoke . . . but now it occurred to Rivas that if he was postulating psychic teeth, then he was talking about psychic resonances, too.

If he was correct, the speakers in tongues were mindlessly relaying not Norton Jaybush's spoken *words*, but his *thoughts*. No wonder the shepherds silenced them, now that he was thinking in English.

So what was that stuff he was thinking in before? A gargling, yodeling, barking sort of language. Rivas remembered once seeing several far-gones all bite their lips at the same instant as they tried to produce some bit of gibberish particularly unsuited to human vocal organs. What language *was* that? How was it that Norton Jaybush, though born of woman, could, as the bald girl back there had pointed out, thrive in, perhaps require, an environment that strangely poisoned human bodies? Rivas had read old journals written in the decade before Sandoval had reorganized Ellay and set himself up as the First Ace, journals kept during the Dark Year, when for a solid year a yellow-brown overcast of smoke and dust masked the sky and made people wonder if the sun and moon were still out there . . . and he'd read about the symptoms the bald girl had described. . . .

Uri—and Jaybush himself, that girl said—are in the sister city, he thought, which I'm now sure is Venice, in his temple, which I'm afraid is probably that terrible nightclub of the damned known as Deviant's Palace. If I'm going in there after her, it would be useful to be able to hear Jaybush's thoughts while I'm doing it.

He climbed back up the ladder and went inside again. He chose the lightest-looking of the five far-gones, a starved boy with no hair or teeth, and gently worked the blood-tap out of his arm. Blood coursed down the bony forearm and dripped from the limp fingers, but the flow seemed to stop when Rivas tied around the elbow a strip of cloth torn from his shirt. Then Rivas unbuckled the straps that held the strengthless body onto the bed, and he lowered it to the floor.

He climbed down the ladder again, grabbed the kid's wrists and hauled him out of the shed, crouched and took the body onto his shoulders. Rivas straightened up and took a couple of steps away from the hut to drag the feet clear, and then he was carrying the boy's full weight.

So, he thought dizzily, can you carry this all the way down to the beach? One way to find out. And if gets too heavy, I can always just drop him and walk on.

As he trudged along under his peacefully sleeping, ruined burden, he was reminded of his very first redemption, four years ago; he'd walked back into Ellay through the South Gate carrying his quarry in just this position.

It had been a favor for a friend. The man who was Rivas's bass player then had told him that his daughter had run off nearly a month earlier with a band of Jaybirds, and Rivas had offered to try to find the girl by pretending to join the faith himself. It wasn't a particularly risky thing for him to do, armed as he was with his drink defense and his *Peter and the Wolf* offense, and he'd managed to find her while her band was still within only a few miles of the Ellay walls, separate her from the band, knock her unconcious and carry her back home.

In fact the most exhausting part of that first redemption had been the subsequent three days, which he'd spent locked in a room with the girl while she raged and wept and broke things and begged to be allowed to return to the Jaybirds and the seductive oblivion of the sacrament. He'd laughed at her, and with his intimate knowledge of the faith he was able to damagingly ridicule its most illogical tenets. When she'd started doing Sanctified Dancing to avoid thinking about what he was saying, he'd brought in his pelican and accompanied her by playing the most insultingly bouncy

and childish dance tunes he knew, and shouting encour-
agements to her like a square-dance caller.

Finally, gratifyingly, she'd come out of it, her eyes lost
the birdy glaze, and she'd thanked him for giving her mind
back to her.

Rivas had asked his grateful bass player not to tell people
about the favor—the Jaybirds were, after all, not a pacifist
crew, and theirs was a jealous god—but the bass player
now had profound sympathy for other parents in the plight
he'd been in, and he couldn't help mentioning to a few of
them the service Rivas was able to perform. Some of these
had offered Rivas so much brandy to repeat his feat that
he'd been unable to refuse, and by the time he was twenty-
eight or so he was making more as a redemptionist than he
was as a musician.

Clouds were scudding more thickly across the sky now,
as he could tell without raising his head by watching their
reflections in the glass under his metronomic feet, and a
damp, chilly breeze tickled his ankles and got in under his
torn shirt. I wonder who this kid was, he thought, and
whether his parents could have afforded the services of a
redemptionist. Unlikely. Brandy's scarce these days, and
even McAn, I've heard, won't go out for less than a hundred
fifths. Too late for this kid now anyway. There's no way
back for far-gones, and even without that, starvation and
sickness seem to have got nearly all there ever was of him.

He squinted sideways at the pale, skeletal hand that flapped
limply at his side with every step. Who were you, kid?

Sometimes the breeze from behind slacked, and when it
did he thought he could hear the sighing crash of surf, far
ahead; and the glass underfoot was frosted-looking now,
and he could feel an increasing grittiness of sand with every
step. He strained his neck to look forward, and saw that the
glass plain ended in a jaggedly shattered edge a few hundred

feet ahead. Beyond that was a paleness that had to be sand, and he thought he glimpsed low ragged buildings and points of dim yellow light.

And then above the scratching of his footsteps and the breathing of himself and the doomed boy, he heard behind him a mix of sounds like a thin stick being whipped back and forth through the air and quick taps on a taut snare drum and the rattling of a length of chain, and it was getting closer fast.

He spun around, automatically going into a sliding crouch so as not to fall, and saw, still a hundred yards away but closing, the jungle-gym-stuffed-with-old-car-parts figure of one of the trash men skating with a weird grace across the glass directly toward him, approaching with such speed that it grew from a distant dot to a noisy, sky-blotting bulk in only a couple of seconds, and only at the last instant did he manage to collect his wits and frog-hop out of its way to one side.

Rivas relaxed into the somersault it turned out he was making, and he rolled to his feet several yards beyond the sprawled looseness of the dying boy and watched the skating trash man, well past him now, flail its lawn-mower arms and lean around in a tight, screeching curve that threw up a starlight-glittering spray of glass chips. When it came looping back toward him, working its aluminum-pipe legs to get back some of its lost speed, he waited until it had a lot of momentum and then he feinted to his right and dove to his left.

The thing reached out an arm for him as it rushed past and succeeded in tearing his shirt, but then like an ungainly top it had spun out in a screeching abrasion of metal on glass, and as Rivas turned toward it it toppled and fell, still sliding.

Run up and try to disable it while it's down, he wondered tensely, or run away? Remembering its speed, and his inert companion, he ran toward it.

The thing was making a terrible racket flailing its junk limbs against the splintering glass, but just as he ran up to it, planning to launch a flying kick at one of its knees, it rolled over and wobbled up onto its wide barbecue-grill feet and faced him.

Rivas skidded hastily to a stop and then just stood and caught his breath, cautiously confident that the thing couldn't, from a dead stop, close the three yards between them more quickly than he could leap aside.

He stared at the roughly man-shaped construction. It was at least a foot taller than he was and twice as broad through the chest, but its legs were so ludicrously thin that looking at it was like looking at some biped bug under a magnifying glass.

Then it spoke, and it had the same sort of wind-in-the-rafters voice as the one that had apparently knocked him out this afternoon. "Brother," it sighed. "Go back to bed. I'll put the bleeder back."

Rivas remembered the sad bald girl saying she'd soon wind up as one of these, and he had no wish to kill it. He noticed that some of its vacuum cleaner hoses and springs had been torn loose in its fall, and he found himself wishing he knew how to put them back. "Go away," he said wearily to the thing. "If you try to stop me, one of us will be seriously hurt. I don't think either of us wants that."

"No," the construction agreed, "but let this go I can't. I'm...*obliged*...to stop you." Starlight glittered remotely in its glass eyes.

"No, you're not," said Rivas. "Go to bed yourself. Do you things sleep? This boy was dying where I found him. I'd die if I stayed here. Roentgens and rads, right? Come on now—you *know* this is a place it'd be healthier to be far away from."

He could hear a valve release a hiss of compressed air

before the thing spoke. "It . . . doesn't matter what I know," it said. "It doesn't matter what you know. Go . . . back to . . . bed."

Exhaustion made Rivas willing to argue with the thing; the only other choice, after all, was to fight. "What will happen if I don't? If I continue?"

"I'll . . . *(hiss)* . . . stop you."

"Would you kill me?"

". . . Not mean to."

Rivas looked beyond it, and then risked a glance over his shoulder at the distant wooden buildings down toward the beach. All this crashing around didn't seem to have attracted any attention yet, but someone was bound to notice this unlikely trio out here on the glass before long.

"Okay," he muttered, slumping. He glanced at its knees and tried to estimate which one had been most weakened in its fall; then he decided, and pivoted and lashed out his left foot in a hard kick. He felt it connect and then he was rolling away over the glass, his shoulder numbed by a blow from one of the thing's arms. He heard a crash behind him.

Scrambling up, he saw that the trash man had fallen over and was stretching its metal arms out toward its broken-off leg, which lay on the plain several yards away. Rivas ran to the leg and kicked it further away—making a noisy clatter—then chased it, crouched, and picked the object up by the knee with his good hand.

The thing was scrapingly hunching toward him, hissing, and he stood still until it was within range and then swung his metal club, banging away the claw hand that was reaching for him, and a moment later, backhanded, he took a solid whack at the bucket head; but even as the club rebounded and Rivas started to hop back, the thing's other arm darted out and caught his ankle. Rivas sat down heavily.

The trash man was pulling him toward itself, ripping his

trouser leg and his skin, and its batted-away other hand
was swinging back, clanking as it opened and closed, and
the trash man was whisper-screeching, over and over,
"Please...please..."

The thing was suddenly too close for Rivas to swing his
club, but he did parry the incoming hand with it. Its other
hand moved up to his knee, and for a moment he believed
it intended to even the score by ripping *his* leg off at the
knee; its grip was like bolt cutters, and Rivas panted through
clenched teeth as he tried not to scream.

The other metal hand closed on his knee too, and the
trash man pulled him so close that Rivas could stare right
into the glass-chip eyes. *"Please...please..."* the thing
was still saying.

He could see wires or tubes under the edge of its chin,
and so he raised his club with one hand—the bucket head
tilted back to see how the blow would fall—and with his
other hand he snatched at the wires and yanked as hard as
he could. They tore out and the thing went limp.

Rivas lay there and he stared into the glass eyes while
he got his breath back, and he thought he saw intelligence
in the two bits of glass, a mind still in there, helpless now
but staring out at him in grieved reproach.

Finally he tried to stand up, but the metal hands were
still clamped onto his knee. He swore, trying not to imagine
another trash man skating in from the horizon right now,
and with panicky haste he wrenched at them. He managed
to open one hand—it looked as if it had originally been a
waffle iron—but the other, some sort of stout caliper, he
had to break off at the wrist. For a while he tried vainly to
work it off over his knee, but then he remembered that the
bald girl had said that trustees only had to wear one leg iron.
A token of captivity, in effect. Perhaps this metal band might
be mistaken for that. Worth a try, he thought; and one *would*
push such a thing up high enough for it to grip, so as not

to have it rattling around one's ankle all day.

He stood up at last, the trash man's hand an eccentric decoration for his shredded pants-leg, and wearily plodded to the boy, who of course had slept through the whole thing. He hoisted him up, got him draped over his shoulders again, and resumed his interrupted walk to the beach.

From far behind he heard a faint, rushing hiss, and he spun around so quickly that he nearly fell over, but it was just rain approaching, so he faced south again and kept walking. It became more audible, a multitudinous pattering behind him, and then swept over and past him, hurrying toward the sea, leaving him to follow more slowly in the downpour.

He was careful not to lose his balance where the glass ended, for before it gave way to the sand a dozen yards ahead, it became an obstacle course of rain-slick, broken, tilted shards, a fall on which would certainly cut a person up. He moved slowly over this broken glass section, but his pace didn't pick up much when he'd got past it, for he was in deep loose sand now.

He squinted up from under his wet eyebrows at the flimsy-looking buildings ahead, and he wished he knew what to anticipate here. What had that girl said? The men are sent to the beach settlement, where they make and repair boats. And they have leg irons welded on. Well, fine, he thought. It sounds like tiring work. I hope they all sleep soundly.

He saw a gap between two buildings, and as he got closer he saw that it was a street that he was looking down the center of; and a moment later, peering through the sheets of rain, he saw agitated human figures. He stopped and tried to see by the faint reflections of yellow light ahead what the people were doing. . . . They seemed to be leaping and whirling in the rain. . . .

Rivas almost grinned. They were doing Sanctified Dancing. And now that he listened for it he could hear over the steady whisper-roar of the rain the rhythmic hand-clapping of the people who stood around watching. No wonder they hadn't heard his battle with the trash man.

Well, he thought as he started forward again, this isn't as convenient as it would have been if they'd all been fast asleep, but it's better than a few quiet watchful guards.

He was wondering whether to sneak around the far side of one of the structures—which would involve carrying his increasingly heavy burden an extra couple of hundred yards—or just stomp right down the street in a nothing-to-hide way, giving a birdy grin and a "Shepherd's orders!" to any inquisitive people . . . when he realized he didn't have the choice. He'd been seen.

A figure with a lantern was striding out toward him, waving, and in a minute he saw that the person wore the robe—and yes, he could see the crooked staff too now—of a shepherd. Rivas knew he was in no shape to outrun anybody, so he just put on a smile and kept trudging forward . . . but he was rehearsing in his mind exactly how he'd throw the kid at the shepherd if trouble arose, and in the same motion draw his knife and try for the man's throat.

But it seemed that wouldn't be necessary. The man smiled at Rivas with a little less contempt than shepherds usually showed for people, and when he was close enough for talk to be possible over the sound of the rain, he pointed at the unconscious young man and said, "Runaway?"

"Evidently," said Rivas without hesitation. He saw the shepherd's gaze go to the boy's ankles and stay there while a wondering frown wrinkled his forehead, so he added, "Got his leg irons off too, somehow, what do you think of that?" He was acutely aware of the pressure which was his knife sheath against the inside of his right wrist.

The shepherd waved Rivas forward and then fell into step beside him. At least the rain was making the sand firmer

underfoot. "I don't like it," the shepherd said. "It's good
for them to dance, of course, when it's that or start thinking
the wrong way, but it's bad that they have to do it so much
lately. And now this . . . sick *kid* got his irons off and tried
to run." He shook his head. "You," he said, giving Rivas
a stern look that, prolonged for just a few more seconds of
silence than it was, would probably have had Rivas tossing
the kid and snatching for his knife, "are supposed to see to
it that this kind of thing doesn't happen. You and the other
trustees."

"Yes," said Rivas cautiously, thankful that his one-leg-
iron trustee disguise seemed to be working. "I know. Well,
this'll spur us to be more diligent."

Rivas found that he'd begun walking in a knock-kneed
way to keep the shepherd from getting a good look at his
leg iron; he realized this would only call attention to it, and
he tried to remember how he'd been walking before.

"Take him straight down the street to the penitence cage,"
the shepherd said. "I'll have the other trustees rounded up.
We've got to talk about how we're going to get this situation
straightened out. I wish the Lord spent more time here."

"Me too," Rivas croaked.

They were almost even with the buildings now, and he
could see that the street between the rows of wooden structures was a cracked, sand-scoured section of some ancient
highway.

The shepherd was lagging behind, but Rivas forced himself to keep walking at the same pace and, much more
difficult, not to turn around constantly to keep an eye on
him. So it was almost a relief when the man said, "Oh,
say," and Rivas had an excuse to stop and look back.

"Yes?"

"Why do you suppose your man ran *north*?"

To see the pretty bald girls, thought Rivas. To go skating
with the trash men. "I don't know," he said.

The shepherd nodded thoughtfully. "Well—see you soon. We'll be in the gun room."

You bet, thought Rivas as he turned back toward the dancers and started walking again. Hold your breath till I get there, okay?

The clapping was loud now, and Rivas could see the spectators lined up on both sides of the street. The dancers were contorting enthusiastically in the rain in spite of the two feet of chain that linked every pair of ankles, waving their arms over their heads, some skipping in short runs across the pavement and some Bo Diddleying in place. Their clothes slapped wetly around their ankles and wrists, and the ones that weren't bald snapped their wet locks and beards around like whips. Most of them had their eyes closed, and on each face was a nearly identical expression of quiet satisfaction.

Rivas walked right down the middle of the street, trying to stay out of everyone's way, for no one gave any sign of seeing him.

The section of highway ended not far beyond the dancers and soon he was walking on wet sand again. He was sure he could hear a faint booming of surf now, and he peered ahead worriedly, fearing that he might not, after all this, be able to find a boat. I'll ditch this kid and swim if I have to, he thought. I wonder where the penitence cage is, and how long it'll take that shepherd to catch on that I'm not coming back.

The sand was giving way to old concrete again under his aching feet, and then to his astonishment he was walking on what appeared to be *new* concrete. In some ways it struck him as more miraculous to be able to make and lay concrete than to be able to manufacture ammunition.

He glanced to his left, which was southeast, and dimly saw tall pale buildings in the distance, made into abstract geometrical shapes by the night and the rain and the miles

that separated him from them. And it came to him that what
he was seeing was the Holy City. The shabby structures on
the glass and sand behind him were like toolsheds tucked
away out of sight at the back of a big estate. . . .

The ocean is the front door, he thought; the gate the
wagon brought me in through was the back door—the serv-
ants' entrance.

Rivas stopped and stared . . . and then felt goose pimples
prickling his arms, for he'd noticed a sphere suspended in
the air above the buildings, and it had to be huge to be
visible at all at this distance, and there was no glint of light
at its bottom to indicate a fire, and he was suddenly sure
that the bald girl *had* meant helium balloons . . . but where
could Jaybush be getting *helium?*

Though slumped as loosely as ever, the boy suddenly
began speaking, and Rivas was so startled that he nearly
dropped him. *"Who is it?"* the boy had burst out. *"Oh,
him. When will the fool learn to come around to where I
can see him, he knows I can't roll over. . . ."*

Rivas was very glad this hadn't happened when he was
talking to the shepherd. There was no mistaking it for anything but genuine speaking in tongues, and far-gones could
no more decide to escape than they could fly.

He'd noticed a dark band parallel to his course on his
right and he'd been slanting toward it, and now he could
tell by the sound of the rain falling there that it was a wide
trench full of water. Looking to his left he saw another one
further away, and now he noticed a similar band ahead that
diagonally connected the two. Canals, he thought. Newly
constructed, too, unlike the ones in Venice. Why is Jaybush
so fond of canals?

When he arrived at the canal edge he crouched and rolled
the young man off his shoulders onto the new concrete, and
then he stood up and simply luxuriated in the ability to stand
up straight and feel cold rain on the back of his neck, before

climbing down into the water. It was warmer than the rain, and he swam out to the middle of the forty-foot-wide watercourse to see how deep it got. He discovered that even out here he could stand on the bottom and still have his chin out of the water. He went back and fetched the kid and then, towing the limp body behind with a collar-grip that kept the sleeping face above the surface of the water, he began moving down the canal toward the sea, sometimes swimming and sometimes wading. The buoyancy the salt water gave them made southward progress much less strenuous, and Rivas wished the canals had extended all the way up to the bleeder huts.

The canal walls tended to throw every splash and gasp back at him as echoes, so he had no hint that he was being pursued until he saw a ten-foot line of blindingly bright yellow light appear high up on the canal wall a dozen yards ahead and then instantly sweep back, past him and well over his head, and recede away northward faster than any bird.

He gaped after it in wonder, and several seconds later realized that it must have been the beam of a searchlight. Rivas had read of such things, and though he wasn't sure whether or not they worked by electricity, he knew they required a level of technology he thought had been lost many Aces ago.

He resumed dog-paddling down the canal with his bobbing, sleeping burden in tow, a little more quickly now.

CHAPTER SEVEN

"CAREFUL WITH that stuff!"

Rivas snapped out of his doze and glanced around at the dark, malodorous space under the pier. Boots slowly thumped against the boards over his head; the men on the pier carried lanterns, but little of their light reflected under the pier and it was more by the phosphorescence of the water that Rivas was able to see that the bald, toothless boy was still moored safely to one of the pilings by the back of his shirt, which Rivas had looped over a projecting nail head. The break-water stopped the waves half a mile out, and the rain tended to flatten what waves there were inside, but Rivas had been worried when he'd moored the unconscious far-gone there that even the gentler rise and fall of the sheltered water might float him loose—in which case, of course, he would quietly have drowned.

Rivas unhooked his own arm from over the cross brace he'd selected for his personal mooring, and as he worked fingers and elbow to get the circulation going, he stared at the dim blur just above the water that was the boy's head. Rivas wondered what he'd do if the kid started speaking again, or even snoring. Drown him? Certainly wouldn't be difficult.

But he knew he couldn't, even though any dog or cat— hell, hamsters, mice, bugs—had more intelligence than a far-gone. Somehow ripping the throat out of that trash man, on top of having tried to knife Frake McAn and having killed Nigel and the two hooters and that shepherd, had broken something in him. He felt crippled by pity, by empathy—he felt that now it would sicken him to kill flies.

It scared him to realize it, as if he'd suddenly discovered he was losing feeling and control in his left hand.

"I said *careful,* damn it," came again the voice that had waked him.

"I'm being careful, brother," came a petulant younger voice. "You want these in the water yet?"

"Nah, they're cool enough in the rain. You can tie the baskets on the rings, though. And use square knots, will you? Like I showed you. Last trip two of the baskets came loose and sank, and I caught all kinds of hell for it."

"Okay."

Slow footsteps and a clinking drag of chain moved from behind Rivas to over his head and then out to the end of the pier, and the strangely cowled hull of the big boat there went down a little and then rose. Low waves spread out through the pilings and gave Rivas a salty slap in the mouth.

For quite a while then there was no noise except for occasional chain clinks and footsteps from the boat and aimless humming from the man on the pier above—Rivas had plenty of time to wish for food and dry clothes, and to decide that his increasing ability to see was due to the imminence of dawn rather than a gradual improvement of his night vision. Then he heard the sudden shifting of a length of chain on the boards over his head.

"Look sharp, Brother Willie. Shepherd."

"Right. Thanks."

Soon Rivas heard hoofbeats . . . and then he heard them with agonizing clarity as the horse was ridden right out onto the pier. "Good morning, brother!" came a new voice, tense but trying not to show it. "Are you alone?"

"There's Brother Willie, too, on the boat, getting the baskets tied to the gunwales. Nobody else."

"Have you seen anyone else tonight?"

"Uh . . . not since the worried lads left for the dance. They through yet?"

"Not yet. Slowing down, though. Well, here, take this thing—don't point it at me! Idiot. It's a flare pistol. If you see anybody but your regular crew, shoot it. You pull the trigger, here, let me show you—that thing. Okay?"

Rivas saw the boat dip and rise again, and guessed Brother Willie had come to the rail to look. Again a little wave surged past, and Rivas glanced worriedly at the far-gone. I hope, he thought, that Jaybush doesn't get up—and start thinking—this early.

"Shoot it at whoever?"

"No. It's a *flare* gun. It shoots flares. Shoot it up into the *sky,* okay?"

"Sure. Who is it we might see?"

"None of—well, why not. We think an impostor may have come in on one of yesterday's wagons. A guy broke out of one of the bunkhouses and apparently killed one of the constructs and kidnapped a donor. I actually saw him last night, but he had a leg band and I thought he was a trustee. So it's important to me personally that we get him back. If you're the ones who first see him . . . I won't forget, understand?"

"Sure, brother. We'll keep our eyes open."

"Be careful. I probably shouldn't be telling you this, but it seems fairly certain that Gregorio Rivas was at the Regroup Tent a couple of days ago. They grabbed him, but he had corrupted a sister, and she freed him. She's in the sister city now, appropriately enough, undergoing remedial discipline. He hasn't been seen anywhere else since, including Ellay, so the guy here last night might be him."

Rivas had winced and bared his teeth during the shepherd's statement, remembering Sister Windchime—her hair the color of the dry brush on the hills, her long athletic legs, her alertness and repressed compassion, and her evident doubts of the faith—and then he made himself stop remembering her.

"Uh . . . sun coming up," put in Brother Willie. "We better be getting the Blood into the baskets and into the water, huh?"

There was a silence then that even Rivas, under the pier, could tell was awkward.

"I mean, uh, the harvest powder," Brother Willie amended nervously.

"What did you call it a minute ago?" asked the shepherd, possibly through clenched teeth.

"I meant to say harv—"

"What?"

"Blood, brother," admitted Brother Willie unhappily.

"Why did you call it that?"

"I don't know, I—"

"Why?"

There was a pause, and then Brother Willie said, sniffling, "I been around. I had Blood once or twice. I know it when I see it."

"Ah." The horse stamped and flapped its lips. "If you are the ones to spot our intruder, I'll *overlook* this." The horse galloped back down the pier, and then the hoofbeats receded away into the steady whisper of the rain on the sea.

"You . . . damned . . . *idiot*."

"Aw, Jesus, brother, all I—"

"Shut up! Say Jaybush if you want to swear! I've met far-gones smarter than you. Yes, get the harvest powder into the baskets and over the sides. And make sure the tarps cover every bit, hear? If sun gets in and ruins one *pinch* of this batch, I think you're gonna wind up manning a hose in a bleeder hut yourself."

For a while there was just a lot of clanking and grunting from above, then a big cubical object wrapped in a tarpaulin descended jerkily into Rivas's view on the end of a rope, hit the water, and with a lot of bubbling and flapping of the tarp sank until three-quarters of its bulk was under the water. Another followed, and then another, until the side of the boat that Rivas could see was adorned from bow to stern with a full dozen bobbing black bales connected to it by taut cables. He could hear the tactless Brother Willie performing the same operation now on the far side of the boat.

Rivas wondered how the boat was rigged. Even with the strange cowling visible around the bow, it seemed to him that it should be impossible to sail with all those bundles hanging along the sides.

"You know," Brother Willie called at one point to his older companion on the pier, "I hope old Rivas does come by here. I'll shoot that flare gun right at his head."

"Ahh," the older man said, and spat, "there's somebody raising hell here, I suppose—but it ain't Gregorio Rivas."

"How do *you* know?"

"Man, there ain't no such person as Gregorio Rivas. That's just a booger man. 'Rivas is here, Rivas was seen there, look out for Rivas.' It's just to keep us all hopping."

Another basket of Blood splashed down in the rain. "Nah," said Brother Willie decisively. "Nah, man, a guy I knew *seen* Rivas! In Ellay."

Rivas could tell the other man had shrugged. "I knew a guy once that swore he talked to Elvis Presley. Had one o' them old liquor bottles, was like a statue of Elvis Presley. Said his ghost lived in it. I listened over an hour, didn't hear nothin'."

Suddenly Rivas had an idea. He hoisted his sleeping cargo down off the nail and then, holding the boy's face up clear of the water, paddled silently out from under the pier and around the wide stern—evidently it was some kind of barge—to the far side. The rain, as heavy as ever, masked any involuntary splashing he might have done, and no doubt made Willie and his companion less likely to stand around peering.

Looking around from behind the sternmost portside basket, Rivas saw for a moment against the paling sky a silhouette that must have been Willie, leaning out over the rail high above Rivas's head to lower a basket up by the bow. The men were still desultorily talking, but from down at water level under the curve of the stern Rivas couldn't hear what they were saying.

Very gingerly he lifted the far-gone, hooked the back of his shirt over one corner of the basket, and then spent a minute gradually letting the mooring cable take the boy's weight so that it wouldn't thrum or move or creak. He then held the basket with one hand and began unlacing the tarpaulin with the other, and when he'd loosened it and peeled it back, he saw that the basket was a metal cage full of boxes made of crude rippled glass, each about a foot long and six inches square at the ends. The basket was held shut by a simple sliding bolt which had been shot through the rings, turned down and wired in place. Rivas began untwisting the wire.

The rain was letting up as the sky brightened, and Rivas forced himself to work both more quietly and more quickly. At last, when the rain had diminished to a misty drizzle,

and Rivas, glancing up, could see the highest soaring sea-
gulls flash bright with sunlight, he was able to work the
bolt back, swing the basket's gate down without dislodging
the sleeping boy, and then gently, one at a time, lift out all
the glass boxes and let them sink away into the sea.

On a sudden impulse he re-caught the last box, worked
it open and looked speculatively at the three screw-top glass
jars inside; and then he looked at his unconscious companion, whose occasional muttering and snarling had, during
the rain, fortunately gone unnoticed. Would a hit of this
stuff shut the boy up?

Worth a try, he decided. It seems like kind of a closed
loop, by-your-bootstraps idea, but I've never heard that
anybody's *immune* to the stuff's effects. And there's certainly more in it than *just* powdered blood—all those tanks
and machineries under the bleeder hut must have been add-
ing something to the raw material.

He took one of the jars out, letting the glass box and the
two remaining jars join the rest of them on the sea floor,
and he unscrewed the lid and carefully held the jar of fine
brown powder to the boy's nostrils and, as the boy's next
inhalation came, Rivas blew on the powder, raising a cloud
of it. He jerked his own face back so as not to get any of
it himself, but the kid seemed to inhale some, so Rivas
twisted the cap back onto the jar and tucked it into his hip
pocket.

Next, with a fervent prayer that neither of the Jaybirds
was looking at this basket's cable just now, he hoisted the
kid off the corner of the basket, pulled him around and
shoved him inside. He pulled up the bony legs and folded
them and pushed them in too, and then he climbed in himself.

Sitting up in the basket, the water swirled around his
chest. He braced himself and leaned way out and down,
ducking his head under the surface, and groped with his

free hand until he found the basket's let-down gate. He heaved on it, dragged it up through the water like a comb through hair and finally got it closed and loosely bolted, and then he managed, with his fingertips poking out between the bars of the basket grating, to twitch the tarpaulin back down over them and pull it straight so that, with luck, the untied lacing wouldn't show.

At last in the darkness he allowed himself to relax. His companion would presumably keep quiet for a while under the influence of the Blood, and was wedged in with his head jammed into one of the top corners so that, though he might succumb to starvation or pneumonia, there was no way he could drown; and Rivas, though anything but comfortable sitting on a steel grating, chest-deep in salt water and tented under an old tarp, at least felt a good deal safer than he had at any time since deciding to follow Uri into the Holy City.

Through the sound conduction achieved by leaning his head against the steel bars which were pressed against the hull, he could hear the slow knocking of footsteps aboard— Brother Willie's, he assumed. Willie seemed to be wandering back and forth aimlessly, sometimes pausing for several minutes at the stern end—Rivas could tell because the knocking sounded louder to him—and probably staring toward the huge distant pale buildings he'd glimpsed last night in the rain. He wished he could see what Willie was seeing.

What on earth, he wondered as he crouched in the lightless cage with the drugged, dying far-gone, do you suppose those buildings are? Dwellings? For whom? Offices? For what work?

Suddenly there was a drum roll of booming knocks, and after his first jump of startlement he realized that the noise must be that of a lot of people coming aboard—and being herded on like cattle, to judge by the commotion. He guessed that at least one more wagonload of Jaybirds had come in through the gate last night. Hadn't that poor baldy girl said that most of the incoming girls were being shipped directly to the sister city?

Hello, girls, he thought sadly, nodding at the hull. Do give my regards to poor Sister Windchime . . . and Uri, too, of course.

The booming of footsteps continued to jar his cage randomly for a while, then settled down. He had just begun to relax again when a deafening rumble started up, setting his teeth on edge and making the cage bars vibrate so violently that it itched to sit on them, and he yanked his head away from contact with the hull and splashed his hands up out of the water to cover his ears. My God, he thought, that's got to be an engine! They've got internal combustion!

A moment later his guess was confirmed, for the hull scraped forward and then the cage tilted as the mooring cable couldn't give any more, and the water that had been a pool around him became a sluicing river, loudly rushing in from around and under the tarp on the forward side and splashing up against the aft side. Suddenly it wasn't at all impossible for his unconscious companion to drown, and Rivas leaned forward to make sure the boy was well braced above the flood.

Well, he thought as he tried to adjust to the idea that this noise and shaking would not be stopping soon, at least it'll cut down on the travel time.

Soon the barge had moved out past the breakwater into the open sea and the real waves, and for several seconds after they breasted the first one he really believed that the basket he was in had been savagely yanked up at least ten feet into the air and then allowed to fall back to the surface, and then yanked up again as soon as it had solidly whacked the water. This toss and plummet effect continued, with no sign of ever coming to an end, and when he'd got himself braced well enough to be able to think, he discovered that the only way he could keep himself from opening the basket and diving out was to promise himself, at each bone-jarring impact, that he would only endure five more.

Slam. Only five more, Greg—hang on! *Slam*. All but five done now. You can take five more. *Slam*. Okay, count 'em down, that was six, here comes five...

Over the Holy City the clouds were disrupted by frequent violent updrafts, and the flying man banked north off them so as to skim the Santa Ana River and the barren beaches south of Hunnington Town rather than actually fly over the glass plain of Irvine, even though most of himself was down there. He didn't know that it was free neutrons that made his soap bubble skin itch, but he knew that flying near the place made him feel bad. He hoped the bulk of himself wouldn't come to harm in there.

Though only five days old, he was getting better at handling his ever-heavier body. Now he skimmed in low over a hill and down the far side, twitching fluff from the bobbing heads of dandelions and startling bees and enjoying being in the shade of the hill.... He was still in direct sunlight, but he was momentarily cut off from the hard, itchy heat radiating from the Holy City.

The hill descended quite a distance, and he was able to surge up fast, lose speed and stall, without rising above its crest. And as he gently drifted down, he wondered why Rivas had to keep pretending he still wanted this Uri creature. The sinking man, his balloon-fingered hands spread to slow his drifting descent, reviewed the scanty memories Rivas had of the woman. Why, he thought as he tap-dancingly touched down—he still didn't have enough weight to bend stiff weeds—why, he hardly remembers her at *all*. She's important to him only as an excuse for... for...

Well, the drifting man didn't quite know. Something like

an alcoholic's attitude toward liquor. Rivas had somehow
got into the position of needing something he didn't
like...no...more precisely, he'd got into the position of
not liking something he needed. Why?

The featherweight man dancing over the tops of the flowers didn't really *care* why, he simply didn't want *Rivas* to
learn why...because if Rivas knew, it might clear up his
confusions and interfere with the dancing man's seduction
of him. And the thistledown man wanted—so very badly!—
to merge with Gregorio Rivas. How else was either of them
to become whole?

All night the rainy wind had been from the north, but
the sun had begun silently to shatter the clouds, and fitful
breezes were occasionally blowing in from the sea. When
the next gust bent the grass and made the balloon man grab
a weed stalk to keep from being tumbled inland, he lifted
his plastic-bag head and snuffed the sea air.

He'd caught a scent of Rivas, but distantly, and in a
strange, bloody-smelling mix. The featherweight man kicked
and rose like a kite launched in a strong wind, and he didn't
mind getting above the hill into the hot region, for he could
see better from up here.

When he was at the top of his jump he spread his arms
and legs to catch the breeze and stay up there, and as he
stared out at the shadow-mottled blue face of the sea he
warped his still ectoplasmic eyes through a dozen round and
oval shapes, trying to focus on what he needed to see.

Then he had it in sight, and his fingers and long toes
lashed madly in the air to keep him steady.

It was a big wide barge with odd projecting cowls and
wings and fins, like an exploded beetle, surging along so
strongly, and leaving such a white wake, that the flying
man knew it was powered by some species of engine. And
it was, his fine-tuned senses told him, crowded inside with
women. The twiddle-fingered airborne man frowned primly.

Well, he thought, I daresay Rivas is enjoying *this* cruise.

There were bales under dark cloths dragging in the water alongside the boat, and the kite man finally caught on that Rivas was in one of the bales. He couldn't have explained how he knew it, only that when he looked at the boat and thought of Rivas he got an impression of cold rushing water and darkness and stale air.

Boy, boy, the flying man thought, clicking his tongue and shaking his translucent head pityingly. You do so *poorly* on your own. It's time you and I had another chat.

The hemogoblin spread flattened arms and, at home on the wind, swooped away toward the sea, leaving the land behind.

Chapter Eight

At first Rivas tried to resist the warm euphoric drowsiness that was stealing over him; he reminded himself of the danger he was in, and the much greater danger Uri was in, and he tried to feel tension and anxiety.

Somehow, though, it all seemed postponeable. After all, what could he do to help or hinder things from inside this ridiculous cage? Perhaps the wisest thing to do would be to go to sleep, in this actually quite comfortable bed of rushing water. The shaking wasn't nearly so bad now that they'd apparently got out past the breakers. It occurred to him that he'd heard of waterbeds, but this was the first *river*bed he knew of.

He laughed heartily, and for quite a while, at the notion.

Singing a song seemed like a good idea for a few moments, but sleep proved more imperative. He snuggled up against the steel bars on the hull side, not forgetting to say good night to all the girls on the other side of the wood—what were they in, anyway, a big barrel? A keg of leg, ho ho, a butt of butts; he was whooping with laughter now—then he subsided and arranged himself for sleep, wondering, with the last spark of awareness, why the sea water tasted so . . . what, not salty . . . *rusty,* that was it. Like blood.

To his own intense annoyance he let himself sink no further toward sleep. Let me sleep, he begged himself; of *course* sea water tastes like blood. It used to *be* blood. No, the other way around, evolutionarily blood was once just a quantity of sea water contained in the hollow body of some early form of life . . . sponges or jellyfish or something. Right. Now that *that's* settled, he thought, let's go to bed.

But again one part of his mind—a part that was becoming seriously alarmed—resisted sleep. Why, he thought muzzily, *should* the sea water have the rusty iron taste of blood? And why is my thumb . . . and the bullet lash down my back too . . . going numb? And what is it that this . . . thought-dissolving blurriness reminds me of?

The answers arrived almost simultaneously. Shifting to a more comfortable position in the hope of tricking himself into sleep, he became aware of two objects in his hip pocket, a big hard lump and a flat hard disk. Irritably he reached down under the turbulent water and dug them out.

By touch he could tell what they were. They were the jar of Blood, evidently empty, that he'd pocketed after giving the dying boy a whiff, and the lid that had once been screwed onto it. Evidently he was sitting right now in a vigorously stirred soup of Blood. And the oblivion that was eroding the awareness out from under him had the same feeling of being *monitored* that his very first long ago receiving of the Jaybird communion had had.

Taking Blood felt like receiving the sacrament.

He knew this was important . . . in a way. Actually, wasn't

it something he'd already guessed? Or would have, soon? Of course it was.

No, insisted the unhappy, struggling part of his mind, it's *important.*

Right, right. Much too important to consider before taking a little nap.

The salty, rusty fluid crashing around him in the darkness was hot, or so it seemed to him now, and he tried to remember where he was but couldn't. Evidently he'd got inside the heart of some huge being.

He wasn't sure who he was himself. The very idea of self seemed odd. He reached up to touch his face and it took all his strength to do it; he fumbled at his own face, feeling the toothless gums, the sunken cheeks, the hairless skull. There was another person too inside the spasming chamber of muscle, a bigger person, one who still had hair, and it warmed him to realize that that was him, too—or he and that person were both equally members of someone higher, the someone whose blood crashed powerfully, sustainingly, around them in the hot darkness. . . . Individual awareness was now recognizable as a kink in an otherwise perfectly smooth fabric. . . .

One of the four hands in the bouncing basket let go of an empty jar and a lid and then drifted to the bars that, through the covering tarpaulin, abraded back and forth across the hull; and with nearly no more intent than a flower has in turning to the sun, the hand tried to wedge its fingers between one of the bars and the hull.

After a while the basket obligingly swung away from the hull for a moment, as the barge crested a bigger than usual wave, and the fingers were able to curl all the way around the steel bar before the sea slammed the basket back against the hull.

As the fingers of his right hand were crushed between the two ponderous weights, Rivas warped back into self-awareness like a stretched-out-straight spring suddenly released. The hotly nauseating agony in his hand was his anchor, and he forced himself to move toward it along his frayed connection with it, away from the blurred state in which even sharing was a meaningless concept because in the long run there was only one entity in the universe. The pain became more definitely *his own* with every bit of progress, until at last he was again aware of being in the churning cold water in the lightless metal basket with himself *here* and the far-gone boy *over there*.

He held his maimed hand under water—the salt stung it savagely for a moment, but then the cold water began numbing it—and he realized he could see if he wanted to.

He was still in the pitch-dark cage; what he could see wasn't anything that was here, and he was aware of that, but it was vivid, and certainly nothing he'd ever seen before.

A miles-high stone wall in glaring purple light, wavy and blobbly and full of holes like a frozen splash, cut off half the horizon and a third of the gray sky, and things were visible gliding on diaphanous wings among the lacy stone pseudopods at the top. Looking down, a movement that covered quite a distance, as if his neck was yards and yards long, he saw a thing like an orange spider or a hundred-legged starfish, and he reached out a . . . Jesus, what *was* that, a sort of unfolding length of dried gut . . . and touched the orange creature.

Strength flowed into him, and out of the spidery thing, apparently, for it curled its legs and its color dimmed and it slowly settled to the sand. Belatedly he noticed that the creature had two shadows, a red one that lay behind it and a blue one that lay out to one side. . . .

. . . And then he was in a volcanic-looking natural amphitheater, smooth as a bubble with the top broken away, and, incapacitated by the consequences of some unimaginable self-indulgence, he was watching a crowd of the

spider-things. They were arranged in a line curled to form
a big spiral, and one of them in the center began walking
out of the coil, pausing in front of each of its motionless
fellows to extend a leg and make a touch ... and at each
touch he felt the strength flow into him as the one touched
dimmed and slowly collapsed. ... This was of course because for the occasion he had *become* the one that was
walking and touching the others. ...

Though Rivas knew he could stop seeing any of this any
time he decided to, the vision faded now by itself. It had
had a flavor of ... memory. A rueful recollection.

"Not so tasty, those weren't," spoke the boy in the darkness. *"Just lucky for me that their glow was more a psychic
than a chemical effect. Too bad the high fliers never came
down. Hard to see, but once I thought I saw one of them
carrying something that seemed to be a tool. They might
have been* tasty."

Another vision was starting up, and Rivas let himself
watch.

A dimly green-lit plain was what he saw, viewed from
above, with clusters of strange, spherical flowers on long
stalks growing up from it. He sensed that he wasn't alone,
and sure enough a moment later a bulbous, streamlined
animal went porpoising past him, downward, followed by
two more. As he watched them recede, their apparent size
diminishing with their increasing distance from him, he saw
that they were still well short of the flower globes, which
must therefore be huge and much more distant than he'd
supposed.

As he started down himself, his ponderous body working
to propel him through the transparent but thick medium, he
saw that the top half of each sphere was silvery, and he
knew that the silver stuff inside was what held each of the
spheres up and kept the mooring lines taut, and as he swam
closer he saw skeletal constructions inside the bottom halves,

and, in the top halves, spots of colored brightness that might
have been fires. . . .

The scene changed then, and he glimpsed a spiral line
of creatures that looked like walruses made of flexible palm-
tree trunks, and again one that he had become extended an
extremity—a sort of catfish whisker—to touch each one
in turn, and the strength flowed into him with each touch. . . .

And when once again he had drained from their minds
enough of the strength, the psychic power to move things
at a distance, he swam back to the secluded grotto which
he had made his own. He had sniffed out some fairly hot
pitchblende and adorned his cavern with it; and though this
seasoning left something to be desired, the *entrée* itself was
as rich as any he'd ever tasted.

The heavy component of the medium through which he
swam was abundant down here in the old quiet valleys, and,
using just a flicker of the vast energy he'd taken from his
flock, he made a globe of vacuum around a slightly smaller
ball of the omnipresent medium. He looked the ball over
to make sure it was perfect, and then, still without touching
it, moved it away from him, deeper into the grotto. Feeding
like this always damaged his body, and though he could
make repairs on it almost as easily as he had caused the
globe of vacuum to appear, there was no sense in putting
the body in a situation where it might be outright destroyed.
Too much trouble would be involved in finding another.

The ball was far enough away now, around several corners; and with his mind, powered now by the vast energy
he'd stolen, he *squeezed* it.

The resistance was strong, but his power was stronger.
He doubled and then redoubled his pressure. The ball, inside
its diminishing shell of vacuum, was now half its original
size, and continuing slowly to shrink.

He squeezed even harder, and now he could feel the
drain on his energy; but what with the local concentration

of the heavy stuff, and the slight head start of the already tremendous pressure down here, and the copious amount of power he'd taken from his flock, he was confident that he'd be able to squeeze it to ignition and then glut himself on the resulting radiation, without having to unmake any bit of the crystal which, unlike the aquatic body he was now temporarily wearing, was himself.

When the ball of heavy water had been compressed down to a tiny fraction of the size it had been, he reached into it with his mind and all at once agitated its atoms furiously, using up nearly the last of his stolen strength to do it—but then a second later he was battered by a blast of nutrition, the entire revitalizing spectrum of radiant energy. Suddenly it was easy to maintain the compression, a physical pleasure to squeeze the stuff; and, as always, he had to resist the temptation to drag more matter in and squeeze even harder as his capability increased, had to fight the perverse inclination to squeeze the products of the first ignition into another, and then the ashes of that one into still another, drawing from each compaction a little less energy than from the one before until, carried away and unable to stop, he would heedlessly pass the point where energy could be derived from the transmutations, and each successive fusion would be *taking* energy from him. He'd done that occasionally, on other worlds than this aquatic one, and though the super-heavy, unstable elements he was left with were pleasant to have around, tickling him with the particles of their decay, they weren't nearly worth the crippling efforts it took to produce them, nor the years of slow recuperation he needed afterward.

The scene changed again, and though the new vision was of the same world as the previous one, Rivas knew that it occurred much later. He was making a long swimming journey across vast extents of the green plain, but finding only empty spheres lying on the ground, the silvery stuff having long since leaked away and the mooring lines curled in limp loops around them. The walrus things were all dead, and the only beings that prowled here were the vampiric facsimiles of them, very hungry now that there were no genuine ones left for them to attach themselves to. One of these voracious, semi-transparent things had been accidentally created each time he had touched one of the walrus creatures that had been in extreme pain; the strength had flowed out from the suffering communicant, but at a sort of psychic slant, so that he'd been unable to catch it and consume it. These stray unabsorbed strengths eventually became a sort of being themselves, solidifying and even acquiring independent wills if they managed to attach themselves to a sufficient number of the genuine, original creatures; and these artificial, hungry things would cling to *him* if they could, and try to drain *him,* and though they'd get more from the disastrous conjunction than they could deal with—a burst of psychic energy that would certainly kill them—it would damage him, too. It was time, regrettably, to leave.

"I should have taken more time with them," said the boy in the dark basket sadly. *"I should have conserved them, bred fresh herds. They were tasty."*

Still in the memory, he swam up out of the warm nourishing levels to the outer surface; and when he splashed out, his borrowed body bursting around him in the inadequate pressure, he separated from the ruptured organic ruin the tough crystal that was himself, and, using up a distressingly large amount of the energy he'd acquired here, he flung himself up into the starry sky at a speed sufficient to get out of the bent space around this world.

And then once again there were simply the aeons of waiting, of remembering past satiations and hoping for more; at rest, with no sensory apparatus with which to perceive the universe wheeling around him. Stuff—dust, pebbles, ice—would gradually collect on him, until he formed the minimally sentient heart of a drifting boulder, a potential comet or meteor . . .

And then, like every time before, after much waiting there would come the shiftings, the stretching . . . with his obsessive self-attention he'd notice the faint stressing of an electron valence here, the tendency of a molecular ring there to become just the slightest bit elliptical . . . and he'd know he was near something.

Most often it would pass; and sometimes he could feel the tickle of hard radiation, and he'd know to propel himself away, for though hot naked nuclei and crowded photon-waves were delicious, it would unmake him to fall into one of the dense furnaces from which they sprayed. And then, too, it often happened that, though there was none of the fusion-heat, the stretching effect would simply become steady, and he'd have to use up more energy to get closer . . . and of course in the heartbreaking majority of cases he'd impacted onto a sterile surface devoid of life, and he had had to spend still more of his own power just to leave and get back out to the eternal sea.

But always before he'd come dangerously close to the point where converting any more of his crystal-self to energy would mean losing some of his personality and memories, he'd found something, if only seas of primitive life that barely repaid the exit fee; and once in a while he found the *tasty* ones, the ones who knew they were ones.

"Sentience," said the far-gone boy smugly. *"That's what Sevatividam likes."*

Always he learned, and eventually even came to *think* in, the language of his hosts . . . though he always thought of himself by his own, real name, which he'd always had, and had by now heard rendered into—it must be—thousands of accents, on waves that had vibrated in air, water, methane, ammonia . . . the name best rendered in the language of these people here in this newest place by the syllables *Sevatividam*.

This place—Rivas caught several scenes at once: the glass plain he'd been on last night, the walls of a canal moving past under a blue sky, a glow of warm nourishing nuclear fire shining up through the water of a harbor at twilight, a rooftop balcony with bent towers beyond it as white and bumpy as the spinal columns of giants—this place was one of the best he'd ever come across.

"Lots of people," the boy said. *"As tasty as any I've found."* He sighed. *"I wish I'd been able to maintain their little local golden age, their little renaissance, a decade or so longer; it wasn't costing me all that much energy and attention to cultivate great artists and doctors and politicians among them, and even though it would have meant postponing the real feasting for a while, how luscious they'd have been after I'd let them fall from a real cultural height, tumble back down to the old despair after a whole generation of confident optimism!"*

The far-gone kid sighed again. *"But of course after only four years of cultivating and fertilizing them, I got carried away."*

The visions were dimming out—or, more accurately, Rivas was losing access to them—but he got a glimpse of a tremendous amount of rock falling from all directions into a point of intolerably bright light. He was squeezing the whole pile through dozens of levels of fusion and he could feel the tickling all through his body—and then everything became the white light, and it was all he could do to make a shell around his body to keep it from being vaporized in the explosion he'd accidentally touched off.

"I never got so carried away before," the far-gone observed in a voice half rueful and half awed. *"I never made quite so much of the heavy unstable stuff. I guess if you have too much of it all piled together at once it begins to*

decay in step or something, or chain reacts like a live coal on a stack of paper . . . for years after that error in judgment I scarcely had strength to move, let alone donate energy and attention to maintain the Ellay renaissance . . . yes, getting the Holy City paved in glass was very expensive. . . ."

For a while the kid was silent, then he laughed softly. *"But even after just four years, they weren't bad; after their precious Sixth Ace was assassinated and all their artists burned out and went mad after being deprived of my unsuspected support, and everybody saw that the brief but tantalizing promise was all a lie. People are so tasty when they're truly embittered, truly despairing . . . and that's when they come to Sevativìdam. They can't stand the bitter rain, so they run in under one of the two awnings—religion or dissipation—and guess who's waiting for them under both awnings at once. . . ."*

The tumbling sea water had flushed the dose of Blood out of the metal basket, and the effects were wearing off. He had lost the ability to see Jaybush's memories. His hand was numb except when anything touched it—when that happened it exploded in a hot flare of pain that shocked, sickened and aged him.

Rivas knew now that pain was just as effective an insulator from Blood as it was from the communion; which made sense, after all, since it seemed that both things were just differently labeled straws for Jaybush to push into the punchbowls of people's psyches. And though it insulated him from the usual unconsciousness and loss of identity and subsequent period of confusion, it certainly didn't prevent an awareness of Jaybush—it seemed to force that. When, six days ago in the Cerritos Stadium, he'd taken the sacrament while pressing the blade of his knife through his thumbnail, he'd been distantly aware of a chilly alien sentience; today's dose of Blood, clarified by the ruining of his right hand, had shown him Jaybush's memories as clearly as if they'd been Rivas's own. Another administration of either agent, accompanied by some further physical damage, might . . .

God knew what it might do. Rivas wasn't eager to find out.

The engine roar, which had been so steady that he'd stopped being aware of it, abruptly lost most of its volume and became a low uneven chugging. The basket rocked and bobbed for a few moments as it collided with the hull and the basket in front of it, and then it hung blessedly steady. Muffled by the tarpaulin, he could hear voices calling, loudly but not excitedly.

What the hell, he thought nervously. Are we docking? But we can't be, I'd have felt the turbulence if we'd moved back into shallow water.

Above him a voice shouted clearly, "Take 'em from the back. Here." Rivas's cage shook. "I'll untie it when you've got it."

Through the hull Rivas could hear the footsteps of the girls shifting uneasily, and it reminded him of something. Yes, in all of Jaybush's memories, even the memories of being the stripped-down crystalline seed drifting through space, he had clearly, implicitly been a *masculine* thing. Evidently gender could be intrinsic, independent of the physical systems of organs and hormones and whatnot that Rivas had always thought dictated it. That must be, he thought, why women can take the sacrament forever without quite reaching the far-gone stage—there must be some kind of core to femaleness which Jaybush, being male, can't consume.

Rivas thought of that meteor shower that legend claimed— and his father had verified—lit the sky one night during the year before Jaybush's birth. He thought, If someone had impossibly known what parasite was riding along among that handful of interstellar debris, could anything have been done then? If the crystal thing can survive huge accelerations and re-entry temperatures and the raw radiations of interstellar space, though, I suppose it wouldn't be bothered by a boot tromp or a hammer blow or being tossed into the fireplace. And how does it get *into* somebody?

Something metal clanked against Rivas's cage, and then right next to his head he heard the tarpaulin tear and metal rasp on metal, and he could see a spot of light where a hook had torn through. The hook rattled a bit, and then he heard, a little more clearly because of the hole, someone call, "Got it solid. Go ahead and untie."

Rivas could feel an agitation in the line that held the basket to the boat—and then the whole basket tilted over, filling up with water, and he knew the far-gone kid must be under the surface, and he lunged downward to hoist him up next to the hook, which seemed destined to become the basket's highest point. His right hand collided horribly with the boy's head and Rivas felt consciousness receding, but he gritted his teeth and forced himself to stay aware. Catching a breath and letting himself tumble to what was now the bottom of the cage, he used his good hand to grab the boy's belt and shove him upward to where, if anywhere in this confinement, there was air.

Rivas braced himself, holding the breath he'd taken, and waited while the cage shook and swung on the hook, and he told himself, *Wait, just a few seconds more. They've got to haul this up out of the water in a moment. Wait. . . .*

His lungs were working in his chest, trying to break the seal of his closed throat and inhale sea water, and again he felt his consciousness fading. Christ, he thought shrilly, you're about to pass *out,* man, you'll drown for sure, struggle to the top while you still can and hook an arm through the bars so that even if you do lose consciousness you'll be held up out of the water, do you want to die for a *far-gone,* who can't even see or think or feel gratitude, do you want to die for this absolutely minimum example of humanity?

He was bitterly disappointed in himself when he realized that he was not going to trade places with the boy. Good job, Greg, he thought—the man hires you to save Uri, and you lose your damn *life* saving a mindless, poisoned kid who's probably got only days to live at *best,* and who'll most likely die right now as soon as you pass out and let go of him.

Abruptly all the water rushed down past him with a racket of bubbling and the kid was suddenly far too heavy and the surface of the water swirled past his face and he was gasping air—and then his left arm buckled and the boy fell down onto him and Rivas's crushed right hand was jammed under the two of them and with a scream that only dogs could have heard he sprang away from consciousness like an arrow from a bow.

Rivas had for a while been dimly aware that he was lying on his back with a weight across his middle on a corrugated surface that, though uncomfortable, he couldn't be bothered to get up from. He didn't care what had awakened him, for he planned to sleep quite a while longer. It was still dark after all.

Some people were up and about, though. Somebody was even whistling.

Then a wet canvas was flapped away somewhere overhead and suddenly there was light beyond his closed eyelids. Without particularly noticing them, he was aware of the smells of beer, sweat and fish.

"Well!"

Rivas didn't open his eyes or move.

"Uh," the voice went on, "this ain't Blood, in this one."

"What's in there, then?" queried another voice irritably.

A finger touched Rivas's sea-chilled cheek. "It's . . . well,

Joe, it's a couple of dead guys."

"Dead guys." Rivas heard a chair scrape on a floor. He kept his eyes shut and held his breath when clumping boots approached. If they think you're dead, he told himself, *be* dead. "Damn me, you're right. Jaybirds trying to escape, I guess. Hell! And we've paid for the stuff that was in here."

"Can we get our money back?"

A pause followed, and then a disgusted exclamation as the boots moved away. "That'll take some considering. Whether we even ask or not, I mean. We could show 'em these two and say, see, these guys dumped the Blood and climbed in in its place, but that'd be awful damn close to admitting we know it's from the Holy City. It ain't just to keep the product cold that they use all the extra fuel it takes to drag these baskets on the outside of their boat—the main reason they do it that way is so guys like us can hook it and run real quick, without getting any kind of look inside their boat. And the stuff's in glass and metal so if there's any mix-up it'll just sink. They don't want rumors getting out about any connection between Irvine and Venice. No, I'm afraid we'll have to eat this loss. That or go asking to eat some bullets."

"Dump 'em?"

There was a sigh. "I guess."

"Out like with the garbage?"

"No point carrying 'em any distance, is there? What'd you want to do, say some prayers over 'em?"

Some gesture may have been the reply, but the next thing Rivas knew the battered metal basket was being noisily pushed across an uneven floor. He braced himself, wondering what the garbage arrangements consisted of around here.

They turned out to be primitive. The man kept pushing the basket across the floor until the bottom edge caught against the sill of a very low, open window, and the basket simply turned over and dumped its two occupants out.

Rivas found himself cartwheeling through empty air—
the sensation reminding him of something—and then he
impacted onto a slanted heap of rotting, feculent trash. As
he rolled dizzily down the slope of broken wood, boxes and
bad old food, he was sure that he and the boy were not the
first bodies to be tossed here.

Dizzy and sick with the pain of his hand, Rivas simply
lay for a while in sunlight at the foot of the garbage heap.
When the pain had backed off a little he sat up, worked his
arms and legs cautiously to see if anything had broken during
his fall—nothing, it seemed, had—and then he looked
around for the far-gone kid. He saw him off to the right,
lying on his back. He was breathing.

Rivas looked at his own right hand. The fingers were
swollen and black, and at least two of them seemed not to
be attached to the hand very securely. Poor old hand, he
thought sadly.

He looked around, ignoring the mildly interested stares
of a couple of children who'd been digging in the trash. He
was in a wide court with high foliage-topped brick walls,
and an arch to his left showed a segment of old alley that
someone had tried to brighten by painting a lot of vividly
blue birds across the surface of it. Certainly seems to be
Venice, he thought.

He got up and limped over to where the boy lay. The
boy's eyes were open, staring straight up into the noon sun,
and Rivas crouched to close them.

"*New girls!*" the boy exclaimed suddenly. "*All right,
gonna give 'em a treat, let 'em receive the sacrament from
the Messiah himself, yes sir. . . .*"

"Good afternoon, Sevatividam," said Rivas wearily.

"*And won't I touch them! Oh my, yes . . .*" the boy said,
and the contrast between the fatuous insinuation of the voice
and the bony, wasted face it issued from was appalling.

"I've come to take one of them away from you."

"Some pretties and some piggies," the boy said judiciously.

"You know," said Rivas hoarsely, leaning forward and bracing himself against the wall with his good hand, "I don't think I can kill people anymore. Animals, even."

"The piggies I'll touch with my finger."

"But I believe I could kill you. I believe I'll try very hard to do that."

As the boy's voice diminished into muttering about how tasty it would be, Rivas tried, one-handed, to pick him up. A week ago he might have been able to do it. After five minutes he gave up and stood up straight.

The two children had resumed digging around in the trash—their ancient shopping cart was half full of junk—and Rivas said, "Hey. Kids."

They looked up warily, their eyes in the wide, unspecific focus of animals ready to bolt in any direction.

"Could you...keep an eye on my friend here for a few minutes?" He knew he might as well be making the request to a couple of the monkeys swinging around and screeching in the wall-top greenery, but he needed to make the gesture, needed to let the universe know that he wasn't ditching the boy.

The children stared at him, and one of them might have nodded before resuming the excavations.

"Thanks." Rivas trudged to the arch and through it to the narrow alley outside. Tall houses, liberally scaffolded with wooden and iron balconies, leaned against each other in the sun, and to his right the alley was shaded by the rooftop connection of two old buildings, one on either side of the alley, that had bowed forward until their tops touched, like a couple of ragged old women exchanging gossip.

He knew where he was; a block or two north would be the Imperial Canal—no, it was Imperial Highway this far inland—and three or four blocks north of that would be the restaurant where he'd first got a job washing dishes. And where had that doctor lived? In a basement only a few buildings away from the restaurant, he recalled. The standards of cleanliness in the restaurant's kitchen had provided the man with plenty of patients. And Rivas had gone back to him a few times during the ensuing years—once for a clap cure and a couple of times to have dueling wounds sewed up.

Rivas set off in that direction, noticing apartments where friends had lived whose names he now couldn't remember, terrace bars where he'd taken young ladies for drinks on long ago late nights, canals he'd fallen into.... Much had changed—there were lots full of charred rubble where he remembered houses, new bars that had been Junk & Relic stores in his day, a new wide hole in the street where some cluster of antique sewer tunnels must have collapsed, over which a gaily beribboned but unsteady bridge had been built—but so much had not changed that he thought the ghost of young Gregorio Rivas must still haunt these streets and alleys and rooftop bridges; a self-consciously cynical ghost, inordinately proud of its skill with both sword and pelican, its capacity for liquor, and all the dues it imagined it had paid. The place was still Venice, where he'd spent his youth, still crowded with old buildings rotting under bright new paint, curbside hot food vendors, shouting parrots and street lunatics, still redolent with the smells of ordure and spicy cooking.

Though the restaurant had mercifully burned down, the doctor's building was still there, but as he scuffed down the steps to the man's door he wondered whether *he* would still be there. It had been—what—six years? He knocked at the door.

After a few seconds it swung open and he felt weak with relief to see that the man peering out of the doorway was the doctor. "Doctor Dendro!" Rivas said. "I'm glad you still live here. Do you still have that thing you used to call a stretcher barrow? There's a—"

The gray-haired man was frowning. "Who are you?" he interrupted.

"Don't you recognize me? I'm Greg Rivas. I came to you several times for—"

"Rivas." The doctor stared at the ceiling. "You had the clap."

"Well," said Rivas, nettled in spite of everything, "yes. Once. But right now I'd appreciate it if you'd—"

Abruptly the doctor saw Rivas's hand. "My *God,* man, what have you done to your *hand?* Come in here and—"

"Doctor," said Rivas loudly, "I'd be grateful if you'd look at my hand." More quietly, he went on, "But first I wish you'd get your stretcher barrow and come look at a friend of mine."

"He worse off than you?"

"Yes."

"All right." The doctor waved him inside, and when Rivas had reeled in and blinked around enough to be able to see in the dimness, he smiled, for the place hadn't noticeably changed since his last visit. Here was still the old wood stove autoclave, here were the window-blocking stacks of terrarium mold gardens, the astrological charts and the live, caged, two-headed snakes which may patients insisted be consulted before they'd accept any medication, the cupboards full of ancient and almost certainly useless bottled pills.

Doctor Dendro had put on his antique white coat with *Doctor, Doctor, Gimme The News* stitched on it, and from a closet rolled out the extended, padded wheelbarrow Rivas remembered. "Your man in much pain?" he asked Rivas.

"Unconscious."

"Won't risk bringing a hypodermic needle, then. Broke one since you were in last. Down to seven now."

He wheeled the device out the door and Rivas followed.

"I can't pay you today," Rivas said, "but as soon as I get back to—"

"I'll take an I.O.U." As they went up the steps the doctor sniffed. "Or will I? Blood's bad stuff, Rivas. You used to have a little more sense."

"It was an accidental dose. I gave some to this friend of mine as a, a sedative, and we both wound up doused in it."

"It's only a sedative to people who want that kind of sedative."

When they got up to street level Rivas swayed dizzily in the sudden blast of sunlight.

"Sure you don't want a ride in this yourself?" Dendro asked dubiously.

"No—thank you—I'd fall asleep, and when I next sleep it's going to be for about twelve hours."

He led the doctor back to the alley, and down it to the arch in the wall, and when he stumbled into the enclosed court the two children were gone but of course the far-gone still lay where he'd been, at the foot of the garbage pile. Rivas pointed, then leaned back against the wall and slid down it until he was sitting.

The doctor trundled his wheelbarrow over to the boy and crouched to look at him. He picked up one of the skeletal wrists, then dropped it and pushed back an eyelid. He looked over at Rivas and then stood up. "Sorry," he said. "Boy's dead."

Rivas nodded and shrugged, and it wasn't until the too bright scene blurred and fragmented that he realized, to his weary horror, that he was crying, for the first time in more years than he could remember. He tried to stop and discovered he couldn't. He was breathing in harsh gasps, tears running down his unshaven cheeks, and he didn't hear the doctor approach.

Dendro put his hand on Rivas's shoulder. "He was a close friend?"

Rivas shook his head. "Just . . . some kid. I don't know

what the hell's the matter with me." He looked up. The doctor had put the wasted corpse in his wheelbarrow.

"I'll take him to the burial pit," Dendro said, "after I've fixed up your hand. Get up now."

Rivas climbed to his feet and plodded after the doctor.

An hour and a half later, his hand a bandaged numbness swinging at his side, Rivas was wandering along the Lennox Street sidewalk, wondering which old acquaintances he might be able to find who'd loan him some money and give him food and a place to sleep. He could remember a number of people, but somehow he couldn't picture any of them being particularly glad to see him, especially since his years of success in Ellay. And of course it was out of the question to consider looking up any of his old girlfriends. He'd never understood how some people could be friends with ex-lovers; his own romances always ended with at least one party feeling nothing but loathing for the other.

A street band on a corner ahead was banging out a melody on instruments made of kitchen utensils and car parts, and Rivas slowed, trying to identify the tune of the song. Then with a shock he realized it was a song he'd written himself, many years ago. He kept trying to remember a lyric before the singer could sing it, and finally managed to, moving his lips silently half a beat ahead of the band:

> Well, I haven't crapped in three weeks,
> Feels like I never will again;
> No, I haven't crapped in three weeks,
> Wonder if I ever will again—
> They tell me Jaybush is gonna end the world soon,
> Maybe I'll do it then.

He had slowed to a stop in front of the musicians, and the singer slid a foot forward to nudge the hat that lay inverted on the pavement. Glancing down, Rivas saw a handful of jigger cards in it. He looked up, met the man's gaze and shrugged apologetically, and the man rolled his eyes in a way that clearly conveyed, *Then take off, hobo*.

Rivas shambled on, but a moment later the music came to an abrupt, twanging halt. He looked back and saw the band hastily packing up, and looking beyond them he saw why.

Half a dozen of the sort of madwomen known locally as pocalocas were striding aggressively down the street, their arms swinging and their ragged skirts sweeping the pavement. Music often threw pocalocas into violent frenzies that abated only when the music stopped, and they'd been known to claw out eyes and bite as ferociously as dogs.

The musicians fled into a nearby bar, and they were swearing angrily, for the bar's owner could certainly charge them for the temporary shelter. Rivas stepped well back out of the path of the wild-eyed women, and as they passed, as a couple of them scowled menacingly at him, it occurred to him for the first time, even though he'd seen them frequently during his years in Venice, that despite their savage restlessness their eyes had a distinctly *birdy* glaze.

He didn't pursue that thought, though, for the sight of them had reminded him of someone who might be willing to help him.

He'd been about twenty-three years old, walking home in the early hours of the morning after the Bom Sheltr had shut down for the night, and from a dark alley he'd heard hard scuffling and the thump of blows and, in the instant when he'd been considering whether to interfere or move on, he'd heard a muffled female voice call for help. He'd drawn his knife, then, and interfered.

It was a band of pocalocas beating a young woman, and without using the blade of his knife—just the pommel as a club—he'd managed to kick and punch and slap them

away. He'd helped the victim to her feet and then escorted
her to her home, and she'd insisted that he sit down and
have a drink while she washed the blood off her face and
changed her clothes and prodded her ribs to see if any had
been cracked.

When she'd reappeared, pleased that a black eye and
some bruises were all she'd suffered, they had talked for a
couple of hours, and young Rivas learned that she was a
free-lance prostitute. He hadn't asked, but he'd been certain
that that explained the pocalocas' attack—the madwomen
reacted to public displays of affection as strongly as they
reacted to music, and if, as he'd guessed, they'd come upon
her consummating a business transaction in the alley, it
would certainly have been enough to provoke the melée
Rivas had broken up; the client, presumably, had made good
his escape.

As he'd left her place at dawn she'd told him she owed
him a big one, and during the next few years he'd taken it,
as he'd phrased it to himself, in pieces, wandering over to
her place whenever he was in the mood and not seeing any
particular young lady. Perhaps because neither of them had
ever thought of the intermittent liaison as significant, nor,
once they'd got to know each other, found any reason to
feel more than a faint, slightly patronizing fondness for the
other, this relationship had not ended in the kind of bitter
acrimony he was used to.

I wonder, he thought now as he tried to remember where
she'd lived, if she'll still be there, and if I entirely used up
the big one.

The building, when he finally found it after several wrong
turns, looked different, but after a moment he realized that
it wasn't; he'd simply never seen it in bright daylight before.
You dog, he told himself. So it was with cautious optimism
that he walked up the steps and knocked at the door. A man
answered the door, though, and the furniture Rivas could

see behind him wasn't any he'd ever seen before.

The man was frowning suspiciously, and Rivas knew what he must look like, bandaged, bearded, exhausted and dirty, so he conjured up his most respectable tone of voice. "Excuse me, sir," he said, "I'm trying to find a young lady that lived in this apartment, uh, eight years ago."

"I only been here three," the man said, not relaxing his frown. "What's her name?"

Rivas felt his face getting red. "I . . . don't remember, but she was kind of pretty, skinny, with dark hair . . ."

The man swore disgustedly and slammed the door.

Feeling obscurely humiliated, Rivas hurried back down the steps and walked briskly around the corner. I guess I could head for the old Bom Sheltr, he thought—assuming it's still there—but when Steve Spink recruited me to play at his place in Ellay, I just went, I didn't even tell old Hanker I was quitting, much less give notice.

But the thought of the Bom Sheltr reminded him that this woman—whatever her name had been—had liked to hang out in a place called, what was it, El Famoso Volcan, down on the Ladybug Canal. Lunchtime in those early years of the Seventh Ace had generally found her at one of the umbrella-shaded tables on the place's canal-front patio. He glanced at the position of the sun above the uneven rooftops. Worth a try, he thought.

When he got there, though, he saw that the old EL FAMOSO VOLCAN sign was gone, replaced by a relic sign—REALIGNMENT AND BALANCING—obviously chosen more for its size and the handsomeness of its lettering than for any meaning in the old, hard-to-read words. It did still seem to be a restaurant, though, so he decided to go in and have a look—but once again he'd forgotten what he presently looked like.

He pushed open the door and had taken two steps into the coolness of the place when a hard hand closed on his shoulder. "Trash bins are out back, Chucko," said a bored, unfriendly voice.

"Excuse me," said Rivas, "I know I'm not dressed appropriately, but I simply want to find out whether—"

"Go somewhere else to find out, Chucko. Right now hit the road."

"I'm Gregorio Rivas," he said angrily, "and I'm the star performer at Spink's in Ellay, which I imagine even you've heard of. Now all I want to do is—"

He was swung around and propelled with surprising force at the door, which slammed open when he hit it, and he was still moving too fast to negotiate the steps, and he wound up thudding into the hot dust and rolling several yards. As he was struggling dizzily to get up, something clanked on the ground near him. "No hard feelings, Chucko," the man said, a moment before closing the door.

Half stunned but at least sitting up, Rivas blinked around stupidly until he saw what the man had thrown after him. It was a half-pint bottle, one-third full and with a few bread crumbs in it, of the cheapest local whiskey. Rivas snatched it up, uncorked it with his loosening teeth and drained it in a series of heroic swallows that sluiced the dust off his bristly chin with dribbled whiskey and made tears cut tracks through the dust on his gaunt cheeks.

"You're looking good, Greg," came a woman's husky voice from right behind him.

He paused, then slowly lowered the bottle. Her voice had brought back her name. "Hello, Lisa," he said.

She walked around to where he could see her. She doesn't look bad, he thought. Some gray in her hair, more lines around her eyes and mouth . . . at least she hasn't got fat. "I heard you were doing real well in Ellay," she said. He couldn't tell whether she was amused or pitying.

"Isn't it obvious?" he asked her. "These clothes, my

grooming, this fine old liquor I'm sipping?"

"The way restauranteurs hasten to serve you," she agreed.

"Serve me to the canalside dogs. Listen, Lisa," he said, wishing he hadn't had the liquor, for he could feel it hitting his abused system hard, "is there any of that big one left?"

She stared down at him. "A little. Not as much as what you're maybe thinking."

"All I want is a place to sleep—a kitchen corner and a blanket is fine—for tonight, and maybe tomorrow night, no longer than that, and a bit of food, and enough jiggers to get some liquor and clothes."

"I'd recommend a bath, too," she said.

"Didn't I say that? I meant to."

She seemed to relax. "Okay, Greg. But that spends it, you understand? Not a drop of change."

"Sure." He wobbled to his feet. "Thanks."

"What are you back here for? And so trashed-looking? It's down this way, along the canal a half mile. Can you walk?"

"Yeah, half a mile, anyway. I'm..." He'd be doing her no favor to let her in on the Irvine-Venice connection. "I'm looking for someone."

"Been looking down sewers, it seems like. What'd you do to your hand?"

"Mashed it. Saw a doctor today. He splinted my first two fingers and had to cut off two."

She stopped. "Jesus, Greg! Can you still play your... what was it, pelican?"

"Right. I don't know. Holding the bow shouldn't be too hard, and as for plucking the strings, I never used the missing fingers much anyway. I guess it depends on how the two I'm left with heal up."

"Huh. Mashing your hand have to do with finding this person?"

"Yes."

"Anybody going to come looking for you? In rough ways?"

"No. This," he said, waving his bandaged hand, "was an accident. Nobody *did* it to me."

"Okay." For a while they trudged along in silence, then she said, "You know, it was a shock to hear your name after all this time. I was with a guy there in the Lancing, and I hear this commotion by the front door, like a bum's trying to get in, and then I hear the bum say he's you. And then I ditch this guy and walk outside and it *is* you, sitting in the dirt and soaking your beard with cheap whiskey! You're lucky I even still recognized you."

"Reckon I am," said Rivas shortly, not relishing this conversation.

"Are you in, like, *disguise,* or are you really this low?"

"I'm in goddamn *disguise,* okay?"

"You're as grouchy as ever, that's for sure."

"I just lost two *fingers,* do you mind? I'm never at my most charming right after amputations."

"Not a drop of change, Rivas. Not the price of a cup of beer." Her tone was amiable but obviously sincere.

She lived in a narrow one-story house that fronted on the canal, with its own tiny pier and a flock of ducks hanging around in case anybody might throw bread crusts. She had obviously prospered, for on the roof he could see a maintained-looking water tank and the pole-mounted propeller of a windmill. She led him in and showed him where the bath was, and when he emerged twenty minutes later she had men's clothes right in the house that fit him well enough. She'd cooked up scrambled eggs with some canal shrimps and onions and garlic while he was in the tub, and he cheered up immensely when he smelled it.

He sat down at her kitchen table, picked up his fork, and

then didn't speak for fifteen minutes. "God," he said finally as he sat back after the last swallow, "thanks. I believe I was about to expire."

"You're welcome. Want a drink?"

"Oh no, I'd better not, I—well—maybe it'll help me sleep."

"Look at it as medicine," she agreed drily. "What, beer, whiskey, tequila? No Currency."

"To hell with Currency. Uh . . . tequila."

"Coming up."

She brought him a big shot with beer and salt and a quartered lemon on the side. He ignored the salt and lemon, bolted the tequila and chased it with the beer.

He looked up at her helplessly. "Somehow I'm still not sleepy."

Her smile was becoming tired, but she refilled the glasses.

When he'd downed the third set he had to admit that, despite how dead for sleep he ought to be, the alcohol was giving him some kind of spurious energy and restlessness. "Maybe a walk," he said, and though it was hard to speak he felt entirely sober, "would relax me a bit."

"Okay, Greg. Can you find your way back here?"

"Sure. Okay if I borrow a couple of jiggers? Just pocket change."

"Of course. I may be out myself when you get back, but if you yank on the fern by the front door—it's plastic, the fern, I mean—it opens the latch. Got that?"

"Yank the fern, right."

"And I'll leave out the stuff you want—a shoulder pouch and a fifth of something, right?"

"That's it. Tequila will be fine."

She cocked her head and gave him a troubled look. "Am I going to have to worry about you, Greg?"

Even with shock, liquor and exhaustion working on him he could see that she wasn't concerned that he might rob her or bring rowdy drunks back to her place; touched, he told her, "Nah, Lisa, I'm okay. Just going to have a drink at the old Bom Sheltr."

"Do be careful. Here's half a pint, which will buy you more than you ought to have, probably. And I can get you more tomorrow, if you need it."

"Thanks, Lisa. I'll pay it all back as soon as—"

"*No*," she said. "No. Pay me back and you've put a bit of tilt on the scales again. Do it my way and we'll be all square, with no reason to even speak to each other if we pass in the street." Her smile had not faltered or become strained.

He knew he wasn't understanding this, so he didn't pretend to be hurt or angry. "Okay." He got up, pocketed the half-pint card and walked, pretty steadily, to the door, and opened it. Somehow the sky had already gone molten in the west behind the tall palm trees, and the long shadows were purple. He turned back to her and said, "But thanks."

She waved. *"Por nada."*

The air had cooled outside, and though at noon it had smelled only of dust and baking pavement, now at twilight it was elusively scented with jasmine and gardenia and the not so distant sea. He scuffed thoughtfully down the canalside path, kicking an occasional pebble into the water, pondering the fact that he'd become a different man since leaving Venice five or six years ago. . . . No, Greg, he told himself, be honest, since leaving Ellay five days ago. Was it an improvement? It didn't feel like it.

The flavors of the breeze changed as he walked toward the sea; now there was smoke in the air, the smoke from a hundred basement Mexican and Chinese kitchens, and though he knew he was probably imagining it he thought he detected tobacco and marijuana and perfume and the quiver of distant music. He remembered having whimsically wondered today whether the ghost of young Rivas might still haunt these bars and bridges and canals. Let's go see, he thought, whether I can catch him out of the corner of my eye.

He smiled almost sadly when he rounded the last corner and saw, in the still vacant paved yard, the dozens of pieces of plexiglass set flush with the old concrete, for they reminded him of his very first days of working here, washing cups and pitchers in the yellow afternoon light that filtered down through the translucent plexiglass skylight. The upright, wedge-shaped shed which was the top of the entry stairs was a little flimsier-looking now, and the lettering on the sign over the doorway had been repainted carelessly at least once; but several more tall poles had been planted in the dirt or nailed to the sides of the shed, and the many lengths of wire and string draped from one to another were lavishly flagged with bits of cloth and colored plastic and tinfoil; and through the soles of his feet he fancied he could feel the bass beat of subterranean music. He pushed his disordered hair back from his forehead, straightened his borrowed coat and crossed the yard to the descending stairs.

The band was noisy and only just competent, but the place had so many tunnels and burrows that it wasn't difficult to find a table from which the music was just a remote crashing. Candles behind colored glass threw tinted shadows, reminding him of one of the worlds he'd seen in Jaybush's memory, the world where the orange spider-things had each cast two shadows, a red and a blue.

A waitress arrived. He'd never seen her before, and she obviously wasn't interested in who he was. He ordered a tequila with water on the side, and she strolled away to get it.

All at once it came to him what it was that he'd been reminded of by the sensation of falling this afternoon, when the Blood dealer had dumped him and the far-gone boy onto the trash pile; for an instant it had taken him back to the at-rest-in-free-fall sensation of being in the long wait between planets. But that wasn't a memory of his own—that was Jaybush's. It didn't please him to find himself sharing the Messiah's recollections.

During his third tequila, just as he was getting ready to leave and walk back to the Ladybug Canal, a lean, grinning middle-aged man walked up to him hesitantly, pointing at him. Rivas couldn't remember ever having seen him before.

"Greg?" the man said. "It's Greg, right? Rivas!"

He could have denied it, but the man at REALIGNMENT AND BALANCING having doubted him and called him Chucko, and the irresponsibility induced by the tequila, made him smile and say, "Right."

"I knew it! You remember me, don't you?" The man dragged a chair over and sat down at Rivas's table.

Ordinarily Rivas would probably have objected to the unsought company, but tonight he wanted reassurance—admiration, if only from this silly little man. "Remind me."

"Jack Frenchfry. I been working here forever. Remember? I helped you arrange some of your first songs—polished 'em for you."

Like hell you ever did, thought Rivas; but, "Sure, I remember you, Jack," he said. "So how's the old place doing?"

"Real good, Greg. Old Hanker died two years ago—he was real mad at you, but I told him, 'Hey, Greg is a genius,' I said, 'and geniuses can't be bothered with things like giving notice.' Am I right? Hah? Yeah, they wanted me to take over the place when he died, but I told 'em I'd rather stay maiterdee, out where I can *meet the people*. I like meeting people, you know? That's the kind of person I am."

"Sure, Jack." The man was beginning to depress him, but before Rivas could kill his drink and go, Frenchfry had ordered him another.

"You know who this guy is, Doris?" Frenchfry said to

the waitress. "This is Greg Rivas from Spink's in Ellay. We're old friends. He comes back to see me every chance he gets, don't you, Greg?"

"Sure," said Rivas, feeling dizzy.

"You don't look like him," the waitress said. "And who needs old Rivas anyway?"

"I don't know," said Rivas, shaking his head.

"Just bring him the drink, will you, Doris?" The unnecessary harshness in Frenchfry's voice made it clear to Rivas that the man had no particular authority over the girl. "If the new boss was here, Greg, he'd let me make it on the house—but he's in Ellay, on business. Sorry. You know how it is trying to deal with damn *clerks* and *cashiers*."

Rivas's chest had gone cold and he fumbled in his pocket to see if he had enough left to cover this unwanted drink. He did, but barely, only if he ludicrously undertipped the waitress. *That'll* impress her with me, he thought.

"Yeah, I just kind of work here part time," said Frenchfry expansively, "in like an *advisory* capacity. Fact is, I quit too, a while ago. This new boss started yelling at me about some crap or other, and I walked out. Who needs 'em, eh?" He leaned forward with raised eyebrows and poked Rivas painfully in the chest. "You know something?"

Rivas's drink was clanked down in front of him, and he pushed all his money across the table to the girl without looking at her. She took it and left with at least no spoken comment.

"You know something?" Frenchfry repeated.

"What," said Rivas dully.

"You and me, Greg—we're two of a kind."

"Jesus." Rivas pushed his chair back and stood up. Why had he come here?

"Hey, Greg, where are you going?" Frenchfry started to get up too. "I know, you want to go to a better place, right? With girls, if I remember *you* correctly, eh? Listen, there's a place I go to a lot nearby where they got girls that'll—"

"You stay here," Rivas said, afraid he might hit the man, or start crying again. "I'm leaving."

"Well, say, Greg, I wasn't going to bring it up right now," Frenchfry said, beginning to sound worried himself, "but I can't break the last, uh, hundred-fifth note they paid me here, and I was wondering—"

"That was it," said Rivas, "for that drink." He pointed at the fresh glass. "All the money I had." He was having trouble taking a deep breath. "But hey, help yourself, man. *Mi tequila es su tequila.*"

He blundered out of the place, aware of the stares of other drinkers. The waitress had obviously told them who he claimed to be. Some seemed to believe it and some didn't, but none of them seemed very impressed.

In the darkness outside he walked quickly, as though trying to outpace the memory. *You and me, Greg—we're two of a kind.* My God, he thought. And everybody there thought we were! So who cares? So *I* care—you are what people think you are, which is why it's so important to get them thinking you're someone who . . . *counts.* Gaah.

By the time he came to the canal, the night breeze seemed to have blown away the worst edges of the tequila and the memory, and he stood on the bank and watched the reflected moon waver on the black water and then separate into glowing white streaks as some swimming thing approached, rippling the water. A rat? No, too many ripples. A dog, conceivably, or some kid.

The low waves subsided as the swimmer stopped in the darkness below Rivas and to his left.

"Greg," came a whisper from the darkness.

"Who's—" he began, but he realized he didn't have to ask. He tried to tell it to go away, but at the moment he didn't have the strength.

"I can restore you," said the whisper. There was a slurrying sound as the thing flapped gently in the black water.

"What do you mean?" Rivas asked angrily, though keeping his voice down. "You couldn't lift up a medium-size stone."

"True. But I'm part of you. Maybe the most important part, the part that makes—used to make—you *you*. You know when I . . . was born?"

"No."

"That day at the Cerritos Stadium, when you gashed your thumb to avoid merging with Jaybush. That works, of course, intense pain does block you from the sacrament, but it splinters a piece of you away—something like a ghost. That's me. And you've noticed qualities missing from yourself since then, haven't you? Weaknesses where there used to be strengths, hesitations and uncertainties where you used to have assurance?"

". . . Yes," Rivas whispered.

"Merge with me and let me make you whole. You don't mind merging with *me*—I'm nothing but yourself."

"But . . . would I be . . ."

"Remember when you threw rocks at me that first day, how I tore apart but grew back together, so you couldn't see I'd ever been cut?" It chuckled out there. "Merge with me and I'll grow back your two fingers for you."

Rivas gasped as if he'd been hit, and before he'd even thought about it he'd taken two steps forward, so that he was standing on the tilted dirt slope of the canal bank. There was more swirling in the water, and then the thing swam out of the shadows of the trees into the moonlight, and Rivas could see that it was a lot solider now than it had been when he'd seen it last.

"How did you *get* here?" he asked, thinking of all the populated urban miles around them.

"Followed your boat up," the thing said, its voice taking on a gobbling sound because of its eagerness. "I caught the new-born ghost that was cast when you used the pain parry against that dose of Blood, so you don't have to worry about where that piece of you went. I ate it. It's in me. And then all day I've been eeling around through the canals, trying to find you. Almost got to you before that damn whore did. You don't need her, do you?"

"Need her. Well, I don't know, I—"

"You—we—don't *need* anybody. Thinking you did is what split us in the first place, isn't it? And it has nearly destroyed you."

The thing had swum in closer, and Rivas didn't have to whisper loudly at all for it to hear him. "I'm not sure that's . . ."

"I was angry, earlier today," the thing said, giggling reproachfully, "when I realized you were in that boat full of women. I was hoping you wouldn't be stupid enough to . . . have congress with any of those *vacas* in the state you're in."

Rivas started to tilt, then took a step back, up the bank, to right himself. "Why . . . shouldn't I?"

"It would diminish you. It always does, but in your present broken, unstrong condition it could make you forget."

The thing had fishtailed closer as he backed off, and now he could see its fingers above the water, gripping the muddy stones and glistening like fat sea creatures in the moonlight.

"Forget what?"

"Who you *are*, man. If we forget we're Rivas, what's left of us?"

Rivas took two more steps back. "Whatever *is* me. That's what's left."

The thing was trembling so violently that a lot of close rings were radiating away from it. The canal water smelled like crushed green leaves. "Come to me," the thing in the water choked.

He was suddenly sure that to go to it would mean leaving behind things that had been too costly to acquire. The sadness in the glass eyes of the broken trash man, back in Irvine. The remembered ache in his arm from holding the dying boy up to the corner of the Blood basket where there was air. His shame at having struck a buyer's-market bargain for saving Uri's life. The grudged respect of Frake McAn.

He stepped all the way back up to the path. "No, thank you," he said politely.

"Your fingers, I can replace your—"

"Get away from me," said Rivas tensely, suddenly aware that he was scared. "Go catch a fish if you need some blood to drink."

"You need me more than I need you, Rivas. I can—"

"Then you don't need me at all."

He turned on his heel and started walking toward Lisa's house, which all at once seemed very far away; and a moment later he was running, for he'd heard splashing behind him and the slap of wet rubbery feet against the packed dirt of the path. The pursuing footfalls stopped after a few seconds and Rivas let himself slow down a little, thinking that the hemogoblin had stopped—he didn't realize it had simply taken off and begun flying until it slammed into his shoulders and sent him tumbling down the slope to splash into the canal.

And then it was on him like a dog that has beaten its companions by only a few seconds to a big piece of meat. As the two of them rolled in the chilly salt water Rivas punched at it with his left fist, feeling jellyfish tissue split apart and spill, but always quickly re-knit, and its entirely solid teeth were greedily tearing at his arms and chest. They were both sobbing with fear and rage, and any time either of them got halfway to his feet the other knocked him down.

Finally Rivas got his knees around its waist and his hands

on the corners of its jaw, and he pulled its face away from him, trying to use only the thumb and heel of his bad right hand.

It blew out a mouthful of water and blood and then, its big milky eyes boring into him in the moonlight, it whispered, *"Please*, Greg."

Gripping it strongly with his legs, he began twisting its head around.

The creature began emitting a sort of whispered scream, but the noise was chopped off abruptly when he'd given the head one full turn. The thing's hands were scrabbling at his chest and arms and sometimes even his face, but it didn't seem to have developed fingernails yet, and the fingers just broke against him in a slimy nastiness that was worse than scratches would have been.

Rivas had been letting his head submerge in the canal water whenever he had a fresh breath and the move would allow him to get a new grip on the creature's slippery head, but at the third full turn the thing's neck began to split and spurt some kind of fluid into the water, and after that he tried to keep his head up out of it. The hemogoblin was heaving about under him so strongly that he was afraid he'd be flung off, and he couldn't believe that the noise of their splashing wasn't being heard, but at last at the eighth or ninth full turn the creature's head, which like a clock-winding key had been getting more difficult to twist, snapped off, and the abruptly released force of his straining arms flipped Rivas right over in the fouled water.

The body of the hemogoblin went limp and, releasing a lot of bad-smelling bubbles, sank beneath him. He struggled to his feet and flung the still quivering head as far down the canal, in the direction away from Lisa's house, as he could. After three seconds he heard it splash in the darkness. Then, leaving the body there, he swam up the canal, away from the two pieces of the creature, rinsing his mouth and hair in the canal water, which was relatively clean compared to what he had been splashing around in.

Before long he began imagining that something was wriggling silently through the water in his wake, and he clambered out onto the canal bank and walked the rest of the way to Lisa's place. She wasn't home, so he went in and took another bath—which exhausted her water supply—and crawled into the bed she'd made up for him.

And out in the sluggish, lightless canal, thin filaments were fingering out from two pieces of organic stuff in the water—a small round lump to the west and a big four-limbed lump to the east. The filaments from one traveled toward those of the other, and in the small hours of the night they touched, and merged . . . and slowly began to pull the two pieces together.

When Rivas awoke next morning at about seven, he was hungover and stiff, but he felt more solidly put together than he had for the past several days. Lisa was nowhere to be seen, so he broke some more eggs into a pan and dumped in the fillings from some tacos he found in her brick evaporation box, stirred the mess up over her re-stoked fire until it was nearly cooked, then folded in the taco shells, piled it all onto a plate, shook *salsa furiosa* over it all and then set to. After washing the meal down with a cool beer, he felt at least a lot less unqualified for the sortie he'd planned for this morning.

After washing the dishes and locking the door behind him he left Lisa's house and walked north to Century and then turned left, toward the deep canals and the waterfront, the pouch with the bottle in it swinging at his side. The narrow sunlit streets were alive with cats, the rooftops with monkeys and the sky with parrots, though the human species was represented only by a few shamblers and some steamy smells of coffee and bacon wisping up from tiny street-level windows.

Nearly all of the items that were offered for sale in Venice's shops or served in her restaurants were, if not made or grown locally, wagoned in from Santa Monica to the north or Ellay to the east; the mile of docks and piers rotting over the sea was the site of none but the most furtive sorts of trade, and the citizens who preferred shorefront property did so because they were in the Blood or birdy girl trade, or preyed on those who were, or liked having a whole ocean to dispose of inconveniences in, or simply were more comfortable swimming from place to place, along the waterfront or up and down the canal network, than trying to walk on limbs that had begun to devolve back toward a simpler way of life.

The waterfront area had been built up more than a century ago, during the days of the First Ace, and all the docks and sea walls and canals had been so determinedly built to last that the architects had not hesitated to add touches simply for the sake of decoration—fancy towers, fairy bridges too high and light for any actual traffic, even a seaside amusement park for children. But construction had stopped during the years of the Second Ace, and even maintenance was discontinued when the Third Ace came to power, and now the constructions were cracked, canted and undercut by the sea, and the towers and lacy bridges and the sun-bleached frameworks of the amusement park rides waved and creaked in the wind like the abandoned toys of a long-departed child.

Palms and hibiscus and vines grew in hybrid profusion here, and folklore had it that it was easier to get from place to place through the clustered treetops than by trying to negotiate the unmapped maze of alleys and canals and wobbly bridges, and that the snakes and bugs and monkeys one would encounter in the jungly heights would be less dangerous than the denizens below.

If he'd had two good hands Rivas might seriously have considered taking the green highroad on his trip to the waterfront. What he wanted to do this morning was get near enough to Deviant's Palace to see if that was, as he feared, the destination of the barges full of Jaybird girls, once the Blood baskets had been sold off. There was, of course, the possibility that the barge he'd stowed away on had been the last for a week or so, and that he'd have to try to get into Deviant's Palace without confirmation of his hunch; but he had heard nothing in the Holy City or from the boy who had spoken Sevatividam's thoughts to indicate that the shipments of girls from Irvine were due to be cut any time soon.

As the sun slowly rose above the buildings at his back, the streets ahead of him became narrower, for lines of little houses and shops had been built down the middle of the old wide streets, and in some cases even the resulting ways had been split by rows of food and drink and fortune-telling and peepshow tents, so that no wagon nor even a very fat person could maneuver through. Some of the food tents and liquor vendors were doing business, but most of Venice had only gone to bed a couple of hours ago.

Closer to the sea the ways became uneven as alleys zigzagged sharply to circumnavigate collapsed buildings, or rose and fell where makeshift bridges had been flung up over gaps in the undercut pavement, and it became hard to keep moving west—it was as though the city itself were trying to prevent him from getting to the waterfront. At last, though, nearer to noon than dawn, Rivas edged his way cautiously out along a tilted, swaying fire escape and, crouching to look under the remains of some ancient gable that had broken free of its original mooring and was now jammed precariously between two roof edges, he saw the

surging, wrinkled darkness of the sea. He shuffled along
his perch, trying to keep the sea in sight, and climbed
through an arched doorway that was in the slow process of
becoming a window as the masonry settled away below it.

On the other side he got to his feet and looked around—
and realized that he'd stumbled onto what appeared to be a
long established scavenger's roost. He was on a gently slanting rooftop with a fancy wrought iron railing along the
seaward edge but not even a length of twine to stop a person
from walking off the north or south edges; a number of the
men on the roof had turned toward the arch as he'd clambered through it, and were now looking at him with a variety
of expressions: alarm, anger, speculation and boredom. One
man near Rivas seemed to be about to launch a kite that
had a spread fish-net for a tail, most of the ones by the
railing held fishing poles or binoculars, several were just
sleeping in the sun, and one white-haired old fellow scampered to the north edge of the roof, crouched and then disappeared below the edge—presumably down a ladder—
when Rivas entered.

"What do you want, *hombre?*" asked one lean old man
whose yellowish beard, as Rivas saw when the man stood
up and drew a knife, hung all the way to his belt.

Rivas grinned. "Just want to look at the ocean—and
maybe find somebody to help me drink this." He pulled the
bottle of tequila out of his pouch.

The tension relaxed a little. The old man put his knife
away, stepped forward and grudgingly took the bottle. He
pulled the cork with his teeth and, holding the cork like a
fat cigar, he sniffed the clear liquor. Evidently satisfied, he
spat the cork over the rail and said, "Okay. But if you're
in Blood—"

"Or birdy girls," added a young man with fine blond hair
curling like golden smoke around his head.

"—Then you'll find you've made a mistake coming here," the old man finished.

"Not me," Rivas assured everyone. "I'm just a . . . a bird-watcher."

"What?" exclaimed the man with the kite.

"He's kidding, Jeremiah," said the yellow-bearded man. He tilted the bottle to his mouth, and bubbles gurgled up in it. "Well," he said when he'd lowered it again, "your credentials are in order, sir." He handed the bottle to someone else.

Rivas walked down the slope of the roof to the rail, but its moorings were so corroded-looking that he didn't lean on it. Glancing left, right, and down, he saw why these men had chosen this place for their eyrie; there was deep water a hundred feet below for fishing, and since they were above most of the surrounding structures the rooftop commanded a wide view of the sea. Holding the rail carefully and glancing to his right, Rivas felt his already fluttery stomach become even colder, for he realized that the white building way off there, looking like a cutaway section of a nautilus shell with long-stemmed mushrooms growing all over it, was Deviant's Palace. He looked away quickly, not wanting to let these men guess that his business had to do with that place.

Gradually all the rooftop businessmen resumed their activities, and as the bottle made the rounds the glances turned on Rivas became less suspicious. The man with the net-bearing kite got the thing up into the air and then began skipping back and forth across the rooftop and whistling peculiarly. Another man was watching the course of one particular rowboat and making notes in a little book, and one of the men with binoculars had found something in a nearby window that absorbed him totally. The blond young man kept looking around worriedly, as though he was sup-

posed to have met someone here a while ago. Rivas just
watched the ocean.

He saw any number of boats—a trio of broad ones with
tall structures on their decks, a refitted ferryboat apparently
operating as a seagoing bar and grill, and many fishing boats
clustered around the dark blue patch of ocean where lay the
submarine pit known as the Ellay-Ex Deep, dropping nets
on long lines to haul up the mutant phosphorescent fish that
were so highly prized in some circles—but none of them
was obviously the sort he was watching for, and it occurred
to him that he'd never gotten any kind of good *look* at the
vessel that had brought him up from Irvine. At least a couple
of these boats he'd seen today *could* have been the same
one, or a duplicate.

The anxious young man with the curly hair peered through
the arch where Rivas had entered, then went to the north
edge of the roof and looked down. At last he turned back
to the company and asked, "Did any of you hear the old
man I was with say where he was going?"

"No, kid," said the yellow-bearded man drunkenly. "Fact
I din hear 'm say anything atall."

Far off to his left, just on the horizon, Rivas could see
some ponderous vessel approaching. The sun had just begun
to fall away from the meridian, and he had to squint against
the flickering needles of reflected sunlight.

It was some kind of barge, with strange cowls and fins
all over it. There were masts and rigged sails, but Rivas
felt certain that it was the boat he'd been watching for. Now
all he had to do was note where it docked.

The boy leaned out over the north edge. "Hey?" he yelled.
Rivas was just about to ask one of the men if he could
borrow his binoculars when the boy added, "Lollypop?"

CHAPTER NINE

RIVAS FORCED HIMSELF to do nothing more than look over at the boy, who was still peering around worriedly. He tried to remember what the old man who had left when he'd arrived had looked like. Jeez, he thought. Not too tall, white hair—could have been the same guy. And he didn't let me see his face, though he must have seen mine. And the kid here warned me that I'd better not be after birdy girls.

I'd better assume it's the same guy—and leave here fast, now.

As he backed away from the railing, trying to seem casual, he caught another glimpse of the barge out on the sea, and he thought he saw a row of dangling ropes along its side.

And then something tore across the top of his head so hard that he was flung forward across the railing, which broke loose at one end and swung out away from the rooftop like an outward-opening door, and then bent downward as the hinge end buckled.

With his legs more than his hands Rivas clung, sideways and nearly upside down, to what had been the railing and was now an ill-moored ladder swinging over an abyss. He'd heard the screams as at least two of the other men had tumbled away toward the sea so far below, and a couple of yards above him he could see one other man clinging to the penduluming railing; and beyond the kicking legs of that man he could see the rage-contorted face of old Lollypop himself, who was jigging wrathfully along the edge of the roof, trying to get off a second shot at Rivas with a slingshot he'd no doubt bought in memory of dear dead Nigel.

The slingshot thrummed, the man above him heaved and screamed, and Rivas unclamped his legs from the iron bars and plummeted toward the sea, spinning and flailing and hoping to land feet first, and he heard the mosquito-buzz of another missile passing very close to his head.

The water felt like concrete shattering under him when he hit it, and it punched the air out of his lungs and left him thrashing, weakly, God knew how far under the surface, in a churning cloud of bubbles. He didn't know which way was up until the bubbles stopped shaking and began wobbling in one direction, and then he flapped and kicked himself up after them.

The first thing he did after he broke the surface and shook the hair out of his eyes was crane his neck to look upward, and his eyes widened in horror, for here came Lollypop bicycling down through the air and getting bigger every instant, in a jump that seemed likely to land him right on top of Rivas.

With nearly the last of his strength Rivas lunged spasmodically toward the shore, throwing a bow-wave that was engulfed by the tremendous booming splash as the old man hit the water directly behind him, and the big surging wave from that swept Rivas even further in, as well as knocking out what little air he'd managed to draw into his stunned lungs.

Ahead of him the sea water splashed in shadow around the stout concrete pillars that evidently supported this entire waterfront block. Old nets and hammocks had been strung from column to column and served as perches for at least a dozen children, who were all staring at him in awe. Even in the sudden dimness Rivas could see their baldness, and as he paddled further in under the overhang he noticed too the suggestive wrinkles on their necks and the webbing between the fingers and long toes. He made it to one of the unoccupied nets, the splashing of his progress echoing among the pillars, and he floundered up into it and turned back to face the wide circle of flat white water. He fumbled his knife out and gripped it in his left hand and then sagged limp to let his lungs get themselves straightened out.

Can I kill him? he asked himself. I *have* to . . . but that doesn't mean I'll be able to.

He realized that some of the wetness on his face was blood, and with his knife hand he clumsily felt the top of his head. There was a long ragged scratch there, as if he'd tried to part his hair in the middle with a saw. He shivered and wondered whether he'd even have felt anything if the missile had struck an inch or two lower. When he brought his hand down he saw that some red had got on the knife blade, and he wondered if soon there might be more on it.

He managed to take a deep, shuddering breath. Back in the breathing game, he thought. But for how much longer? With a clarity of imagination he hadn't known he was capable of, he saw his own arm drive the knife toward the old man's throat, felt the blade cut through gristly resistance until his hilt-gripping fingers hit against the Adam's apple, and saw the twitching body slosh back in the water, saw the spreading stain, the round eyes of all these children. . . .

Very slowly, almost without volition, he tucked his knife back into its sheath and pulled his sleeve down over it.

His eyes were on the patch of sea where a thousand little bubbles were still making the water hiss, though the choppiness had rebounded back in and spoiled the momentary flatness. He felt a calm that wasn't entirely of exhaustion, for he was remembering his rush from behind at Nigel five days ago, and the alarmed expression that had been on Nigel's face in the instant before Rivas's club broke his forehead.

The bubbles had mostly disappeared, and the long leisurely waves resumed their pace . . . and Rivas realized, certainly more with relief than with anything else, that old Lollypop would not be resurfacing. Well, he thought, that was quite a jump, and he *was* an old man . . . and who knows, maybe he couldn't swim, maybe he just wanted to explode my skull with his boot heels before he drowned.

Because of *Nigel*. Huh.

Suddenly he remembered the barge he'd seen. My God, he thought, springing up in the net, I've got to see where it docks! See if Jaybush's "temple in the sister city" really is Deviant's Palace. He glanced around and saw stairs way back in the shadows, and he let himself fall back into the water and began swimming toward them.

Several men were sitting on ledges against the inner wall, and there was a narrow boat rocking in the water near them; clearly their business was salvage, and if much more fell down from above they'd be rowing out. But though they turned their expressionless eyes on Rivas, they had obviously decided he wasn't worth bothering with, and he attained the slimy stone stairs with no obstacle but his own weakness. He didn't allow himself time to rest, but hurried up the stairs.

The stairs extended quite a way up, and after three or four ascending circuits of the stairwell he began to see rays of sunlight lancing through the dimness from gaps in the masonry; he stopped to peer through each one that he came to that faced the sea side, but each time there was some close stone or wooden surface blocking his view of the ocean.

At the first landing he ran out onto a wide concrete terrace where a dozen men were laboring at the cranks and capstan bars of a crane, the chain-supported arm of which stretched thirty feet out over the water, and Rivas looked around wildly, trying to orient himself. After a few seconds he spied the dangling roof-railing, way above him and off to his left. There was no one hanging on it now. He looked northwest, but at this lower level a warehouse wall blocked his view of half the ocean—the half that included the barge and Deviant's Palace. For one impetuous moment he thought of running out along the crane arm like a tightrope walker, but the cable being hauled in lay along the top of the boom, and was wet, and kept hitching and jerking.

The workmen were staring at him apprehensively, and he realized that his scalp must still be bleeding. "What's the," Rivas gasped, "quickest way up to where that railing is hanging?"

One of the men frowned. "Some guys fell off there a few minutes ago."

"I *know*." He waved inexpressively. "One of them was *me*. So how do I get back up there?"

After a pause to think about it the man gave him a string of instructions, including one "really *long* jump," and concluded with, "but they'll just throw you off again."

"I wouldn't be surprised," Rivas agreed, hurrying away.

Five minutes later he was climbing up the ladder down which Lollypop had fled at Rivas's previous arrival, and he paused when he was a foot below the edge of the roof. What, he thought, peek? Or scramble right up?

Scramble up, he decided. He got his feet a couple of rungs higher, then grabbed the roof edge and jackknifed up, rolling to his feet as quickly as he could on the slanting roof.

The old man with the long beard stared at him in fuddled surprise. "Didn't happen to bring another bottle?"

Rivas shook his head and, looking around cautiously, shuffled out to the now unrailed western edge.

"Then," said the old man sadly, "your credentials have expired. Hey, kid! Here's the guy your old buddy dove in after!"

Rivas looked back, and his heart sank to see the blond young man stand up resolutely from beside the arch, cuffing tears from his face.

"Aw, hell, kid," Rivas said in a tone of weary, scared exasperation. "*I* didn't do it. He shot at me and then jumped in, remember?"

"He was," the boy said brokenly as he drew a long knife from his belt, "just beginning to . . . forget about . . . Nigel. And then you had to remind him . . . and now he's *dead*."

Rivas flipped back his cuff and got his own knife into his left hand and waved it around, just to make the boy back off. The boy kept advancing. Rivas swore, then turned to look northeast.

The strange barge was, as perhaps he should simply have assumed, at rest beside the white stone centipede of a dock in front of Deviant's Palace.

Quickly he turned back to the roof, and saw that if there had been a chance of getting back down the ladder without a fight, it was gone now. Lollypop's young friend was only a few steps away, clearly waiting for Rivas to move away from the roof edge, and he was warily watching Rivas's knife.

Rivas wondered how the Rivas of a week ago would have handled this. The footing wasn't the greatest up here—

probably he'd have tried a long kick at the boy's knife hand
and, as close to simultaneously as possible, a wide, unaimed
slash that could be relied on to strike somewhere between
forehead and throat.

What he did was smile, sheathe his knife and step off
the edge of the roof.

His fall was controlled this time—he was careful to keep
his body straight and his feet together, and as he took and
held a breath he wondered if the workman by the crane was
watching. When he hit the water and was under it he spread
his arms and kicked to keep from hitting the bottom. He
was pleased with the unruffled way he'd handled it until he
remembered that old Lollypop was drifting around down
here somewhere in the dark water—maybe above him right
now, grinning and reaching for him with cold hands—and
he flinched to the side, swam spasmodically for a few strokes
and then did a panicky thrash up to the surface. This time
when he surfaced and shook the wet hair out of his face,
he looked anxiously *down*. He swam fairly hastily toward
the pillars and when he was in among them in the shadow
of the massive overhanging masonry he became aware of a
spattering sound.

He paused to lift his head and blink around, and he
realized that the mutant children perched in the nets and
hammocks were clapping their webbed hands, clearly hoping he'd do it one more time.

Lisa was standing out on the little pier in front of her
house when Rivas came trudging up the canalside path.
He'd stopped dripping, and his hair wasn't as damply spiky
now, but his shoes still squished when he walked.

"Afternoon, Greg. I gather you fell into the canal last
night; do it again today?"

"The ocean," he said. "Twice."

He'd decided not to approach Deviant's Palace from the

seaward side, not at first, anyway, but to reconnoiter the place by simply walking in the front door. Beyond that he wasn't sure. Order a drink? If the legends were accurate, the place was as much a bar as it was anything else. Ask for a job? He shuddered.

"What are you doing out here?" he asked.

"I keep thinking I hear a hurt animal in the canal. This is the third time I've been out to look." She shrugged and started toward the house. "Oh well." She squinted back at him over her shoulder. "You don't look like you found your person."

"No." Thinking of her carpet, he kicked off his mud-caked shoes on the porch and peeled off his socks.

She looked surprised at the courtesy, but didn't remark on it. "Well," she said, "while you were off looking for somebody, somebody was here looking for you. He left a—" She stopped, and looked at him.

He had frozen in the act of hanging the socks on the porch rail. "A . . . hurt animal," he said.

She nodded. "In the canal. Do you know something about it?"

"Maybe." Jesus, he thought, what does it take to kill one of those things? And I've led it here. "Have you ever heard of, uh, hemogoblins?"

"Yeah," she said, her eyebrows halfway up to her hairline. "Vampire ghosts in the southern hills, right? Is that what I've got in my canal, one of those?"

He straightened up and spread his hands helplessly. "Well, I—yeah, if I had to make a guess. I thought I killed it last night. I twisted its *head* off, for God's sake." He sat on the rail, next to his socks, and stared unhappily at the floor. "I'm sorry, Lisa. I didn't mean to lead it to your place. It's been following me around for days, sneaking up and saying disgusting things to me. I think it'll follow me when I go, but just in case, if you can get any screens for your windows, just for a couple of days, I'd—"

He stopped, for he'd finally looked up at her, and the mixture of pity and apprehension in her eyes startled him. He reviewed the last few things he'd been saying, and suddenly, after one flash of indignant anger, he was laughing— and then a moment later the laughter was shaking him as if it were a pack of invisible dogs, and he had to fall off the rail on one side or the other so he let himself fall in, and he sat rocking and hooting on the boards of the porch floor while tears coursed into his beard and Lisa, backed up to the far rail, smiled twitchily in an effort to keep from joining him; but soon she was laughing as hard as he was.

As the laughter subsided, Lisa stepped away from the rail, pushed a stray lock of hair back from her forehead, and sighed. "Screens," she said weakly. "And some of that spray. Isn't there a spray?"

Rivas snapped his fingers. "Now why didn't I think of this earlier? We'll get a leash on the thing and sell it to somebody as a guard dog."

She giggled. "And . . . and what, something about blood. Do they say pure-blood dogs? I guess not. Still, there's a joke there somewhere." Her smile had worn off. "In the old days, you'd *never* have thought it was funny that somebody thought you were crazy."

"I nearly didn't today."

"But you're not, are you? Crazy?"

"I'm afraid not."

"You *did* twist the head off a vampire out there last night?"

He nodded. "Not easy, with this bad hand."

"What a world." She opened the front door. "There's screens in the shed. I'll put 'em up. Oh, I started to tell you—a guy came looking for you and left a note."

"Not Jack Frenchfry," Rivas groaned, getting to his feet. "Middle-aged, skinny, lechy grin?"

"No," said Lisa from inside the house. "Where'd I put it—here we go." He'd followed her into the kitchen and she handed him an envelope. "This guy had a beard and only looked about twenty-five."

Shaking his head blankly, Rivas tore open the envelope and took out the enclosed card. "Nice paper, hm?" he said.

On the front of the card, in handsome calligraphy, was written, "Mister Gregorio Rivas". He flipped it open. " . . . is invited," the card went on, "to have dinner at eight o'clock tonight at the Venice house of his one-time spiritual father . . . if he knows where the place is; and I can't believe he does not." It was signed, in a different and messy scrawl, "SEV."

Lisa had been peering over his shoulder. "This Sev wouldn't be who you're looking for, would he, Greg?"

"Uh," said Rivas, reflecting that he'd been a fool to let himself be recognized last night. "No. But he knows where she is." His heart was thumping too quickly and his mouth was dry. His hand began to shake and he put the invitation down.

"What's wrong, Greg?" He didn't answer, so Lisa turned to the liquor cabinet and asked as casually as she could, "Will you be accepting this invitation?"

Mechanically Rivas took and drank deeply from the glass of whiskey she handed him. "Aaahrrr," he said quietly, almost conversationally. His face was pale. "Maybe I will," he said wonderingly. "God help me, maybe there isn't any other way . . ."

She looked uneasily at the invitation and then back at Rivas. "Where *is* the place?"

He gave her the ghost of a smile. "Promise not to try to do anything about it?"

"Well . . . okay."

He sighed. "It's Deviant's Palace."

Lisa sat down and had a drink herself, from the neck of the bottle.

A lot of its substance had been lost in the canal—it had been set back *days*. It had expected resistance, certainly, some obstinacy on Rivas's part, but it had not expected *treachery*—for he had taken two steps toward it, obviously intending to cooperate, before suddenly backing away and making that remark about go suck a fish—nor had it expected sudden senseless *violence*.

It bobbed again to the surface and noticed that the sun had set. It rolled its milky eyes toward the house and bared its teeth in a smile. He was back! He must have returned while it had been brooding on the canal bottom. With a lot less effort than would have been required yesterday, the thing kicked its diminished body up into the air, glancing sadly back down at the canal. So much hard-won blood wasted, just spilled into the water! And so much of the thing's substance—intelligence, even, it admitted—gone with it. Well, it promised itself as it drifted back down, I'll catch up with him again, and this time it won't be seduction. It'll be rape.

Suddenly the thing came to a stop in midair, undulating like a fish to stay in one place. There he was! Rivas was leaving the house! The thing spread itself to catch the breeze, and followed.

You can still turn back, Rivas told himself hopefully as he walked away from Lisa's house. More truly than ever, you've earned Barrows's five thousand fifths. Getting this far has all but destroyed you, and now the enemy even knows who and where you are!

But I know who and where he is, too. And at this point I'm afraid I simply can't back away. I don't think it's even for Uri's sake anymore. It's for my own sake. Too many hard-won things will have turned out to be worthless if I don't read the last page. Too many people, including a substantial amount of Gregorio Rivas, will have died for nothing.

He knew that if he hadn't been so devastated by the events of this past week he'd never have dreamed of following this present course, but that knowledge didn't slow his steps. Maybe, he thought wryly, a released stone falls because it *chooses* to.

He'd transferred his knife to a makeshift pocket in the collar of his shirt. It would probably be overlooked in a quick search, and if it should come to seem necessary, one hard slap at his own chest would send it up into his jugular.

There were still streaks of orange in the western sky, though squares and dots of yellow light were beginning to appear in the dark structures around him, and he smiled at the flashy, vulgar, colorful, vital town. I'm not sure I appreciated the place when I lived here, he thought. My focus was always too narrow.

A chair scraped on a darkening second floor balcony, and in the early evening stillness he heard the clink of a bottle on a cup edge, and then a faint splashing. "Evening, man," said a courteous voice.

"Evening," said Rivas, waving up at the balcony.

At Inglewood Street he turned north, and, not having the remotest idea what Jaybush's dinner might consist of, he climbed up onto the wagon of a traveling kushi seller. With a glass of cool beer he munched his way through two skewers of hot teriyaki beef and green onions. The beer and food cost only three jiggers but it tasted wonderful, and as he climbed back down to the pavement Rivas wondered if he'd ever really paid enough attention to food.

He continued north, over a couple of torch-lit canal bridges, and he was glad he'd thought of food when he had, for he'd have been reluctant to eat at any of the ubiquitous restaurants and snack stands in this area. The stuff sizzling in these pans was highly spiced and often couldn't even be distinguished as meat rather than fish or fowl—as if, and it wasn't inconceivable, these cooks had access to some hitherto unknown class of animal. Rivas had always been told to avoid dining spots that didn't have dogs hanging around the kitchen door, but he'd never understood whether the advice meant you'd be better off not eating the product of kitchens that smelled so bad as to repel even dogs, or if it meant that the lack of dogs was the result of the cook's policy of catching any that chanced by and cooking them. In any case he couldn't see any dogs around these places.

Women, and persons who were probably men dressed up as women, smiled peculiarly at him from open doorways, and children with knives offered to give him a cheap shave, and several old Blood freaks who had very evidently not taken off any article of clothing for any purpose for quite a while shambled up and asked him if he had any brandy to spare. As politely as he could, Rivas managed to elude all of them.

The buildings were tall in this area and crowded together with just grudged alleys between, and Rivas knew that direct sunlight probably never got down this far. The pavement was uneven cobbles, either individual stones or crumbled asphalt, and the eternal mud between the pieces was faintly luminous, so that he seemed to be walking on a ghostly spiderweb. Vibrations like bouts of fast drumming shook the walls from time to time, and once he thought he heard a lot of awkward voices raised in atonal song, and always there was the sleepy smack and buzz of the huge flies that nested way up under the eaves.

Rivas had his knife out now and was tapping the blade along the wall as he walked, to let the dwellers within earshot know that he was armed, but after turning west near

Arbor Vitae and winding his way down another hundred
yards of alleys and ladders and half-roofed courts he stopped
doing it, for it was assumed that everyone here was armed,
or else so horribly diseased that their mere proximity was
dangerous.

The pavement had been getting muddier, and when one
of his feet sank to the ankle he knew that there was now
no pavement at all, though the walls crowded in just as
closely on either side. At the frequent cross alleys he looked
both ways, but the few lights he could see were dim and
far away. Somewhere behind him human conversation had
stopped being an element of this dark cityscape. The only
voice sounds he heard now were occasional shouts, screams,
curses and insane laughter, and he couldn't decide whether
he was being paced by someone who paused frequently to
vomit or if there were simply a lot of upset Venetian stomachs tonight.

Finally he came to a section where the mud was uncom-
fortably warm and the walls were a soft claylike stuff that
would hold the tracks of fingers dragged along it, and some
fluid was bubbling out of the cracks between the soggy
bricks. There were hundreds of little shelled animals like
barnacles on the walls and underfoot, waving cilia that stung
when they touched his skin. The entire tunnel—for a flexing, fibrous roof had been put up over the alleys here—
was dimly glowing, and the wet breeze kept changing direction at regular intervals, blowing into his face for several
seconds and then fumbling at the hair on the back of his
head.

There was a collage of smells—hot metal, mildew, bad
teeth—and then the tunnel narrowed to a small ragged opening that he had to scramble up a slope to get to, and then
he'd squeezed through it and leaped clear and was rolling
on cold, gritty, *normal* pavement.

He scrambled to his feet and for a moment he was tempted

to bless himself as his mother had taught him decades ago, for here, separated from him by only one high-arching canal bridge, and beyond that an ascending flight of steps, was Deviant's Palace itself.

CHAPTER TEN

TALL RIDES WHIRLED out front, glaringly lit, as was the building itself, by apparently genuine electric lights that cast a multicolored noon radiance over the waterfront. A big incandescent orange sign crawled across the front of the edifice, and even as Rivas read it, dizzy with incredulity, he wondered if it could have been put up solely for his own benefit, for the words were in the complicated old-time spelling:

DEVIANT'S PALACE
Steaks, Unconventional Seafood, Progressive Cocktails
Meditation Chapel! Petting Zoo! Souvenir Shop!
GIRLS! GIRLS! GIRLS!
Explicit Scenes & Offensive Sounds

A million big flying bugs were battering themselves against the glowing glass tubes.

The stories he'd heard had prepared him for the size of the place—it was huge, stretching away out of sight in either direction, and six or seven stories tall in some places—but had not quite prepared him for the lunacy of the architecture. Everything was rounded or tapering out to spiny points; there were no planes or right angles, and the lavishly applied stucco had the appearance of leathery hide. The many unsymmetrical windows and doors were inset, in arches so ragged and so randomly placed that they seemed to have been made by firing cannons at the walls from within—though each window was covered by an intricately worked grille; a profusion of apparently ornamental arches gave the place a morbidly skeletal appearance, which was not entirely relieved by the hundreds of banners and giant pinwheels and weathervanes. Most of the windows glowed with colored light, and the big front doors were wide open and spilling out a loud two-toned singing, not unlike the Jaybirds' mind-blurring hum.

Rivas ran trembling fingers through his hair and took the invitation out of his pocket. This must be the place, he thought, and started forward. He walked slowly, for each step required an individual choice between continuing and fleeing.

At the top of the bridge he paused to look around. Deviant's Palace, he saw, was the hub of a dozen canals, which all disappeared inside the place through high arches. He descended the far side of the bridge and approached the stairs.

A fat, hooded person scrambled out of a manhole in front of him and blocked his way. In glowing letters on the person's robe front was spelled out: I GOT MY ASHES HAULED AT DEVIANT'S PALACE. "Sorry, sir, invitation only tonight," piped up a sexless voice.

Rivas held up his invitation.

The hooded figure peered at it in the bright electric light. "Well, excuse me, the guest of honor! Just head right on in—you're expected."

The situation had already had a fever-dream unreality to it, but this grotesque courtesy totally disoriented Rivas. "Thank you," he said, and as he went up the steps he actually caught himself wishing he'd shaved.

From overhead he heard a windy sighing, and looking up he saw the wooden gargoyles he'd once heard described. They were writhing and stretching out splintery arms and rolling their heads. Rivas had been told that when the things cried out it was with human voices, but tonight it was just a whispery roaring that he heard, like the voices of the trash men in Irvine.

Through the open doors he could see a carpeted hallway. He shrugged and stepped inside.

In a loop of a canal a few hundred feet from the structure, ripples spread as a corpse drained of blood floated to the surface.

That's a little better, thought the thing under the water. I can think a little more clearly now. So he thinks he can lose me by going into that place, does he? Think again, Gregorio.

It swam closer, already faintly uncomfortable with the burning and itching, in spite of the shielding water around it. He *knows* I hate these places, it thought. That's why he keeps going to them. But once I've got him, we'll go where *I* want to go.

It looked back and up at the floating corpse, wishing the old drunk had had more vitality. That's what I need, it thought. If I could drain somebody strong, then I could become so strong myself, and solid, that I could simply beat Rivas into submission.

The thing shivered with pleasure at the thought.

Well, it told itself, get moving. You don't want Rivas to die before you can catch up to him. It kicked its froggy feet and swam toward one of the arches in the wall of Deviant's Palace.

Another hooded figure approached Rivas as soon as he'd entered the low hall.

"We meet again, Mister Rivas!" came a woman's voice from inside the cowl. "The Lord will be pleased that you could attend on such short notice." The hood was flung back and Sister Sue smiled crazily at him. "You should be flattered," she said. "He nearly never troubles himself to invite anyone. Generally he just lets them *drift* west."

Rivas had managed to control, and, he hoped, conceal, his instant impulse to run. Right at the moment, he told himself firmly, there are many more dire things to fear than this girl. "Well hello, Sister Sue," he said, deciding he might as well enter into the spirit of the evening. "Uh . . . what an unexpected pleasure."

With a clever but completely unconvincing imitation of vivacity she took his arm and led him up the hall. "During our brief acquaintance," she said, "I've gathered that you're fond of music and drink. The former, as you perceive, is provided." Evidently she meant the two-tone hum. "Might we furnish you with some of the latter?"

All at once the whole awkwardly stilted pretense, from the calligraphic invitation to Sister Sue's nearly impenetrable imitation of high society speech, made Rivas vaguely sick. "Yes, thanks," he said tiredly. "Tequila neat, please." At least the offer of a drink was an indication that they didn't intend to hit him with the sacrament. The smell of the sea seemed to be even stronger inside the building.

She led him down the hall to a flight of stairs and down these to a beautifully tiled but lopsided arch, and simultaneously a drink was put into his hand and he stepped through the arch.

He nearly dropped the glass. He was standing on a sort of dock at the bottom of a vast cathedral of a chamber, and he almost thought he was outside again because of the damp chill and a faint mist that made the ceiling hard to see. Colored lamps dangling on long chains set the mist aglow and cast highlights on the broad and apparently deep pool that was most of the floor. Wide tiers with tables and chairs on them ringed the ascending walls at uneven intervals, and bridges spanned the gulf in several places. The arch Rivas had walked out through was the smallest of at least a dozen that ringed the chamber, and with a thrill of panic Rivas realized that the whole place looked inadequately supported—the tiers, the bridges, the vast expanses of inward-sloping stone far above his head; the structure, it seemed to Rivas, needed many more pillars.

Big polygonal rafts drifted on the surface of the lagoon like leaves on a pond, and as Rivas's eyes grew accustomed to the soaring volume of the place and able to focus on smaller things, he saw that there were chairs and a table and candles, and in most cases a party of diners, on each raft. Waiters in little gondolas sculled among them, occasionally raising waves and drawing curses from the diners.

One raft held steady, perhaps anchored, way out in the middle of the lagoon, and instead of a table it had a ring of holes cut in it. All the holes were empty except the bigger central one, in which bobbed something that Rivas thought was a leather beanbag chair. The smell on the chilly air, he noticed, was the same one he'd encountered in Irvine—a mix of fish and garbage.

Sister Sue rang a bell mounted on the arch beside them, and though the silvery note wasn't loud, conversation stopped at all the tables. The monotonous singing stopped too, and the thing Rivas had thought was a beanbag chair straightened up, revealing itself to be the unsubmerged top half of a man—bald, brown, and fatter than Rivas would have thought a person could get.

"Mister Rivas," came a glutinous whisper that echoed among the canal arches. "So good of you to come." And Rivas realized that this must be his host, Norton Jaybush himself, Lord of Irvine and Venice.

Rivas remembered the drink in his hand, and took a sip of it. It was tequila all right, and the peppery bite of it was reassuring, evidence that a sane world did still exist somewhere outside. "Mister Jaybush, I think," he said loudly; but when his voice echoed back at him he realized that he could speak in a conversational tone and still be heard throughout the enormous chamber—evidently the place had been built with acoustics in mind. "Or should I say Mister Sevatividam? High time we met." Cool, he thought with some cautious satisfaction. Very cool.

One of the gondolas swept up to the dock, and the boatman's pole flexed as he brought the boat to a halt. With a smile, Rivas solicitously took Sister Sue's elbow as if to help her aboard, but she smiled back—with such joyful malice that his smile became a wince—and said, "You first, brother."

The boatman held the gondola steady while Rivas maneuvered himself and his drink into it, and then Sister Sue swung in behind him. She prodded his back with something hard, and said cheerfully, "The Lord wants you alive, so I won't shoot to kill—but if you want to mess around, I'll be happy to ruin your elbow."

"I'm sure it'd get you all excited," Rivas agreed.

Again the gondolier flexed the long pole against the pool wall, and the little boat surged smoothly out onto the face of the water. They passed a raft of diners, and Rivas glanced at them curiously. They were an oddly mixed lot—some were just filthy Blood freaks that somebody had dressed up in tinfoil hats and red monkey jackets, but others had the narrow faces and elegant dinner clothes of aristocracy—but for some reason the faces of all the alert ones wore expressions of alarm as they returned Rivas's stare.

Though he was keeping his face twisted in a smile that he hoped looked more confident than nervous, he was estimating how many ways there might be to get out of here. Somehow the idea of drawing his knife and using Jaybush as a hostage didn't seem feasible; the man was far too fat to be moved readily, and touching him would probably subject one to an unsought dose of the sacrament. Sue, and no doubt others too, had guns, so swimming back to the dock entrance was out. But these arches obviously connected this lagoon to the canals outside. It might be possible to swim out through one of them.

And in through one of the eastern arches a thing came swimming, several yards under the water's surface, its big eyes peering at the wobbling patches of light overhead. It paused, its head turning on its stalk neck as it scanned the many rafts up there.

The gondola was nearing Jaybush's raft, and Rivas reluctantly met the gaze of his host. The man's eyes were nearly hidden in folds of fat, but Rivas could see mild humor in them, as though Jaybush was finding tonight's proceedings tolerably amusing. A parent attending a school play, thought Rivas.

"You've learned some things, sir," Jaybush rumbled. "But be careful. Knowledge is a toxin. Why, just the fact of your having spoken my true name means that quite a number of these people must die tonight." A smile widened

the huge pumpkin head as Jaybush looked around at the
many rafts. Rivas was a little surprised that none of the
diners did anything more than look unhappy at this news.

The gondola bumped up alongside the raft. "Out you go,
brother," said Sister Sue.

Rivas finished his drink, leaned out and set the glass
down on the wooden surface of the raft, and then managed
to follow it without falling into the water. He crouched
awkwardly on the raft, hoping that everyone couldn't see
how it made him tremble to be this close to the thing called
Jaybush.

There was, he could see now, a submerged chair hung
below each of the round holes cut in Jaybush's raft. "Do
please be seated," his host told him.

"Uh...right. Thanks." Rivas lowered himself into one,
now feeling ridiculous as well as scared. The water was
cold.

Sister Sue climbed out of the gondola with effortless
agility and slithered into another hole across the raft from
him. Her smile was as sunny as ever, and she held an
automatic pistol with relaxed familiarity.

Jaybush, bobbing in the big central hole like some disagreeable centerpiece, beamed at him. "Well!" said the Messiah. "As you say, it is high time we met. I believe, in fact,
sir, that you know me better than anyone else does. A
number of people have taken both Blood and the sacrament,
but you are the very first, I believe, to have developed
procedures to shield yourself from their effects! Even in,"
he paused to wink ponderously, *"other places,* no one ever
attained the insight into my nature that you have."

Rivas grinned unhappily, for he'd just recognized an
important reason for his having accepted the invitation—
to show off. He had wanted to let this interstellar limpet
eel know that he had indeed learned its secrets. If he had

simply ignored the invitation and gone back to Ellay, not only would Uri be doomed, but Sevatividam would think Rivas hadn't been bright enough to figure the invitation out.

"Do you see the men with rifles on the small rafts around the pool's periphery?" Jaybush went on. "They are, like the jaybush you encountered at the Cerritos Stadium, deaf. Not for the same reason, but just so that, in case the very direst sort of secrets are revealed here tonight, requiring the deaths of all hearers except myself and conceivably you, I won't be left unattended." He caught Rivas's glance at Sister Sue. "Yes, my boy," Jaybush said, "even our dear Sister Sue will have to die if certain things are spoken aloud."

Sister Sue's smile didn't falter.

Rivas discovered that he was not tempted to shout, for example, *He's a psychic vampire from outer space!* . . . and he thought he caught a glint of surprise in her eyes.

"And," said Jaybush, "since you have learned such an unprecedented amount about me, I'm going to make an unprecedented offer to you." He was smiling—everybody at the table was smiling—and Rivas couldn't tell if he really did have some kind of offer to make or was simply playing with him. God, the man was fat! "I want you to join me," Jaybush said.

"Merge with the Lord?" Rivas asked drily.

"No, not merge with—*link* with. I'm sure you've often seen people with undeveloped twins attached to or imbedded in their bodies. I'm offering you the opportunity to become such an appendage—psychic rather than physical, of course—to me." He chuckled. "And another five or six of our guests have become dead people."

Several of the guests called for drinks, and Rivas raised his hand, too. "Why don't we let the remaining people go?" he asked, wishing he'd thought of it before.

"How many of you would like to leave?" Jaybush asked.

No one spoke and no hands were raised. He waited until Rivas's fresh tequila was brought, then said, "How does my offer sound?"

Rivas took a long thoughtful sip. "Let's see," he said finally. "It sounds insincere, impossible, and definitely, absolutely unattractive."

There were gasps from the surrounding rafts, and even Sister Sue looked a little shocked.

Jaybush, though, just laughed good-naturedly, the fruity *ho-ho-ho* echoing away into the upper reaches of the huge chamber, where other imperiled guests peered down from the high tiers and bridges. "Ah. Well, I'll explain it to you more fully—to the further decimation of our guests—over dinner, eh?"

That must have been a cue, for a waiter now piloted a gondola up to the raft and deftly laid big plastic-sealed menus in front of Sister Sue, Rivas, Jaybush and two of the presently empty holes. Rivas looked at Jaybush and cocked an eyebrow.

"Ah, my dear fellow," Jaybush said, "you and Sister Sue being old friends, I was beginning to feel left out! So there will be some feminine company for myself, too—and since there's so much of me, heh heh heh, I get *two* girls."

Rivas's instant suspicion was confirmed when he looked beyond the grinning Messiah. A bigger gondola was being sculled toward Jaybush's dining raft, and the two women passengers were Sister Windchime and—though he had to squint and wait until it got closer to be sure—Urania Barrows. Uri had obviously been weeping recently; Sister Windchime looked paler and more drawn than she had when she and Rivas had ridden together to the Regroup Tent, but her mouth was a firm, straight line.

"*Ah,* but I see you know these young ladies also! You *do* get around, don't you, sir?" Jaybush leaned back and indulged in a fit of laughter that set his corpulent body jiggling like a rack of *carne asada* on a windy day in the meat market.

"Why are they here," Rivas asked in a voice he managed to keep even.

"Simply to brighten the conversation," said Jaybush, spreading his palms ingenuously, "and to serve as examples and illustrations in a story or two I might tell."

When their gondola stopped beside the raft the gondolier whispered to the two women, and Sister Windchime climbed across and settled into one of the vacant holes, but Uri shook her head and fresh tears ran down her cheeks.

"Please," she said brokenly, "couldn't I just go back to the—"

The boatman touched the back of her neck, and she gasped in sudden pain and then climbed obediently onto the raft and, with a splash that wetted her four raft mates, seated herself.

Rivas's left hand had gone to his right sleeve before he remembered that he'd transferred his knife to the improvised pocket under his collar; and now the boatman was poling his craft away and all Rivas could do was clench his jaws together very hard.

"There we are," said Jaybush fondly. He picked up his menu and then glanced around with raised eyebrows, so the others, even Uri, did the same.

Rivas was not surprised to see, when he glanced at the menu, that Deviant's Palace specialized in the more *outré* forms of Venetian dining.

"I think," said Jaybush to the waiter, who had been holding his little boat steady since presenting the menus, "that I'll have the sport bass livers in film-darkening sauce. Though," he added genially to the others, "I don't think I'd recommend such hot food for the rest of you." He turned to Sister Sue.

"Un plato de legumbres," she said, handing her menu to the waiter.

Sister Windchime had been studying the menu, and Rivas realized that she could read—like her horseback riding, it was not a common skill. *"Y para mi la gallena en mole, por favor,"* she said.

Uri was blinking around unhappily. Clearly she hadn't recognized Rivas. "I don't know," she quavered; "I guess a couple of tacos. Soft shell, and with extra cheese but no salsa." And it occured to Rivas that he couldn't remember whether Uri knew how to read or not.

It was his turn. May as well get something good, he thought, since it's probably my last meal. "Let's see," he said, raising one eyebrow like an actor trying to look judicious. The incongruity of the whole scene—the possibly naked fat man in front of him, the underwater chairs, the handsomely printed menus, the formal clothes and tinfoil hats of the diners on the other rafts, the prospect of eating poisonous food with the finest spices and sauces—made him want to giggle hysterically. "I'd like the *camarones al diablo,* please."

"Ah, sir," said the waiter with a regretful smile, "that is available only with sport shrimp." He held up his hands to show how big the sport shrimp were.

"Fine," said Rivas with an airy wave. "And with that, a couple of bottles of Dos Equis."

"And a bottle of Santa Barbara Riesling for the ladies," added Jaybush, "and for myself and the gentleman a bottle of tequila and a pitcher of *sangrita."*

The man nodded, collected the rest of the menus and poled the gondola away.

"Though I didn't know what it was at the time," remarked Jaybush to Rivas, "I could feel you participating in my memories when you used agony to clarify and disarm your inadvertent dose of Blood." He pointed his finger at a couple of guests in turn, his thumb vertical and bending as he said, "Bang, bang." Turning back to Rivas he went on, "So I think you'll understand what I'm about to say. I have found knowledge in this place—technology—which, though presently neglected and disordered, leads me to believe that the shedding of the host body and the expenditure of personal energy involved in . . . leaving a place, can be avoided. You see? I'm convinced that it's possible to preserve the body, to construct a machine to shelter it and carry it to . . . the next place."

Rivas just managed to restrain himself from saying, *Space travel!* Instead he just nodded.

"You understand what I mean," said Jaybush with an approving nod. "And if you happened to glance southeast during your trek through the Holy City's back yard, you probably saw my Cape Canaveral. Bang! Bang! Bang! And I know you've had conversations with one of the inadvertent castings known as . . . well, you know what I mean. And you know the healing and recuperative powers it has, through me. So you see what I'm offering you, dear boy, is immortality, and unimaginable travel, and more knowledge than any entity other than myself has ever had!"

Rivas took another sip of his drink, and shook his head more in wonder than refusal. "Perhaps I," he said slowly, "withdraw the 'impossible.' Let's look at the 'insincere.' Why *me?* What's in it for *you?*"

"Well! As far as what's in it for me, I'll tell you frankly that I'm spread just a bit thin at the moment, a trifle overextended; like a farmer with vast fields of ripe crop but no field hands or horses and only a couple of bushel baskets. And, too, ten years ago I foolishly indulged in the, uh, *extravagance* that left the Holy City paved in glass. Bang! Bang!"

Rivas nodded, remembering Jaybush's memory of the sudden unexpected white flash.

"So," the Messiah went on, "I'd find it useful to have a full partner, rather than just a lot of uninformed employees, who could travel back and forth between here and Irvine—bang!—and make sure everything's proceeding efficiently, and perhaps give me useful advice from the point of view of an intelligent and informed native. We could present you as a sort of latter-day Saint Paul—once a merciless scourge of the true faith, but now, enlightened and forgiven, one of its stoutest pillars! I like it. Greg, Greg, why do you persecute me?" He chuckled hugely.

"And," he said, "as to the question of why *you*—my dear fellow, you underestimate yourself! I learned something about you, too, during our brief psychic linking. Why, in all my travels, I swear to you, never have I encountered such a fellow soul! Confess, confess—you too find other entities interesting only to the extent that they might give you pleasure or hindrance. Like me you consume with greedy haste everything you can get from them, and are indifferent to what may become of them afterward; you are in fact sickened by the sight of them afterward, like being forced to linger over the chilling, congealing remains of a dinner! And, like me, your real focus of attention, shorn of peripheral poses and pretences, is the one thing, the only thing, worth an eternity of regarding—*yourself*. You and I understand each other perfectly, boy. We could, without *having* to simulate any *affection* for each other, help each other considerably. *We* don't merge with anyone, boy. We consume. You and I are always distinct, undiluted, individual. Quanta rather than arbitrary segments of a continuum." Jaybush laughed harshly. "We're two of a kind."

Rivas stared across the deck table at the fat smiling face and knew that no one had ever understood him as thoroughly.

"And is," said Jaybush, "the offer still—how did you put it—'definitely, absolutely unattractive'?"

"No," said Rivas.

Neither of the women at the table had seemed to be paying any particular attention to the conversation—Uri had been staring earnestly into Jaybush's face whether he was speaking or not, and Sister Windchime had been just as intently staring at her hands, wearing the expression of pained tenseness of someone who's just swallowed a too-big mouthful—but now Sister Windchime looked up and met Rivas's glance, and the look of hurt and betrayal in her eyes had doubled.

Jeez, kid, thought Rivas, I'm *agreeing* with your damned Messiah, your precious god.

The gondola was back, laden with steaming trays, and the waiter dextrously put the right plates in front of the right people and set out the drinks.

"But I'm afraid," Rivas added, touching the sewn-in lump under his collar for reassurance, "I'm going to refuse."

Jaybush, a forkful of some glowing trash halfway to his bulging mouth, paused to smile tolerantly. "Are you *sure*, my boy? Tell papa why."

Rivas downed the remainder of his tequila and refilled his glass. "Well," he said almost comfortably, sure now that he would never leave Deviant's Palace alive and that nothing he could say would change anything, "because of . . . a bald boy who died on a garbage heap. And a pile of old stove parts that died on a glass plain. And a murdering pimp who evoked, and died out of, loyalty. And a whore with a sense of justice. Am I boring you? And because of Sister Windchime, who has compassion, though you've tried hard to stamp it out of her. And because the hard selfish part of Greg Rivas is swimming around in a canal someplace."

"I understand, my boy," said Jaybush gently, putting down his fork. "What you need is to see a little show, isn't it?"

"No," said Rivas unsteadily.

"I know you don't mean that." Jaybush smiled and clapped his blubbery hands and raised his voice and called, "I need some volunteers from the audience!" As if all twitched by the same string, half a dozen people leaped up from chairs at various tables.

"One of the waiters is bringing around a boat," Jaybush called to them. "I'd appreciate it if you'd all get into it, and he'll bring it to a spot right in front of this raft."

Rivas watched as the six people, three of whom were women, stepped one by one into the boat the waiter was towing around the lagoon behind his gondola. At last the boat, with all of them on it now, was left rocking gently in front of Jaybush's raft table.

"Hi!" Jaybush called to the boat's occupants.

"Hi," they all responded.

"How's everybody feeling? Glad to be here?"

An overlapping chorus replied, "Sure!" "You bet!" "Damn right!"

"Glad to hear it," Jaybush assured them. "Now I want all of you to pay attention, okay? Please stand up—carefully, don't want you all tumbling into the water—and each of you look straight at me and hold out your hands, palms up, as if you were carrying a dish."

Smiling cheerfully, the six people did as they were told, and after some jostling and elbowing they all stood facing Jaybush's raft and holding out cupped hands.

"Do you know what you're holding?" Jaybush asked.

They shook their heads, glanced at each other, shook their heads again. Rivas suspected that they'd been hypnotized.

"What each of you is holding is his or her own face," said Jaybush forcefully. "You're all standing there holding your faces in your hands, and the fronts of your heads are

as smooth as eggs! You're all absolutely identical! Good
heavens, don't any of you *drop* your face, or get it switched
with someone else's!"

None of the people moved, beyond some shiftings of
weight and licking of lips, but now they were agitated, tense.
Their hands were claws.

"You can't even speak!" marveled Jaybush. "You're just
egg things." He picked up a salt shaker and tossed it into
the water. His face was placid, but he put panic into his
voice as he said, "You dropped them! You've all dropped
your faces in the water!"

All six of the people instantly leaped into the water,
splashing Jaybush's raft and sending their boat rocking away.

"And are you, sir," asked Jaybush, turning to Rivas,
"holding on securely to your own face?"

"Yes." Rivas peered down at the agitated water.

"Ah. Never any uncertainty about who it is in the mirror?
Here's a question—if there's no mirror around, do you still
have a face? Are you sure?" He followed the direction of
Rivas's gaze. "Oh! Oh, no, my boy, they won't be coming
back up. Would you?"

Involuntarily Rivas again touched the lump under his
collar. "I . . . don't know."

"Identities can erode," Jaybush said. "I'm offering you
the chance to armor yours and preserve it forever—but they
can erode." He extended one fat finger and leaned toward
Sister Windchime. "Merge with the—"

"No," said Rivas sharply.

Urania had stopped chewing her taco and was looking
alarmed again.

Jaybush glanced at Rivas in feigned surprise. "I beg your
pardon?"

"Don't give her the sacrament."

Sister Windchime hadn't moved, but was staring hard at

nothing and holding her fork so tightly that her knuckles were white.

"But you'd benefit too," Jaybush told Rivas. "We'd share, if we were linked. I'm in a mood to consume both these girls tonight, right down to the core, and bequeath two more pocalocas to the Venice streets. Bang! Bang! Of course, if my *partner* objected, I wouldn't do it. Are you my partner?"

Rivas was somehow certain that if he said "Yes" now, he would not be able to take it back later; so he pursed his lips and rapidly whistled the first ten notes of *Peter and the Wolf* while simultaneously doing a gunning drum accompaniment with his knife and fork against the tabletop—and then a number of things happened all at once: Jaybush collapsed unconscious, Sister Sue registered clear surprise for the first time that evening, and a slingshot-propelled stone the size of a golf ball slammed hard into Rivas's solar plexus. He was knocked back almost out of his seat, and for a moment he hung half off the raft, staring down—then his pain-clenched muscles relaxed and he slumped back down and forward across his plate, sending huge sport shrimps rolling away across the table, and he lay that way for a while, gagging and retching to get air into his abused lungs. He'd glimpsed something in the water below him, but the agony in his chest left him no attention for it.

When, still wheezing, Rivas straightened up, Jaybush had recovered and was blinking around. "Well!" said the fat man with somewhat forced joviality. "You did it, boy. As surely as if you'd cut her throat with a knife. I'm sorry, Sister Sue, but Rivas has killed you."

Sister Sue smiled brilliantly at Rivas and caressed her automatic.

Urania, who didn't seem to be following much of this, stared. "Rivas? Greg?"

Rivas nodded, and then managed to choke out, "Yes."

A moment later he was able to add, "Came to . . . rescue you." He looked at Jaybush. "That's why . . . no musicians in the renaissance you . . . artificially induced for us? Because music . . . renders you unconscious?"

Jaybush waved his massive arms. "You're all dead!" he called up to the people on the tiers and bridges. He waved at the people on the other rafts. "Everyone!" He lowered his arms and remarked to Rivas, "Yes, that's why. And it's why I still try to suppress it, and why the pocalocas stomp anybody who even whistles a tune. It isn't *all* music that does it, but I believe a blanket policy is best. It's mainly the irregular rhythms you call *gunning,* and melodies with the kind of notes they used to call accidentals. Apparently my brain waves correspond in some fashion to your musical scale and times, and are damped out by certain violations of them. If you do that again, of course, my deaf guards will silence you again, and I'll have them bind and gag you so that you needn't feel called upon to interfere when I set about draining these two ladies in the most pleasurable way." He smiled. "You know, in the buoyancy of salt water I am surprisingly agile, which of course is why I like to have a lot of canals available to me." His smile grew broader and more kindly. "I really think we understand each other. And I don't see why you should need time to consider my really very generous offer, so I won't give you any time."

He extended his finger again toward Sister Windchime. "Will you link with me or not? Answer!"

Rivas remembered the glimpse he'd got of the water under the raft, and belatedly he realized what he'd seen down there. At first he'd assumed that it was the drifting corpse of one of the face-divers . . . but it had been moving.

He remembered Sevatividam's unease—outright fear, in fact—when the planet of the floating globes and walruslike creatures had been picked clean; the walrus things were all dead, but there were hungry things swimming among the fallen globes . . . sentient replicas of the original creatures, each one accidentally formed when one of the originals had received Sevatividam's touch while in extreme pain . . . and Sevatividam had feared them, for though attempting to drain *him* would kill any venturesome replica, totally overload it, the process would harm Sevatividam too . . .

Rivas bit his middle knuckle thoughtfully—and bit a section of skin right off, though he was careful not to wince. Then he lowered his hand into the water below his submerged chair and let the blood leak into the water.

Forgive me, he thought, trying to project the thought, as thoughts had been projected at him when, four days ago, his soul had hung bodiless in the sky over the Regroup Tent. *I'm yours,* he thought now, *come and take me. I'm sorry I hurt you, sorry I fled from you. Come take my blood.*

Sevatividam's finger moved closer to Sister Windchime.

"Wait," Rivas snapped. He'd felt a surge in the water under his hand. "I'll give me to you—the part of me you're interested in, anyway."

"My dear boy," said Sevatividam, lowering his hand.

Rivas felt teeth clamp onto his hand. He turned his surprised gasp into a smile—and then, contorting like a man trying very hard to strike a match on the seat of his pants, he yanked the hemogoblin up through the hole.

In the instant of general stunned surprise he flung the squealing thing directly into Sevatividam's face, and as a follow-through to the action he rolled forward out of his submerged seat, somersaulted across the raft—aware of the *bang* and aspirated *thop* of bullets being lashed past very close to him—and dove into the water, drawing his knife with his bitten left hand as he sank.

He had no idea what to do now. He had probably got himself and Uri and Sister Windchime killed, but he was certain they'd all been doomed anyway.

Then he was jarred by a solid boom and rattle of bubbles. Something big had impacted very hard with the water. There were further booms as more stuff crashed in, and thinking that whatever was going on might at least be distracting the gunmen, he kicked up to the surface.

It was even noisier out in the air than it had been under water. There were mountainous rendings and crackings from overhead, and the long screams of people falling, and the evidently random pop and ricochet of gunfire, but Rivas's attention was drawn to the raft he'd vacated moments ago—and not just because of the pain-convulsed figure of Sister Sue, who had clearly caught at least one of the bullets meant for Rivas.

A man trying to scream while inflating a balloon would probably have produced sounds like the ones Sevatividam was making now, and as Rivas blinked up at the spectacle he saw Sevatividam's bulk visibly diminishing. The Messiah's narrowing arms were tearing at a luminous membrane that covered his head, and during the couple of seconds it took Rivas to swim to the raft and scramble back aboard, the membrane—which was twitching and pulsing independent of Sevatividam's wrenching at it—doubled the intensity of its glow, then tripled it, and then began actually to flicker with pale flames.

Another thing rushed down through the smoky air and exploded a splash when it hit the water, and Rivas realized that it was masonry, that the whole structure was coming down. Because Sevatividam was losing power?

Sister Windchime had already got up out of her chair, and Rivas shouted at Uri, "Up! Come on! We've got to get out of here!"

Uri sobbed and extended her hands—one of which still clutched the remains of a taco—toward Jaybush. "Lord, save us!" she wailed.

Rivas put down his knife, drew back his left hand and balled it into a fist, and then carefully gave her a solid downward punch next to her chin. Her mouth was knocked open, but clacked shut again when her head hit the table. "Get a boat," he shouted to Sister Windchime, "and get her and you into it." He retrieved his knife and turned to Jaybush. A bullet sang past and actually stung the end of his nose, so he crowded closer to the Messiah, almost hugging him.

It hurt to be that close, for the hemogoblin was definitely burning now, but through its dazzlingly vaporizing substance Rivas could see Sevatividam's eyes glaring specifically up at him, full of agony but full of promise too.

Rivas winked at him and drove the knife blade through the clinging hemogoblin into the tanned slab of chest, digging around a bit before finding a gap between the ribs.

A strange thing happened when he drew the blade out; as if he'd reached into a tub of water and stabbed a hole in the bottom, the burning hemogoblin began draining into Sevatividam. Now there was fear in the pouchy eyes, and something like . . . pleading?

Not certain that it was by his own volition, Rivas now swiped the blade across the corded throat, and after the first hard-propelled gout of blood had burst out and rocked him back, and he'd dragged his sleeve across his eyes to be able to see again, he saw an angular object about the size of a thumb joint emerge from the opened throat and hover unsupported in the air in front of his face.

It quivered, and the blood disappeared from it in a fine spray, and he saw that it was a crystal.

Behind him Sister Windchime had found a gondola and wrestled Uri's bulk into it—the gunfire had stopped, but the rain of stone was getting worse, the water was choppy, the air full of splash spray, and the night sky more and more visible beyond the buckling walls and ceiling—but Rivas slowly reached out and took hold of the crystal.

Instantly there was a voice in his head: *Swallow me. You win. You're the boss. I'll work for you. Swallow me.*

He knew what it would mean—to live forever, always knowing who he was, with a cozy border between what was himself and what wasn't, never to be hurt; in fact, never to be touched.

A week ago he might have been tempted. He pushed the crystal into the tequila bottle and firmly corked it.

He turned around. Sister Windchime was in the gondola with Uri and was clutching the edge of the raft, but not patiently. Rivas tossed the bottle into the little boat and started forward. The light was bad with most of the hanging lamps extinguished, and so though he heard the hollow coughlike sound of another section of roof giving way, and even looked up in useless alarm, he never saw the piece of stone that came tumbling down through the smoke-fouled air and broke his head.

Chapter Eleven

THE GANG OF pocalocas, most of them squinting in the noonday sun but a few staring wide-eyed, hurried wrathfully down the street where the singing had seemed to come from. People skipped out of their way into doorways, and then when they'd passed peered after them nervously.

Crouched on a fire escape high above them, Urania Barrows watched them disappear around the corner. When they were gone she shivered, and clung more tightly to her perch because her eyes weren't focusing. The pocalocas were gross dirty creatures, Urania knew that, but every time a gang of them strode past she found herself wanting to join them, graft herself smoothly onto the group. She sensed that they had something she used to have, something she missed now.

After some length of time the blurriness passed and she

uncramped her hands, and she remembered how mean Barbara could get when she dawdled around like this, so she scrambled hastily back down the old iron ladders to the street, and then walked quickly in the direction opposite to the course of the pocalocas until she came to Barbara's donut wagon.

Barbara must have been watching for her, for when Urania was two strides away from the wagon she opened the rear door and reached down a hand to help her in.

"Thanks, Sister Windch—" Urania began.

"It's Barbara now," the other woman said when Urania had climbed inside and shut the door. "You've got to remember that. Did you take 'em far?"

"Three, four blocks," said Urania, leaning against the wall across from the occupied bunk and blinking in the sudden dimness.

"In which direction?"

Urania shook her head tiredly. "I don't know about directions, I—"

"West is behind us," interrupted Barbara. "East is forward. North is toward the canal and south is toward the grocery shop."

"I thought north was always straight ahead."

Barbara closed her eyes for a moment. She opened them and repeated, "In which direction?"

"Uh . . . behind us . . . toward the ocean."

"That's lucky, anyway." Barbara glanced at the unconscious bandaged head of Rivas, then frowned and crossed to the bunk he was lying in.

Urania had begun to drift toward the sugar-powdery *churros* that Barbara had cooked this morning, but paused to see what she was doing. "Is he dead?"

"I thought he moved," said Barbara. "Get me a damp cloth."

"Okay, in a minute. *Ow!* Okay! Jeez, you don't have

to . . ." She lost the thought, looked around blankly, and then started toward the *churros* again.

"Damp cloth! Now!"

"Jeez, you just got to ask." Urania dipped a towel in a bucket, wrung it out and brought it over to the bunk. "Here, Sis—I mean, Barbara." She smiled happily at having got the name right.

"Thank you." Windchime wiped the parts of Rivas's face not covered by the bandage.

Urania got her donut at last, then watched. "You ever figure out whether it's him that keeps drawing the pocalocas, or that?" She pointed to the shelf where stood the half-full bottle of tequila with the crystal suspended in it.

"I'm not sure. I think it's the thing in the bottle. I think they can sense where it is."

"Well, why don't we throw it away?"

"Because," said Barbara, obviously tired of repeating this, "he saved it. It may be important. We've got to hold it for him until he wakes up."

Urania swallowed some donut. "He's real sick. Shouldn't we just leave him and the bottle with a doctor? We can't take care of him as well as a doctor. He'd thank us for leaving him with one, I bet."

"The doctor we took him to told us everything that needs to be done. He said that he actually has a better chance under our care than he would in that awful hospital."

"But taking care of sick people isn't our job! Jeez, it's been two days he just lays there and needs cleaning up like a damn baby."

Barbara rounded on her. "He *saved your life!* He's trashed himself—starved, sick, fingers missing, split head—to save you. He wound up saving me, too, and maybe himself, maybe to some extent himself . . . but he *did* it for *you.* He—" She looked down at Rivas with an unreadable expression and added in a whisper, "he killed God for you."

"Well excuse me for living," said Urania indignantly.

"You knew him?" asked Barbara after a pause. "From what he said at the dinner I gathered you knew each other once."

Urania nodded. "A long time ago."

"Arf barf," said Rivas.

Windchime turned back to him and crouched beside the bunk. "Rivas?" she asked urgently. "Can you hear me?"

Rivas muttered indistinctly and seemed to laugh.

Barbara turned to Urania. "Why don't you try talking to him."

Urania took her place. "Hi, Greg. This is Uri, remember?"

There was such a long pause that she was about to speak again, but finally he said, "Yeah." He opened his eyes, narrowly, as if the wagon's interior was very brightly lit. "Long time," he croaked. His voice was rusty, but there seemed to be contempt in it. "Thirteen years. I've been unconscious thirteen years."

"Oh, naw, Greg," said Urania. "It's just been two days."

"Jaybush," he said softly. "And I thought I left him behind when I was twenty-one. Ten years ago. But I've just been sort of a . . . what, wandering disciple or something." He subsided, then suddenly opened his eyes and tried to sit up. "Jesus," he choked, nearly passing out, "where's his crystal, where is he? That can't—"

Barbara touched his shoulder and pointed at the bottle on the shelf. "There."

"Ah." He relaxed, sweating with relief. "Good. Don't uncork it."

"What is it?" Urania asked. "You said 'he'? Is that the Lord, in that tequila bottle?"

Rivas glanced from Urania to Barbara. "How birdy are you ladies?" he asked.

Barbara frowned deeply. "Coming out of it," she said. "Now I . . . *know* he w-w-wasn't really God. I mean, I *know* it, but . . ."

Urania shook her head sadly, staring at the tequila bottle. "So I have to go home and marry Joe Montecruz."

"You're what, Uri," said Rivas, "thirty? You can do what you want. You don't have to marry this guy if you don't want to."

Urania shook her head dubiously.

"I remember some of the dinner, Sister Windchime," said Rivas. "But how did we get out of there? And . . . what happened to me?" He touched his bandaged head.

"You're supposed to call her Barbara," said Urania virtuously.

"People might remember the, uh, birdy name," Barbara explained. "Well, the place started collapsing as soon as you threw that squid thing at him, and then bullets were flying so thick you'd get hit if you moved. Sister Sue moved, tried to pull the thing off the L—off Jaybush. Then after you . . . cut him up, a rock hit you in the head. I was sure you were dead, or dying anyway, but I got you into the boat and then just headed for one of the arches. I thought one of those bridges was going to come right down on us and mash us all—that was happening to most of the people on the rafts, it looked like—but I figured why not keep moving. Anyway, I got us through the arch into a little tunnel and then it wasn't so bad, the tunnel roof was just dropping pebbles and sand, and the waves from the pool in the big room helped move us along."

She shook her head. "Do you remember when h-he told all those people they were going to die? Well, even though he seemed to be dead, they didn't want any change in plans. Some had wound up in under the arch with us, but they didn't try to get into our boat, or swim out—they were trying to drown, and getting mad when they'd come up and take a breath in spite of themselves.

"I paddled us along the tunnel, and when we came outside we were in one of the canals, so I just kept going. After a while I found an old pier hidden under a big pepper tree, so I left the two of you there and went back."

Urania was listening avidly, and Rivas wondered if this could be the first time she'd heard the story. Could she have been too incurious to ask?

"The building had mostly fallen down by that time," Barbara went on, "and I could hear sounds something like seals barking, or honking geese, from the big pool inside the crumbled walls, but it was like they were speaking with mouths and throats that weren't any good for speaking with. It seemed like they kept trying to say, 'Where are you, Lord?' And some of the voices were coming from the sky, where things were flying around; they sounded so awful, just the noise of them flying, I mean, like big wet wings slapping, that I was glad it was dark and I couldn't see them. Anyway, a lot of bodies had floated out of the tunnel into the canal, and I went through the pockets of three or four of the better-dressed ones." Her voice was still matter of fact, but Rivas could see tears in her eyes and her hands were clenched on his blanket, pulling a section of it drumhead taut. "A couple of them had quite a lot of money. I took it and came back to where you two were." The blanket tore with a sound like a spitting cat, startling all three of them. "Urania was still crying. You still looked like every breath was your last. We all waited there until morning, then I got us a room and got a doctor for you. And then I used nearly all the rest of the money to buy this donut wagon and two horses, and we've been doing well enough since." Staring down at the torn blanket, she added, "My f-father owns a bakery, so I . . . know how to . . ."

"Except we have to move around a lot," put in Urania.

"The pocalocas keep zeroing in on us," Barbara explained. "I've tried to keep moving east, figuring to get to Ellay, but those damned women make us backtrack a lot of the time. They'll march past quickly, then back again not so quick, and then if we don't rouse the horses and get the wagon out of there they start just milling around, looking everywhere, like they're not even sure what they're looking for. I've been having Urania decoy them away by singing in a street in the other direction—they hate music—but lately they haven't been as easy to deflect. I think they want what's left of . . . their god," she said, looking at the tequila bottle, "or the guy that killed him," she said, looking at Rivas. "Or, more likely, both."

Rivas shivered. He raised his right hand and tried to make a fist; he could, but he couldn't have crushed a sponge in it. God, I'm weak, he thought. A single pocaloca could kill me right now, easy as killing a bug. I'm going to have to get some exercise . . . and some food.

With the thought of food came an awareness of ravenous hunger—and of the smell that filled the wagon. "Could I have some of your donuts?" he asked.

"Of course," Barbara said. "But there's some soup, if you'd rather. Bean and onion, and the guy I bought it from thins it with sherry." She said this a bit primly, as if she still couldn't bring herself to approve of alcohol.

"Oh, yes, please," said Rivas fervently.

Barbara went to the front part of the wagon, which was evidently a tiny kitchen, clattered around for a minute, and then returned with a steaming bowl and a spoon. "I'd better feed you," she said.

"My God, I'm not a baby," Rivas said. "I can feed myself. Here, give me the spoon, I'll show you."

She did, and he could hold it, but his hand shook so badly that most of the soup spilled out of the spoon, and then he dropped the spoon in. It sank out of sight.

"God damn it," he grated, afraid for a moment that he might cry at this defeat.

Barbara fished it out, wiped it off, dipped up some soup and held it to his mouth. "It's no disgrace," she whispered. "Eat, dummy."

He did, and it was delicious, and in a few minutes she'd scraped the last spoonful out of the bowl.

"Would you like something to drink?" she asked him as she stood up.

"Sure, thanks," he said. "What have you got?"

"Nothing, but there's a market a block away, and the donuts made some money this morning."

"Okay, I'll, uh, pay you back," he ventured.

"Don't be silly. What would you like?"

"Beer?"

She pressed her lips together, but said, "Okay. Back in five. Uri, anybody knocks, make sure it's me before you open up, right?"

"Sure, sure."

"See you." Barbara left, drawing the door closed behind her.

Rivas turned and stared at Uri. She did look much better now than she had at the Regroup Tent and the disastrous dinner; her hair was clean and she seemed to have got enough sleep lately. He didn't need a mirror to know that she must look ten years younger than he did. But she wasn't *Uri*, the girl he'd dreamed of and written songs to for thirteen years, the girl that had made all other girls seem coarse and in-sensitive and stupid by comparison. And he realized at last that what had made her so enduring an obsession was his deprivation of her. If her father hadn't separated them after that birthday party, she'd simply have been his first girl-friend. It was the drama of frustrated love—and the safety of it, too, of course, for frustrated love is never subjected to the daily patch-and-make-do reality of a marriage—that had made him base his life on it.

He remembered, suddenly, what he'd been dreaming of, just before he woke up. Probably prompted by hearing Uri's voice, he'd been dreaming of the birthday party. It was a dream he'd had before, but always before in it he'd been young Rivas, winding up barking in drunken apprehension behind the bushes. This time he'd been the present day thirty-one-year-old Rivas, somehow transported back through time to be an observer of that traumatic evening thirteen years ago.

He'd seen the kid who was his younger self come lurching out of the Barrows house, pale and sweaty and unhappy-looking, and go reeling toward the road—then stop, slap a hand across his mouth and go lunging into the bushes. There had followed the inelegant racket of someone being violently ill.

An elderly couple had strolled out of the house, and registered startlement at these sounds. "What on earth is that, Henry?" the woman asked.

"Oh," said the man, smiling tolerantly, "it sounds like a dog, behind the bushes there. Nothing we need concern ourselves with." They'd started to wander away then.

But a moment later a strange new sound arose from behind the bushes. *"Rowf. Rowf. Arf barf. Owooo—*Oh, God, *gaaak*—oh, *rowf, rowf . . ."*

Urania, who had fetched herself another donut, looked up and caught Rivas's eye just as he began laughing. He was too weak to laugh very hard, but he did it for quite a while.

"You laughing at me?" Urania asked when he'd subsided somewhat.

He sniffed and weakly wiped tears away from his eyes. "No, Uri. Me." He looked at her fondly. "It's been thirteen years, Uri. Did you think about me much?"

"Some," she said. "Of course I've been busy. Uh . . . did you think about me much?"

He shrugged. "I thought so."

"Would you like one of these donuts?"

"I guess not, thank you."

Abruptly there was a hard knock at the wagon's door, and, overlapping that noise, Barbara's voice, quiet but tense: "Lemme in, quick. That last gang of pocalocas is back."

Urania let her in, and Barbara hurried forward and crouched by Rivas. "Can we let them have that?" she asked, pointing at the bottle with the crystal in it.

Starkly aware of his own helplessness, Rivas shook his head. "No. That's Jaybush dormant in there, that crystal. It they can get it, he'll be alive again."

"Okay, we run." She turned to Urania. "Uri, they're coming from behind us. Do you remember how to drain the deep fryer?"

"Well, you only showed me once. You turn the—"

"You've got to do it. And then take the broom, hop down and quickly sweep the oil off to both sides of the street. Go!"

"But why do—"

"Now, damn it!"

Uri went, grumbling, to the front of the wagon.

"Can I help at all?" asked Rivas.

Barbara dropped the bar across the flimsy door. "Of course not," she said with the briefest backward glance. She peered through a narrow hole in the door, sunlight making a luminous slash across her smooth cheek. Without feeling the least bit less useless, Rivas found himself growing excited by the sight of her.

Brilliantly appropriate response to peril, you idiot, he told himself.

Urania came puffing back in through the kitchen. "There, it's all—"

"Bring me the broom," snapped Barbara.

Rolling her eyes like a martyr, Urania went back to the kitchen. Rivas could hear a sort of unsynchronized marching outside, getting louder. Urania returned with the broom, which was dripping and reeked of cooking oil.

Barbara straightened and snatched it from her. "Now when I say go," she said quickly to Urania, "you fling the back door open—lift the bar first—and then instantly run forward and whip up the horses and get us out of here fast, it doesn't matter where. Got it?"

"Yes," said Urania, moving forward and taking hold of the bar.

"Go."

The bar clanked back, the door was flung open, and Rivas, raising his head in the bunk, was sure he glimpsed the pain-gaunt face of Sister Sue in the moment when Barbara held the broom head to the candle and the oil-soaked straw brush blazed into flame. Then the wagon lurched forward and Barbara blocked his view as she leaned out the door to toss the burning broom to the pavement.

Over the rattling of the wheels and his own pounding heartbeat he didn't hear any *whoosh* of sudden ignition, but he did hear screams of surprise and pain and rage. Barbara lost her balance and had to grab the door frame, and Rivas watched her swing out and around, her white teeth bared with effort, and then he saw muscles flex in her brown arms and legs as she dragged herself back inside. She gave him a taut grin as she pushed the door shut.

"We're away from 'em," she said, "but now we don't dare stop. They'll remember this wagon."

"And I'll bet one of them recognized you, and probably me too," Rivas told her, letting his head fall back onto the pillow. "I think their leader was Sister Sue."

"Oh. Yes." She grabbed the bunk to brace herself, and a pan fell in the kitchen, as Urania took a fast turn. "Are you sure? I didn't look at any of them closely."

"I'm afraid I'm sure."

"Huh. Well, I hope we all—including the horses—like donuts, because I think we're going to have to just make one long burn straight to Ellay. Objections?"

He spread his hands. "It's your show." The wagon took another sharp turn and this time there were angry yells from outside as well as pans falling in the kitchen, and Barbara started forward but stopped when Rivas said, "Oh, one thing..."

"What's that?"

"Did you get my beer?"

She frowned, then reached into the big pocket of her skirt. "Well, yes," she said, producing a bottle. "Can you drink it?"

"I think with it balanced on my chest I could."

"All right." She uncorked it and set it on his chest and braced his hands around it. "You okay?"

"Yeah," said Rivas. "Thanks." He tilted the bottle to his mouth, and got a good sip in spite of the wagon's rocking.

She smiled. "Good. You really did look terrible when I got you out of there. The doctor who put your head back together knew you, by the way. He said, 'Rivas is rapidly using himself up.' I told him there was lots more to you than met the eye." She patted his bony shoulder and went forward to help Urania with the driving.

Rivas spent most of that day eating and drowsing, and when it became imperative that he either call for a bedpan or visit the wagon's bathroom—a tiny closet between the head of the bunk and the back kitchen wall—he managed to stand up and make the trip himself, though when he reeled back to the bunk he collapsed limply into it, nauseous, cold, sweating, and almost fainting from exhaustion. He slept several hours after that, and when he woke up Barbara had halted the wagon for the night in what she assured him was a well-concealed spot. The three fugitives made the last of the soup serve as dinner, though dessert was lavish, and then, over Rivas's weak protests, the two women stretched out on the floor to go to sleep.

Rivas slept too, but fitfully, and a tiny *clink* in the middle of the night brought him instantly awake.

The wall across from his bunk could be unlatched and folded down on hinges to provide a window and flat counter for selling donuts, and by the faint moonlight filtering in through the cracks he could see someone holding the tequila bottle. She turned half toward his bunk as she held the bottle up to peer into it, and he saw that it was Urania. Even as he opened his mouth to tell her to put it back, she licked the glass, sliding her tongue up toward the cork.

"Uri!" Rivas croaked in alarm, "put that *down*, you—"

When he spoke she jumped, then with feverish haste clamped her teeth over the whole neck of the bottle.

Rivas flung himself out of the bunk and managed to collide with her and knock her against the hinged wall, but a moment later he had tumbled helplessly to the floor, blinking his eyes and breathing deeply to fight off unconsciousness.

Barbara was on her feet and looking around jerkily, aware that there was an emergency but not what it was; she seemed to think someone was trying to break in, and Rivas didn't have enough strength in his lungs and jaws to speak.

The cork came out of the bottle with a pop, and then Barbara knew what was happening, and she lunged at Urania. Her shoulder thudded into Urania's stomach and they both crashed into the hinged wall, which came unlatched and fell open with a series of loud wood-on-wood whacks and a sudden glare of moonlight. Both women had fallen and as they gasped and struggled on the floor, the tequila bottle rolled past Rivas's face. There was still some tequila sloshing around in it, but no crystal.

Rivas rolled over and propped himself up on one elbow to see what was going on. Barbara was kneeling on Urania's back and strangling her; Uri was thrashing furiously, but one of her arms was pinned under her and she could only claw ineffectively at Barbara's wrists with the other. Rivas might have interfered, at least to stop Barbara from being quite so rough, if he hadn't seen Uri's eyes blazing at him out of her darkening face, for in that instant he was sure that it was Jaybush glaring through her eyes at him.

"*Spit—it—out—or—die—Uri,*" grated Barbara.

For another three seconds it looked as though Uri had decided to die, but then her mouth opened and the crystal was spat out; Barbara rolled off her and Uri went limp, panting rapidly in harsh whistling gasps.

Rivas picked up the crystal. *You win,* it said in his mind. *You're the boss. I'll work for you. Swallow me.*

Barbara was helping him up. He had to keep blinking, for blood was running down his forehead from his reopened wound.

"That would have," said Barbara tightly as she rolled him back up onto the bunk, but she began coughing before she could finish the sentence, and had to sit down on the foot of the bunk.

"What?" The monotonous voice in Rivas's head made him speak too loudly. Uri kept on wheezing.

"If she'd swallowed it," said Barbara. "That would have harmed it, harmed him?"

Rivas looked at her with something close to despair, then closed his eyes. The pillow was wet with blood against his cheek. "I can't do this . . . by myself," he said. "You've got to help. Do you want him to come back? Do you want to take the sacrament again?"

"...No," Barbara said slowly. "No, I don't want him...*back* again, but I somehow don't want him dead either." She stood up and went to the kitchen and came back with a lit lamp, which she put down on the floor in order to step over Urania. She unfolded the counter wall, lifted it back into place and latched it shut. Urania, incredibly, was snoring, evidently fast asleep.

"Do *you* want him dead?" Barbara asked when she sat down again on the bunk.

"Yes," said Rivas.

Barbara smiled at him. "Really? There isn't any little bit of you that would like to...merge with the Lord, stop being you?"

Swallow me. You win. You're the boss. Rivas reached out and put the crystal down on the torn blanket between them, and it was a relief for him to stop hearing the voice. "Okay, maybe there is. And when I took a huge dose of Blood recently, there was a part of me that wanted to just relax and go down. But have you seen any real Blood freaks? Well, you've seen real far-gones."

"Sure, but their outward form, we're told, isn't the whole story. If I take a boat to get somewhere, and then later you find the boat all rotted and decrepit on some shore, you can't tell anything about where I've gone or how I am."

She touched the crystal, and her eyes widened in shock. After a few seconds she took her finger away. "What *would* have happened if Uri had swallowed it?"

"She would have become Jaybush."

"He'd have been with us again?"

Rivas nodded unhappily. It was very late, and he was exhausted and scared and his head hurt.

"Swallow it," said Barbara suddenly. "Quick, without

thinking about it. You know you want to."

"No," snapped Rivas, "I want—" He paused, thinking about what he'd started to say, and then he said it quietly, with a smile. "I want *you* to."

"Me? But then *I'd* be him. And you're the guy who killed him."

"If I wanted him back that wouldn't make any difference to me, the fact that he might kill me right away."

She nodded sadly. "I know what you mean. Better that your parents find you and beat the daylights out of you than that you spend the night lost."

Rivas laughed softly. "We both . . . sort of . . . want him back, but neither of us wants to *be* him." He looked down at Uri. "We shouldn't have stopped her." He smiled at Barbara, and said, "We should wake her up and feed it to her."

And then suddenly his words weren't a joke at all. Barbara snatched the crystal and stood up. Rivas thought he should say something to stop her, and he meant to, but not right away. He had to catch his breath first.

At that moment a voice spoke from outside the wagon. *"Swallow me. You win."*

Barbara dropped to her knees, and Rivas fell back onto his soggy pillow, his eyes tightly shut.

"You're the boss," the voice went on. *"I'll work for you . . ."*

It's him, Rivas thought dizzily, somehow he's right outside, he's gonna break down the wall and get us, he'll burn us to ash just by looking at us, consume the souls out of our bodies like a big spider emptying a couple of captured flies, we'll absolutely cease to be and *what is he waiting for?*

Abruptly the familiar litany stopped; Rivas opened his eyes; and then it started up again—*"Swallow me. You win . . ."*—but in a different voice.

Barbara stood up and tottered to the back door. She lifted the bar and pulled the door open and peered around outside.

Rivas could hear other voices now. "He isn't gone!" someone exclaimed. "His spirit is still with us!"

"Tell us how to find you, Lord!" cried a woman's voice.

"*Swallow me . . .*" the second voice droned on.

Barbara closed the door and came back to the bunk. "It's a gang of Jaybirds," she told Rivas, "evidently without a shepherd. Why are their far-gones saying the same things as this?" She held up the crystal.

"They're picking up his thoughts," Rivas said. "Evidently without a brain to project them the thoughts don't carry very far." He sighed. "Do you still want to feed it to Uri?"

Barbara's shoulders slumped with loss. "No. Not right now."

"Is this moon bright enough to drive by?"

"I don't know," she said dully. "I guess so."

"Then I think maybe we ought to get a head start on the morning."

On the floor Uri snored on.

Chapter Twelve

DESPITE BEING SHY one pedal, the bicycle ratcheted rapidly up the street and a couple of doors east of Serena's Cantina the boy laid the bike down in a controlled slide that left him, after a couple of running steps, right in front of the place. The boy peered into the bar from the doorway until he'd spotted Fracas McAn, and then he darted in and yanked on McAn's sleeve before the bartender could yell at him to get out.

When McAn saw who it was, he raised his hand to prevent the bartender's outburst. "What is it, Modesto?" he asked the boy. "Have you seen him?"

"I think so, man. He's traveling with two women."

"Two of them? I don't see—well, no, that sounds like Rivas, actually," he said. "Afoot? On horseback?"

"In a donut wagon."

"A . . . a donut wagon."

"*Si.*"

"Coming from the south, is it?" McAn asked hopefully. "He's at the army checkpoint?"

The boy looked apologetic. "No, man. He's coming in from the west, on the Ten Highway."

"Like from *Venice?* Hell, I'd like to be able to let you have the fifth, Modesto, but I don't see how this—"

"The kid really can't hang around in here, Frake," said the bartender. "Sorry, but you'll have to take it outside."

McAn looked indecisive for a moment, then shrugged. "Okay, Modesto," he sighed. "I'll listen." He drained his glass of Ellay Red and tossed a couple of jiggers onto the bar. "Uh, don't put the bottle away, Sam," he said. "Okay, come on," he added to the boy.

Outside the air was cool with early evening, and rats could be seen in silhouette scampering along roof edges. "Well now," said McAn to Modesto, "what makes you think it's Rivas?"

"Well, he looks like Rivas, in a beat-up way—he looks even worse than you said he would, big bandage on the head—and he's with at least one lady who's not wife or girlfriend . . . and there is a haste about them, hurry to get here. I asked to buy a donut, but they didn't have any."

McAn glanced toward the western wall of the city. Torches were already flickering by the newly erected barracks, and tomorrow it might be difficult to get in or out. "How near are they?"

"Maybe at the gate by now," Modesto said. "I rode my bicycle as fast as I could, but, as I told you, this is not a donut wagon that stops to sell donuts."

"May as well go see, I guess."

McAn started walking west, Modesto wobbling along slowly on his bicycle beside him. Twice, as they made their way toward the gate, kids looked up from scavenger labors and called fast questions in Spanish and then swore when Modesto grinned and nodded. Each of them was of course hoping to be the first to sight the San Berdoo army, but private watch-for-'ems like McAn's paid a lot better than the Ellay government's.

The boy's confidence began to infect McAn. "Well, if this *isn't* Rivas," he said, mostly to himself, "then I doubt if he'll be coming back at all. Tomorrow it'll be a week since I saw him in Irvine."

Ahead of them they could see the high black band that was the wall, its uneven top edge indenting the orange sky. In one of the palm trees overhead a parrot exclaimed, "Hooray, it's Gregorio Rivas!" McAn grinned at Modesto and held up crossed fingers.

"Ah, *mira*, man, there is the wagon now!"

The boy was pointing at a wagon that was just entering the gate, being pulled by one overworked horse. When the two of them got closer to it, McAn sprinted to the curb to be able to see it better than just as a head-on silhouette. It was battered and powdered with dust, but he could read DA-DOO-RON-RON DONUTS on the side of it.

"It's who you described," McAn admitted, trotting back to the center of the road. "Let's see if it's who I'm after."

The horse was panting deeply and seemed to be letting the wagon coast, and McAn guessed that simply getting inside the Ellay walls had been these people's goal.

He strolled up to it as it waveringly approached, and he smiled up at the exhausted-looking young lady on the driver's bench. "Hi!" he said. "I have an important message for Greg Rivas. Would he happen to be aboard?"

There was a pause, then, "Who are you?" the girl asked.

"My name is Fracas McAn."

The wagon had zigzagged to a halt now, and the girl got up and disappeared inside. Modesto nudged McAn, who dutifully dug a fifth-card out of his pocket but held onto it.

After fully two minutes the girl reappeared, her arm around a tottering, unsteady figure with a bandaged head. The bandaged man sat down and smiled weakly at McAn, but it was several long seconds before McAn handed the fifth-card to the boy. Modesto snatched it, kicked his bike around and cranked it away up the street.

Rivas's smile remained in place but turned a bit sour when he became aware of the way McAn was staring at him. Damn it, he thought, you'd think I was an embalmed corpse. "Hello, Frake," he said, glad that at least his voice hadn't deteriorated. "This is a coincidence, running into you first thing."

"Well, actually, Greg," said McAn, "it isn't. Could I hop up there and talk to you for a minute?"

"Sure. Barbara, could you step back so Frake can have the other half of the bench?"

McAn climbed up and perched beside Rivas. "I've got some important information for you, Greg," he said. "I've had kids watching for you for days, 'cause I figure I owe you one for helping me get my quarry away last week. But first, tell me . . . tell me what *happened!* What's behind the walls of the Holy City? How did you get hurt? Why are you coming back from the *west?*"

Rivas smiled. "I'll tell you the whole story over a pitcher of beer at Spink's, after I deliver my quarry to her father. But I can tell you this—I'm afraid you're out of a job. Jaybush is—if not dead exactly—certainly out of the Messiah business."

McAn blinked. "You mean . . . how . . ." A slow grin built up on his face. "No kidding! I do want to hear about it. But let's have that pitcher *before* you deliver Miss Barrows. There are some aspects of that situation that I know and you need to be aware of."

"How do you know her name?"

"I can see Spink's from here. I'll tell you when we're at a table. It isn't really," he said, rolling his eyes toward the rear of the wagon, "a story for the ladies."

"Okay."

McAn hopped down to the pavement. "I'll meet you there," he said, and started walking.

Barbara guided the wagon to Spink's, but their remaining horse was so tired that McAn got to the place first and was holding the front door open when Rivas stepped carefully down from the wagon.

"Thank you, Frake," he said, "but I'm really not quite as frail as I look." Once inside, he looked around. The chandeliers were lit and raised, though they were swinging a little, implying that Mojo had only recently cranked them up. The shadows of Noah Almondine's paper dolls seemed to Rivas to be waving at him. A young man he'd never seen before was sitting on the stage, tuning a pelican and exchanging desultory jokes with Tommy Fandango. Mojo was behind the bar, muttering weary curses and trying to unjam a clogged sink with a piece of wire.

"I can't believe it's been only ten days," Rivas said, shaking his head gently. "Uh, could you buy the pitcher, Frake? I've got a fortune in the spirit bank but not a jigger on me."

"Sure, Greg. How's this one?" asked McAn, indicating a table by the window.

Rivas grinned, for it was the table Joe Montecruz had been sitting at when he'd originally tried to talk Rivas into this redemption. "Appropriate," he said, pulling out a chair before McAn could do it for him.

When they were both seated, Mojo ceased his labors and came puffing over. "What'll it be, gents," he recited.

"A pitcher of beer and two glasses, Mojo," said Rivas.

The old man looked at him disinterestedly, and then his eyes went wide in recognition. "Leaping Moses, *Greg!*" he exclaimed. "Damn, boy, what happened to you?"

"Nothing some beer won't start to fix."

Mojo turned to the stage. "Hey, Tommy, look who's back! With a full beard!"

Fandango peered across the room at them. "Oh, hi, Greg...uh..." He wiped his mouth uncertainly and glanced at the pelicanist, who was now staring at Rivas with alarmed hostility. "Are you back, then?"

Rivas smiled and waved. "No, no. I'm...retired." I keep sitting at this table and telling people I'm retired, he thought. "So," he said, turning to McAn. "What's up? Why did you post a watch-for-'em on me?"

McAn said, "I've been hired to do the breaking and restoring of Urania Barrows."

Mojo brought the pitcher and glasses, and Rivas didn't reply until the old man had bumbled off and they'd filled the glasses. "Well, you're welcome to it, as it happens," he said, "but old Irwin Barrows doesn't know that. When we made the deal, I insisted on doing that part too. Doesn't he think I'll object?"

McAn frowned, as if trying to think of a civilized way to say something uncivilized, then obviously gave up and just said, "Irwin Barrows intends to have you killed as soon as you've brought his daughter back."

Rivas laughed softly and took a long sip of the beer. "Does he indeed," he said, letting the heavy glass clank back down onto the table. "Because he thinks we'll be wanting to run off together?"

"Right. So, uh, what I want to tell you is, if you *do* want to run off with her, just get what money you've got, and go, right away. Don't go near his place."

Rivas stared at McAn, then looked around the bar. "*I've* been recognized," he said, "and even though it's not crowded right now, it's a safe bet that you have too. He'd know you warned me."

"As I said, I owe you one."

"Thanks, Frake." Rivas had another pull at the beer. At least he was making the glass easier to lift. "But as a matter of fact, I don't want to run off with her. I'd *like* to return her to him. How does he plan to do it, anyway?"

"He's pinning his main hopes on you being killed in a duel with her fiancé. I gather you called him out before you left, and he's going to insist on satisfaction."

"Ah. Yeah, I called him sport. You've seen him?"

McAn nodded. "Not even eyebrows. Of course, in the shape you're in, you'd certainly be justified in asking for an extension on the date of the duel. I'm not sure what Barrows would think of that. I guess if you're not interested in his daughter anymore—and haven't messed with her during this redemption—"

"I haven't."

"—Then he probably won't care what you do. Unless you insulted him, too . . . ?"

"Maybe I did. It all happened a long time ago." He reached out, hoisted the heavy pitcher and topped up his glass, reflecting that all this weight-lifting ought to help him get back in shape.

"In any case, if you *had* wanted to marry her, and managed to kill Montecruz, I'm pretty sure Barrows would have fixed up a fatal accident for you to have. I'm just saying this to let you know what kind of scene is waiting for you up on that hill."

Rivas shook his head wonderingly. "And he was appointed distiller of the treasury by the Sixth Ace! Incredible. I've always known he was tough, but . . ."

"You tapped the stressed part of his personality and it broke."

"Can happen," Rivas said. "Not always a bad thing, maybe."

McAn shrugged. "Anyway—if you're staying, want me to be your second?"

"I'd appreciate it, Frake. Let's not rush this beer, though— the ladies will stay in the wagon, and even though I'm not a big fan of bugwalk, I'd like to hear this pelicanist." As he drank, his fingers absently toyed with the bulky lead- wrapped pendant he'd made the day before, which hung now on a wire around his neck.

After a tiring visit to the commander of the Ellay forces to warn him that the San Berdoo army would probably attack from the south, Rivas borrowed some money from McAn and bought some clothes to replace the ones Barbara had bought for him in Venice, and they managed to get enough food, despite the widespread pre-siege hoarding, to cook up some dinner in the wagon's kitchen. Urania ate sparingly and hardly spoke at all, though McAn tried to draw her out, and it was obvious to Rivas that he was looking for anxieties and weak spots that he'd be able to use against her in their upcoming breaking and restoration sessions. Finally there were no more excuses for delay, so two fresh horses were hired and Rivas, McAn, Barbara and Urania set out for the Hollywood Hills and the Barrows estate.

The air was chilly up in the hills, away from the street pavement that would hold the sun's warmth nearly until dawn, and as the horses pulled the battered old wagon around the last steep bend, Rivas shivered and pulled the blanket closer around himself. He had insisted on joining McAn on the driver's bench, and as McAn flicked the reins again, Rivas shook his head. "I think we passed the place," he said, squinting around at the trees made visible by the wag- on's swinging lantern.

McAn looked over at him. "No, it's still ahead of us."

Urania was braced in the kitchen doorway behind Rivas,

and he felt her shift her feet. Yeah, Uri, he thought—I'm a little surprised too that I forgot.

"Here we are," McAn said, slanting the horses sharply left onto an ascending brick-paved driveway. An iron gate blocked the way ahead, bracketed by two lamps on short stone pillars.

"We could still go away together, Greg," said Urania suddenly. "It's still a few yards short of being too late."

McAn reined in the horses and put on the brake, then looked away, out into the darkness. Rivas heard the creak of the bunk in the wagon as Barbara stood up to listen.

"No, Uri," he said.

After a pause the brake squeaked off, the reins flapped and the wagon got moving again.

A restored telephone booth stood beside the driveway ahead, and when the wagon halted in front of the gate an officious fat man hurried out of it toward them. "I'm sorry," he was saying in tones of satisfaction, "I wasn't told to expect any donuts tonight. I'm sorry, but you'll have to leave."

"We're Fracas McAn," said McAn evenly, "and Gregorio Rivas, and Urania Barrows."

"And a friend," put in Rivas.

The guard, startled, peered more closely—then, albeit with ill grace, walked back to the gate and unlocked it. "You might have had the thoughtfulness," he remarked stiffly, "to have brought the young lady home in a less shabby vehicle."

Rivas laughed, with an edge of hysteria. "Hell, he's right. What were we thinking of? Something with, like, bells and ribbons and a pipe organ. . . ."

The gate was open, and McAn flicked the reins. "Cool off, Greg," he muttered as they moved forward and the gate was drawn closed behind them.

The guard commenced clanging a bell, and the racket was kept up, raising a sympathetic chorus of bird cries in the surrounding shrubbery, until the driveway leveled out under the wagon's wheels and they were in the paved front yard, where a grander wagon was half loaded with furniture and crates. The front door of the big old house was open and several men were hurrying down the steps and toward the newly arrived wagon.

"Uri!" came Irwin Barrows's well-remembered voice. "Uri! Damn me, if that fool grabbed the wrong bell by mistake—"

"It says donuts, Mister Barrows," pointed out another voice dubiously.

"Donuts! Damn me! I'll—"

"Urania is here, Mister Barrows," called Rivas.

The tall, white-haired old man walked slowly forward, after having waved someone else back. "Mister Rivas," he said. "You've come for your final five thousand fifths."

McAn glanced at Rivas in surprise.

"No," said Rivas.

"I see," said Barrows, a weary harshness in his voice. "You think you'll go away with her, is that it? And you think that waiving the second half of your fee will make me more—"

"No," Rivas interrupted. "Urania and I have no plans for getting married or going anywhere together. But I overcharged you eleven days ago, in the . . . heat of the moment. Here's your daughter. We're square."

"Uri!" Barrows called, a new suspicion evidently having occurred to him. "She's hurt, badly hurt, is that it? Or no, a babbling idiot because of having repeatedly taken the sacrament, right? God damn you, you—"

"Maybe he just brought back her corpse, Mister Barrows," helpfully suggested the other man, whom Rivas recognized now as the bald Joe Montecruz.

"No, dad, I'm okay," said Uri in a loud but listless voice. She edged behind Rivas and dropped to the ground, then plodded across the paving stones to Montecruz, who took her into his arms with an ostentatious show of emotion.

Barrows slowly walked the rest of the way to the donut wagon. He was frowning thoughtfully as he stared up at Rivas's face, which, under its bandage, was lit in craggy chiaroscuro by the wagon's lantern. "You've suffered, sir," he said.

"Redemptions are never easy," said Rivas.

"He . . . *killed* Norton Jaybush," McAn told Barrows, awe putting a slight quaver in his voice.

"You did?" asked Barrows, startled.

"More or less."

Barbara was standing behind Rivas now, and she put her hands on his shoulders. "He cut Jaybush's throat," she said.

Barrows hesitated; then, "Perhaps neither of us is quite the same person he was two weeks ago," he said. His uncertain gaze slid away from Rivas to the big old house and the grounds, and Rivas belatedly realized that Barrows and his people were in the process of leaving to take refuge inside the city walls, and that soon this house and these vineyards might very well be sacked by the San Berdoo army. "Thank you for my child," Barrows said. "Now please go."

Rivas lifted his head and looked past Barrows. "I think Mister Montecruz has something to say to me."

Montecruz looked up, blinking as he changed his focus, then released Urania and walked toward the wagon. His walk was uncertain, as though he were dutifully taking part in a ritual that had been improperly prepared. Finally he stopped and stared impassively at Rivas. "You insulted me," he said flatly.

Rivas, huddled in his blanket, smiled. "You're right. I did."

"I . . . *must* demand satisfaction."

"And I'll give it," said Rivas. "I apologize. I was wrong to say what I said. The speech you made, which goaded me into insult, was the truth, which of course is why it stung me so deeply." Rivas spread his hands. "You were right. I was wrong. I mean that."

Again McAn was staring incredulously at Rivas.

Montecruz was at a loss. "You're a coward," he said, loudly but without conviction.

"No, he's not," said McAn. Night insects sang in the darkness.

"No," echoed Irwin Barrows tiredly, "he's not." To Rivas he added, "Please go."

"*Adios*," said Rivas. "Goodbye, Uri."

There was no reply. McAn urged the horses forward and around, awkwardly because of the other wagon. Lamps were lit in the house but the curtains were gone, and Rivas looked in at the dining hall as they inched past the front window. All the furniture was gone, and nothing looked familiar.

At last McAn had the old wagon facing downhill, and, leaning on the brake, began to guide it down the sloping driveway.

"See those bushes there, to the right?" Rivas remarked to him quietly. "Before the night's out, have me tell you what I once did behind them."

Epilogue

AT NOON THE next day, Rivas was sitting on the roof of his apartment, gripping the neck of his new pelican and skating the bow across the strings to produce various chords.

It was sounding better. At first he'd produced only squawks that had raised protesting howls from the dogs in the street below, but now he was getting his maimed hand to hold the bow properly . . . though he still didn't have the heart to try any strumming.

Gripping the instrument with his chin to free his right hand, he reached down, snagged his jug of beer, raised it— and then paused, baffled.

"What shall I take?" asked Barbara drily.

"Uh . . . the pelican."

She stood up from the shaded wicker chair, reached out and took the instrument by the neck.

"Thanks," he said. Free now to tip his head back, he took a long sip of the beer, which had stayed fairly cool in the shadow of his chair. He put the jug down and took the pelican back.

He took a deep breath and then sawed out the opening of *Peter and the Wolf*. Doesn't sound half bad, he thought.

"That's what you whistled, isn't it?" Barbara asked. "That night."

"Sure is," said Rivas. He could feel the sun-heated weight of the leaden pendant resting on his chest, and he remembered yesterday's dawn when, once Urania was safely tied up in the wagon's bunk, he'd made Barbara go out and pry the lead balancing weights off the wheel rims of a dozen of the ubiquitous old car shells; when she'd returned with a handful he had helped her heat them and watched critically as she had hammered them into a sheet to wrap the crystal in.

"Uri *was* quieter after we wrapped the crystal up," said Barbara now. "Did the lead stop his . . . influence?"

Rivas shrugged. "Maybe. I mainly wanted to block out any radiation that might strengthen him." He squinted at the sun. "Even warmth is something. I'll have to dunk him in cold water later."

Barbara shuddered. "I wish you could ditch him."

"You don't wish it any more than I do." He supposed that whatever was left of the hemogoblin was in there too.

Barbara shifted in her chair. "You said the quality of food inside the city is going to be dropping pretty quickly," she reminded him. "What time is it?"

Rivas grinned and lowered the instrument. "Not till we're actually besieged," he told her. "In fact they're stripping the fields now and crowding cattle into the whole South Gate area, so for a couple of days, at least until the perishables perish, we'll be eating better than usual. But you're right, it is lunchtime." He stood up—almost lithely!—and shut the pelican up in its case, slipped the bow under the strap he'd had made for it, and picked up the case by the handle.

"What, are you bringing that along?"

He started to put it down, then straightened again. He could feel his face reddening. "Well," he said awkwardly, "you never know. They might ask me to play."

After a moment she grinned, and if her eyes were a little brighter than usual, at least no tears brimmed over. "Oh, I suppose," she said derisively. "And you'll have had so many beers by then that you won't be able to get a single note right."

"And then I'll fall off the stage," he agreed, "confirming everything they say about me."

"Maybe we should sell tickets."

They went down the stairs—Rivas vowing to himself that within a week he'd take the steps two at a time, and that *tomorrow* he'd stop this hobbling, both feet on one step before going on to the next routine—and then started walking toward Spink's.

She glanced at him. "You going to keep the beard?"

Rivas felt his furred chin. "As long as the siege lasts, I guess. Hot water and sharp blades won't be wasted on whiskers for a while."

"No hardship for old Joe Montecruz," observed Barbara.

Rivas laughed. "That's right. For a while the baldy-sports will be the only really aristocratic-looking citizens. I'm sure that'll be a consolation to Uri."

"How long do you think the siege will last?"

"I don't know. The San Berdoo guys have to be banking on a quick victory, 'cause they sure couldn't have set up any useful supply lines in that roundabout route they took. Frankly, I think they're crazy."

After several blocks they rounded the corner onto Wool-shirt, and Spink's was visible ahead. Rivas peered at the place through the wavering mirages. "They've got a window broken," he said. "No, two windows! Christ," he said, trying to walk faster. "They can't be outside the walls already, can they? With a catapult?"

"I don't know," said Barbara tensely, obviously restraining herself from running on ahead of him. "Can they?"

"No, no," Rivas said, more calmly, "we'd have heard the bells. When the San Berdoo army is sighted, every bell in the city is going to be rung like crazy. No, there must just have been a fight."

When they got to the restaurant they saw that a long board had been nailed across the doorway. A man Rivas had never seen before leaned against the wall and shook his head at them. "Sorry, folks," he said. "Closed for repairs."

"I w—" Rivas began. "I used to work here."

"Sorry. Big mess inside."

"Oh hell," said Rivas, stepping forward and putting his hands on the board. Someone inside was sweeping with slow strokes. "Mojo! Hey, Mojo, it's Greg. Tell this guy to let us in."

The sweeping stopped, and in a few moments Mojo appeared in the doorway. "Hi, Greg. Sure, Tony, they can come in. What do you think of this, eh, Greg?"

Rivas and Barbara ducked under the board and peered around the dim room. Chairs were overturned and broken, glass shards crunched underfoot, and on the floor by the stage there was a tangle of strings and wood strips that Rivas eventually recognized as having once been a pelican.

"What the hell *happened?*" he asked.

"Some ladies objected to the music," said Mojo.

Rivas and Barbara exchanged a frightened look. "What do you mean?" Rivas asked quickly.

"Well, they were—but wait, you used to live in Venice, Greg, maybe you've seen 'em. A guy said they've had 'em in Venice for years. They just arrived here this morning, and by bad luck musta just made it inside before the gates were closed to general traffic. They're all crazy and dirty and wild-eyed, marching like they got God's own orders to carry out, and they purely kick the living crap out of whoever they please. That new pelicanist lost some teeth."

"Pocalocas," said Rivas.

"Yeah!" exclaimed Mojo. "That's what this guy said they were called. He said they hate music."

"They sure do. How did they look? The trip from Venice seem to have worn them down at all?" Suddenly Rivas looked much frailer.

"Oh sure, they were all dusty, hair like greasy old yarn, but God, they got energy! One of them was real thin-faced and sick-looking, but she busted Jeff's pelican with her bare hands, smiling all the while like a big mean cat."

Rivas touched his leaden pendant. "Which way did they go from here?"

"North. Matter of fact, Greg, they were headed your way. How'd you come here?"

"Straight down Flower and then west on Woolshirt."

"Oh, well, you must have passed 'em, two blocks west of 'em. They went up Grand. Man, I hope never to see nothing like that again. But say, you don't think they're *here* now, do you, like them big ants that just appeared half a dozen summers ago and now can't be got rid of?"

Rivas looked out through the broken window at the street. A dog was asleep under an awning across the way, and a couple of children clattered past on low wooden tricycles, raising a cloud of dust that hung nearly motionless in the air.

"No," Rivas grated wearily, almost in a whisper. "No . . . I imagine they'll be . . . moving on." He looked around the room, as if to fix it in his memory. "How late can first-class citizens leave the city, Mojo?"

"Well...you know, Greg. Until the bells. Until they see the enemy. And after that, *nobody* can leave."

"I've got time for one more beer."

"Always, Greg," said Mojo, glancing at him in mild surprise. "Hey, and this afternoon it's on the house. I mean, it's gonna go flat otherwise, right?"

The swish and rattle of Mojo's broom in the debris started up again, and then there was also the echoing *click click, click click* of Rivas working the beer pump; and the next sound was booted footsteps approaching from the office.

Steve Spink's grin relaxed when he saw Rivas sitting cross-legged on the bar. He walked over, nodded curtly to Barbara, and then said, "Howdy, Greg."

"Hullo, Steve," said Rivas, lowering his glass and wiping foam from his moustache. "Sorry your place got busted up."

"We'll live. Two weeks ago we lost our Venetian pelicanist, but at least now we got genuine Venetian madwomen." He looked from Rivas's pelican case to his leaned and bearded face. "I found out who that old guy was, who was in here a week ago, remember? The guy that told me you were latently birdy. And now I hear he's got his daughter back from that gang."

Rivas nodded over the rim of his glass.

"Well—assuming the Berdoos don't take us—any time you want your job back, just say." He turned and walked back toward the office.

"Thanks, Steve!" Rivas called.

Spink waved over his shoulder without looking around.

Rivas finished his beer and lowered himself down from the bar. "You know why I'd better get moving," he told Barbara. "Luckily the spirit bank is south of here. Reckon I'll get a bank draft and then see how far respect for Ellay money extends. A horse, food, liquor, a weapon—I should be out of the city in under an hour. Come to the bank with

me and I'll loan you some money to get settled with, and
then when you do, leave your address with, say, Mojo over
there, and when I can—"

"You're sure leaving is the only way?" Barbara asked,
stretching her long legs to keep up with him as he strode
across the littered floor. "It *is* just a gang of crazy women."

"Led by Sister Sue, of fond memory." He ducked under
the board across the doorway, and she followed. "No, Barbara, I can't spend the siege locked up in the same city with
them; I'd rather run than have to slingshot every birdy-eyed
lady I see . . . and of course if one of them *got* me and was
to swallow this," he touched the crumpled gray pendant,
"Jaybush would be back. And, hell, this is just the gang
that followed us most *closely*. If I hang around, they'll *all*
drift here, and even after the Berdoos go home nobody'll
dare open the gates."

"Are you *sure* you can't destroy the crystal?"

They were moving energetically south on Grand, Rivas
forcing himself to maintain a brisk pace. "I'm pretty sure.
Remember when you laid it on the pavement and took a
hammer to it? The pavement broke. And I happen to know
that, short of shooting it into the heart of the sun, heat's no
problem to it. If I could find a really *deep*, really *cold* well,
I might risk dropping it in and then devoting the rest of my
life to filling the well with the heaviest rocks I could
find . . . but even then I'd worry. He obviously wasn't ready
to become . . . discorporated . . . when he did—he weakened
himself drastically ten years ago, and way too much of what
energy he had was externally invested, like a millionaire
who's a pauper if you time the audit just right, and so he
can't do his fly away into outer space trick—but I think
with years to work he could *move* a pile of stones." They
rounded a corner, and the white pillars of the spirit bank
wavered in the sunlight ahead. "No, I think I have to just
carry it, and try to keep it cold, and if I should ever have

any children, pass the duty on to them."

Barbara grabbed him by the arm and stopped him. "You want company?"

He squinted at her. "Company. Do you mean you'd—"

"Like to come with you. Yes."

He put his hand on her shoulder. "No," he said gently. "Thank you, I appreciate it, but no, Barbara. Get yourself a nice place and a good job, and keep some extra blankets and liquor for when I pass through, okay? Dammit, girl, you've *had* your stroll through hell."

"You haven't? Anyway, what's so safe about staying here?"

"It's better than what I'll be doing. Until the last pocaloca dies, I'll be hiding, running, hunting, going hungry—making only furtive, hurried visits to civilization—and even after they all die, I'll still have *him*." He touched the pendant.

"To pass on to your children," said Barbara sarcastically. "Where are you going to find *them?* I guess you'll just have to dally with one of the pocalocas, huh?"

Rivas blinked. His chest was hollow, and though the light didn't change, he felt as if he'd just stepped out of a dark stuffy room into breezy sunshine. He opened his mouth to speak. . . .

And a bell began ringing on the east wall, and a moment later bells were ringing everywhere, church bells, wagon bells, chimes like excited parakeets, even just randomly snatched up pieces of metal banged clangorously together. Up on the wall soldiers were shouting orders, and a number of people in the streets were just screaming wordlessly. Rivas felt the dark stuffy room close in on him again.

There was no point in trying to talk over the racket. Rivas took Barbara's hand so that together they could make their way through the surging crowd toward the Dogtown section of the city wall.

The stairs leading up to the catwalk were already jammed with denizens of Dogtown, and it took two burly soldiers to keep them off the catwalk. Every few seconds one of the people fell, flailing and perhaps screaming, down into the crowd.

One soldier was shouting down through a bullhorn. *"Get away from the wall!"* he was yelling. *"There is nothing to see! They are still across the river, at least a mile away! The device they've got is* not *a cannon! Repeat,* not *a cannon!"*

Then Rivas saw several of the wall-top soldiers stare in sudden startlement out to the east—and a couple of seconds later a section of the wall to his right exploded, the flying stones knocking down people and shacks and then the boiling dust-cloud considerably veiling the view of splintered wood, broken stone and torn flesh.

Rivas felt a flicker of wild elation, the breezy sunshine feeling again, as the wash of sour dust blew over them and he inventoried what he had with him: his pelican, some pocket change, and a girl who wanted—of all the unheard-of things—to share his life.

He gave her a wild, challenging grin. "Leave by the Dogtown gate?"

She grinned back in sheer delight. "High time."

Hand in hand they ran forward, and hopped and clambered and slid over the tumbled masonry, coughing in the dust and the acid smell of broken stone, and then, out in the sunshine, they ran down the slope toward the river and the abandoned boats.

AWARD-WINNING

Science Fiction!

The following titles are winners of the prestigious Nebula or Hugo Award for excellence in Science Fiction. A must for lovers of good science fiction everywhere!

☐ 77421-0	**SOLDIER ASK NOT,** Gordon R. Dickson	$2.95
☐ 47809-3	**THE LEFT HAND OF DARKNESS,** Ursula K. Le Guin	$2.95
☐ 06223-7	**THE BIG TIME,** Fritz Leiber	$2.50
☐ 16651-2	**THE DRAGON MASTERS,** Jack Vance	$1.95
☐ 16706-3	**THE DREAM MASTER,** Roger Zelazny	$2.25
☐ 24905-1	**FOUR FOR TOMORROW,** Roger Zelazny	$2.25
☐ 80698-8	**THIS IMMORTAL,** Roger Zelazny	$2.75

Prices may be slightly higher in Canada.

Available at your local bookstore or return this form to:

ACE SCIENCE FICTION
Book Mailing Service
P.O. Box 690, Rockville Centre, NY 11571

Please send me the titles checked above. I enclose _____ . Include 75¢ for postage and handling if one book is ordered; 25¢ per book for two or more not to exceed $1.75. California, Illinois, New York and Tennessee residents please add sales tax.

NAME_____

ADDRESS_____

CITY_____STATE/ZIP_____

(allow six weeks for delivery)   **SF-3**